DAVID LONDON

SUN DANCER

SIMON & SCHUSTER

SIMON & SCHUSTER
Rockefeller Center
1230 Avenue of the Americas
New York, NY 10020

SIMON & SCHUSTER and colophon are registered trademarks
of Simon & Schuster Inc.

Designed by Kathryn Parise

Manufactured in the United States of America

10 9 8 7 6 5 4 3 2 1

LIBRARY OF CONGRESS CATALOGING-IN-PUBLICATION DATA
London, David (David T.)
Sun dancer / David London.
p.   cm.
1. Indians of North America—Black Hills (S.D. and Wyo.)—Fiction.
I. Title.
PS3562.0486S86   1996
813'.54—dc20   96-7409
CIP
ISBN 0-684-81458-7

For My Parents

Acknowledgments

I would like to thank Nick Janis and Linda Yellow Elk, and their sons—Harold, Erik, and Vaughn—for their kindness and hospitality. I'm also grateful to Leonard Yellow Elk for all his great stories, Tom Raymond and Karen Raymond for their many kindnesses and hospitality, Tom Meyer, Seymour Jack, Stanley Young, the incredibly beautiful Jennifer Young, Stanley Jr., Shorty Lamont and his boy Hawk Raising Hell. Thanks for shelter, laughter, and great food.

For their guidance and support, I wish to thank Leslie Epstein, Frank Conroy, and Connie Brothers.

Great thanks to Mary Ann Naples and Laurie Chittenden, and to Toni Rachiele and Beth Greenfeld, who don't seem to miss a thing. A big thank-you to Kim Witherspoon and Larry Kaltman.

I am especially grateful to Michael Korda.

I wish to thank the Henfield Foundation for the Transatlantic Review Award, and the Maytag Endowment for its generous support. I am also grateful to the Washington Prize for Fiction organization for its kind support.

A deep thanks to Samantha Harvey, who still walks the Branch, and most of all to my parents and brother for Everything.

History is a mysterious approach to closeness. Every spiral of its path leads us into deeper corruption and at the same time into more fundamental return.

Martin Buber, *I and Thou*

PART I

THE RETURN OF CLEMENT BLUE CHEST

The cow never saw it coming. Clem walked up to her in the moonlight with a sledgehammer over his shoulder. He lifted it above his head, real high, like he was about to chop wood, split a billet. I wondered what kind of sound the skull would make and how much she would feel.

He held the hammer up there for damn near ten seconds. The moon shimmered off the blunt metal head, and off the stubble in the fields behind them. It gleamed in the wetness of her eyes. She looked at him like she expected to be fed. Some stars were out, too. It was all quite pretty. I stepped forward and shot her through the side of the head with my AR-15. She crumpled into the grass before the echo returned from the Badlands.

"The hell's *with* you, Joe? They'll hear it in goddamned Montana," said Clem, letting the hammer down to his shoulder. In the moonlight, he looked younger. I could hardly make out the gray in his braids or the lines in his face. But his gut was still there. He turned to check the road, which runs straight through these prairies and plains for hundreds of miles without a bend. We had put Eli Jr. on the crest of a rise about a mile up the road, and Shorty Shangreaux's boy on the crest of another in the op-

posite direction. We gave them each a light so they could give us plenty
of warning if a vehicle approached.

McLaren's ranch was out of earshot, about ten miles off the reservation, so the shooting wasn't really a risk. But we had agreed to take her
as quiet as possible, on account of McLaren's hands sometimes rode
fences at night. They do that in pickups now from along the road.
McLaren leased land from the tribe because his herd got too big for his
own spread and was getting bigger every year. Lots of ranchers do that,
and get it for a song. You just can't get much for this kind of prairie. And
the lease gives them the right to come on the reservation whenever they
want—to check on their stock and fences.

She wasn't down two seconds before Elijah Hunts Alone dropped to
one knee and started cutting the brand out of her hide. Eli's your man
when he's sober.

"Probably heard it in fucking Russia," Clem said.

"Relax, Clem, you got the pants," Elijah said, without looking up from
under his ten-gallon. I laughed. We were always busting on Clem's pants.
He had these lemon-yellow corduroys that he picked up at the Goodwill
in Rapid City. They were way too big, but that didn't bother Clem. He
just hitched them up with a rope. Everyone ragged on those pants, but
Clem would always shake his head and say, "Hey, nothing go wrong
when I wear these pants. These lucky pants." But nothing went that right
for Clem.

"Give a punk a gun and he just gotta *let* it off," Clem grumbled, opening the door of the pickup and getting in. He flashed the headlights three
times and pumped the brake lights three times.

"Why you giving the signal? We still need 'em on lookout," I said.

"Shut up, Joey," he said, getting out of the truck.

"Take it *eeeeez*y, Clementine. Ain't Joey's fault you froze," Elijah said.

"Froze?" Clem gave Elijah his what-the-hell-you-talking-about look,
but Eli was busy with the hide.

"She had you licked," I said. "You looked in her eyes, you sorry sack
of—"

"Froze, my ass. She too damn big. It hit me when I raised the hammer, how we gonna get her in the truck. We needed a yearling or
younger."

"A yearling won't feed enough," I said. "And what we *need* is to keep
those boys on lookout."

Eli finished cutting out the brand, rolled it into a bloody ball, and tossed it into some deep grass. I thought of fetching it and making a wallet later. That'd be wild, a wallet with McLaren's brand in it. But this was like patrol, like a mission; you can't be screwing around on patrol. It always surprised me how I missed the war at times, that feeling of being part of a team, having to not screw around.

"Without those boys we'll never lift her," Clem said. "Have to butcher her right here, at least into quarters, and that means another hour with our asses in the wind for McLaren to see." He turned back to the truck to get the bandsaw and send the reverse signal.

"Well, shit then," said Elijah, cleaning his knife on his boot, "let's wait till they get back 'fore we start making a mess."

The first boy to make it back was Eli Jr. A couple minutes later, Shorty Shangreaux's kid, Tattoo, came in from the opposite direction. Both were sweaty and panting, so we gave 'em a minute to catch their breath. I went and lay in a patch of high grass and watched the road. The Milky Way reached all the way down like a great arm to the distant horizon of the Black Hills. The road was still. There was the far-off yelp of coyotes, but that was it. There was no one out.

"Let's go," said Clem. We gathered around her, grabbed her legs, and tried lifting. He was right; we never would have budged her without the boys. We managed to get her head and neck onto the tailgate of the pickup, then her shoulders. It was a matter of inching her bit by bit the rest of the way. We were almost there when lights came up over the northern rise. We couldn't tell if it was a truck or a car, just two headlights floating on the endless straightaway. They were moving slow, which was not a good sign. We lay low in some tall grass. As the vehicle got closer, we could see there was a side beam, too, the kind they mount on the door for checking fences. The guy would have to be looking the other way not to see our truck or where we cut the wire to back into the field. When they came within a hundred yards, they slowed down and flicked the brights on. It was a pickup, all right, and the little orange lights on top of the cabin meant it was probably one of McLaren's.

"Shit," groaned Clem.

It slowed to a crawl, two wheels on the asphalt, two skimming the gravel shoulder.

"What are we gonna do?" I said.

"Depends on them. Might have to open up," Clem said. He threw a braid back over his shoulder, then screwed up his face and put his eye to the sighting piece of his rifle. Fucking Clem, only one of us who hadn't served, didn't want to fight no white man's war, and now here he is doing some cross between John Wayne and De Niro.

I looked over at Eli, hoping he'd agree that Clem was nuts, but he was busy lining them up in the sights of his thirty-thirty. There wasn't much choice.

They came within forty yards of us and pulled off the road onto the shoulder, their high beams all over Elijah's pickup. They couldn't see us, as we were lying low in tall grass, but we were right in the path of their beams, a few feet in front of Eli's pickup. I looked over at Eli, his face tiger-striped in grass shadows and light. He turned his head and whispered to the kids to crawl under the pickup and out the other side, then get as far away as possible. We'd pick them up along the way or meet them home in Wambli. Young Elijah didn't want to leave his dad.

"It'll be all right, Junior," Eli whispered. The boy hesitated. "Now," said Elijah in a harsher whisper. The two boys slithered backwards through the grass and beneath the pickup, then away.

From the direction of the rancher pickup came the sound of a door opening, then shutting, then a second one. We couldn't see them or know if they were armed, on account of their high beams in our eyes, but it was a fair guess they had rifles.

"We got no choice," whispered Clem. He was right. They were forcing our hand by coming that close. And the thing is, what we did wasn't any skin off a rancher's nose; all the cattle these days are insured. Plus it's not a regular thing with us. It was only on account of our mother's wake, Clem's and mine, that we did it. Clem's my half brother, and our mother had just died.

"You in that field, come on out slow," came a voice that tried to sound steady.

Clem let one off, deliberately high. There was the sound of bodies hitting the dirt. "This is Sioux land," Clem shouted. There was silence. He got up from the grass and fired at the pickup from a standing position. Of course, his pants lighted up like yellow neon in the high beams. I don't think he was drunk. We all swore to be sober, took an oath. I think he wanted to go out the old way, with a gun in his hand and a bullet in his chest, instead of hooked up to the dialysis machine at Rosebud.

"Get *down!*" yelled Eli, but Clem remained standing and taking aim at the truck, firing, dinging the grille. They returned fire and Clem was plain lucky he didn't get it. "This is too much," said Elijah, taking aim quickly. With two shots he plugged both headlights. Everything went dark. We could hear boots scrambling on the shoulder of the road, then doors opening, creating momentary light in the cabin. Their heads were ducked below the dashboard. The doors slammed, putting out the cabin light. We heard the engine thrown into reverse, tires tearing up dirt, then screeching on asphalt. They pulled back like that, patching rubber, maybe fifty yards, then turned and sped off into the night, red taillights aglow between the land and sky.

The next day, we were over at Bob Walking Eagle's, drinking beers and butchering the cow in his yard. He had the same kind of place as the rest of us: two-room shack with a bathroom. We were out in his yard, which was basically parched dirt, weeds, crumpled cans, and some busted bottles for color. We all had that kind of a garden, except for the various preachers who moved in to save us. Theirs were very prim and pretty, with lovely fences. They're big on fences.

In the back of the yard, we set up a couple of tables—that is, old doors laid over rusty oil drums—and it was on them that we cut up the cow. It's hard work with just knives. We didn't have cleavers or butcher blades. Some of the muscles were cased in sheaths that were way tougher than hide and took the edge off your knife in no time. Same with the tendons and ligaments. So the work was slow and we had to keep sharpening our blades on the whetstone, which was getting ugly with Elijah's tobacco juice.

The sun was hot and we wanted to get her butchered and cooked before she started stinking. Flies were all over the place. Armies of them. Blood and parts everywhere. The flies never had it so good. Suzy Walking Eagle had her little transistor going by the door to the house. The music and the beer helped you not feel the blisters that were starting in your knife hand.

Eli had a couple coolers in his pickup. Whenever someone was out of beer, Eli would catch Eli Jr.'s eye and point with his chin at the man with the empty can. Eli Jr. would go to the truck and come back with cold ones, offering them silently.

Elijah Hunts Alone had some income because he had a patch of land—not the tribe's, his own. There was some scrub pine on it. He sold wood to the ranchers now and then when he needed cash. It's not like he was rich. The Hunts Alones lived in a government-built shack like the rest of us, but they ate other foods than surplus cheese and butter, and their clothes never looked too tired. Eli and Eli Jr. dressed like ranchers—boots and fresh jeans, western shirts, and always a tin of Skoal in Eli's left pocket. They both kept their hair short. Junior had a rodeo buckle and Elijah wore about the biggest ten-gallon I ever saw. It was black, and there was no denying it looked good on him. He looked like a dark, handsome cowboy, 'cept for the beginnings of a gut. He had been a sharpshooter in the Marines and I guess maybe that's when he got into all the redneck shit, but he never forgot he's Sioux. No one ever accused him of that. In any case, I was pleased as hell he could shoot.

Eli Jr. was good-looking, too, clean-cut like his dad but real lean like a runner. He was fifteen and his main worry in life was whether the Crazy Horse School would have enough money for a football team again. He had a hell of an arm and maybe a future.

Clem put his knife down and accepted a beer from Eli Jr. He opened it with his bloody fingers and took a deep swig, then watched young Eli return to his stool, where his 7Up was waiting. "Don't you let the boy drink yet?" Clem said across the table to Elijah.

"He don't want to," said Elijah.

"Not with us old farts," said Shorty Shangreaux, "but I'll bet he go into the Badlands with his buddies and get plenty shitty. Don'tcha, Junior?"

Eli Jr. smiled timidly. "Yeah, in the Badlands," he said, but you could tell he never touched the stuff. Clem was still looking at him and I know what was going through his mind; he was remembering himself as a kid, how he had to pass the beers out to his dad's friends, fill their coffee mugs up with whiskey, listen to their drunken bullshit. And he remembered how determined he had been to never follow in that way.

He put down the can and picked up his knife, then started on a big section of the rib cage. "I want to build a scaffold," he said.

Shorty Shangreaux chuckled. "Shit, Clem."

Elijah Hunts Alone shook his head under the ten-gallon hat and said, "I don't know about you, Clementine."

Old Isaac Sky Elk, who's the tallest, most broad-shouldered sixty-year-old you'll ever see, laughed. "Old Clem think he some kind of a *bush* Injun now."

"You still fixin' to sun-dance, ain't you, Clem? One of these years when you're all dried out?" said Elijah. They all laughed or said shit, Shorty spraying beer as he said it and giggled.

"Go dance it today. They ain't gonna run no piss test on you, won't give you no balloon to blow, neither," said Shorty. It was late June; Speckled Hawk's sun dance was going on near the Butte. You had Sioux and Cheyennes from all over come for it—most to watch, and a handful to dance.

Clem ignored them. "What about it, Joey?" he asked, as if he had been talking to nobody but me all along. In a sense, I *was* the only one who mattered, because Clem and I were her sons, not them. Both our fathers were dead, so it was up to us and only us to make the funeral happen, provide the feast, do whatever else would be done. We killed the cow because we didn't have the money to buy that kind of meat. And that was serious enough in itself. But putting up a scaffold was another matter. They outlawed that long ago, and they take it a damn sight more serious than rustling beef. They say they outlawed scaffolds for sanitary reasons, but it was priests and missionaries who leaned on the government. Not doctors.

In the Lakota way, you wrapped the dead person in a hide and placed the body on a scaffold high above the ground, so no animals could get it. You left it there for two weeks to give the spirit time to quit the body and rise into the Milky Way. After two weeks, you put the body in the ground. That last bit is a compromise. The real old way was to just leave it on the scaffold for the wind, sun, and rain to reclaim.

"Joey, let's do it right, the old way," Clem said. "We'll bury her in the sky." He had nine years on me and he was looking wrinkled and pathetic with his swollen eyes and his braids gone gray.

"I'll do whatever you want," I said.

He nodded.

Walking Eagle's dog, Ooly, came over and started sniffing the cow legs, which had been sawed above the knees and stacked in a pile. The legs were skinned within a few inches of the hooves, and there were flies walking the length of the tendons and ligaments, looking for beads of blood. Ooly was a yellow Lab, very skinny. You could count her ribs from down the road. I figured she was going to scamper off with one of those legs, but she didn't. She just lay down next to the pile and shut her eyes. She was a sweet dog, always wagged her tail at everybody. But the first thing you always noticed about Ooly was her open sores and wounds. She's got the mange real bad and a few gashes in her ears that won't close, and on her shoulders, too. There's always a cloud of flies around her, settling in her sores and cuts, but she doesn't notice—or else she knows there's no point in resisting. Just too many keep coming.

The new Mormon missionary in town said hello from the dirt road.

Bob Walking Eagle murmured, "Hey ya." The preacher took this as an invitation and strolled into the yard. Elijah squirted tobacco juice, which kind of spoke for us all.

The preacher smiled real warm and wide, proud of how straight his teeth were. He was in his fifties, I'd say, and handsome. Usually, Salt Lake sends us kids who are just out of high school. The church calls them "Elders," which makes it easier for them to lecture us on the mysteries of God. Even to our old people, they lecture. Of course, there's not much mystery the way they tell it. It's all quite pat. Anyway, the last "Elder" knocked up a Wambli girl, so now we've been sent this older fellow who is married and is supposed to have his shit in one boot.

"How are you, gents?" he asked, coming up to the table.

"All right, Preacher," Bob said.

"My name's Cyrus Blake. Call me Cy or Brother Blake. We Mormons are missionaries, not preachers."

"Didn't know there was a difference," said Eli.

"It's about *acts,* not words."

"We'll call you Action Man, how's that?" said Elijah with a friendly smile.

"Yeah, the last one, he got some action, too," Bob said. Shorty Shangreaux and I cracked up. Cyrus Blake acted like he didn't hear the crack.

"So, what are you all up to?" he asked.

Old Isaac looked down at the knife in his big bloody hand, at the rump and ribs on the table, then over at the hide, spine, and guts in the yard. "Cutting meat," he said, like he was talking to a slow child.

The preacher blushed and looked down at his shoes. "Say, this poor pooch has some awful-looking sores. He yours, Bob?"

"She. Yep."

"I believe I saw a veterinarian's sign when I was in Kadoka last. I'm sure he could put some salve and medicine in these wounds, close 'em right up," said the Mormon.

"That'd be great," said Bob. "Only problem is the last preacher who took an interest in Ooly was a Christian Scientist. He kind of won her over. Ain't that right, Ooly?" Ooly wagged her tail against the ground and blinked her eyes open, then back shut. The Mormon blushed a second time. He must figure old Ooly's on Blue Shield/Blue Cross. Preachers always think everybody has an allowance just 'cause they do. And they always think they got the salve and the medicine. They're more like the flies, though, always looking for the wound, settling in, sponging an existence. We've got 'em all, Lutherans, Episcopalians, Wesleyans, Catholics, Seventh-Day Adventists, and everything else, and all of them with the exclusive path to Christ and Paradise. They're always nice and kind till they realize you ain't gonna buy. Then they got to fix your wagon somehow. With a vengeance.

"I'll just rub her down with motor oil," said Bob. The preacher smiled like he thought Bob was joking, but motor oil ain't a bad way to beat the mange. "That holy oil go a long way with Ooly. Guess that makes you Catholic, don't it, Ooly?" She thumped her tail and blinked her dark eyes again, closed them quick before the flies got in. Bob shook his head. "She don't know what she is, no more."

"A rancher named McLaren phoned me," said the preacher. "His people believe somebody rustled one of their cows."

"Is that right?" said Clem.

"Yes, it is. I don't believe we've met. I'm Cyrus Blake."

Clem just kept cutting. The silence was hard to take.

The song on the radio had a nice slow beat and a girl was singing about how now that her boyfriend was gone she could have her dinner in a fancy restaurant, she could go anywhere, do whatever she want . . . *but nothing compares, nah, nothing compares to him* was her big line. Old Isaac Sky Elk broke the silence. "Damn, she's good. These black girls can *sing.* Ain't heard nothing that sweet since the Supremes."

"That ain't a black girl. That'sa Irish chick," said Frankie, one of the Walking Eagle boys. He had spent the summer on the East Coast going to some kind of science program for minority kids. "Half the chicks in Boston got their heads shaved 'cause of her."

We all looked at him, even the preacher.

"Okay, a quarter," said Frankie. "Seriously, some guy told her what beautiful, thick hair she had, how pretty and feminine it made her look, so she went and shaved it off. Clean as a cue ball."

"Shit," said Elijah from under his ten-gallon. "Hope nobody tell her she got pretty tits."

The preacher laughed a bit with us, like he was a good old boy, but not too hard 'cause of the holy act. When the laughing died, he said, "You can tell me, boys. You know I wouldn't do anything to fall out of your good graces. *Is* this McLaren's cow?"

We sipped our beers, listened to the radio, and kept cutting. "Man, if she don't sound like a piece of brown sugar, then I don't know shit," said Isaac Sky Elk.

Frankie and the other Walking Eagle boys took the pieces of meat that we cut and threw them in the huge kettle, which was actually an old metal watering trough about five feet long and three feet deep. We had dug a pit in the yard and built a fire in it, then placed the kettle over the flames. The water was bubbling like mad and we had about half the cow in already, with canned onions, peas, carrots, and stuff.

"The point is," said the Mormon, "if it's McLaren's cow, it's got to be paid for."

"This cow *been* paid for," said Clem.

"Who'd you buy it from?"

"And it wasn't cheap," Clem said. There was another long silence. There was just the black-sounding Irish chick on the radio and the sound of the knives working. The preacher folded his arms and looked at his shoes, then looked up at Isaac, as he was the oldest of us, so maybe the most reasonable. "What I'm proposing to you is this: If you men were to see fit to pay for the cow, I would be only too happy to deliver the money to the McLarens, and that would be the end of it. No questions asked. And if you can't put together that kind of money right away, why I would be willing to pay McLaren myself and be paid back by you over time, at no more interest than a bank would charge."

"What's a McLaren?" said Clem.

The preacher tried another approach. "Elijah, that's a handsome pickup you got. Tell me, though, what would happen if Bob's boys were to take it and sell it, or go joyriding and crack it up? Put a strain on the friendship with Bob, don't you think?"

"Oh, Bob and I been through thick and thin," said Elijah.

The preacher continued. "Yes, but when you take someone's property, it destroys the fabric of community and fellowship. I think any man who has as much to be proud of as does a Sioux would be ashamed to—well, let's call it by its proper name—ashamed to steal."

"Don't be talking property and shit to us," said Clem. "No white fucker asked permission before you wiped out all the buffalo. Prairies was dark with them, and hunting was our way. You couldn't beat us in battle, so you killed all our food out from under us. You wiped 'em out so that we couldn't *live* no more."

"So we couldn't *resist* them no longer, Clem. But you can't tell me we ain't *alive*," I said. I was feeling sorry for the preacher. It wasn't his fault, all that history, and I could tell Clem was about to lay on him the part about how when we had no more buffalo robes to keep us warm, we had to go to their trading posts and trade for blankets, blankets that they'd infected with pox and typhoid deliberately.

Clem shot me a look of disgust and pity. "Alive? McLaren got more cattle on his ranch than you got Sioux on this side," he said. *This side* meant the world of the living. In the old way, the next world is on the other side of an invisible screen. You go through the screen when you die, through the skin of this world, to the *other side,* the spirit side, which is everywhere around us. Clem put his knife down and wiped his fingers on a rag, then said, "Anyway, you alive, Joey?" like that was his big punch.

"I've been more alive than you could guess."

"Yeah, shooting gooks from a chopper, big fucking deal," he said.

"No shame whatsoever?" said the preacher.

Clem looked at him impatiently, as if he'd forgotten the guy was still there, then he said, "What shames me is that Sioux got to slaughter creatures that got the sense of a rock and the speed of a tree. Sioux were *hunters.* Buffalo are gone, antelope gone, elk gone, deer gone. What the hell else is there? And don't be talking stealing till you give us back the Black Hills and all the lands that were guaranteed by treaty, then stole. To call it by its proper name."

When we got the rest of the meat chopped and into the kettle, we left two of Bob Walking Eagle's boys with a shovel so that they could stir it. We had a few hours to kill before the wake, so we decided to drive out to the big prairie north of Eagle Nest Butte and watch the sun dancers. Elijah drove us out in his pickup, just him, Clem, and me—and the last of the Budweisers. Instead of parking in the field by the other trucks and cars, Eli pulled off the dirt road early and stopped a hundred yards or so from the dance. We were on a slight rise and could see the crowd gathered below in a circle around the mystery circle. We glanced around to see if anybody was nearby, then chugged the beers and hid the cans under the seat. I passed around some mint Life Savers, then Eli doled out some cherry cough drops. We got out of the truck and walked down to the dance.

There were a hundred people, I'd say, and a lot of our friends were in the crowd. The only greeting was a nod or a smile. People were quiet and still. The only sound was the eagle-bone whistles that the dancers blew. They're shrill and give you shivers. Mostly, it was Oglala Sioux like us in the crowd, but also some Burnt Thighs from the Rosebud. And there were a few Cheyennes. Cheyennes are good sun dancers and might as well be Sioux. They've always been close to us, and helped us rub out Custer. There were a couple of canvas tepees set up beyond the mystery circle, and a sweat lodge made up of bent branches and hides.

We made our way through the crowd and reached the front row. I got down on one knee. Clem hovered behind me. "Look at that dancer!" he said, bending down near me and pointing with his finger. He was trying to whisper, but it was more of a shriek. "He's a fucking *white* fucker!" A few people turned and looked at us. I was glad Clem was down low with me so that they couldn't smell his breath. We would have never lived it down.

"That's one crazy white guy," I said in a quieter whisper. This blond dancer was lean and toned, didn't grow up on surplus cheese and butter.

There were twelve dancers strung to the pole. This white dude was pulling just as hard on his cord as the others, but I doubted he could really have visions. This was the fourth and final day of the dance. For the first three days, they just dance untethered from sunup to sundown without rest or food or water. At night, they rest but continue to fast. At dawn on the fourth day, they pierce. The medicine man cuts a vertical gash in the chest of the dancer and then a second gash a few inches to the side of the first. He pushes a stick through the first slit and passes it sideways under the skin till it comes out the second slit. The skewer is then fastened to a cord, and the cord is attached to the top of the sun-dance pole, which usually stands about thirty feet high. The pole is a freshly harvested cottonwood tree, cut down with great ceremony and then planted upright in the center of the mystery circle. Leashed to the pole, you dance all day, pulling away from it, jerking the cord to increase the pain. You blow an eagle-bone whistle so the shrillness takes your mind off the pain some. In time, you slip into sort of a trance. The point is to acquire wakan, to have a vision, and go to the land of the spirits. Then you pull so hard that your chest rips and you break free. There's sort of a rebirth in that moment, like ripping free of the placenta, or so it's said. The spirit that visited you in the vision will guide you through this new life. And if the spirit is strong, it will protect you in battle and create an aura about you that will inspire men to follow you. If you get wounded, it will heal you. This is wakan. And all that is mysterious and unexplainable is wakan.

It seemed strange to see a white guy undergoing all this. On one hand,

I figured the spirits, if there were any, would never talk to a white; on the other hand, I couldn't see any white dude falling for this stuff.

I had sun-danced before I went into the Army, because I knew I would be going to Vietnam. Originally, it was a warrior's dance of thanksgiving. If you had escaped death in battle, you would endure the dance as a sign of thanks to Wakan Tanka, the Great Mysterious, for having spared you so that you could go on providing for your family. For it was His hand, not chance, that saved you. At some point, warriors started doing it before battles, to seek God's protection, to hedge their bets. That's why I danced. But now it's got less to do with being a warrior and more to do with becoming revered as a traditional, one who keeps the culture going. It's ritual. Such things have no meaning to me now, but Clem would give anything to have my scars. The problem is you've got to prepare under the supervision of a medicine man, got to purge your system of all poisons for twelve months before dancing. You've got to be pure. Clem never dropped the bottle for more than two weeks.

"How much that whore Speckled Hawk making to let this white fucker dance?" Clem asked.

Speckled Hawk was the medicine man running this sun dance. He had married a rich white woman and was always off in the East being wined and dined by professors and so-called mystics who want to say they know a Sioux medicine man. Some would come back to the rez with him and take notes, then come out with books on the mighty Sioux, always dedicated to their dear friend, Mr. Speckled Hawk.

"Now they gonna steal the religion, too," Clem whimpered.

"Ah, get off it, Clem. It beats the hell out of before, when they tried to kill it completely. At least the dance is legal now. So you got a white who's interested, sees something in Lakota way. Cut the fucker some slack."

"Fuck you, Joey, he's probably a anthro. It's a book to him."

Missionaries live on us year-round, but the anthropologists are a seasonal pest, swarming us each summer like locusts. I guess the priests are right that man always has choice, even on Pine Ridge. Those who refuse to be saved can choose to be *explained*. "Anthro or not," I said. "I bet he ain't a fall-down drunk."

"You're telling me he pre*pared* twelve months?"

I took Clem by the arm and led him away from the crowd and back to the truck. "Either do it or shut up about it, Clem. We're tired of your bullshit. Drop the booze and dance, or let it rest."

"You're a *hard* fucker, Joey."

"Yeah, and maybe you drink so you always got an excuse not to pierce."

He looked at me, mouth open, eyes welling. "On the day we're burying our mother."

"A hard-ass bush would've swung at me, or he'd be home building the scaffold he been talking about."

"I never swung on a brother."

He always does that. He always wins by changing the rules. My anger melted. "Look, you're always saying how the dance is gonna make you feel complete. I don't think it does, or maybe the war undid it. But if that's what you want, Clem, you gotta make it happen. You gotta take steps."

"I'm down to just beer now, Joey. Soon, I'll be dry."

"That's good," I said, wondering how many times I'd heard it. "Let's find Eli and get back."

Eli was kneeling at the front of the crowd. A couple of the dancers had broken free. The white dude was just a few feet away, with his back to us. Like the others, he wore a sage wreath on his head and a wraparound ankle-length skirt. He was sort of hopping from foot to foot but leaning back away from the pole. His eagle bone was very loud and his head started rocking from side to side against the back of his shoulder blades, almost like his neck had been snapped. One arm flailed and the other hung limp. We could see his eyes, and above his eyes his nose and mouth, the mouth tight around the whistle, the chin skyward. For a moment, he looked right at us, then his eyes rolled back into his skull and went completely white. He kept hopping and leaning back. The eagle-bone whistle flew from his lips, but he kept blowing like it was still there. Then a smile appeared. A smile upside down is a weird-looking thing.

"Yes," he shouted. "Of course. Always." He flew back into us and might have broken his neck but for Elijah catching his head before it hit the ground. He was lying back in our arms, bleeding freely from the chest, fresh red over sunbaked crusts of black. A thick flap of skin hung down from the wound like a wet flag. It had stretched a good deal before ripping. His body quivered, his chest rising and falling. His hand clenched my forearm very tight. His eyes were open, beaming, then closing, then opening again. His other hand was squeezing Eli's hand. His blond head was in the crook of my elbow. His mouth was a strange thing to look upon because it bore a deep scar that ran perpendicular to the lips, extending from one nostril down the better part of his chin. It was like he had a big *X* or a cross in his face, at least when his mouth was shut. I felt very close to him, whoever he was. I could also feel Clem standing behind me, but I couldn't bear to look up at him. Clem let out a strange sound that reminded me of a rabbit I had started to skin once that I thought was dead. I turned. His fists were clenched at his sides, knuckles white, and his eyes were a red mess.

We got into Elijah's truck and headed for Wambli. "Eli, I need saplings for scaffold poles," said Clem.

"You're not gonna build no scaffold," said Elijah.

"You gonna let me cut some or do I gotta drive to Rosebud?"

"I'll charge you what I do the ranchers. It's lumber, Clem. It don't grow on trees." Elijah laughed and looked over at me for a laugh.

"How much?" said Clem.

"Six bucks a pine, eight for a cottonwood. But I mean saplings."

"Shit, Eli, I guess you don't have enough in life," said Clem. He turned to me. "You gonna kick in?"

"If Eli'll give me credit," I said.

Eli stopped the truck and looked Clem in the eye, the brim of his Stetson brushing Clem's forehead. "I don't want your money, Clem. I just want you to understand nothing's free no more. Ain't no fat of the land. Everything cost. You wanna build a scaffold like an old-timer, *fine;* but if you don't pick it up, means I got to. Everything's property now. Like that fucking cow."

"Elijah, you're a saint," said Clem, smiling. "A reg'lar latter-day."

We went out to Elijah's woods and chopped some saplings. Clem branched them with Elijah's ax, then we loaded them in the pickup.

We unloaded by Clem's trailer house, about half a mile out of Wambli. He didn't like having neighbors. Linda leaned on the doorjamb, watching us with her arms crossed. Her hair was still black and she had a decent shape after shucking four kids. She turned and went inside. When we entered, she was wrapping our mom from head to toe in a blanket. She tied it tight with clothesline, tying loops around the ankles, knees, working upward. It was starting to smell and I was glad Linda's kids were over at her sister's.

The walls of the house were covered with my mom's paintings. Mom loved sketching scenes of the old life, men on the hunt, horses pulling travois, women making pemmican, embroidering their husbands' war shirts. *If you can't live it no more,* she used to say, *keep it alive some other way.* One sad thing about her death is that it came just when she started having some success. A store in Omaha was selling her pictures. They sent her small checks and supplied her with canvases and paper and paints. They also sent her poster tubes of hard plastic so she could mail them her latest pieces.

On the wall was her unfinished sketch of Crazy Horse. Unlike other chiefs, he had never sat for a photo. He had also never signed a treaty and never took a drink. Some say he thought the camera might steal his wakan. Other chiefs, after all, had sat with whites, had their portraits taken, and lost their fighting spirit. So Mom had to rely on descriptions that had been handed down. Crazy Horse was lighter-skinned than most and had been called Curly because of his wavy hair. He wore only one eagle feather out of modesty, rather than the war bonnet that was his due. He was lean and wiry, because of his many fasts. He fasted so there'd be more food for the children, and to increase his wakan. He got to the point where bullets melted in the air around him. His wakan sometimes showed itself, shimmering about him like an aura as he rode into the enemy. That was the part that stumped Mom. She didn't know how to paint the wakan. The face on the paper was handsome and strong, but she was sure it was not yet Crazy Horse. Clem said there was plenty of wakan in the eyes and that the picture was a sacred thing.

Linda placed a hairbrush into the blanket before tying it up all the way. Clem handed her some paintbrushes to put in. It was customary to send the dead off with things that would serve them on the other side. He took down the picture of Crazy Horse, rolled it up and put it in the largest of the plastic tubes, which was about three feet long and five inches in diameter. He screwed the top on and handed the tube to Linda. "Put this in. She's got lots of time to finish it now."

"It won't fit, Clem," said Linda, looking up at him.

He untied the ropes and slipped the tube down deep in the blanket, so that it rested on the chest and legs. They retied the loops.

"Be better if we had some hides," she said.

"We got a hide," said Clem. "We can wrap it right over the blanket."

"It ain't cured," I said.

"We'll dry it on the fire."

Bob Walking Eagle had lashed a wooden broom handle to a metal pot, making a giant ladle. His sons had done the same. They ladled stew out of the trough into two aluminum trash cans that the tribe loaned out for feasts and occasions like this. With the three of them working, it went fast.

We took the empty trough off the fire pit, which was mostly embers and hot rocks now. Clem laid the hide down, letting the blood and fat sizzle off. Then we took it back to his house and wrapped it around our blanketed mom, tying it tight as we had the blanket. The burnt smell was good, overpowering the other.

Clem and I carried the cottonwood poles and some tools up the hill in back of his house. We stopped at the crest by Wenonah's grave. A few feet from Wenonah's was an open one, more than six feet deep. The pile of earth by it was moist. Clem and I looked at each other, puzzled. Linda was still making her way up the hill. He looked down at her.

"That's right, Clem," she said. "Somebody had to. I couldn't exactly count on you for a scaffold."

Clem laid the poles down and started pacing out a rectangle, marking the corners with his heel in the dirt. When he marked all four, he took a swig from a flask of cherry liqueur.

"Jesus, not by our daughter's grave," said Linda.

Clem pocketed the bottle and looked at me. "There's no missing Mom when you're married to Linda."

"Yeah, make jokes," said Linda. "But don't gimme no more talk about bringing back the warrior societies, or any more of your bull about '73 and AIM and being tight with Peltier. Only warriors now are the women."

There was a shoot-out with the FBI in '73 at Wounded Knee. It was a siege, really, that went on for months and was the high point of Clem's life. I was still in the Army, so I don't know how involved he really was, but he talks like he was a major player. I guess her point was that there was a lot of booze between then and now and that the warriors had become wastes again. But the bit about women being the new warriors was a hell of a leap. I looked at her, wondering if I should mention Elijah's bronze star, Isaac Sky Elk's Congressional Medal of Honor from the Korean conflict, or Bobby Red Cloud and the other guys that never came back, or my own Purple Hearts, or Shorty Shangreaux's brother, Buddy, who survived Vietnam just to get picked off by an FBI sniper at Wounded Knee.

She returned my gaze and said, "Maybe you ain't a drunk, Joey. But tin soldiers and warriors ain't the same thing. There's a world of difference."

"Is that right?"

"Yeah, like wakan and knowing what you're fighting for. Nobody got to give orders to a warrior."

I decided not to get into it with her, because she wasn't altogether wrong. I picked up Elijah's fencepost digger and started to sink some holes where Clem had marked off the corners. "Not here," she said. "They'll see it from the road." We moved twenty feet down the far side of the hill, low enough so that we couldn't see the road. I sank four holes that made a rectangle of about six feet by three feet. We stood a pole in each. Clem and I lashed four cross-poles that connected the four standing ones. We lashed them at about seven feet up, then laid branches across them, making a high bed.

When we returned to the house, the Walking Eagles were unloading the trash cans of stew from their rickety pickup. As the sun went down, people started showing up. They came from towns all over Pine Ridge, and some from Rosebud. Everyone brought their own bowl and spoon, then ate steady and remembered our mother fondly. Good thing we shot a big cow. Young drummers sat around a big drum, beating it slowly and wailing with the old people.

Clem sat in a chair in the yard with his elbows on his knees and his face in his hands, sobbing. Soon he started wailing with the others, then above them. I guess the booze was wearing off him and her death was sinking in. I wanted to let loose and do the same, but it wasn't there. My numbness was different from Clem's, and had nothing to do with booze.

Something brushed the side of my knee, then tugged at my jeans. I looked down and saw my nephew Jeb. He was about five or six then, and he was clutching my jeans at the knee and staring off at his father. Then he looked up at me, wide-eyed. He seemed frightened. I reached down and picked him up. "Is Daddy okay?" he asked.

"Yeah, he's okay, Jeb."

Linda walked up behind Clem with a hunting knife in her left hand. She brought it to the nape of his neck. With her other hand she took hold of one of his braids. She started cutting it at the base. He turned and held his hand open. She gave him the knife. He cut about five inches off of each braid, leaving a good four inches dangling, which was four inches more than she would have left. It was a mark of grief to cut your hair, but Clem didn't want it so short that people would think he was nontraditional. He didn't want to look like no Cowboy Eli. He removed the leather ties from the shorn braids and tied them to the stumpy braids that remained, then he tossed the cut ones into the fire. Stars began to light the sky.

Still standing behind the chair, Linda started massaging Clem's neck. Then she rubbed his temples. When he leaned forward in convulsions, she walked around the chair and kneeled by him, kissing his brow. Jeb saw all this, then turned and looked me in the eye. "He's okay," I said. "He's just sad." I was leaning back against Eli's pickup. So were Bob, Isaac, and Eli. After a few minutes, Linda left Clem's side and walked over to us. "Did you guys get enough stew?" she asked. Everyone said he had. "How about you, little one, did you get enough?" she said, taking Jeb's hand in hers. He nodded. "You sure you don't want more?" Jeb shook his head. "Okay," she said and gave his hand a kiss. Then she noticed Eli's bottle. "It's a wake, Elijah."

"So I'm Irish," he said, flashing a pearly grin. We laughed. Little Jeb laughed along, the way kids do.

"Okay, you're Irish," she said, and she took her son into her arms and turned her back on us in one motion.

Just then Ray Bright Cloud floated onto the scene in one of the new cruisers. I looked up the hill to make sure the scaffold was not in view. Ray was a reservation cop and proud of it. If they paid him nothing, he would still do it just for the uniform. He looked a bit like Marlon Brando, and almost as heavy. He eased the cruiser to a stop and put his elbow and head out the window. His hair was short and thinning. Ray had some white blood that he made the most of, put Vitalis in his hair and grew a mustache. "Hey, fellas," he said. "I don't wanna see you out on the roads tonight. McLaren say he got it on good authority Clem popped a cow of his. You gonna start a war with that shi-tuff." Ever since he became a deacon at the Episcopal church in Kadoka, Ray's been replacing *shit* with *stuff,* but sometimes his tongue ain't up to speed. "Don't think 'cause you're a bunch of good old boys I won't hand you to the State Troopers if I catch you messin' with fences."

"Yeah okay, Ray," said Elijah, as the cruiser rolled away. "You fat shit."

The red brake lights lit up and the car rolled back. Ray put his window down again. "Joey, I'm sorry about your mom. Tell Clem, will ya?"

"Sure, Ray."

"And, Elijah."

"Yeah, Ray?"

"Your gut's looking pretty good yourself."

Elijah cracked up. "Okay, Ray."

"How *are* you, Raymond?" said Linda, walking up to the cruiser with Jeb still in her arms. "Doing the double shift?"

"You know it."

"Well, have some food before you go," she said.

"Junior, go get Ray a bowl," said Elijah to Eli Jr. "And make it chunky. Bring some salt back, too." Junior took off for the trash cans. Ray put the car in park.

The boy came back with a plastic margarine bowl filled with stew. He gave it to his father, and Elijah passed it gently through the window to Ray. Then he handed him a spoon and the salt bag.

Ray tasted it. "It's good," he said, then sprinkled salt on.

"Try the chunks. They're tender," said Eli.

It wasn't long before Ray was scraping the bottom of the bowl. "Why don't you get out?" said Linda. "Stretch your legs, have some more, say a word to Clem. It'll mean the world to him, Ray."

"Maybe I will," he said, opening the door.

"Might as well eat your fill," she said, smiling warmly. "Now that you're an accessory after the fact."

Ray pulled the door shut and started the engine back up. "Very clever, Linda," he said through the window. "Crafty as a coyote. I guess you have a receipt from some rancher proving you bought that cow."

"Wakan Tanka sent us a buffalo," she said. "Everybody knows buffalo is what you serve at wakes. Been that way since the beginning. Even if He had sent us a cow and we didn't have a receipt, that wouldn't prove it was a McLaren cow." She put her hand on his arm, flattening the razor crease in his polyester uniform. "If you get hungry later, Ray, you just stop by. I'll save you some." She smiled. It was a sincere invitation to a man who was rarely included, largely because he chose to be separate. Ray lived off the rez with his white wife. He was only here to police us. He tried not to return her smile. Linda's smile was never easy to resist. With red eyes and smudged cheeks, it was harder still.

He shook his head and grinned. "Little coyote," he said, then put the cruiser in gear and drove off.

◆

Isaac, Elijah, Clem, and I carried the body up the hill. Everyone followed us, the drummers still hitting the drum slowly as they walked, and the old people still wailing. The load was light enough. My only fear was that Clem would go into convulsions again. We passed by Wenonah's grave and the open one, then came to the scaffold. Clem and I lifted the bundle to our shoulders. We looked sideways at each other under the load. "Now," I said. We stepped up onto the chairs. One of Clem's feet came off the chair and swung in space. Linda rushed up and supported him. We lifted the bundle off our shoulders and maneuvered it onto the platform of branches beneath the stars.

Linda hung one of Mom's favorite shirts on a corner of the scaffold. My aunt tied a pair of moccasins with pretty beadwork to one of the poles. Speckled Hawk tied a sacred bundle to another pole, and so on.

Her burial in the stars was complete. People went down to the house, some for more talk and stew, others to wail and mourn. The wailing started getting to me, so I left. But I heard it from far off, right through the night.

It wasn't just for my mother that I mourned that night but for Wenonah again. She had been Clem and Linda's first child. And she was my mother's greatest work, for it was mostly Mom who had raised and shaped her.

The last time I saw Wenonah, I had just finished Door Gunner School and gone home to South Dakota for a few days before shipping out to Vietnam. I was scared. Everything I looked at on the rez, every shack, every parched field, made me wonder if I was looking at it all for the last time. It all became beautiful. Even from the plane on the way in to Rapid City, it had struck me that way. A boy in the seat in front of me kept telling his dad there were diamond fields glittering below us, and green sparkles, fields of emeralds. I knew it was just years of busted bottles and Bud cans around our little shack towns, but as I looked down over the sparkling rez, I was sick with the fear that I would never see my home again. There was a feast where I said my goodbyes. Then Clem and I got in this old pickup so he could take me back to Rapid. I wanted that truck to break down. But the engine started up and we began to roll. "Uncle Joey, Uncle Joey," came a voice. It was Wenonah running to us. We stopped, and I opened the door. She had some flowers and roots that she had picked from the top of Eagle Nest Butte. She was stuffing them into a drawstring pouch. I had seen her sewing it earlier in the week but figured she was just making herself a purse. She scrunched all the petals into it and drew the string tight. "Wear it like a medicine bag," she said. "Like Crazy Horse did, to turn away the bullets. But be careful, Uncle Joey. It might not be real medicine at all." She was almost ten.

"Wenonah," I said in Lakota, kneeling in front of her on the dirt road. "It seems a truly sacred bundle. I'll see *you* in thirteen moons."

She smiled her toothy smile and hugged me around the neck tightly with her skinny arms. She held me like that a few seconds, then placed the drawstring over my head and around my collar. I tucked the pouch inside my uniform and felt it against my breast. I can't say if it kept the bullets from my heart like Crazy Horse's did, but more than once it kept me from cracking up.

◆

Two days after Mom's funeral, I woke up in Bob's yard with Elijah, Isaac, and Shorty. It was a shrill and high-pitched thunder that woke us: "Free Sugar-Daddies and Snickers for all who come to morning mass." The amps and speakers mounted on the Ford were turned up full blast, crackling and squawking to wake the dead.

"There goes that faggot O'Reilly." Bob yawned.

"He ain't a fag," said Shorty. "Is he?"

"Let's just say he likes it up the rectory," said Bob.

Old Isaac chuckled, the lines in his face deepening into a grin. "The rectory, eh?" He shook his head and rubbed his eyes awake.

Eli called out, "Hey, Father, what time's the show?"

"Ten o'clock," screeched the speakers on the Ford.

Old Isaac's chest shook with a little laugh, then he got up and stepped over Shorty's legs to reach into the flatbed of Eli's pickup. There were still beers in Eli's emergency cooler, so we took some hair of the dog to clear our heads.

The Lutheran and his wife were coming up the road in a shiny blue

Ram Charger, also fitted out with speakers. In his honey voice, Reverend Swensen exclaimed, "Hershey's Kisses and Musketeers for all who come to sermon." Joe Conquering Bear's little whelps ran out of the house, the screen door slapping behind them. Swensen slowed down and the kids climbed in the back.

Isaac hummed a few bars of "Swing Low, Sweet Chariot" from deep down in his barrel chest.

"Yeah, how low can you go?" said Elijah, pushing back his Stetson.

"Makes you miss the old days when they just got the BIA cops to nab 'em, beat 'em, and haul 'em in. That was ugly but honest," said Isaac. He swallowed some beer and lulled softly, almost under his breath, "*A band full of angels chasing after me, coming for to carry me . . .*" His deep voice made the high notes effortlessly and trailed off. I was struck at how beautiful a singing voice he had, how spiritual it sounded. I guess Shorty was, too, because he said, "Shit, Isaac, you shoulda been a nigger."

Isaac smiled, then sipped some beer. "That's what your old lady tells me."

Shorty laughed and squirted chew on Isaac's boot.

"Hey, where the hell's Clem?" asked Bob.

"Haven't seen him since the funeral," I said.

They all looked at me like I'd fallen asleep on watch. "We gotta hang together till this thing blows over," said Elijah. "McLaren could have him hanging from a tree."

The Lutheran and his wife slowed down to say hello, she through the window, he through the speakers. "Morning, boys."

"Halle*lu*jah *to* ya," said Shorty. He patted the hood of the shiny new truck and exclaimed in a Baptist twang, "What a friend we have in Jesus."

"How goes the roundup?" called Isaac with a big smile. The wife turned red but kept waving little stiff waves, like the queen. With her other hand, she jabbed her husband's leg to make sure he kept rolling. A cloud of dust rose behind them as the little Conquering Bear kids and some others waved to us, feeling special in the shiny truck.

We sat around and sipped our beers. My stomach started knotting up. "What am I supposed to do, put him on a leash?" I said.

A few minutes later, Shorty said, "He's probably fine. Probably came across a bottle and wanted it for himself is all."

Just then, from out of the Lutheran's dust cloud way down the road, appeared the sloping shoulders I knew so well. Clem was stooped and looking dog-tired, but shuffling along faster than usual. Thank God, I whispered.

He reached us and fell to his knees. "You won't believe it," he sputtered in Lakota.

We put a beer in his hand but he dropped it and picked up the cooler, tipped it back and drank a gallon of melted ice.

"Was it McLaren?" asked Isaac.

"Much more," said Clem.

"Catch your breath, keep it simple," said Isaac. "Don't give us some shit we saw on TV." Clem was famous for his bullshit, specially after boozing.

"Drove out to Kadoka last night on a juice mission," said Clem, still in Lakota but using bits of English. "A great weirdness happened, maybe a vision."

"What you talking Indian for?" asked Shorty. Clem and I had been raised on Lakota, and old Isaac spoke it, but the others didn't. Clem just kept jabbering. When it was clear he wasn't switching to English, Isaac and I started translating. It took both of us to piece together his scattered rambling. The best we could make of it was this:

Clem had grabbed a twelve-pack of Buds the previous night from the cooler of Jenkins's general store and placed it on the counter. As he went through his wallet and counted bills and coins, he could feel Jenkins's daughter behind the register looking at him, at his graying braids and at the creased, sunburnt leather of his face. He knew his face was tired and lined, and he could feel her eyes finding ugliness in his every feature.

"How you doin'?" he had said as he placed the money on top of the twelve-pack.

She took the cash and rang it up without a word. She was blond and thin-lipped, twenty-five years old and had the world figured out. He didn't care what she thought. He knew he couldn't change people. He was more interested in the dull glow of bottles on the shelf behind her, where they kept the good stuff, the green and brown bottles from Scotland and Canada, and the Jim Beam and Jack Daniel's. The stuff he'd sworn off. He took two more fives out of his wallet and put them on the counter. "And I'll take ten bucks of unleaded."

She nodded and set the meter. He slid the twelve-pack into his Boy Scouts of America knapsack, slung it over his shoulder, and said goodnight.

His Impala waited out by the pumps, dented, rusty, without hubcaps. He unhooked the hose. An old man, a rancher type, replaced the other hose and said, "Evening," exhaling whiskey fumes that shot Clem back to childhood, to J&B bear hugs and that feeling of strong arms and love coming through a blanket, scratchy kisses on his cheeks. There had been the downside, too, like finding his father passed out on the road, the disappointment of missing camping trips because his dad would be in a stupor for days. But never had there been any beatings or ugliness. His dad was never an ugly drunk, yet Clem had decided early on that he would not follow in that way. His would be the old way, the Lakota way. He would hunt and trap, as our uncle Jesse had tried to do. But there just wasn't enough game. Even so, he could keep clean, work, have a family, do right by them, take his kids camping in the Badlands now and then. And for a number of years, he did just that, until Wenonah got killed.

The nozzle dangled from his hand and felt like a heavy six-shooter, a flamethrower. He wanted to erase the general store and the ugly little buildings from the face of the prairies. Prairies had always cleaned themselves with fire, he thought. Instead, he replaced the nozzle and went inside. "Forget the gas and gimme one of them J&B bottles." He counted out his last six dollars and added them to the ten she already had.

She checked the meter to make sure, then took a bottle down and placed it on the counter. She snuck a look at him as she took the last of his cash. *Dumb-ass Indian,* he could feel her thinking.

You don't know shit, little girl, he thought right back. He waited for his change and for her to bag the bottle like she's supposed to, like her fat-assed father would have done. But she didn't, probably figured what's the point with these Indians. He didn't say a thing, just opened up his Scout bag and put the bottle in with the twelve-pack.

"Good night," he said for the second time.

"Night," she said, and then added something he couldn't fully hear but that he thought was, *Be Prepared.* And she gave him this sarcastic little two-fingered Boy Scout salute.

He turned the engine over and pulled onto 73 South. It was a twenty-seven-mile drive home to Wambli through wasted prairie and Badlands. The needle was on E, but he had the most forgiving gauge ever made. He always said it was like a softhearted parent who warns of danger and threatens to punish but never does. Never had it run dry. He guessed there was probably still a good fifty miles of juice left. In the morning, he could fill up on the rez.

As he drove into the night and entered the Badlands, barren and eerie, he thought of the girl in the general store. How's a person get so rude? he wondered. He thought of cracking some beers and putting her out of his mind, but he wasn't on the rez yet and didn't need a third DWI. So rude so young, he thought, and she don't even know me from Adam. It struck him then that she was about the age Wenonah would have been, which was proof that there's no justice in the world, and that there's nothing higher and nothing after.

I should tell you quickly about Wenonah. She got killed by a car at the age of ten. It was toward the end of my thirteen months in Vietnam, and two months before Clem was to dance the sun dance. She'd been walking on the road with a girlfriend when a car shot over a hill and clipped them both. It happened just out of town, on 44, a couple hundred yards past the Crazy Horse School.

A drunken Burnt Thigh from the Rosebud did it. Fucker hit the girls and just kept going. When he sobered up a day later, he turned himself in. There were no witnesses but his own conscience, so you got to give him that, at least. Clem wanted to kill him, and started making plans. But our mother and Linda, and even friends like Eli and Shorty, talked him out of it, even notified the reservation cops. So instead, Clem bought a bottle. His first. Soon he sold his rifles to keep the feeling going. The Burnt Thigh later hung himself anyway. The reservation cops had turned him over to the State Troopers, to get him out of Clem's reach. The Troopers, not figuring an Indian to have a conscience, didn't bother to take away his belt and laces.

When Wenonah was born, they named her Sally. By the time she was nine, though, everyone called her Wenonah, because that's how wonderful she was. You only give that name to the exceptional girl, to a girl who has all the virtues of the ideal Sioux maiden. Maybe once every two generations a girl in the tribe will be given that name.

The way little Sally had been visiting and caring for the old folks after school, combing their hair, dressing their sores, and the way she always shared what she had with the other kids, the way she never got mad and never got mean, and the way she blushed or ran away when you paid her a compliment, well, there just wasn't any question. People were calling her Wenonah before she even had her naming ceremony. Clem was the proudest man alive the day it became her official name before the whole tribe. He wanted so bad for so long to be a traditional Indian, and maybe he was, and maybe he wasn't, I don't know, but one thing nobody could take away from him was the fact that he had the ideal Indian daughter.

His Impala started sputtering. Soon it died altogether. He looked at the gauge with disgust. He tapped the glass a few times as if the needle might be sticky and all he would need do is unstick it. Then he slammed his hand on the dashboard and cursed Detroit to hell. He wasn't even out of the Badlands yet, which meant he had a twelve-mile walk before reaching the reservation, then another five miles to Wambli. He pushed the car over to the shoulder of the road and down into the drainage gully.

The highway was empty. The only thing to do, he decided, was start on foot and try to hitch. But he had not seen another vehicle on the road all night, so he was less than optimistic. He reached in the window of the passenger side and pulled out the knapsack. There was no way he could walk all that distance. It had been years since he was in shape.

He decided there was nothing to lose by saying a prayer. No atheists in foxholes, or in highway drainage gullies. He sat down a few yards from the car, looked at the stars, and prayed to our mother. Some believe the dead can help your prayers get through. I wonder, though, if Clem simply believed more in our mom than in any notion of the Great Spirit—for she, at least, had never failed to stand by us. Never disappeared.

He asked her to send a friendly ride his way. Failing this, he asked that she steer him to a place of shelter for the night, where he could have food and hospitality. It was a mystery to me where he expected such hospitality to materialize, as McLaren's ranch was the only thing out there between him and the reservation. Everything else was Badlands and prairie.

"So what'd she do, build you a Holiday Inn for the night?" said Isaac.

"She answered my prayer with a memory," Clem said, switching into English. "She gave me a memory from way back, like it was a vision that I needed. I'd long forgot about this, but Joey, do you remember when you were a kid, like nine years old, and the priests at Mission picked you to go to that summer camp in Minnesota? And Mom was afraid the white kids would pick on you 'cause you only had that one pair of underwear, hand-me-downs from me, remember? And they were full of holes? Remember that?"

I nodded. I remembered it well. We had no vehicle back then. No one in Wambli did, nor horses. Clem was laid up with an infected toe, so Mom walked twenty-five miles to Kadoka, carrying an old coffee can full of pennies and other coins. She bought me Fruit of the Loom underwear, briefs and T-shirts, three of each, brand new, in plastic wrapping. Knowing that no one in Kadoka would take her in for the night, she turned around and headed home. It took her all night and most of the morning. Her feet were blistered and bleeding when she returned. She stayed in bed for a week and was still in it when I left for that camp. Fifty miles for my underwear.

"Well, on the road last night," said Clem, "Mom reminded me of that trek, how she'd done it both ways. It was like she was saying, If I can do it, Clem, you can do it." He slipped back into Lakota and continued his story. Isaac and I translated again for the others.

He put the knapsack on, said goodbye to the Impala, and set out for Wambli. After two miles of walking, or what he reckoned was two miles, he became hungry. At three miles, he had forgotten hunger on account of thirst. Despite a brief thunderstorm in the afternoon, it had been a hot day and much of the heat lingered into the night. He was sweating hard as he followed the highway up a gentle incline. Clem hadn't walked any kind of distance in years, and he wasn't used to carrying such a heavy load for more than a few steps. The coldness of the Buds came through the canvas and through his shirt, cooling his back. He took off the knapsack and opened it, reasoning that a beer would not only kill his thirst but lighten his load. But he decided it was too soon after praying. It might seem disrespectful to our mom, who had always hated the drinking. And the prayer, after all, was not addressed only to her. He rolled the can across his face a few times and pressed it against his forehead, then put it back in the pack.

About a mile later, he was so dry he had trouble swallowing. He wondered if enough time had passed that he could drink a beer. No, he decided, and there was the larger danger of drinking all twelve and then the whiskey, then passing out and getting hit. He kept the pack on and tried to think of other things.

A couple miles later, he noticed something shimmering in the road, on the other side of the yellow divider. He walked out to check what it was and found a puddle in a pothole. Clem put down the pack and knelt by the hole, cupping his hands in the water and bringing it to his lips. It wasn't cold, but it was soft. It soothed his throat. He put some on the back of his neck. He splashed his face, sprinkled his scalp. Then he drank many handfuls for the road. He wondered about impurities and parasites, but he was too thirsty to care.

A half hour later, as the highway led out of the Badlands and into the prairies, Clem noticed in the corner of his eye three glowing colors. He turned to look at them directly. Floating six feet above the ground were three lights, a red and a purple, each the size of a basketball, and a white one about the size of a grapefruit. He blinked his eyes, but the lights remained. He closed them and counted to ten. When he opened them, he found the lights not only remained but had begun revolving around each other. Was he *that* beat, or was it the water? He rubbed his eyes. Still the glowing colors remained. He raced fifty paces up the road then spun around. They floated up the road after him. He started flashing on *Close Encounters,* which we had seen years back in Rapid. He sprinted all out for a quarter mile. When he caught his breath and opened his eyes, the lights hovered off his right shoulder. He thought of waving them off, as you would a fly, but didn't dare. *Treat them like bees,* he thought. *Don't bother them and they won't bother you.* A little farther down the road, he opened the pack and counted the cans, hoping to find empties, proof that it was a drunken dream; but all twelve were there and the bottle was sealed. Forget them, he decided. Put them out of your mind. You're cracking up; definitely bad germs in that water, or some rancher's coyote poison.

He kneeled on the highway and stuck his finger down his throat, but only dry-heaved. The lights were still there, glowing, hovering. He would either die like a dog on the road, he figured, or wake up in some far corner of the universe, having experiments done on him. He started praying, begging the Lord to send a saving car or truck to deliver him from this evil. And he prayed to Jesus now. When you're that scared, he explained to us, you go with the one that's kicked the most ass.

He was still on his knees when headlights cleared the crest of a hill about a mile away. They were coming toward him down the other side of the highway. *Thank you, Jesus.* He stood up immediately, ran out onto the yellow divider line, and started waving his arms above his head.

When the truck was about a hundred yards off, it came to a complete stop and flicked on its brights. Clem turned to see if the colored orbs were still over his shoulder. Maybe they were visible to others, too, and had spooked the driver. But the glowing lights were directly behind him now, as if hiding. He heard the engine being gunned and then the truck jolted out into the center of the road, roaring down the yellow line, gears shifting upward.

Clem figured it must be ranchers having fun. He pictured them in the cab sucking beers and laughing about how they were gonna scare shit out of this Indian. As it neared, he noticed the orange lights on top of the cab; it was one of McLaren's. That's when he realized he was wearing his lucky pants. They made him. They had him in their sights.

The truck screamed forward. One of three things would happen, he figured; the truck would either take him out so quickly he wouldn't feel a thing, or it would screech to a halt at the last moment, giving Clem a victory—in a life, I might add, that had known mostly defeats. The third possibility was that McLaren would swerve at the last moment and maybe roll the truck. It kept nearing, coming on fast. Faster. Bearing straight down on him. Clem thought of the old No Flight societies, like the Badgers and the Plain Lance Owners, who used to wear long sashes into battle that they would stake into the ground. They would win or they would die on the spot, but never retreat, never take flight. Never give ground.

His last thought before it happened, he said, was that he could count on me to look out for his kids and Linda. Then the white light shot over his shoulder and up the road like a huge tracer bullet, a comet. It exploded silently on the windshield, showering a canopy of sparks over the entire truck, like fifty thousand sparklers at once. He couldn't see the truck through the brightness of the sparkler canopy, but he heard it screech and skid. It came to a stop thirty feet from where he stood. The blinding light and sparks burned a few seconds, then faded. The windshield and hood appeared unscratched but covered in soot. The driver leaned his head out the window and threw the truck in reverse. It shot back fifty yards, turned around, then sped off.

Clem turned in circles looking for the red and purple lights. They were gone. Chills rippled up his back and into his scalp. A wave of joy moved through his chest, lifting his heart. *Spirit lights,* he thought. Adrenaline surged into his legs and he set off for home at a fast clip. When he came to the small bridge over White River, he took off the pack full of booze and flung it over the railing without breaking stride.

◆

Elijah laughed and shook his head. "That's the best you spun yet, Clementine. You keep with the space movies 'stead of the westerns. Definitely better shit."

"Guess the J&B helps some, too," said Shorty.

"It wasn't no aliens," said Clem, slipping back into English. "Don't ya see? Wenonah was the white light. She's like a angel of the road now. The

41

red and purple musta been Mom and maybe her mom."

It was another of his drunken-ass tales, only this time he tied in Wenonah to make sure we couldn't rag on it. We sipped our beers quietly and shot one another looks.

The Mormon preacher was out on his morning walk before sermon. He waved and came over. Bob started telling the preacher Clem's story just for kicks, to embarrass Clem, I guess. "Oh, come on, son, are you saying you think Jesus had a hand in your *vision*?" said the preacher when he heard the part about praying to Jesus on the highway.

"Jesus got nothing to do with it," said Clem, "unless he stole McLaren's truck last night and went joyriding. But ain't it like that blind guy in the Bible who say he don't know if Jesus be a sinner or not; he only know that before he was blind and now he can see?"

The preacher laughed, understanding nothing, showing his perfect teeth, finding such humor in my simple brother, in all us simple men.

"You people, man," said Clem, "you got your latter-day saints and your latter-day miracles, and it's all gospel, your seas dividing, your saints rising, your loaves into fishes, your walking on water, your one in three and three in one and whatever Joe Smith did. It's always real. But if it happens to us it ain't nothing but childish dreams, right? It wasn't no *vision* and your Jesus ain't the only spirit who cares. Your loaves into fishes, how about some cheese into meat, buddy? Can you swing that one? Hey, but your yard sure is looking tidy, Preacher. We do all appreciate the example."

Old Isaac Sky Elk dropped his Bud can and crunched it into the dirt with his heel. So did Elijah with his cowboy boot, and then Bob Walking Eagle dropped his and crunched it into his weed garden. Mine was pretty much full so I held on to it. And Clem didn't have one, being it was the first day of his new life. The preacher, though, he took the hint.

We sat around, talking about the plump butt cheeks on that preacher's wife. "You know what makes them so fine?" said Isaac.

"What's that?" said Shorty.

"Indi'n owned and Indi'n operated," Isaac said. He said that about everything: his car, his TV, his dog, everything. The image of big Isaac giving it on the sly to that fussy woman, digging his big red hands into those milk-white cheeks as he humped away and they lost their breath was a hard picture not to laugh at. But the laughter was killed by a sky-ripping thunder. A huge chopper shot overhead, not more than a hundred feet up. It circled Wambli twice, then buzzed us again before setting down three hundred yards behind Bob's house, out on the ridgeline. It was a Chinook, double-rotor troop transport.

"What the fuck is this?" said Shorty.

A few seconds later, a beige Ford rolled up the road and stopped forty feet from where we were standing. Two guys in suits got out. One of them spoke into a walkie-talkie, while the other, a tall black wearing a gray suit, crossed the road in our direction. A Jeep and a blue Ford barreled up from the other direction, sending up tails of dust. They stopped in front of the first Ford. Two more guys in suits got out of the Jeep. Four guys in blue windbreakers that said FBI in white block letters across their backs got out of the blue car. They wore blue caps with visors. I could hear dispatchers crackling on their radio.

"That must've been one sacred fucking cow we shot," said Elijah.

The guys in the windbreakers and visor caps looked athletic. I knew by their eyes what they were: former Lerps, SEALs, Green Berets, recruited out of the service. It went without saying all agents wore handguns, but these guys stood next to the trunk of their car. They were the muscle behind the suits, the big artillery.

The black guy in the gray suit walked up to Isaac and said he was Agent Dexter, flashed his ID. He was tall as Isaac but reedy. His shirt was crisp and white, his collar starched like a banker's, the tie dark blue with red stripes. The hair was short, a part beveled into it. "We have a warrant to search Wanblee," he said. Wanblee is the white way of saying Wambli.

Isaac let some tobacco juice fall into the dust. "What the hell for?"

This Agent Dexter looked at Isaac for a moment, taking in his size, his shoulders. "Someone's stirring up trouble again, only with bigger guns."

"What do you mean?" said Isaac, hoping there might be something to it, that another uprising had started in Kyle or Porcupine and just hadn't hit Wambli yet.

"I don't suppose you men would know anything about any bazookas or other shoulder-launched weapons floating about?"

We all looked at each other, wondering if he was joking.

"Where can I find Clem Blue Chest?" he asked.

"That's me," said Clem.

Agent Dexter looked him over. "What were you doing last night on Highway 73?"

"Making my way home."

Dexter nodded. "What exactly did you fire at that pickup?" he asked.

So we knew right there that there wasn't any uprising. But it also seemed Clem hadn't been completely full of shit about seeing *some*thing on the road.

"Didn't even have my rifle," said Clem.

Dexter looked over at the four guys in windbreakers. They had the trunk open now. He nodded at his partner, who said something into the walkie-talkie. It crackled back to him, "Ah . . . that's a roger." Dexter turned back to Clem and read him his rights. I looked back at the chopper. About another twenty of these windbreaker guys were pouring out of the hatches, toting M-16s and fanning out as they approached. The four by the open trunk of the car decided there was no more point in being cute. One of them passed M-16s to the other three, then took up his own and shut the trunk. They pointed them either at the ground or skyward, trying not to provoke.

"You can't come on a rez with fucking airships and troops," I shouted. "This ain't Honduras. We got rights."

Dexter turned to me. "Those aren't troops. They're federal agents. And as for airpower, let's just say we remember '75 like you remember '73." A couple of years after Wounded Knee, two feds had driven onto the rez to arrest a guy. They killed an Indian and both got killed. So now they come like the 101st. This wasn't the first time, either. In '76 they used choppers and commando shit on us at Crow Dog's Paradise on the Rosebud, an army of them terrorizing a bunch of old men and ladies.

"You don't mind if we start with your house, do you, Mr. Blue Chest?"

"It's kind of messy," said Clem. "I'd like some time to clean it up."

"No doubt," said Dexter. He spoke in a clipped, superior way.

His partner perked up as something came in over his walkie-talkie. He mumbled into it, then nodded at Dexter. Dexter looked at his watch and then at the south horizon, like he was lost in thought.

"Did you want to meet me there?" asked Clem.

Dexter smiled. "We'll give you a lift, when the time comes."

Another chopper roared a hundred feet overhead, a Huey, blowing the road up in our eyes. It set down in the field, fifty yards away. Two men in suits and an Army colonel hopped out, followed by six more FBI windbreakers.

The new suits and the colonel made their way to where we were standing. "Special Agent Maxwell, good to see you, sir," said Dexter as he reached his hand out to a strong-shouldered man in a blue suit. This new guy, Maxwell, had black hair, cut short and going gray at the temples. His eyes moved around and seemed to take in everything. He was clearly the man.

"Agent Dexter," said Maxwell, "this is Colonel Mavor from Fort Benning. And this is Captain Higgins of the Royal Canadian Mounted Police." The Mountie didn't have the red jacket, but he had orange-red hair and a droopy mustache.

Dexter and these guys walked across the road to talk privately. Dexter swept his arm out in an arc that covered one-half of the town and then again covering the other half. Maxwell nodded. There were only about forty shacks in Wambli. I couldn't see it taking long.

Maxwell set up a command post at the Crazy Horse School. It was the only real structure around. Ten of the windbreakers started on the east side of town and ten started from the west. The idea being, I guess, that any weapons being shuttled from house to house as the search progressed would eventually get caught in the tightening noose. The men presented warrants, then looked in every room, under every bed, under every shack and burnt-out car.

"Let's check out your place," said Dexter to Clem, holding open the back door of the car. Dexter's partner was already inside, and a windbreaker GOON was sitting on the backseat. Clem looked scared. "I'm coming, too," I said to Dexter. "I'm his brother." Elijah and Shorty said they'd follow us, and they did, but one of the other fed cars, driven by windbreakers, pulled in front of them.

At Clem's, the four of us watched Agent Dexter and his partner search the place while two windbreakers lifted the planks of the floor and opened a wall. A third windbreaker kept an eye on us and tried not to look menacing with his M-16. He kept looking at my mother's paintings and then over at us apologetically. Those feds were lucky that Linda was at her sister's.

After looking under the house and in the yard, Dexter took the walkie-talkie. "Dexter at Blue Chest's." He sighed. "Nothing."

Clem wanted compensation for the damage to his house.

"Let's wait and see if you're so lily white," said Dexter.

He escorted us to the school. Special Agent Maxwell wanted to question us. Shorty Shangreaux's wife, Jenny, brought me a coffee while I waited. She was a secretary in the school office and had been bringing these bastards coffee for the last hour and a half. She said some kind of weapon was missing from Fort Benning. Something fancy, she said.

The door to the principal's office opened. A guy in an olive-colored suit said, "Joey Moves Camp?"

I got up and went in. Special Agent Maxwell sat in his blue suit behind the principal's desk, on which sat a field radio. The colonel and the Canadian sat a few feet off on either side of him. Higgins, the Canadian, was rolling one end of his mustache between his thumb and forefinger. Maxwell asked me to sit in the chair facing the desk, then offered me a smoke. I shook my head. "Joey, we're well aware of the fact you served overseas, that you volunteered is all the more commendable. We understand your indignation at our coming here in such force. We did it because we thought it the best way to avoid conflict. Any hothead will think twice when he's outgunned."

"Why'd you arrest my brother?"

"He's not quite the patriot you are, not that that's a crime, of course." He smiled. "But when you were overseas, he was involved with the AIM agitators. We think he still is."

"Since when's it a crime to join the American Indian Movement?"

Maxwell smiled, the other two looked bored. "It's not," said Maxwell. "But theft of government property is, and so is international trafficking of stolen arms."

"What's that supposed to mean?"

"Five weeks ago, a number of shoulder-launched armor-piercing weapons disappeared from Fort Benning without a trace—"

"So why not hang it on the nearest Indians to beat a court-martial, right?" I said. "I suppose it happened on the colonel's watch."

The colonel made no answer, just gave me his steel-gray hard-ass look.

"Without a trace," continued Maxwell, "until the Kadoka Sheriff's Department reported a truck that was attacked by a bazooka-type weapon. They've ID'd your brother."

"The guy must'a bought Japanese if he survived a bazooka."

"It's not hard to lighten a round," said the colonel. "Or empty it altogether. We train with dummy rounds all the time."

"And isn't it interesting," said the Royal Mountie, "that the ringleaders of the rebel Mohawks up around Montreal are not only AIM members but they've got A.T.4s and LAWs pointed at our hardware—"

"You mean at the tanks you're moving on them."

"You must agree it puts your brother in a rather pivotal position," he said.

Maxwell started in again. "Joey, we're offering you a chance to help him, help the tribe, and once again help your country."

I nodded. "I help you recover the weapons in exchange for some kind of a leniency deal for Clem?"

He nodded.

"I must look like I just fell off the turnip truck. You think I believe that you believe that Clem could walk onto a military post and know what the fuck was up, or what kind of uniform to wear, or where to go, how to salute, or who to contact and bribe? I suppose he was wearing his braids up under his hat. You think I don't know you know I'm in AIM? You thought you were so close you could taste it. Let's just play Moves Camp for a fool, then bust him later. I don't know what this bazooka shit is, but you aren't gonna find shit in Wambli. And I don't know what happened on the highway, but you can bet your last buck the guys in that truck were as fucked up as Clem. You got nothing on him and nothing on me or any of us, 'cause this whole thing's a joke. And in a few hours you're gonna have to go, or else it becomes a siege, and we call in the press."

The red light on the radio went on. He picked up the receiver. "Maxwell . . . right." He recradled it. "They finished," he said to the colonel. "Just rifles." Then he turned to me: "What are you doing with a semiautomatic assault rifle?" They must've found my AR-15. I smiled because they couldn't touch me. "I'm a sportsman." I pulled my wallet out and showed him my NRA membership.

"They could have buried them anywhere," blurted the Mountie.

"Well, that's true," I said. "What with all the booze and kids about, we thought it best not to keep the armor-piercing stuff in the house."

"We're talking about hundreds of square miles here, Captain Higgins," said Maxwell. "Where would you propose we start digging?" Then, turning to me, he said, "But you mark my words, Joey, we'll be running surveillance flights and taking satellite shots of every inch of this place. Your dog digs up an arrowhead and we'll know it before you do."

There was a clamor outside in the front office. "I want to talk to them *now,*" a voice was saying. "It's a matter of great urgency." The door opened and there stood Preacher Blake, the Mormon. Maxwell gave me a nod, meaning I could go. The preacher avoided my eyes as I passed him on the way out. The door closed behind me.

I sat in the couch by the door and listened. The preacher was excited. "Well, there's one federal offense happening that you *can* do something about: this filthy habit of not burying the dead, putting up a scaffold to better blow pestilence around. My *God,* they're so backward."

"Mr. Blake, we're here on pressing business. You'll have to employ the reservation police. We simply haven't time," I heard Maxwell say.

"The rez cops are worthless. Now, I'm not a man without influence. Do I have to tell my senators and congressmen that you were here on the spot and chose to do nothing?"

"Mr. Blake, you do what you have to do."

"Listen, it's just a mile out of town, behind the house of this Clement Blue Chest. You can follow me in your car."

There was a long silence, then Higgins said, "Wouldn't hurt to go there and make sure Dexter was thorough."

I took off. When I got to Bob's place, agents on the road were showing little kids pictures of the LAWs, light armor weapons, the A.T.4 Fire-and-Forget, and the Gustav, asking them if any of them had seen stuff like that. The kids shook their heads, and I heard one windbreaker say to another, "Gooks is gooks."

"Just don't burn the hootches," I said over my shoulder as I turned into Bob's yard. I found Eli and Bob in the kitchen. We piled into Eli's pickup and headed for Clem's.

There was a rez cruiser out front. We could hear Linda screaming about the way the house was ripped up. I opened the door. Ray Bright Cloud was in there trying to reason with her.

"Well, if it ain't the freakin' deacon," said Elijah as he came in behind me.

"I had nothing to do with this," said Ray, then he turned back to Linda. "I'm telling you the body has to go in the ground. They could make you do time for that."

"Fuck you, Ray," said Linda, her voice cracking. "Fuck you, fuck you, fuck you. And fuck the FBI."

The two Fords and the Jeep pulled up in front of the house. Dexter and Maxwell walked up to the door, the Mountie and the colonel stood uselessly in the weeds. Linda opened the screen door and stood there with her arms crossed. "Where's my husband?"

"He's still being questioned," said Maxwell. He cleared his throat. "We understand there's an improperly disposed-of corpse on the premises. Could you take us to it, please?"

"Sure, when you fix my floor and walls."

"You'll be recompensed."

She snorted. "I guess the Sioux never heard that before."

"It's just over the hill," called the Mormon from the car.

We followed them up the hill, while one of the agents rolled slowly behind us in the Jeep. The scaffold stood motionless, looking beautiful and ancient against the prairie and the distant Badlands, part of something timeless. Even Maxwell and Dexter and the others stood in silence.

The preacher came up the hill. He must've decided he was safer with the feds than alone in the car. "Well, are we going to just look at it all day?"

"You better ask Salt Lake for a new assignment," I said. "Your work here is done."

"Are you threatening me?" he said.

"Who is it?" asked Maxwell.

"Clem's and my mother."

He nodded. "I'm sorry." Then he asked Elijah and Shorty to please take it down and put it in the grave. They looked at me. I didn't know what to say.

"Would you rather two FBI men did it? One way or the other she's got to get buried," said Maxwell.

"Clem should be here," I said. Maxwell nodded and had Dexter call it in on the walkie-talkie. We stood around in the sun, waiting for Clem's arrival.

The word must've gotten out that that's where the action was, because people from the town started showing. Even Speckled Hawk and some of his sun dancers appeared.

Soon we heard a chopper, then it was on top of us. It was the Huey. The scaffold started shaking. It swayed back and forth and the moccasins and things that people had tied on were blowing all over the place. Linda and I ran over to brace the legs. The branches rattled on the cross-poles and the body shifted. Eli ran over to catch it in case it fell. Maxwell was waving off the chopper and shouting in the walkie-talkie. The Huey moved off and set down farther up the ridge.

Clem got out, flanked by agents. He looked shook up, but that might have been from flying for the first time.

Eli and Shorty tried to get her off the platform, but Shorty couldn't reach. I took his place. Eli and I managed to slide the bundle sideways off the platform. The body inside was stiff and so was the hide itself. It was like carrying a log. Elijah's face was twisted as he tried not to breathe. I was also holding my breath. And there were flies.

Clem and Linda had stuffed the blanket so full with things for Mom to have with her on the other side that it made for a pretty shapeless package. I think Eli had the ankles and I the other end.

We laid her on the buffalo grass while an agent went to the chopper for rope. Speckled Hawk came over to Clem and me. He knelt by the hide for a moment, then stood. "Don't be sad. You're good sons. You acted well. It's strange, though."

"What is?" said Clem.

"I feel tremendous wakan here, by your mother's body. She was a holy woman, I think," said Speckled Hawk. I looked at his small eyes and beakish nose.

"I'm sorry for your loss," someone said from behind us. We turned. It was the white guy who had danced in Speckled Hawk's sun dance. I nodded. Clem said nothing. The agent came back with red rappelling line and it was with this that we lowered the body into the grave.

Dexter and Maxwell were talking quietly a few yards away. Dexter seemed excited but speaking in hushed tones, urging, pleading, trying to convince Maxwell of something. They came over and Maxwell told two agents to pull the body back up. I wondered for a moment if they were going to blow the preacher off and let us do it the Lakota way.

They got her up and laid her on the hood of the Jeep.

"What's going on?" said Clem.

"I'll be able to answer that better when I see what's inside the hide," said Maxwell.

"What are you, sick?" cried Clem.

"You could fit a couple of A.T.4s in there, or a batch of LAWs and then hide the shape with rags."

"Can't you smell it?" I said.

"So you put a leg of beef in, or any dead animal," said the Mountie. "They smell the same."

Clem shot his fist out, hit the Mountie square in the face, then Dexter shoved him back. The Mountie got up, clenching his nose. He looked at the blood in his hand. "Wasn't meant the way it sounded," he said, his mustache crimson now and drooping more than before.

"Any more shit like that," said Dexter to Clem, "and we'll take you out hog-tied." There were three windbreakers with M-16s trained on us now.

All kinds of people had turned up and were standing around. Clem pulled away from Dexter and yelled to them, "Are we gonna take this shit? Are we gonna let them open our graves and strip our dead?"

Maxwell stepped away from the commotion and talked into the

walkie-talkie. Within minutes, the huge Chinook chopper appeared. It circled low around the hill, hovering here and there, ten feet off the ground, inserting the Lerp types at strategic points on the scaffold side of the hill. I wondered if they had their safeties on.

"I'm the law on this rez," said Ray Bright Cloud, stepping up to the hood of the Jeep. "Taking a body off a scaffold is one thing. Stripping it of its winding sheet is another. That's desecration of a grave, and I won't have it. Come back with a warrant and you can exhume and inspect all you want."

Maxwell smiled at the challenge, or maybe just amused by all these big words from an Indian. Then he put the smile away. "My jurisdiction supersedes yours, and I outrank you, sergeant."

"Jesus, just pass a metal detector over it," I said, my voice cracking.

"Stand aside," Maxwell said to Bright Cloud.

"Clem, Joey, put your mother back in the grave," said Ray, staring Maxwell down. "They can't do shit. Too many witnesses." We walked around to either side of the Jeep and lifted the body.

"You can even *see* it," cried Dexter, pointing with his long, black finger to where the hide stretched smoothly over the plastic art tube. "It's an A.T.4."

"Put it down!" commanded Maxwell in a lethal tone. It sounded like a saber pulling from a scabbard, the way he said it. I froze. There were Lerp guys all over the backside of the hill; some had pulled their hats around backward so the visors wouldn't get in their sights.

"Sergeant, you're under arrest if you don't stand aside," said Maxwell. Ray didn't move. "Okay," said Maxwell to Dexter. Dexter took Ray's gun from his holster, then cuffed him.

"On what charge?" demanded Ray.

"Until we're out of here."

"What *charge?*"

"Obstructing justice," said Maxwell. He nodded to two windbreakers, who came over to take the hide from us. Clem didn't let go, so I didn't either. Four others had to come in to hold us down while the first two pried our fingers. Clem and I stared at each other as they worked us over. Then Clem's face changed. He smiled. "Let 'em have it. They want it so bad, let's let 'em have it." He went limp and let them overpower him. They put the body on the hood of the Jeep. Maxwell, Dexter, the Mountie, and the colonel gathered around the hide like coyotes.

"Why?" I asked Clem.

He looked at me and smiled. "Wait'll you see what happens when they open that tube. The wakan, she caught it. It's in there. We're gonna be counting coups, man. Very big victory about to happen."

I didn't know who looked stupider, the feds for seeing bazookas under every rock, or Clem for believing in all the wakan and spirit stuff. I walked closer to the Jeep. A guy in a windbreaker with a Rambo knife cut a long gash at one end of the hide, then cut through the blanket. Everyone who had a handkerchief clutched it to his nose and mouth, others pressed the backs of their forearms against their nostrils. The guy laid the knife on the hood, turned to take a deep breath, then, using both hands, ripped the blanket. A small foot with a yellow nail popped out. My knees buckled and I fell to all fours, vomiting, flashing on a time when I spent a whole afternoon unzipping body bags and checking tags on toes. White ones, black ones, brown ones, some with long nails, some with no nails from boot rot, some hairy, some blistered, others scaly, and others still smooth like the toes of children.

When I looked up again, they were inspecting the tube with disappointment. Clearly, it was not the barrel of an A.T.4. But they went right ahead and unscrewed the top anyway. Maybe they thought there were shells inside it, the famous missing shell from Route 73. I looked over at Clem. He was staring at the tube, waiting for I don't know what, maybe a big eagle to fly out, or Crazy Horse himself. As Dexter pulled out the unfinished portrait, a shrill yell came from down near Clem's house. One of the windbreaker guys walked up the hill with his hands on his head; behind him walked Eli Jr. with a Winchester in the guy's back. Little fifteen-year-old Eli Jr. Everyone watched in silence. "Get away from that grave," yelled Junior. Elijah ran over to Agent Maxwell. "He's fifteen years old. He don't know what he's doing. If they pick him off I'll hunt you down. I'll see you fry, Maxwell."

"He's got my man."

"He isn't gonna do shit to your man. You get on your radio and tell *all* your men to hold their fire. That's a boy out there."

Maxwell shook his head. "We've got a situation here."

I'd never seen Elijah Hunts Alone scared. He spun around toward his son. "Don't come any closer, Junior," he yelled. "Get down. You got a shield, use it." He sounded like he was crying almost.

Junior and his prisoner stopped halfway up the hill. Junior crouched. I saw a Lerp lying in the buffalo grass like a sharpshooter, lining up a shot.

Someone dashed by and slammed into him, sent the scope flying off the gun. It was the blond guy, the dancer. He slammed into him so hard that he kept rolling and slid a few yards through the buffalo grass. The Lerp quickly lined his shot up again, without the scope. The dancer doubled back and dove to his knees, putting his chest right in front of the barrel. The Lerp, still on his belly, rolled laterally and lined up a new shot, but the dancer darted over and blocked the view again. In one fluid motion and with great speed, the Lerp rose to his knees and butted the dancer's face with the stock of his M-16. The poor bastard teetered on his knees, trying to stay conscious and hold his ground. Another windbreaker ran up from the side and butted him over the head with his weapon.

Eli got up on the Jeep. "Don't *any*body fire. I'm going down to take care of this. You hear me? I'm taking care of this. Don't you fire at my boy," he said, looking at Maxwell. "Anybody!" he said again. He hopped off the Jeep and said to Maxwell, "He's a minor. You can't do shit to him."

Eli went down and told Junior it was all over, said they didn't find what they wanted and now they got to go. "Gimme the gun, son, and run like hell. Stay hid till I come find you." Junior gave his dad the weapon and bolted down the hill, half deer, half rocket. A windbreaker took off in pursuit, but Maxwell raised his walkie-talkie to his jaw and said, "Let him go."

The blond guy was brought over to Maxwell by two windbreakers. "What's your name?" said Maxwell.

"Father Bacon. Quinn Bacon."

"You're a *priest?*"

The guy nodded, blood trickling from his scalp down his forehead.

"A *Catholic* priest?"

"Yes."

"Well, that's great," Maxwell said, looking over at Agent Dexter and the Mountie. I looked back at the priest, at his face. He was older than his lean body suggested.

"And what exactly are you doing on Pine Ridge Reservation?" Maxwell asked him.

"Learning."

"A word to the wise, Father. Don't ever pull a stunt like that again—"

"*You* pulled the stunt," the blond guy said.

"And how's that?"

"Searching an entire neighborhood at gunpoint. That's an illegal search."

"I've got a warrant, my friend."

"Not for an entire town, you don't. Maybe one house, two tops. You'd never pull that in a white town."

Maxwell smiled. "If you think you've got a case, go talk to a lawyer." He turned away from Father Bacon, signaled for the chopper, then said to Clem and me, "It isn't over, gentlemen. Not by a long shot." The Huey started up. For a few seconds, we all watched the blades pick up speed. Then Maxwell bent forward, hunching his big shoulders into the down-draft of the rotors as he approached the open bay door. The Army colonel and the Mountie followed him in, then the chopper flew off at a steep angle. All the pretty feds vanished as quickly as they had come.

Elijah took the arm of the bleeding dancer-priest and Speckled Hawk came alongside and took his other arm. They helped him down the hill.

Clem and I reclosed the hide, bound it tight, and put it back on the scaffold. I walked him down to his house, both of us silent, in shock.

I took a drive to clear my head, and soon found myself at the bridge over White River. I stopped and got out, went down to the water's edge and started hunting around for something. Then I realized I was look-ing for Clem's knapsack. Of course it wasn't there. As I turned to climb back up to the road, though, something flashed pink from under the wa-ter. I waded out a little ways and pulled up a can of Budweiser. It was full, the tab unbroken. I reached down again, feeling here and there until I touched wet canvas.

On the riverbank, I emptied the bag out. There was a total of twelve unopened Buds, plus a bottle of J&B, the seal unbroken. My eyes started to burn. I could see it now. It stopped being drunken bullshit and I could *see* Clem's hulking frame kneeling in the middle of the black highway, stooped over a pothole, drinking from a dirty puddle, as humble and faithful as any saint. I wedged two Buds sideways against my eyelids till the cool aluminum stopped the burning.

The label on the J&B hadn't come off. It was soggy but still on there pretty good. I let it dry in the sun. Then I drove to Kadoka to ask Jenk-ins if I could get a couple of steaks and some o.j. in exchange for the whiskey. His daughter was giving directions to some tourists. "Take 73 South for twenty miles, then follow the Pampers and the beer cans."

I put the bottle on the counter and suggested the swap to Jenkins.

"No," he said, looking up at me, then over at his white Wenonah. "No, we couldn't do that. But you can take a pack of them frozen sausages."

On the rez, I could have sold that bottle for twenty-five bucks, at night for thirty-five. I looked at him hard and wished I had my brother's braids. Jenkins had red eyelids from smoking all day, and a gut from sitting behind his register eating Fritos and taking nips from a flask. It was easier than hunting and it sure beat work. "Now, there's a trade," I said, leaving the bottle and turning for home.

"What about your sausages?" he called from behind the counter.

But as I stepped out the door and into the light, I was staggered by the hugeness of the sky, and by the sudden understanding that my mother was gone.

The next Saturday I was in Kadoka. Went to Harlow's because I was through with Jenkins. Then I went to the Broken Spur to use the phone. It's a long, dark room and the bar runs the length of it. There's a pool table and a pinball in the back. Light came in through the window by the door, but didn't reach far. It was the only window in the place. Behind the bar was a Miller High Life sign in yellow neon and a glowing plastic statue of Johnnie Walker, tipping his hat. That was it for light.

"Hey ya, Joey," someone said.

I made out a patch of red fuzz, big Dori's bleached hair, frizzy and aglow in the light of Johnnie Walker's jacket. "How you doin', Dori?" I said, my eyes adjusting to the darkness. She was wearing a gray sweatshirt with the sleeves cut off and was leaning back on one of the ice chests. Her meaty arms were folded across her small breasts. She didn't try to pull her stomach in. There were three or four people down the bar, one in a straw ten-gallon. I nodded and grabbed a stool.

"What'll it be?" Dori said, stepping forward and wiping the bar with one swipe of a rag. The flab of her arm jiggled after she tossed the rag onto the ice chest. A whiff of her armpit wafted over.

"Just some change for the phone, if I could." I handed her a dollar. She headed for the register.

Behind the ascending rows of bottles, you had antlers mounted on the wall. Quite a few sets of them, like somebody was a true shot. A set directly in front of me had visor caps hanging on it. There was a red one that said Winchester Repeating Rifles, a gold one that said Colt. A little lower was a green one that said John Deere Combines. They hung on the antlers like Christmas ornaments.

There were a couple mirrors on the wall, too, the bottom halves of which were factory-painted with scenes of handsome pointers and setters flushing grouse and wild turkey out of amber fields. On the opposite wall, above the jukebox and lighted up by it, was a Yukon Jack poster of a solitary guy in a snowy, moonlit wilderness. He wore a full-length bearskin coat and fur hat and he stood over a campfire, his chiseled face glowing in it, his sled dogs worshiping his self-sufficiency. A Marlboro poster of the square-jawed cowboy up in the Rockies hung on the other wall: Clearly, Clem was not the only one who longed for a culture that seemed locked in the past. Theirs was about conquering the wild. Fine, they did it. But now they just drink, watch videos, and pretend their bellies are hard like their fathers' were.

Dori came back from the register and slapped the coins on the bar. "What was all the commotion on the rez?" she asked. A couple heads down the bar turned slightly.

"Oh, you know, the feds thought AIM was back. Thought they're up to mischief again."

"Ain't it a shame the way a few bad apples spoil it for the whole pack of you?" she said. "Same old shit. Agitators and agents. Gorby quits on Communism, says he wants the airlift, yeah truck it in, he says, give us the Pepsi, but does he tell his agents in the States that the show's over? Shit no. They still stirring up shit with the unions and the Mexicans and they still using the ACLU and they still got AIM on the payroll."

"I guess," I said, picking up the quarters. "But I got the feeling AIM's pretty much dead and buried, at least on Pine Ridge."

"I dunno," said a guy with a straw ten-gallon. "Heard they got their hands on some bazookas. Word is they gonna start hitting Brink's trucks." He shook his head, chuckling. "I'd trade my skin to be in on that. All them trucks do is ship the cash east to Jew York. You Indians got the right idea."

"Yeah, we got it covered," I said, getting up to head for the phone. I crossed the room and went down the little dark hall that leads to the bathrooms. I dialed Francine's number, let it ring twice, then hung up. I waited a few minutes. It didn't ring back, so I returned to the bar and asked Dori for a beer. As I sipped it, I pictured Francine out riding, her red-blond hair flying back off her shoulders.

"Oh Jesus!" shouted Dori, throwing back the piece of the bartop that's on a hinge. She ran out from behind the bar and bolted out the door onto the street. "What did I tell you?" she shouted at the top of her lungs.

We all hustled over to the window. She was yelling at her daughter, who was on the opposite corner with another girl. Dori's daughter looked a lot like Dori—same stubby nose, same body—but the other girl was hot. "You get home right now or I'll give you a thrashing. Now! Right now." Dori waddled across the rest of the road, her big butt shifting from side to side, the dimples showing right through the pink polyester pants. She grabbed her daughter by the arm and shoved her in the direction of home. The other girl backed off a few steps and waved slightly to Dori's daughter. Dori pointed her finger at her child and shouted, "I'm 'onna phone home in five minutes. If you ain't there to pick up, you gonna be one sorry young lady. The'll be hell to pay." Her daughter scurried off. Dori came back in the bar, muttering curses and sweating freely under the arms. "Goddamn her, dragging me out into the sun like that. If I tol' her once I tol' her a thousand times not to hang out with that Tammy Wortz. Talk about your bad apples."

I went back to my seat and so did the cowboy and the other two. They were chuckling at Dori's cowboy mouth. She snapped at them for mocking her, letting out another string of curses about how they were no-good layabouts and drunks, but you could tell she was delighted. Dori loves thinking she's a frontier woman, made hard by a hard country. And she loves thinking others see her that way.

"That Tammy Wortz is poison," she continued. "She'll be selling it on the street 'fore long."

"Which one? I'm there," said the cowboy.

"You *would* be, too," said Dori. She was just working herself up out of boredom. Kadoka's too small and churchgoing for anything like hooking. The town is just seven streets, a hardware store, Jenkins's general, Harlow's grocery, a couple bars, and some truck stops for the interstate. "She ain't gonna poison my Sherry, so help me God," Dori said, pouring herself a shot of Wild Turkey and stopping to knock it back. "I don't know what to do. I told Sherry never to talk to that girl again. I gave her the belt over it, locked her in her room for a weekend, made her swear with her hand on the King James. I done everything I know from beating her to bribing her but there they were on Main in broad day, like two harlots for the world to see." She poured another shot. "Hell, I don't know how to bring up kids, and I can't be a father, too." She sighed, then knocked back the shot, made a sour face, exhaled loudly and looked at me. "What else am I supposed to do? What do *you* do with problem kids?"

"I got no kids," I said.

"I mean the Sioux."

"Well, kids are kids, right? What *can* you do?" I said, smiling. There was no point in telling her that we never beat children. At least in the old way we never did. Dori and the others would have just looked at each other and said, Well, that explains it.

"Have you tried the Church of Latter-day Saints?" I asked.

"I ain't no Mormon," she said.

"The Mormons work miracles with kids. Teach 'em love of family."

"What, and Lutherans don't care about family, I suppose?"

"Luther was good in Europe," I said. "But Jesus wants America to have its own religion, one that springs from this wonderful land." I didn't bat an eye. She didn't know what to say. She just poured herself another Wild Turkey, gulped it, and said to the others, "Get a load of this Injun."

I went and tried the phone again, let it ring twice, and hung up. Within twenty seconds, Frannie called back. "It's good to hear from you," she said. I paused as the cowboy walked past me on his way to the men's room.

"Good to be heard from."

"Yeah, what's been happening out there?"

"Long story."

"I missed you so bad last Sunday," she said.

"Me, too."

"Can you make it?"

"I'll leave straightaway."

I hung up and went back to the bar to pay up. "Hey, Dori," called a voice from behind me. It was the cowboy. He was doing up his belt as he stepped out of the head. He had one of those huge rodeo buckles and he was having trouble hooking the notch into the leather. He walked to his stool, spurs dragging on the floor and a big grin across his face.

"When'd you install that rubber machine?" he said, jerking his thumb over his shoulder.

"Had it put in yesterday," she said.

"What's the reverend gonna say?"

"I don't know, but I say better safe 'n sorry."

"Well, I don't know what's so safe about a rubber. I've known them to break on more 'n one occasion."

"Well, aren't you God's gift to heifers. That's why you're supposed to use 'em with something else. Part of a combination."

"Like with one of them creams, I suppose."

"I suppose," she said.

"Is that what you recommend, Dori?" he said, grinning, hoping to make her blush.

"I'm sure I wouldn't know, Wade," she said, drying a glass thoroughly and intently with a rag. "What do the gals on the rez use, Joey?" she said, trying to get the focus off herself.

"Well, it's different," I said.

"How's that?" said Wade.

"Lot of our women been sterilized."

"You got the life, man," said the cowboy. "No fumbling with rubbers, then losing your rod. How you sterilize 'em exactly?" He really looked excited, like maybe he could make it a new rodeo event.

I gulped some beer and thought about my sister, about how she gave birth to my nephew at the BIA hospital and then noticed her cycle was gone. She went back and they said, "Well, you remember we had to do a C-section, right? Well, we saw tumors on your ovaries. Had to take them out to be safe." It was happening a lot. I guess they didn't want too many wards of the state. Anyway, girls are squatting in the bush again, and no one's dying of tumors.

"I'm just kidding," I said. "There ain't no sterilization." They wouldn't have believed it and I didn't want to get into a fight.

"Well, short of that," said Wade, tipping up his hat. "There's only one contraceptive combo that's a hundred percent."

"And what's that?" said Dori.

"A good alias and a wrong address." He slammed his hand on the bar and threw his head back in a big guffaw.

Dori shook her head. "Who you got writing your lines, Wade?"

"Well, I do admit I got that one from Sherry's dad." He reared back to howl at the ceiling. She rat-tailed him so hard with her dishrag that he fell off his stool and landed on the planks. He looked quite startled.

"Just like in the rodeo, Wade. Always landing on yur trailer hitch," she said, tossing the rag back on the ice chest.

I left a couple bucks on the bar. As I stood up to go, I gave him a hand getting up. He dusted off his hat, put it on, then nodded.

"Who you ranchin' for?" I asked.

"Colonel McLaren," he said.

"You like it?"

"So far."

I wondered if he was one of the fuckers who tried to run my brother over. "Well, see ya," I said.

"Right," he said.

Dori had moved down the bar and was talking to the guy in front of her. She caught my wave and raised her volume. "Imagine the nerve of that redskin. Preaching to me like I'm some fat-lipped African."

"Dori, if you had fat lips," said Wade, getting back onto his stool, "you wouldn't be so lonely at night. And if you wasn't so lonely at night, you wouldn't be so ornery by day."

"Gimme that," she said, swiping the hat off his head and tossing it toward the door. "Take him with ya, Joey, will ya? And stay out of the ruts." I tossed him back his hat and left.

◆

I went back into Harlow's to pick up some hot dogs and marshmallows. Frannie loves roasted marshmallows. As I tucked a bag of them under my arm, I heard a high-pitched voice with an Irish lilt. "Aren't you the fellow who danced in Speckled Hawk's sun dance the other day?"

"I *did* have that honor, yes," said another voice.

I peered around the corner of the aisle into the tiny produce section of the store. Father O'Reilly stood in profile, dressed in his black outfit, hunched a bit, cradling a head of lettuce in his arm. Facing him was the blond guy, Quinn Bacon. He wore jeans and a green T-shirt, nothing to suggest he was also a priest.

"What were you *think*ing, man?" challenged O'Reilly.

"How do you mean?"

"What possessed you to take part in those mutilation rites? It only encourages them, don't you know, when they see a white man do it."

The blond guy made no answer.

"Have you any idea how long we've been trying to wean them off such backwardness?"

"I do," said the blond guy, looking up. "And of your methods, too."

"Oh, please," said Father O'Reilly. He snorted and walked away, shaking his head with disgust. I walked over into the produce section. "I figured all you priests knew each other," I said to this Quinn Bacon fellow.

"Happily, no," he said.

"Kind of interesting that you didn't tell him *you're* a priest?"

"Are you kidding?" he said with a laugh and a shake of his head. "He would have had a coronary. At the very least, he would call my order back East, tell them to yank me *before the lad goes completely native,*" he said, putting on O'Reilly's Irish accent.

I nodded, but something didn't add up with this guy. Anyway, I was more concerned at that moment with hooking up with Frannie, couldn't wait to see her. "See you around," I said. I paid and left.

◆

Near White River, I took a small road heading west. After ten miles, the asphalt ended and I followed a rutted dirt road through the tall grasses. Every time I thought about Frannie, my foot pressed the gas harder, then I would have to brake to make sure the wheels didn't slip into the ruts. They were much too deep and would have ruined the bottom of the car. As it was, my floor had rusted through in a few spots. I followed those ruts to where the White River skirts the Badlands, and there I stopped and got out.

There's nothing around for miles, for tens of miles. Francine and I snuck out there most every Saturday. Sometimes we swam, sometimes we hoofed it into the Badlands, and sometimes we just slept in the sun. I lay down near the bank of the river, closed my eyes, and drifted off.

The sound of choppers woke me with a start. I bolted to an upright position. The sky, though, was blue and empty, the sun getting lower. I scanned the northwest horizon for Frannie and tried not to think on the events of the last week and of what they stirred up in me—that feeling of thundering in low, skimming the canopy, lining up Stone Age peasants in the sights of my door-mounted 60. I imagined Francine's body against mine, her breath in my ear, blowing away these other things. I tried to remember every detail of how she looked and what she wore when we met a year and a half earlier.

It was my first day on the job and I was shoveling out the stables. She rode in on a mottled stallion. A thick braid of reddish-blond hair hung in front of her shoulder like a gleaming brass cable. Her cheeks were flushed and her eyes were green, so was her shirt. She ducked slightly, passing under the door frame, then smiled from her high perch and said, "Hi." She quickly dismounted. I remember thinking that she got down off her horse as quick as she did because she didn't like talking down to people. A person on a horse is a general. "My name's Frannie," she said. "You must be the new hand."

"Well, I'm new. Don't know about being a hand yet," I said. *Hand* was a term worn like a badge, meant you'd proved your worth. If nothing else, it meant you could ride and rope. So far, I'd just been shoveling stables and scrubbing pots and pickups. "I'm Joey Moves Camp," I said.

She sparkled at that. "What a great name!" She put her hand out, so I shook it. It was a firm grip and her eyes didn't look away. Her shoulders were square and strong. "Are you staying with the others in the bunkhouse?" she asked.

"I'll be driving in. I live on the rez."

"In that old Mustang out there?" she asked with a smile.

"In a house."

"I just meant is that your car?" she said, flushing red. "Is that what you'll be driving in in?"

I nodded. It was a '68 that I had bought from a guy when I got back to the States in '73. "Yeah, it should've given up the ghost years back. Keeps hanging on, though," I said.

Just then her dad walked in the other end of the stable. "Frannie, let that man do his work. Where's Pogo?"

"Rounding up strays by the crick last I saw'm," she said, turning toward her father. He nodded and said, "Let him work," then ducked back out.

She turned back to me with a smile. "The Supreme Commander has spoken. Did he tell you to call him 'Colonel'? I'll bet he did."

"As a matter of fact." I nodded.

She smiled again. "Well, it's real nice to meet you, Joey. I hope you like the ranch."

"It's nice," I said.

"I mean, I hope you stick it out. I'm just back from the Peace Corps and I'm already bored outa my mind. Be good to have some new blood around."

I stuck it out, all right, and had the best summer of my life. That's when we started sneaking off to White River. Eventually, though, her old man started suspecting and he let me go. That's when she and I worked out the system with the pay phone at the Broken Spur.

I had met her dad, "the Colonel," two days before meeting her. It was on the interstate. On my way back from Rapid, I spotted a handsome pickup on the shoulder of the highway. The hood was up and a tall man was bent over the engine. I pulled over, got out, and asked him if he needed a hand.

He had on a straw ten-gallon with the brim broken down over his eyes. He tipped the hat up a notch with his thumb and looked at me. His eyes were powder-blue and distrusting, his face weathered and full of lines, his chin square and heavy. He gave me the once-over, probably looking for the bulge of a gun, figuring I was going to bushwhack him. "You know engines?" he said.

"My whole damn family is." That scored half a smile. "I've kept that one going for a dog's life," I said, pointing with my chin at my rusty Mustang.

"Be my guest." He stepped aside a bit so I could check it out. "You in the Air Cavalry?" he asked. I was wearing my old service jacket and my shoulder patch with the horse head was facing him as I checked his fuel line.

"Yeah, I was."

"Me, I was with the Eighty-second in Korea," he said. Then he shook his head: "Best years of my life." I couldn't tell if he meant *made* the best years or *took* the best years. "How about you?"

"I was in Vietnam," I said.

"Look about ten years too young for that."

I smiled. My whole life people have been saying I look too young for this and too young for that. "Went over in early '72. Vietnamization mostly."

I found a clogged valve, took it off, and cleaned it with my jackknife. I could feel him watching me work, watching the blade mostly.

"Didn't you want to stay in?"

I looked up at him. It was an odd question. I mean, who the hell wants to stay in?

"Well, look at you," he said. "Short hair, the field jacket, shine on your boots. Tidiest Indian I've ever seen. Didn't you like it?"

I shrugged. "Why'd *you* leave?"

"I didn't," he said. "Not altogether. I'm a colonel in the Guard."

So while I was in Vietnam, he was on Pine Ridge with the FBI, the U.S.

Marshals, the GOONs, and every redneck who had a gun.

"Air Cav's a good outfit, I understand. Not paratroopers exactly, but a good outfit," he said. "Got the job done a hell of a lot more than the Marines, according to my son."

"Hell, yes," I said. "Half the time we were saving their asses. He was in the Cav?"

"No, he went Marines. Lost a leg to friendly fire."

"Sorry."

"Not yours. Marine artillery."

"I meant, sorry about his leg, is all."

"Oh, he's fine. Got even more spunk than before. Tossed his VA leg and got an ivory stump. Claims it's easier for walking and better for fighting. Hell, he busts broncos now and rides bulls. Had a spur mounted on it. You'd think he was nineteen the way he raises hell."

I screwed the valve back and told him to try it. It started right up.

"Much obliged," he said, after I lowered the hood. I walked around to his window to give him back his rag. He rubbed his chin as though lost in thought, searching his soul, it seemed, as to how much, if at all, he should tip me. "'Seventy-two. That was after the draft; you must've signed up."

I nodded.

"And you got an honorable?"

"Yep."

"You need a job?"

"I ain't joining the Guard."

He smiled. "I just lost a hand. You done any ranch work?"

"Some."

"Just stay clean-cut and don't ever let me smell booze on you. You a Pine Ridger or a Rosebud?"

"Pine Ridge. Name's Joey Moves Camp."

"You can call me 'Colonel.' Follow me, son."

At the ranch, he explained that I would be low man on the totem pole for a while, so I should expect the nigger work, then he gave me a shovel and led me to the stables. That's how I met her old man and got started at the ranch.

I heard the hoofbeats coming up through the earth, so I closed my eyes and pretended to sleep. I heard her dismount. Next thing I knew, she put a plum to my lips. "Jo-eeey," she whispered.

"Fran-eee," I whispered back and opened one eye. She took a bite of the plum, then put the rest in my mouth. It was juicy. I looked into her green eyes and smiling lips. We kissed and I slipped her the pit. "Oh, thanks a lot," she said.

"Don't ever say I'm not a good provider."

"Don't ever think I'm lookin' for one."

She had a roast chicken and some peeled carrots and celery in her saddlebags. I went and got some blankets from the car and spread them out on the sand. I grabbed the twelve-pack of beer and put it in the river to cool. Then I built a little fire out of dried grass, twigs, and driftwood. We warmed the chicken over it and had a nice dinner as the sun went down. "Did you have an okay week?" she asked.

"It was different."

"You mean the FBI? They were at the ranch, too," she said. She started to laugh. "Two of my dad's men think an Oglala shot a bazooka at them on the highway. They swear to it. All these hands do is drink. There's not a scratch on the truck, just a lot of soot, but these agents were taking it seriously, going over the truck with brushes and chemicals. The FBI don't know cowboys, I'll tell you that."

"Your dad and the boys know who it was on the highway?"

"Some guy who killed one of our cows. A guy named Blue Chest. Goes around wearing yellow pants. You know him?"

I nodded. Clem wasn't the kind of relation you went out of your way to boast about, specially not to whites.

"They want to pay him back for the cow," she said.

"How do you mean?" I asked, getting up on one elbow so I could read her face better. "How they gonna pay him back?"

She shrugged. "Some kind of prank is all. So people don't take to popping cows."

"When're they gonna do this prank?"

"Dunno. Why? You like him? He a nice guy, this Blue Chest?"

"Yeah. Nice enough." We were silent for a while. I could feel her wanting to ask how well I knew him, and what was he like. "Anyway," I said, "Blue Chest didn't shoot the cow. I did."

She laughed and said, "Sure, Joey," then kissed my neck. We unrolled the sleeping bags and the blankets and made love under the first of the stars, then again under all of them. Then we lay awake on our backs and watched for shooters. "Man, Joey, you should see the stars in Mauritania." She sighed. "It's just below the Sahara, you know, I mean talk about *clear.* You've never seen so many stars."

"You really miss it, eh?"

"I miss the freedom."

"Yeah, must be tough being back, I mean being white and over twenty-one," I said. She laughed good-naturedly and pinched me. "Seriously, Fran, you can't get much freer than that."

"Away from home, you can. Didn't you feel freer at Berkeley? I mean, you could do what you wanted, be what you wanted. Not like everyone you ever grew up with on the rez saw your every move. Look at the way we sneak around. That's not freedom."

"I guess it isn't," I said. Soon she drifted off. I watched the stars awhile, hunting the constellations that I used to know so well, and I listened to her gentle breathing. Then, it came out of nowhere, a woman's voice. So clearly a woman's voice, and so well trained. It was beautiful and controlled, at least the first two notes were. "*Good night*," she sang in a high falsetto. The syllable *night* was sung at even a higher note than *Good,* and was held a long time. As she held the note, she increased the volume. A crash of cymbals punctuated her crescendo. Then her voice came again but harshly, shrill and taunting: "*Stooooooooopid.*" Kettledrums thundered, then faded. Then silence. I bolted up and looked at Frannie, but she slept soundly under all her hair.

I looked up at the stars and told myself that it hadn't happened. You imagined it. Nobody said, "*Good night, stupid,*" much less sang it. But I knew the difference between real and imagined sound. I closed my eyes and played it over in my mind's ear. It had been months since I had heard her sing, or heard the popping noises or the explosions, so I had started convincing myself that I had never *really* heard these things, only imagined hearing them. I convinced myself I was healthy.

At sunup, we took a quick dip in the river. Frannie threw on her clothes and saddled up her horse in a hurry. It was Sunday, so she wanted to get back and make breakfast for her dad and brother before they woke up. Then she would go to church with her dad. It was the same every Sunday. I made a little fire for the hell of it, but there was nothing to cook. As she positioned the bit in her horse's mouth, she was singing lightly, "*Modern love, modern love, gets me to the church on time,*" then she broke off the melody and said, "God, wouldn't it feel good to drive to Kadoka and have breakfast together at the diner?"

"I can just see it."

"Well, what about the Bright Clouds?" she said, meaning Ray and his white wife.

"First of all, he's a breed."

"Oh, like you're a pure blood. You're as much a breed as Ray is."

"And second," I continued, ignoring the interruption, "Ray's wife ain't no daughter of Hank McLaren."

"Oh give it a rest."

"And while we're on it, Frannie, half-breed and pure blood mean more than what's in your veins. You can be a hundred percent Lakota and still be a half breed. And likewise you can have mixed blood in your veins and be a pure blood."

"That's quite a trick."

"It's about outlook, how you see the world. Ray's a progressive, wants to work with the man."

"And I suppose you're a traditional."

"My mother was."

Frannie was silent. She was sassy, but knew when to lay off.

"And third," I said, "Ray and Kay are legally married."

"Well, this town and my old dad could stand a little shaking up."

"Won't be your house, though, gets shot up."

"We don't have to stay in Kadoka, Joey. You got your degree. I got mine. We could go anywhere. Hell, we could do a stint in the Peace Corps together. I been thinking a lot about going back in."

My degree was a B.A. from Berkeley, thanks to the GI Bill. It was at Berkeley that the voice had started. First I denied it was happening, then I tried to block it out with a tape deck and constant studying. I was an astronomy major, but then switched to psych to learn about what was happening to me, studied around the clock and received a fellowship to grad school. I told no one about the voice, except over at the VA, but I learned about the condition, and about the hopelessness of it. Fast or slow, it would be a tailspin, a fragmenting of the mind, a splintering of the personality. Most of them ended up on the street, arguing back. So after a year of grad school, I returned to Pine Ridge for a life of quiet disintegration. At least on the rez I would never end up on the street or homeless, and I could blend into the larger disintegration and despair. But the tailspin never came. I hung on, year in and year out, convincing myself I'd be okay. I could live with it, disguise it, overrule it. And there was no question that for a long time it had backed off.

"You'd love Africa," she said.

"Sounds real fine, Frannie, but a bit escapist."

"Escapist?" she said defensively.

"Seems whatever we could do for the Zulus or whoever needs just as bad to be done on the rez."

"But don't you ever wanna bust outa here? The world's a big place."

"You like different cultures so much, Fran, move onto the rez with me. I'll show you a world right here, I'll teach you Lakota." She was silent. Her specialty in the Peace Corps had been digging wells, so I added, "Half the families still don't have plumbing or water. We could do a lot of good and be happy."

"You won't even eat in a diner with me," she said.

"That's off rez."

"Oh, like we'd never have to go to town."

"They'll leave us alone if we tell 'em we're married," I said.

She laughed and got on her horse, then bent down for a kiss. "Let's aim for Wednesday, okay? Saturday's too far," she said, meaning our next river date.

"Yeah, we'll aim for it," I said. "And don't forget the Fourth of July either."

◆

When I got back to Wambli, 'most everybody was still asleep. Ooly came out into the road to say hello. She put her front paws up on the car door and her face through the open window, blinked her dark eyes and smiled. She licked her nose and the side of her yellow snout. It looked like Bob had finally put some STP into her coat. "How's my girl? You bored? You wanna come for a ride, sweetie?" She yawned deeply, contentedly. I wish I could yawn like that. I opened the door and let her hop in over me. She curled up on the passenger seat, then put her head on my lap. The gash in her ear hadn't closed at all, neither had the one on her shoulder, but she didn't seem to be in any pain or bad temper.

I headed out of Wambli in the direction of Clem's house. Linda often got up early and made coffee, so I figured I'd drop in.

Ooly hopped out and ran to the door, nudged it open with her nose. "Well, hello there," I could hear Linda saying. "What're you doin' here, sweet thing?" Ooly wagged her tail, holding the screen door open a few inches with her snout. Linda opened it all the way to let the dog in, and only noticed me then. "Morning, Joey," she said with her lovely smile and a little wave of the hand. "Whadya, smell the coffee?" She was talking kind of hushed, so I figured Clem and the kids weren't up.

"Does smell good," I said. "He up?"

"No, but he ain't dead to the world neither. He's off the bottle, and I got a good feeling about it this time," she said. "Hey, why's it you sleep late all week, but Sundays you're up at the crack of dawn?"

"Sunday belongs to the Lord," I said. She laughed over her shoulder as I followed her in. Linda had picked up most of the mess the feds had made. She makes a good home for her kids, and she stays on top of it.

"You know where the cups are. Help yourself." She disappeared into the bedroom. I poured two cups. She returned with her baby in her arms and her shirt unbuttoned most of the way. She had pretty breasts. The baby seemed happy with them, too. "Say hi to your uncle Joey, Jennifer," said Linda, tilting and turning so that I would come into the child's view. I handed Linda her coffee. She sipped and I sipped and the child made little suckling noises. "You're gonna hook her on caffeine," I said.

"Gosh, you think it gets through?" she said, putting the cup down on the counter. I smiled and shrugged. Knowing Linda, she probably wouldn't touch another drop till Jen entered high school. I thought of the Vietnamese lady just then, saw her running at me. Every now and then Linda reminds me of her, very similar faces. We were taking a village that was hiding NVA weapons. The pilot set the chopper down and a woman bolted from a hootch with a blanketed baby in her arms. She ran straight at the open bay door, like we were her saviors and the hounds of hell were at her heels. This was late in the war and we'd learned their tricks, like running up with babies that were bombs. It had happened to more than one chopper. *You protect your bird. You protect your crew. It's the only survival.* I didn't even have time to shoot the ground in front of her. That's how close, how fast she was. I cut her down. That damn 60 cut her in half, and the bundle she held was no bomb. Still, it felt like self-defense when it happened. I was pumped. Everyone agreed it was sad but self-defense. The problem is time. Time starts twisting things in your head.

Jenny started crying. Linda burped her over her shoulder but the crying continued. "Her teeth are coming in," Linda explained. She stood and said we should go outside so that Clem could sleep a bit more.

We sat on chairs that were still out there from the wake. Around the corner of the house I could see a canvas tepee set up. "Are Rafe and Jeb in there?" I whispered. She nodded with a smile. Rafe was my other nephew. They were eight and five years old.

"That's *your* old tepee," she said. My mom used to set a tepee up in summer so that Clem and I could sleep and spend time within the power of a circle. Tepees form circles on the earth, and the circle has force. It protects you and can give you wakan, Mom told us. I used to love sleeping in the tepee and I was happy that Linda was raising Rafe and Jeb this way.

My cup was empty. "You sure you don't want your coffee?" I asked, getting up to go in the house and grab the cup she'd abandoned on the counter. She didn't seem to hear me. She was looking up the hill and squinting.

"Joey, you see anything up there?"

I looked up but didn't notice anything. "Like what?"

"I could've sworn I saw a wisp of smoke. There it is again!" she cried.

I turned and looked. There was a very faint wisp of smoke, almost white, rising from behind the hill. Or so it seemed, and then it was gone. I wondered whether she had just imagined it and if I had fallen for the power of suggestion. "I don't see it anymore," I said.

"You don't think that's the spirit rising, do you?" she said in an excited voice. I looked at her, expecting a sly smile and a wink. I mean, Linda's traditional as far as keeping the rituals alive and speaking some Lakota, but she's not a child. "I gotta get Clem," she said, her face turning pale.

She went inside, so I followed and refilled my cup. She came out of the bedroom, carrying the baby in one arm and towing Clem with the other. His eyes were still puffy with sleep. She had him by the hand and dragged him out into the yard. He'd only had time to put his pants on so his gut was out in full glory. "Look," she said pointing. He rubbed his eyes but couldn't make out any smoke. Neither could I anymore. She took him by the hand again and marched him up the hill. Ooly followed us, then ran ahead. I walked alongside and offered Clem some of my coffee, which he accepted with a nod.

When we got near the crest, we came across a red gasoline canister. I picked it up and shook it, but it was empty. Linda, who had shot ahead and reached the crest first, shrieked. We ran up to where she was. Below us were two more gas cans and the smoking remains of scaffold poles and some kind of charred bones. Ooly circled the smoldering coals but didn't get too close, put off, probably, by the gasoline fumes. I walked closer, then knelt by what was left. A prank, Frannie had said. They must have moved the body or put it safely in the grave, then burnt some old goat bones on the scaffold. But the blackened teeth looked human, and crowded in a familiar way.

I heard the coffee mug hit the earth, then Clem was at my side on his knees. "No way," he whispered. I turned and looked at him as he took it all in. His eyes became round with astonishment, then glassy and wet. My own vision blurred till I blinked and cleared my lids with the back of my wrist. Clem's hand groped out over the smoking remains, his fingers trembling as they neared the blackened skull. The closer his hand got to her head, the slower it moved. I thought it would always approach and never get there. Finally, the tip of his longest finger touched her charred teeth, then swept lightly across them. It paused on a front tooth that jutted out slightly. This unevenness had given her smile an extra charm. Then his finger paused on a chipped tooth that we also knew from the broadness of her smile. The finger doubled back to where it had begun, then moved from left to right across the row again, and again, like the fingers of a blind man reading a line of madness.

Finally, he withdrew his hand and sat back on his heels. "I'm gonna get that Mormon bastard," he said quietly. "I'm gonna burn his church and him in it." He said it softly so that Linda couldn't hear, and that's what scared me. It was Linda and Mom that had talked him out of killing the Burnt Thigh who had clipped Wenonah fifteen years back. I guess he'd learned at least one lesson: Don't tell the women.

It may sound rash, what he wanted to do, but going to the authorities was no answer. Going to the authorities was a joke. In '72, just to give you a for instance, two whites, over the border in Gordon, Nebraska, beat up Raymond Yellow Thunder for the fun of it, stripped him in front of an American Legion dance, then got a pack of spectators to help kick his head in. They locked him in the trunk of a car, where he died. They were released without bail on charges of second-degree *manslaughter*. And even those charges were about to be dropped altogether but for Raymond's family calling AIM in to create a situation. Even so, the murderers barely did a year. Because it's always Sioux season in the Dakotas and Nebraska.

And this, this wasn't even murder or manslaughter, just body burning.

Clem didn't notice the small, circular impressions in the dirt that were left by the ivory peg leg—and I wasn't about to show him. The last thing I needed was for Clem to drive to McLaren's and shoot Frannie's brother, or shoot the whole damn family. I would take care of Pogo in my own way, in my own time.

He was armed with a rifle and a five-gallon can of gas that he'd siphoned from my car. "Clem, you should go to a holy man first. Make sure this is right with the spirits," I said as we walked toward Wambli. In my pocket, I had a sock filled with coins from Linda's piggy bank. I was getting ready to knock him out with it and carry him home if he didn't come to his senses.

He looked at me, surprised at my suggesting he see a holy man. "I thought that was all bull to you."

"Hell, no," I lied. "Just some of them."

He stopped walking and looked at me, then said, "Maybe I'll talk to No Horse." No Horse was a young medicine man. He was my age. Some thought the *Wakinyan,* or Thunder Beings, gave him his power, because he was said to do amazing things. But it was never firsthand, always a friend of a friend.

"This is bigger than No Horse," I said. "Go to a *holy* man." I didn't want Clem seeing a young firebrand like No Horse who would just say, Yeah, do it, burn the church. I wanted Clem to talk to someone old, like Bear Dreamer Bordeaux, who had learned under Fools Crow. These older guys don't like violence and they don't like vengeance. There was no point in Clem throwing away his life. And there was no point in that Mormon getting killed for something he didn't do. An old-timer like Bordeaux would set Clem straight, make him see that only federal invasion and bloodshed would result from a church burning.

Bear Dreamer Bordeaux lived on the other end of the reservation, between Wounded Knee and Batesland. We drove to Wounded Knee and got directions from some old guys, then took a dirt road three miles before we got to a shack. The field it sat in was parched but clean, no cans or papers about. An old woman in the shack told us in Lakota that Bear Dreamer was in a thicket on the other side of the next hill. We left the car and walked. At the top of the hill we saw below us, maybe sixty yards away, a man with long white hair gathering branches. He was wearing just a breechcloth and moccasins. As he cut willow branches with a knife, the muscles in his back rippled in the sun. He looked lean and hard, especially for an old coot. And he must've had the ears of a deer, because he turned slowly around and looked right up the hill at us, as if we'd called to him. He made no motion, just stood there with his arms full of branches. I was spooked.

Clem took the first step and I followed at his side. The old man remained still. Only a strand of his white hair moved in a momentary breeze. His face was chiseled and angular, and covered with leathery skin. The white hair that framed his face made his dark eyes seem black. They were the eyes of a much younger man, I thought.

Clem unfolded the doeskin that was wrapped around the pipe he'd brought. "I'm Clement Blue Chest," he said, holding out the long pipe and some tobacco wrapped in a paper twist. Clem had carved the pipe some years back out of catlinite, and was very proud of it.

The old man nodded. "And you must be the brother, Moves Camp," he said in Lakota.

I nodded and shifted my weight from one boot to the other, trying to disguise my astonishment. Wambli was almost two hours away by car. Clem was a nobody and so was I, and we hadn't told anyone we were coming.

Bear Dreamer handed me the willow branches and accepted the pipe from Clem, laying the head of it in his palm and the stem along the inside of his forearm. Then he accepted the tobacco pouch into the other hand. He cradled the pipe with respect, which made Clem swell with pride. "I've been cutting these willows to build you a sweat lodge, Blue Chest," said the old man. It was the end of June and almost a hundred

74

degrees out; an extra sweat was just what we needed.

"We just came to ask your opinion on something," I said.

Bear Dreamer nodded and said to Clem, "I know why you've come." Then he turned to me and said, "And why you've come." He had scars all over his chest and arms from years of piercing and others on his arms from making flesh offerings. Maybe a hundred or more of these little scars along the length of his arms. It reminded me of a junkie I knew in the VA who shot himself everywhere in search of fresh veins.

"You know about the Mormon?" asked Clem.

Bear Dreamer nodded as though he was thinking of something very sad: "These Mormons have brought great bloodshed."

"How's that?" I asked.

He shook his head. "Let us build the sweat lodge. The answer Blue Chest seeks is not with me but with Wakan Tanka. So first you must make yourself pure, Blue Chest."

Bear Dreamer took twelve willow branches, skinned them of their bark, then bent them into the framework of a dome, tying the branches together with strips of bark and staking the ends down in the earth. Over the frame we laid pine boughs, then blankets and tarps and hides. It wasn't more than four feet tall and had the look of an igloo.

"You see the way it makes a circle, like a tepee does? That's what gives it power. Circle has no beginning and no end, like the world. A square lodge can make you sweat but it won't purify ya. Got no power. Circle is balance, wholeness. We try to live in the circle, live in balance with the world. This keeps us whole, the people whole. We're not shells of men. This is what we call the sacred hoop of the people."

A few yards away, we built a huge fire out of wood that Bear Dreamer had already prepared. He placed twelve large rocks in it. Then he made a flap door out of the blanket on the west side of the lodge. In the center of the lodge, we dug a pit, more than a foot deep and two feet wide. We dug with sharp stones that he gave us, and the earth smelled good. "This pit will contain the *workers*," he said in Lakota. That was his name for the heated rocks. We dug a chute that descended gently from the flap door to the pit. Bear Dreamer placed sage around the pit for us to sit on. Then he gave us each a section of deer antler and said that the workers were ready and we should bring them into the lodge.

Pushing and prodding with the antlers, we rolled the workers out of the fire and coals over to the entrance of the lodge, then down the chute into the pit. Before we brought in six, the lodge began to bake. Clem and

I stripped to our shorts. I realized then Bear Dreamer's breechcloth wasn't such a bad idea.

The sage and pine boughs and sweetgrass released their fragrances. I felt them in my sinuses, as I did the heat. Bear Dreamer took my antler and began arranging the rocks in the pit. They had to be in a certain order, it seemed. When we finished rolling in the other six workers, he told us to put the flap door down and come sit by him on the sage. Clem put the flap down and all light vanished. We could have been underground or in a cave it was so dark. Bear Dreamer lit a match, then the pipe.

He said the kinnikinnick was good, then passed the pipe to Clem, then to me. It's a sweet-smelling smoke, kinnikinnick, made from the inner bark of the red willow and from a root. We had bought it from a guy in Wambli that morning. It's what you smoke for sacred rituals, and Clem wanted to do it right. The smoke is supposed to carry your prayers up to Wakan Tanka, but the sweet aroma just carried me back fifteen years to the reefer that got us through the war.

In the few minutes it took us to smoke the bowl, I must have sweated a pound or more. My eyes stung with sweat and I could hear Clem's breathing become wheezy.

I heard Bear Dreamer move. A moment later, light poured in as he opened the flap door and went out. He came back with something in his hand, but I couldn't see what exactly. He shut the flap, made his way over in the darkness, then sat back down between us. He began mumbling in Lakota, but it was hard to understand. Then he took a bite of something that sounded like an apple. I asked him what he was eating.

"I'm not eating," he said, then kept chewing. *My ass, you're not eating,* I thought. *We're sweating buckets and this old coot is slurping a juicy apple and doesn't want to share.* Clem kept wheezing. A moment later, Bear Dreamer said, with his mouth full, "You might want to open that flap a little. It's about to become very hot in here."

I didn't know what that meant because I don't think I'd ever experienced anything near as hot as it already was. In college, I had used the sauna a few times and that was nothing next to this. "What do you mean?" I said.

"It's about to become very hot," he repeated. I crawled over to the flap and opened it. The outer world was shockingly bright, and cool. I wanted to go out but crawled back to my place. He took another bite of what appeared now in the light to be a root of some kind. He chewed carefully, took still another bite, and chewed some more. With full cheeks, he mumbled again, this time, I think, invoking the powers of the four directions, then he leaned over and squirted this stuff onto two of the rocks in the pit. The rocks sizzled and seemed almost to talk excitedly, then they began to glow red, then orange. He squirted drops onto each of the rocks and then sprayed them with what remained in his mouth. All twelve workers chattered against each other like excited atoms, and all twelve glowed bright orange. Brighter than neon. The heat in the lodge became unbearable. It was as if something was hitting us, beating our skulls and whipping our limbs. My throat and lungs stung, as if by bees. I kept looking at my hands to see if the skin was blistering or shriveling. My vision blurred.

"You like that?" said Bear Dreamer. "Fools Crow taught it to me last year, before he died."

Whether it was the trick itself or the resulting blast of heat, I was too stunned to answer. Clem's breathing was loud and wheezy. I hoped he would complain, so I wouldn't be the one to break. I was ripped at Bear Dreamer. I don't know how he did what he did, but we had been sweating just fine without the extra spit-and-glow trick to impress us. I wanted to suggest that we open the flap wider, but I had trouble talking, as I had to take such tiny breaths in order not to burn my lungs. Clem's breathing was short and getting wheezier. I was afraid he was going to have a heart attack. Slowly, he got to his knees and crawled toward the flap door. *Thank God,* I thought. When he reached the flap, he did something astonishing. He closed it and crawled back to the pit. All outer light was sealed out, but the orange glow of the workers lit up our wet skin. The angles of Bear Dreamer's face were all the more striking in this lighting from below. He dashed some water on the rocks, causing an explosion of steam that gave new bite to the heat, especially in the lungs. I tried breathing through my nose, thinking the longer route to the chest might cool the air a bit, but succeeded only in burning my nostrils and sinuses.

"Why have you prepared this cleansing ceremony?" came a whisper in Lakota. I panicked at the thought that it was happening again. Would it now become a daily haunting? Would I soon be talking back, yelling back like the guys on the ward in the VA, and on the street? But it seemed to come from the rocks this time. It came again and this time like a chorus of many whispers. "Why are you having this purification?" Then I figured it out and smiled with relief; the old coot could throw his voice. I turned and watched his lips. He was good. No movement. Maybe a little by the Adam's apple, I thought, but I had so much sweat in my eyes

I couldn't see too well. Clem leaned forward, rubbing the sweat from his own eyes and looking intently at the workers, as if the rocks had really spoken.

Clem answered slowly in Lakota, pausing between words to take in shallow breaths: "I am a drunk . . . and a fool. Whenever I do something . . . I always know I'm right . . . then I learn I'm wrong. I need . . . guidance now." I had often wondered if Clem knew what people thought of him. It broke my heart to hear he did, and that he agreed. Bear Dreamer put his hand on Clem's forearm in a gentle way that suggested he thought Clem was being too hard on himself and that he should be silent now. *"Hanbleceyapi,"* said Bear Dreamer to the workers. "We have one who will go on the hill to cry for a vision from Wakan Tanka. This is why we have built this lodge."

"Then we will cleanse you," came the chorus of whispers.

I wanted to ask Bear Dreamer if he could do it while drinking a glass of water, but thought better of it. I also wanted to lift up the blanket wall and see who was out there. Probably the old nag from the shack and some friends of hers. No way a tape recorder would work in this heat. After our little exchange with the spirit world, we sat in silence for a long time.

I tried to ask Bear Dreamer what he meant before about the Mormons, but I was having as much trouble speaking as Clem had had. I thought I would pass out before finishing the sentence. Bear Dreamer lit his own pipe and passed it to me. It tasted like kinnikinnick but different from the stuff we brought. It felt good in my mouth, so I inhaled. It soothed the throat and lungs. He smiled and nodded for me to pass it on to Clem. I found I could breathe deep and freely now. I took another pull and passed it to my brother. In a moment, Clem's wheezing stopped. "What did you mean before when you said the Mormons brought bloodshed to us?" I asked.

The old man wiped the sweat out of his eyes and said, "It's how the wars started. A butchered cow and a Mormon. Cow wandered into a Sioux camp, brave shot her, shared the meat out to the families. Everyone thanked Wakan Tanka for sending them this strange game. Soon some whites from a wagon train enter the camp, and one of them is barking mad, keeps pointing at the remains of the animal.

"The brave ignores their rudeness, 'cause he figures they're mad with hunger, see, and he offers them a choice piece of rump. This only feeds the wasitchu's anger. He picks up the hide and points at the brand. Now, you gotta remember our fathers did not *own* the buffalo, or deer, or elk, so it was hard for them to understand what this fella was driving at. Men owned ponies, not game. Finally, they get his drift and offer him three of their best ponies. This was overly generous, but it was considered kind among our fathers to indulge those who had lost their reason. Should've been the end of it, but this wasitchu says no to the ponies, demands money and the right to punish the brave. Our grandfathers didn't know about money, and they sure weren't about to hand no one over. They offered a fourth pony. But the Mormons went off in a huff to Fort Laramie and demanded the Army enforce the 1851 treaty by punishing the *thieves*. The officer said four ponies was more than fair and they should go back and accept. But the Mormon didn't want ponies, wanted satisfaction. Said that if the Army didn't enforce the treaty, he would write to the government. So finally the officer decides to satisfy these saints."

Old Bear Dreamer wiped the sweat from his eyes again, then dripped it off his finger onto the orange workers. The sweat sputtered into little balls like mercury, then disappeared. "Sends out Lieutenant Grattan," said Bear Dreamer. As soon as he said the name Grattan, I realized he was talking about the Grattan massacre. "This Grattan, he sets out with thirty men and two howitzers, finds the camp, enters, demands the surrender of the thieves, has blacksmiths ready with chains and shackles. The chiefs refuse to give over anyone, repeat their pony offer. Grattan pulls back his outfit a short distance, then opens fire on the camp without warning, mowing people down with howitzers, including two chiefs. Soon, though, the braves flank them and rub 'em out. All thirty of them. That was how the Sioux wars started, thirty-six years of extermination war on our villages," said Bear Dreamer. "Right up to the final massacre at Wounded Knee."

We sat there for a while listening to the chatter of the workers.

"Maybe the Sioux wars would have happened anyway," said Bear Dreamer. "All I know for sure is it started with them Mormons wanting to teach us a lesson. And they're still trying to teach us lessons." He shrugged. "Just Catholics, really."

This was *not* the kind of help I wanted from Bear Dreamer. It could only increase Clem's urge to torch Blake's church. "That was a long time ago," I said.

Bear Dreamer nodded.

"And you said before that it is Wakan Tanka who must show Clem which path."

"Yes," he said, smiling gently. "Let us pray before we go on the hill."

We chanted with him in Lakota, then he suggested each of us pray silently. I closed my eyes and thought about swimming with Frannie in the White River, and about her smile and the taste of her mouth. Then I thought about the cow I shot, and about the one some ancestor shot long ago, and I wondered if we were on the brink of war, on the brink of some corny spiral in history. I wondered if Clem would be hungry and dehydrated enough after four days on the hill to hallucinate, to have a vision, and whether that vision would get him and others killed. Finally, despite myself, I prayed. I put away my dignity and begged favors from a nonexistent being. I prayed for Clem and his vision quest. Grant him a vision, please. Let him see something beautiful and interpret it positively. I prayed, too, that my own mind would not splinter. Let me hear no more voices. Let my center hold, like the sacred hoop of the people. But of course I knew that the sacred hoop of the people had been broken, shattered and never mended.

"What you waiting for?" said Bear Dreamer, looking at me. He had slipped a black sack over Clem's head and placed him in the car. I got in and we headed out for the Yellow Bear area. I was thinking about how best to kill Pogo, and whether I should let him see it coming so he'd know what it's about. Maiming might be better.

We left the car and walked up the vision hill with Clem between us, each of us guiding him by an elbow.

Near the top stood a young cottonwood tree, very straight and leafy. Four strips of cloth, red, yellow, white, and black, the colors of the four winds, dangled from its branches. Nearby, gaping skyward, was the mouth of the questing pit. It's basically a cave dug into the hill.

"You should empty yourself," said Bear Dreamer.

Clem shrugged. "I didn't eat this morning."

"Just the same, go into the thicket and try."

We then helped Clem lower himself into the pit. It was a close fit at the belly, but he made it through and disappeared. We sealed up the mouth by stretching a buffalo hide over it and driving some pegs through into the earth. "Can you hear me, Blue Chest?" said the old man. "I'll come get you in four days. Even if you receive a vision before then, don't leave the pit. Wakan Tanka may send you many. This is why you never leave early. Okay?"

"Okay," said Clem, his voice a bit muffled.

"Hey, too bad you're gonna miss the Fourth, Clem. I'll save you some tube steaks," I said.

"Hey, Joey," he said.

"Yeah?"

"Check in on Linda, yuh? See if she needs help with the kids, yuh?"

"She'll never know you're gone, Clemmy."

Bear Dreamer was already heading down the hill. There was the sound of dried grass and weeds crunching underfoot, and the wing-grinding call of grasshoppers to one another. "You should learn to value your brother," said Bear Dreamer as I came abreast of him.

You should write fortune cookies, old-timer, I almost said out loud. *You really should.*

◆

When I got back to Wambli, old Isaac Sky Elk said some guys from Oglala had been around looking for me and for Elijah. Later, Elijah dropped by my place and asked if I wanted to ride into Oglala with him and Eli Jr. "What's in Oglala?" I asked.

"Seems you, me, and Junior been invited to some kind of a secret meeting."

"By who?"

"Dwight Laughing Horse was one of them. And Kaleb Holy Dance was the other," said Eli. That stumped me because I knew those guys and to my knowledge neither of them had been with the Movement.

Around dusk, we got in Eli's pickup and headed west. It was dark before we were halfway there. As we neared Oglala, we saw another pickup on the side of the road and a few men standing there with rifles, roadblock style. One of them flagged us with a flashlight. Elijah slowed gradually with his left foot while keeping his right over the gas so that he could floor it in case these were drunk teenagers shooting up passersby, which was happening a lot around Oglala. I had Eli's shotgun ready and my window down. In the light of the high beams, we could see they weren't teenagers. Eli rolled down his window and came to a full stop. The dude with the flashlight put it in Eli's face. "Moves Camp?"

"That's me," I said.

"Then you Elijah Hunts Alone?"

"That's right," said Eli.

"And that your boy?"

"That's right."

"You guys wanna follow us?"

"Depends where to and who the hell you are," said Eli.

"The Badlands."

"What the hell for?"

"You'll know soon enough."

"I ain't taking my boy into the Badlands at night, following a bunch of armed yahoos that I don't know," said Elijah.

"Eli," called another voice. A dark form walked up next to the guy with the light, took it from him, and shined it up under his own chin. A round face and a nose that must've been busted more than once, and a wide grin full of chipped teeth, glowed at us. With the light going up his nostrils and chipped grin, he looked like a jack-o'-lantern, half menacing, half comic.

"Well, I'll be goddamned," said Elijah. "Harry fucking Pawnee-Killer. Where you *bin?*" Eli got out of the truck. The flashlight swung through the dark, then disappeared. I think they were hugging each other. A moment later, Eli leaned in the window. "Junior, Joey, get on out here and meet Pumpkinhead Pawnee-Killer."

Over the years, I had heard all kinds of Pawnee-Killer stories. He and Eli had been through Tet together, then done sniper missions, just the two of them, taking out Communist mayors and organizers in hamlets deep behind the lines. They'd been through all kinds of scrapes and had saved each other's hide more than once. It was always Pumpkinhead this and Pumpkinhead that.

"Where the hell you been?" Eli said again.

"Been around the world and I'm goin' again." Pawnee-Killer grinned.

Junior and I got out and shook hands with him. His hand was big and meaty, full of muscle. He was about six foot, like me, but extremely broad-shouldered. He looked at Junior after shaking hands with him. "Hell, last time I saw you, your Pampers was leaking on my shirt."

Junior smiled and looked down, while his dad said, "Christ's it been *that* long?"

"Been bobbin' and weavin' ever since '75, mostly up in the Arctic Circle. But I'm back now and staying, and they ain't takin' me," he said.

After the two feds got killed on the rez in '75, the FBI started hunting down and railroading every leader in the Movement. It didn't matter to them that it was a kid who shot those agents and that he wasn't even part of AIM, or that he was right to do it. Those agents had come onto the rez looking to get it on, gunned a man down cold. So this kid takes an AR-15 and gives it right back to them. But the feds used the killing to railroad every AIM leader they could get their hands on. Leonard Peltier was their big catch, but they wanted Pawnee-Killer just as bad. He knew how to bring people together and mobilize them, so the feds wanted his ass bad.

"C'mon, I'll ride with you guys," he said. We all wedged in, sitting four across, and followed the other pickup into the Badlands. After a good number of miles on the road, we turned off and went through ravines and between small but very steep mountains of clay and ash. We listened to Harry's descriptions of life up in different parts of Canada, among the Cree and the Eskimos, always staying a step ahead of the Mounties.

It was a bumpy ride and Eli cursed whenever something hit the bottom of the truck. The Badlands are an eerie place, stranger than the surface of the moon, a range of clay and volcanic dust carved into huge dribble castles and gigantic anthills by aeons of wind and rain. It feels like another planet, an endless and barren maze of rising mounds and falling cliffs.

The pickup we'd been following finally stopped. We could make out ten or a dozen other vehicles, but no people. We got out. In front of us rose a cliff, about forty feet high, and on either side of it some mountainous formations of silt and ash. "This way," said the guy who had flagged us down on the road. He led us through a tight space between the cliff and one of the steep silt mounds, through sort of a "hole in the wall." We descended into a miniature canyon. It was about the size of a basketball court. There were earth walls all around us now, protecting and concealing. In the center of this space, more than twenty men were seated around a fire. Above, the stars were bright. We approached the circle. There were faces I recognized from other towns on the rez, and some from Rosebud. Someone stood up and dropped a blanket from his shoulders. He wore moccasins, a breechcloth, and a bone breastplate. I was ready to laugh till I saw it was No Horse. He was cut up like a gymnast, abs rippling in the firelight. His hair was unbraided and flowing down his shoulders and back. He walked past the fire and toward us, half athlete, half god.

No Horse and I had gone to the Mission school together as kids. In sixth grade, he was having visions and starting to acquire power, or so they said. The priests were not pleased. Watching them was like watching cowboys try to bust a bronc, except that after they'd been thrown a few times, they decided to just whip it instead of ride it. No Horse would always talk to me in Lakota because I was one of the few who knew it, but I always answered in English. I was a smart "laddie" who was going to go all the way, football on Saturday, choir on Sunday, then glory someday in the Army, and maybe college and a life of dignity in a city with a cathedral. Man, I bought the program. But not Johnny No Horse. No matter how hard they whipped him with that willow switch, he kept talking Lakota. They must have feared he might eventually sway the class, because when he stopped coming to school in seventh grade, they didn't send the BIA cops to fetch him and beat his old man like they did with everybody else who tried to stay in the bush. They let John No Horse put himself out to pasture early. Let him rot in the bush. He's the Devil's own, they said. Their motto was *Kill the Indian to save the man,* those gentle fathers, but they knew whom they could warp and whom they couldn't. They knew they couldn't kill the Indian in No Horse, and he was just a boy. What they feared was that as he grew stronger, he might bend the rest of us back, undo all their fine twisting that they had achieved with bodily punishment and the constant threat of hell and eternal suffering. A spirit as strong as No Horse could take away the shame they had so labored to create in us. So they let him go. He grew up out in the sticks, hunting and trapping, just barely surviving, and he started his spiritual training early, under Frank Little Wound, a great holy man.

No Horse stopped in front of me and looked me in the eye. We were the same height and weight, even our faces were similar. I wondered if he would say something snide. Instead, he said, "*Kola,*" which is *friend,* and he continued in Lakota, "I was saddened by the news of your mother."

I thanked him.

"How is Clem?" he asked.

"He's questing," I said. "Under Bear Dreamer."

No Horse nodded, then turned to Eli and Junior and spoke in English. "Welcome, brothers." Junior looked down at his boots and Elijah nodded a bit nervously, perhaps because he had as little idea as I had of what we were being welcomed to. No Horse took a step back and raised his arms in a gesture that embraced all three of us, and he said, "Welcome to the Kit Foxes."

I was stunned.

There were several *akicitas,* or warrior societies, in the old days. There were the Crow Owners, the Badgers, the Sotka Yuhas, or Plain Lance Owners, and others whose names I've forgotten. But the one society whose name is impossible to forget is the Tokalas, or Kit Foxes, and this is because Crazy Horse himself had been Tokala.

Young men who had proved their mettle were invited to join these *akicitas*. The *akicitas* competed for glory. While fighting a common enemy, the societies tried to outdo each other in acts of valor. A warrior would ride right into the enemy and touch them lightly with his coup stick. Counting coups was more important than killing. To count coups was to humiliate your enemy. The more you counted, the more honor you won for your society, because it meant getting in close and increasing the risk of getting shot, and it often meant fighting hand-to-hand.

The last I had heard about any of the societies actually existing was from my grandfather. He told me about what it was like coming home from France in 1918 and being judged by the *akicitas*. They comprised then mostly old men, guys who hadn't fought since the Little Big Horn. So he and the other boys returning from the Ardennes and the Somme, having been mustard-gassed, shot up by machine guns, blasted by howitzers and artillery, and maimed by grenades, were invited by some of the societies to come tell of their deeds. Naturally, they were hoping to be inducted into these timeless brotherhoods, which could connect them to a past that would make sense of their present and give meaning to their wounds. But when each man told of his actions, there came always the same question: "Did you touch the enemy? Did you count coups? Did you fight hand-to-hand?" Most of them had been bombed or shot by men in other trenches, and had killed men in distant trenches, so they were deemed not worthy. A few who had killed with bayonets were invited to join, but that was it. I always figured that with attitudes like that and with this reservation life that forbade pony raids and skirmishes and even free hunting—well, I always figured the *akicitas* had just gone the way of the buffalo.

No Horse invited us to sit in the inner circle around the fire. A pipe was lit and passed around. I scanned the faces as I waited for it to come to me. There were men I recognized as traditionals, others I didn't know, probably because they lived way out in the bush. Some I recognized as AIMers and others not. There was even one guy who had been a GOON fifteen years back. There were some holy types who were said to have never taken a drink and others I'd gotten faced with, so I didn't know how the hell they chose their people. It was probably just like any lodge: if you could pay your dues, you were in.

I saw old Speckled Hawk sitting on the other side of the circle with one of his sun dancers by his side. And to my amazement, I saw sitting on his other side the blond sun dancer, Bacon, who had slammed into the FBI windbreaker who was lining up the shot on Junior. The pipe came to No Horse. He inhaled deeply and passed it to me. I took a drag and passed it to Junior, who took a couple puffs, then gave it to his dad. I kept looking across at the blond guy, the priest, wondering who he really was and what the hell he was doing there.

No Horse stood and addressed everyone in the cave. "Tokalas, tonight we are here for three reasons." He turned slowly as he spoke, taking small pivot steps so that he addressed the whole gathering. The blue-and-white beadwork on his moccasins was beautiful, catching the light of the fire softly. "First, we are here to honor a natural warrior who acted bravely and for the good of the people. He risked his life and achieved a great coup for the Oglala Sioux, a great humiliation for the FBIs. More important, he helped keep alive something sacred of the way of our fathers." Then, with increased volume and deeper resonance, No Horse asked, "Is there anyone who doubts that Elijah Hunts Alone, Jr. is Tokala?"

I looked at Junior and saw Eli looking at him, too. The boy was wide-eyed and absolutely still, not even breathing. A long silence ensued as no one voiced opposition. No Horse continued, "And does anyone doubt that he has also won his first feather?" Again, a long silence. No Horse beckoned Junior to rise, then led him by the hand past the fire to old Speckled Hawk, who was now standing. In his cowboy boots, Junior was almost as tall as No Horse and taller than Speckled Hawk, but still a gangly kid. He looked funny all decked out like a rancher next to these two guys in breechcloths. They fixed a large eagle feather to his short hair, then No Horse walked him back to his place between Eli and me.

"The next order of business," said No Horse. "How will we respond to this body burning?"

Speckled Hawk stood up again. "I ask Joey Moves Camp if it is true that the Mormon led the FBIs to your mother's scaffold?"

I stood and said, "Yes," my voice shaky. I realized they wanted a fuller answer. "He was the one who told them about it. Then he brought them to Clem's, told them it was behind the hill. Led them right to it."

Speckled Hawk moved his eyes from me to Elijah. "Were you there, too, Elijah Hunts Alone, when the FBIs arrived?"

Eli cleared his throat as he rose to his feet. "It was like Joey said."

There was a clamor of voices all talking at once. With a nod, No Horse gave the floor to some kid. He had a ripped jean jacket and pimples, but when he got to his feet he stood straight. "They burn what's sacred to us, I say let's burn what's sacred to them. Let's burn their goddamned churches down."

That was seconded by an older man with a call to burn all Mormon churches on all Sioux reservations, not just Pine Ridge and Rosebud but Standing Rock and the others.

No Horse held a hand up, commanding silence. He then recognized someone in the back who had gotten up on one knee. When the man stood into the light, I realized it was Isaac Sky Elk. Eli and I looked at each other.

Old Isaac coughed into his big fist, his shoulders throwing up monstrous shadows on the wall behind him. "Why are we pickin' on the Mormons? We got twenty-six denominations on this rez, hundred sixty-three churches all told. More religion than the Holy Land, for cryin' out loud. Did we invite *any* 'em? I say we invite 'em *off* our rez. All of 'em. Or we'll never have control of our lives. Holy Rosary is the largest landowner on Pine Ridge. Jesuits own more than the tribe. Of *course* they control the BIA and the council. Of *course* they run us. I say we run 'em off, the whole pack of 'em. Gently, of course," he said with a smile.

There was a lot of Ooo-rah and cheering, but when it quieted down, a guy from Rosebud said, "Some of the priests have helped us. They ain't all bad."

"True enough," said Isaac. "And I guess it's hard to imagine chasing 'em off when we all growed up with one church or another. But you whippers don't even know *why* your families are Christian. You just are. The priests sure as shit won't tell you, but it goes like this. Government wanted to pen us on the rezes. With no game, we were starving. No need to die, they said. Just go onto the rez and we'll feed you. They wrote it into the treaty. Also wrote the Army would distribute the food. But right away the missionaries come, tell the government, Hey, you'll always have Sioux uprisings long as the Sioux got their own religion, it's the heart of their resistance. They say to Washington, Give *us* the food to distribute and we'll turn 'em into Christian sheep. So, suddenly, only the baptized get food. Skip a Sunday and your family starves that week. Them fine men of the cloth used starvation tactics."

"That was turn of the century. They're not like that today. They're helpful."

"The Episcopals, too," said another man. "They help us deal with government forms."

Harry Little Wound got to his feet. He was the brother of Frank Little Wound, who had rescued No Horse out in the sticks and taught him his medicine. Harry had short, white hair and a flattened nose. His voice was raspy but sure of itself. "My father was a healer, so our family was in a bad grace with the priests there in St. Francis. They used to burn our ration tickets over a candle when we came for them. This ain't no turn of the century I'm talking about. It was the late thirties, just before the war with Hitler, and I was a boy. One night the priests show up with the BIA cops. Drag us from our beds, middle of the night, and drive us from our home with clubs and guns into a February blizzard. Drove us off the settlement onto the open plains. They call it St. Francis like it's theirs, but it's our land, *our* rez. Drove us off with guns and clubs. My littlest brother, he did not survive that. Died of exposure. We also got separated from my older sister, found her later in a snowdrift, clubbed, frozen, dead—"

"Still, that's fifty years ago," a man shouted. "They wouldn't do that now."

"No, they wouldn't," I said, suddenly on my feet. "Today, they would not. Today, they don't use food as a weapon and they don't beat our kids. They just sucker them into cars with candy, take them to church where everything Lakota is attacked and ridiculed. Good ones or bad ones, they've got no business here. Why should our lives be steered by Rome or Salt Lake? What is Rome to us? We don't need to go through priests to talk to God. We've got the pipe and we've got the land." I felt hypocritical talking that way when I hadn't believed in so many years, but I couldn't stomach that guy defending priests. When I sat down, several voices burst forth, calling for the running off of missionaries from the reservations. I was puzzled at my behavior. I had gone out of my way to take Clem to Bear Dreamer instead of to a young firebrand like No Horse, because I wanted to make sure he would not harm that Mormon, and now it seemed I had helped fire these men up to burn all 163 churches across the rez, which would surely mean a federal invasion and war. I got back to my feet to tell them how it probably wasn't the Mormon but Pogo McLaren who burned my mother's body, but before I got a word out, Pumpkinhead Pawnee-Killer was already standing over the fire and clearing his throat.

"Brothers," he said in a booming voice that silenced all chatter. "What was done to the corpse of a Lakota woman is sad and criminal, and my sympathy is with her family," he said, looking at me. "But we should not lose sight of our purpose. Did we bring back this society simply to become arsonists and church burners, or did we do it as the first step toward retaking the twenty thousand acres of Pine Ridge that Dickie Wilson illegally signed away to the feds in '72?" He paused. His wide face, lit from below by the fire, was haunting and somewhat beautiful in its heaviness. Everyone was silent, waiting for him to continue. "Did we invite Joey Moves Camp to join the Kit Foxes because his mother was burned and so we think he'll pour gasoline with more feeling than the next guy, or did we invite him and Elijah Hunts Alone because they're combat veterans who can help us retake and defend the land that is ours?"

I looked up at No Horse, who seemed pleased with Pumpkinhead's reasoning and air of command. It was clear by the silence that everyone understood now why the feds wanted to nail this guy. He could cut through all the bullshit and remind you of what you always knew, that before it was about religion, culture, language, or skin, or anything else, it was about land. The oldest story in the world.

On the Fourth of July, everyone in Kadoka became a cowboy. Happens every year. Grocers, bank clerks, grease monkeys, they all squeeze into boots, get under Stetsons, strap on the biggest rodeo buckles they can find, then mosey down to Main Street and watch the parade.

I wished I had shades and a tank-top shirt. That's how bright and hot it was.

Decked out in red, white, and blue streamers, a Ford pickup led the parade, rolling down Main Street and clanging a huge bell that was mounted in back on the flatbed. It was a harsh tone, lacking the richness and resonance you might expect from a bell that size. Through the back window of his cabin, the driver yanked a cord that pulled on the tongue of the bell. Posters on the sides of the truck read, "Ring Liberty. Liberty Rings." For a grown man, he was having a lot of fun, waving and yanking, waving and yanking. Also in the flatbed were two teenagers tossing candies onto the road for kids to pick up.

Next was a girl in a lion suit riding a three-wheel all-terrain vehicle. It was too hot to wear the lion's head, so she had it mounted on the handlebars. There was a poster across her chest that said Lions Club. Hitched to her ATV was a little red wagon with a grown man sitting cross-legged in it, wearing a fez with a tassel. He looked about sixty years old and tired as hell. He was tossing out bubble gum and Tootsie Rolls with a slow backhand motion like he was sowing seeds.

Then came an orange VW bug with a huge American flag sticking out of the sunroof on a pole. Smaller flags were fixed to the windshield wipers and they were going back and forth. A poster mounted on the door of the VW said, "My heart is in America. America is in my heart. I am an American." Another poster taped to the back of the bug said, "Freedom, like everything made in America, lasts forever." And I really don't think it was a joke. A wave of cheering and whistling went up as the VW passed. The parade announcer said over the PA, "Take your cover off when the flag of our great country passes." Off came the ten-gallons, and they stayed off till the VW was well down the road.

Next was a float depicting a section of the Black Hills. It showed coal- and gold-mining operations going on, the Hills laid bare from strip mining, tailings all over the place, artificial mountains of ore. A poster hanging from the side of the float said "Before." In train was a second float, marked "After." It showed the same section of the Hills looking pristine, lush, undisturbed. The announcer crooned into the mike, "Give a warm Kadoki welcome to these good boys from the South Dakota Mining and Land Reclamation Association. They come all the way from Deadwood with their wonderful floats to remind you that we *can* get the minerals and still restore the land. Hell, we can make it purtier than it ever was. So don't let the environmentalists mix up your brain on that. Thanky, boys."

I scanned around the crowd for Frannie, but didn't see her. To my left, sitting on the curb, was an old Lakota lady. There was a little Indian kid with her, too, probably her grandson. He was about eight or nine and real bucky, shy. He had thick shiny hair almost down to his shoulders, topped off with a purple baseball cap that said Knights of Columbus. He looked kind of serious for such a squeak. He had a black T-shirt that said Crazy Horse Student of the Month, but I didn't recognize either of them from Wambli. He kept darting out into the road to pick up candy, then walking back and dumping it into a brown paper bag near the old lady. Now and then—for no more than a split second—he would begin to smile, unable to contain his joy, I think, at the rising level of sweets in the bag, and perhaps his pride in being such a good provider. He was scooping up Tootsie Rolls and bubble gum like they were nuts and berries.

I sat down on the curb next to the old lady. When she noticed me at her side, she picked up the bag and offered me some, smiling silently. She would have done the same if I were white or black. It's a reflex with the old people. I thanked her and put a Tootsie Roll in my shirt pocket.

She wore plastic shoes that were blue, but sun-faded and cracking. Her small toe poked out of a split in the side. She took off the shoe and rubbed her foot. There were sores on the tops of her toes, deep cracks in the calluses on the balls of her foot. It made me think of Mom and the fifty-mile trek for my underwear.

The town's two fire trucks rolled by, decked in streamers of red-white-and-blue, bells ringing, lights flashing, volunteer firemen tossing candy, waving flags. Off came all the hats again. I was glad I wasn't wearing one. The little boy ran out to gather candy. I stood for a moment to scan for Frannie, then sat back down on the curb. A colonial fife-and-drum trio limped after the fire trucks, playing "Yankee Doodle Dandy" in diesel fumes.

Then, at the far end of town, a monster truck, olive-green, started creeping up Main Street, inching closer, looming larger. It must have been four times the size of the fire trucks. I'd never seen anything so large on wheels. In white letters, it said "U.S. Air Force." In his down-homi-est voice, the announcer said, "And let's have an extra-warm Kadoki welcome for this fine crew, drove all the way from Ellsworth AFB to share their Minuteman missile with Kadoka on our nation's birthday. Peace through superior firepower. It's the old way, the only way, the way the West was won. Don't forget to take your cover off for our fine service-men." Off came the Stetsons again, and there was a lot of clapping and whistling. The tires were as tall as a man, and the driver sat as high as the second floor of a house. I couldn't believe there was a nuclear missile in Kadoka. It was suddenly like one of those Red Square celebrations where they parade out ICBMs and all the weapons they can put on wheels. This launcher was practically bigger than the whole podunk town. The mayor must've been tight with some brass at Ellsworth to get them to drive a missile three hours on the highway to a cow town like this.

Mine eyes have seen the coming of the engines of the war. They have crushed every serpent on this and every shore, the diva sang in high falsetto. At the same moment, I saw the purple cap of the boy under one of the colossal wheels. I darted into the street, looking for him. I was sure the slow-moving wheels would reveal his pulp. When the truck passed, I picked up the hat and searched the road some more. I turned around and saw him standing between his grandmother's knees. She had her hand around his belly and was pulling him in close, protectively, waiting for the monster launcher to be well down the road. I walked back, handed him his hat, and sat back down to wait for Frannie, but I'd broken a sweat and I kept thinking about the kid crushed under the huge wheels, kept seeing it and thinking of Wenonah. Was I becoming delusional, I wondered, or was it like a warning vision from deep in my brain? I mean, the kid wore a Crazy Horse shirt; Crazy Horse was a Kit Fox, and even Crazy Horse was finally no match for the superior weapons of the whites. Now their weapons were space-age. How could the "Kit Foxes" of today expect anything but crushing defeat?

Bringing up the rear was an armored personnel carrier. The driver was a handsome blond dude in a snappy black beret and Ray-Bans. A guy who could have been his twin was manning a swivel-mounted M-60 and trying to keep a bad-ass poker face, like he wasn't getting off on all the attention. Because of the heat, the hatch doors in back were open, and I glimpsed some black airmen packed inside. It was their teeth and the whites of their eyes mostly that stood out in the semidarkness of the compartment. Looked about as hot and cramped in there as a slave ship. And they looked sheepish, like they weren't even supposed to have the hatch open. Kadoka's all white. The Nordic coloring of the driver and gunner made for a better parade.

I felt something tap my butt lightly. I turned around and saw Frannie standing over me, smiling. I stood up and said hello. "Let's get out of the sun," she said. We walked north behind the spectators.

"Would you like something cold to drink?" I asked. We were right near the Broken Spur.

"Maybe later," she said without breaking stride.

I followed her off Main onto one of the little side streets. Soon we were in front of the Lutheran Congregational Church. She floated up the stairs and turned around. "It's cooler than out here," she explained. The inside was white and simple. No weepy statues and paintings like Holy Rosary. The door shut behind us quietly. Frannie sat on a pew, but immediately stood up and walked to the pulpit, then back, then back again. "What's wrong?" I asked.

"Just not in a Fourth of July mood."

"Still beats church, though, don'tcha think?"

"Go on, if you want to."

"Something happen?"

"No, I just . . ." She shook her head. "It's the same scene every year, same idiots throwing firecrackers, stuffing their faces with tube steaks, waving flags—like it's a big contest who can act the most American. If it was just the kids, that'd be one thing, you know, but it's everybody. And I'm getting older, Joey. I should be changing somehow, not just getting lines in my face. But I'm stuck, stuck in this dumb-ass scene from childhood."

"That's it?"

"What do I need, a death in the family?"

"I just meant . . . did something happen, something specific?"

"I had another blowout with my dad."

" 'Bout what?"

She shook her head and let out something between a sigh and a laugh. "You wouldn't believe it."

"I used to work for the guy."

"Red meat. Believe that? He takes it personal that I don't eat red meat anymore, says it's trendy bullshit and I'm putting on airs. Just cut the fat away, he says, if you don't want cholesterol. So I tell him it's not about fat, it's about the land. Spoliation of the land. Well, that sent him through the roof. See, Joey, ranching was a good life, but it's got to stop, gotta at least rein itself in or it'll die altogether. It's destroying the topsoil of the entire West. I started quoting these environmental reports and that really sent him through the roof. He can't see past his nose. He can see yesterday and today but that's it. And the fact is, Joey, the West as we know it is coming to an end."

"Seems to happen every hundred years," I said.

"Fair enough." She smiled for a moment to show she took my meaning. "But this still concerns you. See, ranchers have free grazing rights on federal lands, so they let their herds grow and grow—it costs them nothing. Then they spread onto Indian lands for a pittance. So all across the West the land gets pounded by hooves, so there's no aeration of the soil. And it's all because we love beef so much. I mean, to overpopulate the world is one thing, but to overpopulate it with beef lovers is just plain suicide."

"The buffalo herds were in the tens of millions," I said.

"But they were migratory."

I bit my lip, wondering how much of her liberal do-gooder impulse was genuine and how much was fueled by the need to upset her dad. She even admitted once she entered the Peace Corps partly to piss him off, though mostly to assert her independence. I wouldn't be surprised if she tormented him with details about the natives she slept with there—which made me wonder about my own standing.

She walked over to the winding staircase that led up to the pulpit. I followed. Halfway up, she turned around and kissed me, which sort of came out of the blue. "I like the way you use silence," she said.

"And how's that?"

"You know when to say nothing. You're just *there* for me." She sat on one of the steps and took my hand. "I swear, you've made this year so much happier for me." What she meant by "this year" was the fifteen months that had passed since she left Africa early to make her mother's funeral. Being back on the ranch after the freedoms of university and life abroad was hard for her.

Through the railing, she pointed to the second row of pews. "That's where we sit. When I was little, it was the four of us. Pogo stopped coming after the war. Now it's just Dad and me. He doesn't even believe. Neither do I much. It was Mom, the big Lutheran. He just misses her, is all. That's why I go. I remind him of her." Frannie pulled me gently to her and kissed me again. I felt nervous fooling around in church, but she felt wonderful. I touched her thick braid as we kissed, and I closed my hand around it. The possibility that someone could walk in on us added a thrill. I put a knee down on one of the steps between her knees. "It's so cool in here we wouldn't even break a sweat," she said, smiling.

I thought of Raymond Yellow Thunder, the one who got kicked to death by a crowd outside the American Legion dance in Gordon, Nebraska. "I could get lynched—or worse," I said.

She looked me in the eye. "They'd have to come through me first," she said. She paused to let it sink in, then shifted into a lighter tone. "Anyway, everyone's at the parade." She pulled me close and we kissed more, but I started wondering what her reaction would really be if we got caught in the act. She was gutsy, but was she gutsy enough to tell the whole community it wasn't rape in the least but consensual fornication in church?

Every now and then, she pulled away and looked through the bars of the banister at the second pew, as if her dad were there shocked and clutching his chest, then she would turn back to me with renewed fervor.

"What about the pastor?" I said.

"He's running the cotton candy machine. Relax."

"Don't you want him watching, too?"

She laughed and shook her head. "All I need is the spider magic. Spark me." I looked around, but there was no way I could give her the spider magic. It's this trick I have.

"No," I said firmly. Then I lied, "It would never work in a place like this."

Four days after leaving Clem on the vision hill, I drove back to see how he had made out. Bear Dreamer was walking along the dirt road. He was wearing jeans, a white undershirt, and moccasins, unbeaded. I turned the engine off and walked up the hill with him. The hide was still stretched over the mouth of the pit.

"Blue Chest, cover your eyes," called Bear Dreamer. "It's gonna be bright." He unstaked the hide and yanked it, then rolled it up. There was no sound from inside. I wondered if Clem had passed out from hunger, or if he was sleeping. Maybe he had started getting the shakes and run off to find a bottle in Wounded Knee and been clever enough to stake the hide back down. "Hey, Clem, you down there?" I called.

After a few seconds, we heard a moan.

I lowered myself in through the mouth. He was at the other end, in the dark.

"Oh, man, don't tell me I'm back," came his voice.

"Let's go." I held my hand out.

"No, Joey. It was beautiful. I gotta go back to where I was."

"It was a dream, Clem. You can never pick 'em up where you left off. And Linda and the kids need you home now."

97

"I wasn't dreaming. I was *there.* It was so much more beautiful than here."

"Well, you're in a dirt hole."

He shook his head. "I was with eagles. I mean really high up, and we were rolling and diving and climbing."

"We'll call you Eagle, then, okay? Or Blue-Chested Eagle, whatever you want. But let's go. Bear Dreamer's waiting."

We got him out of the cave into the daylight. I was struck at how lean his face had become after the four days of fasting. It reminded me of how handsome he was when he was a young man and I was a kid, before the bottle.

The three of us drove to Bear Dreamer's shack. His old lady gave us each a jar of water. She stirred a couple spoonfuls of sugar into Clem's water. He downed it right away and looked up at her. She spooned in some more sugar and took the jar out to the pump.

"Did your vision show a path?" asked Bordeaux.

Clem scratched his scalp. "Don't know, but it was beautiful." The old woman put the filled jar on the table in front of him. He thanked her in Lakota. She smiled. The jar trembled as he brought it to his lips. He swallowed some, then said, "I was flying with eagles, and I guess I was one of them, and they were trying to settle into these crags in a cliff face on a mountain. But then it started getting weird. There were buzzards swooping down on us and tearing at us, trying to get us out of the nesting places. We weren't fighting back was the crazy part. It was like we were too proud or something, but we weren't giving up the cliff neither. Thing is, there was more and more of these buzzards coming all the time."

"Then what?" asked old Bear Dreamer.

Clem shrugged. "Then Joey yanked me back."

"And there was nothing about the Mormon or his church? Nothing about fire?" I asked.

"Nope."

Bear Dreamer went into the other room and returned with a big piece of cardboard and a thick carpenter's pencil. He got a knife from the sink and began sharpening the pencil. He placed the cardboard on the table in front of Clem, handed him the pencil, and said, "Blue Chest, I want you to draw this cliff." Clem closed his eyes for the better part of a minute, then started making very light marks here and there, to get the dimensions right before pressing hard. He's great at drawing, maybe as good as Mom was. Mom made us draw when we were kids, to teach us how to concentrate. A lot of Clem's drawings were still hanging around the house when I was growing up. I couldn't hold a candle to him at that, but she still made me do an hour every day till I left for the Army. Clem hadn't drawn in many years, not since Wenonah died.

I went outside to take a leak, then I played fetch with Bear Dreamer's dog, an old wolf mutt with goo in his eyes. I was thinking maybe I would stop off at Interior on the way home and pick up some cold ones. I went inside to see if Clem was done with his drawing. Bear Dreamer was studying it. "You put in all the details you can remember?" he asked, scratching his chin.

"Pretty sure," said Clem.

"I know this place," said Bear Dreamer. "But the meaning is not yet clear. I, too, have been there when visiting the spirit world, and I was there once as a small child."

"What about the Mormon?" asked Clem.

Bear Dreamer laughed. "You're so beyond Mormons now it's . . ." His voice trailed off and he shook his head. "Forget the Mormon. Something is moving through you from the other side. Something wonderful. From the other side, to the people, through you, Blue Chest."

Well, that was fine with me. He could tell Clem whatever nonsense he wanted so long as it got him off the plan to shoot the Mormon and burn his church. The only thing I knew for sure was it was Pogo McLaren, not the Mormon, who torched our mother's body. I also knew I didn't want to get saddled with Clem's wife and kids while he watched cable every night in prison.

"Blue Chest, you gotta return to the spirit world, go deeper into this vision. You'll have to pierce. Pierce deep."

"But I haven't prepared," stammered Clem. "I haven't been off the poison twelve moons, haven't been off it two *weeks*," he pleaded.

"Anyone can seek Wakan Tanka *any* time," said the old man. "You seem open to the spirits, and they have found you worthy. Already they have purged you of the poison."

Clem shook his head. "I'm scared."

"There's more strength in you than you know. Or they would not have showed you this vision."

He told us to go outside and wait in the field. A few minutes later, he came out carrying two buffalo skulls by the horns, one in each hand. The skulls were huge and sun-bleached. He laid them down in the grass. "Take off your shirt, Blue Chest."

Clem hesitated, then peeled off his shirt. His gut was definitely smaller, but he still had a fair amount of fat on him. He was trembling and sweating, and his sweat smelled of fear. Bear Dreamer gave him a couple of pegs, and a folding knife, told him to put a sharp point on each peg. "The sharper you make it," he said. "The quicker they'll punch through."

Most sun-dance intercessors these days use a surgical scalpel and even put on latex gloves. They make parallel cuts, an inch or so apart, no deeper than the skin, and then they slip the peg in one cut and out the other. It's neat and it's shallow. Bear Dreamer didn't go in for that new stuff, though. He liked doing things the old way.

While Clem whittled the skewers, Bear Dreamer took a leather cord, fifteen feet long, and threaded it through the eye sockets of one of the skulls. He gave me some cord and a skull and told me to do the same. The skull must have weighed thirty pounds.

Clem's hands were shaking as he carved the points on the pegs. Once, he bobbled the knife and almost slit his wrist.

Bear Dreamer tied a slipknot at the other end of the cord and opened the loops up to about the size of a volleyball.

"Okay, Blue Chest," he said, taking the skewers from Clem's sweaty hands. "Turn around." Clem turned his back to us. The old man grabbed a handful of flesh and pulled it away from Clem's shoulder blade. With his other hand, he punched a skewer through one side of the fold and out the other. But he really put his shoulder and weight into the motion. Clem stifled a yelp. The old man took one of the cords and placed the loop over the exposed ends of the skewer, then tightened the noose. There must have been six inches of skin and fat riding over that peg—I mean six inches from the insertion wound to the exit wound. Then he grabbed another handful of flesh, this time from the other shoulder blade, and pulled it. He gave me a skewer and told me to punch it through. I looked at the point on the peg, then at the fleshy fold in Bear Dreamer's fist. Suddenly, the scalpel method seemed rather nice.

"Sometime today," Bear Dreamer said.

I stepped closer and punched it in, feeling the skin break. It only broke once, though. The skewer didn't come out the other side. You could see it pushing outward but not breaking through. Clem still had a fair amount of fat under his skin, which not only made it hard for me to punch the skewer through but also would make it hard for him to rip free. His fists were clenched at his sides, and he was making a high-pitched growl that sounded like it came through clenched teeth. "Come on, boy!" Bear Dreamer said. "Fast and clean." I adjusted my grip and jammed the peg with more force. The white point popped into the sunlight, streaked lightly with blood. Bear Dreamer placed the loop of the second cord over the ends of the skewer, then tightened it. Clem was hitched to both skulls.

"That should hold you awhile, Blue Chest. They're set deep, and they're set long. Ought to be plenty of time for a vision now. Why don't you walk home to Wambli—"

"That's pretty funny," I said. We were three miles from Wounded Knee. From there, it was nine miles to Porcupine, then thirteen to Sharps Corner, another twelve to Kyle, then thirty-odd miles to Wambli. "You're talking sixty miles or more!" I said.

"Well, he'll break free before then, or drop. But you may as well head in *some* direction, right?"

I couldn't tell if he was joking or just senile.

"Since you won't be needing your car, I'd like to borrow it," he said, holding out his hand for the keys without batting an eye.

He was definitely not playing with a full deck, so I didn't feel like loaning out my car to him.

"Give him the keys," Clem said, then he started walking toward the dirt road. Two or three steps later the cords went taut, Clem screamed, and the skulls shivered but didn't move.

"At least give him a whistle," I said.

Bear Dreamer slapped his forehead. "Hold up, Blue Chest," he called. Then under his breath he muttered, "Where's my head?" He hurried to the shack, coming back a minute later with two eagle-bone whistles and a wreath of sage. He gave a whistle to each of us and placed the wreath on Clem's head. I gave him the keys to the car and told him he should head out before Clem got on the dirt road; that way, Clem wouldn't have to drag the skulls out of the ruts to let him pass. "Good idea," he said, taking the keys. "Just gotta find my library card first." He turned for the shack again.

"Your what?!" I said, but he was already in the shack.

◆

As soon as Bear Dreamer and my car disappeared down the road, I flipped the skulls right side up without Clem knowing. The underside of the skull is smooth and sleds along more easily. I told Clem to blow the whistle loud as he could to block the pain. He leaned forward and started pulling. The skin in his back stretched grotesquely, but the skulls began to slide over the weeds and grass and into the ruts. I came up alongside him. He blasted the whistle as he leaned into each step. His face was contorted and grimacing, but when he saw me alongside him, he managed, for a fraction of a second, to smile. And I think he was thinking, *Yeah, I'm finally doing it. I'm a sun dancer.*

It took two hours before we reached the village of Wounded Knee. People there pointed and waved. Some came over and asked what was up. I told them Bear Dreamer was having my brother go deeper into a vision. Children ran up with jars of water but I didn't know if he should take any or not. When you're tethered to the cottonwood pole, you don't, so I said he shouldn't. It seemed Clem was blocking out the pain or getting used to it. I was afraid water would snap him out of whatever state he'd achieved. Some of the people followed us and cheered Clem on.

From Wounded Knee we headed north in the direction of Porcupine. Clem dragged the skulls along the dirt shoulder of the road. He stopped at one point, blinded by sweat. I gave him my shirt to wipe his eyes. When he gave it back to me, he saw the skulls and said, "They must've flipped. Take care of that, will ya?" I turned the skulls horns down, resigning myself to the fact that there was no way I was going to make my meeting with Frannie. Clem blew his whistle and pushed on, staring up at the midday sun.

It was dark when we reached Porcupine. Some folks there waved and came over, offering portions of their dinner to me and to those who had followed from Wounded Knee. I was weak with hunger but afraid of how it would look if I ate while Clem was fasting and pulling skulls. I've got to admit, I never dreamt he had it in him.

Again, some of the people of the village joined us, bringing our following up to twenty-five or thirty. Some of them brought their own eagle-bone whistles, to help Clem break through to the other side.

Slightly before dawn, we turned east at Sharps Corner. Hardly any whistles were piping now, except for Clem's, which had weakened into a soft peep, a lonely cricket sound. My head kept falling on my chest as I battled sleep. Then the sun broke over the east horizon and hit us square in the eyes. Clem's whistle fell from his lips. I picked it up and tried to give it to him, but his arms shot out horizontally. He started jabbering in Lakota, "Strange man, high runs your spotted pony . . . softly into thunder."

He mumbled that kind of stuff on and off for the better part of two hours. The skin on the right shoulder blade was almost torn through. At around ten o'clock, it gave out. People cheered. I picked up the skewer and wrapped the cord around the skull, then slipped it all under my arm.

The remaining skull, without the counterdrag of the one that broke free, was pulling Clem's torso around to the left. He had to walk in a twisted way now. So, while his load was lighter, his task was harder. The cord pulled his skin at a new angle, tearing into a different group of nerves, it seemed.

Coming down the highway from the other direction were about ten or fifteen old cars and pickups. They started beeping as they approached. When they pulled up alongside us, I could see they were from Kyle. They said folks in Porcupine called and told them about the trek. So they came out to meet us and bring food for everyone, and to escort us into Kyle. Clem was oblivious to them, to everything. He was soaring, I suppose, with his eagles in never-never land, while down on earth his body became more twisted and stooped, his walk more lumbering, his babble more hoarse and bellowing. I kept thinking of Charles Laughton getting whipped in front of the cathedral.

When we reached Kyle, a lot of people stopped to eat canned beans that some families there had put out for us. But Clem just kept trudging along, heading east out of town toward Wambli. Let him go, I thought. You can always catch up. My feet were killing and I was hungrier than hell. I took my boots off to check my blisters and that's when Elijah, Shorty, and old Isaac drove up in Eli's pickup. "Yo, Joey, what you doin'?" said Eli, getting out of the truck.

"Don't ask. How about you?"

"We just come from Porcupine. Heard some nut was dragging skulls all the way from there to here."

Old Isaac got out the other door and walked around, saying, "These two clowns got money riding on how far the guy'll get. Eli put five on less than halfway and Shorty put five on more than halfway. And if he makes it all the way here to Kyle, Shorty gets double."

"Well, Shorty, you're buying the beers tonight, 'cause the guy made Kyle. Made it about ten minutes ago."

Shorty made a high-pitched yell.

"Bullshit! Where is he, then?" Eli said.

"On the road for Wambli."

"You mean he ain't finished?" he said.

"Nope."

"And he's trying for Wambli?"

"Yep."

"It's thirty miles off," he said.

"What's it, some medicine man?" asked Shorty.

"Nope."

"Who?" said Elijah.

"Clem."

"Bu-ull-shit," said Eli and Shorty together.

Old Isaac, though, he took off his hat, sponged his sleeve across his forehead and smiled. "Whadaya know?"

"Damn, that reminds me," said Elijah. "You got to call Linda. She's running around Wambli madder than a wet hen."

I realized then that I had forgotten to stop in on her like I promised Clem. So she knew nothing about the four-day sweat. I guess it was all that stuff with the Kit Fox Society that made me forget. And now this buffalo-skull trek made it a total of almost six days. I threw my boots on and used the phone in the Kyle grocery. She picked up on the first ring.

"Where the *hell* are you and where's *he*?" she said. "He better be laid up in the goddamn hospital or he's gonna be."

"Linda—"

"Passed out in a ditch, I'll bet. I knew it couldn't last. I knew it." She began to cry.

"Linda, he ain't in the hospital. He ain't in a ditch."

"Joey, don't you dare tell me he's dead. Oh God, don't tell me."

"Not yet."

"What do you mean not yet!"

"Look, leave the kids with your sister and get on the road for Kyle. Better yet, bring the kids." I hung up quick before she could start squawking.

Eli, Shorty, Isaac, and I shoveled down some beans, then piled into Eli's pickup and headed up the road for Wambli. Two miles out of Kyle, we came on the crowd following Clem. Maybe fifty or sixty. Some inched along in jalopies and pickups and others walked, and a couple kids rode ponies. Kids and old folks who got tired would get on the hoods and trunks of cars, or on the tailgates of pickups. Quite a few were blowing whistles. "Triple or nothing he makes another six miles," said Shorty.

"You're on," said Eli.

Elijah crossed the yellow line into the other lane and rolled us up to the head of the procession, where we inched back over the line, just behind the dragging skull. The skin in Clem's back was stretched far, looking so rubbery I wondered if it would ever break or just keep stretching.

"Jesus, he looks like some monster freak or something," said Eli.

Shorty started to say something about distance and their bet, then he stopped. I think he was silenced by what we saw—the twisted back, the skewer, the limp, the trickle of blood running down the back and seeping into the yellow pants, and the endless highway that wiggled in heat waves, floating on them, riding them slightly into the sky as if overshooting the horizon.

Elijah sighed. "He's got a lot of sack. Who'd've guessed he had so much sack?"

Half an hour later, I saw a tan speck coming down that black ribbon, growing larger quickly. It was Linda in Clem's shitbox. She must've been doing ninety, and then must've thought she was having a mirage as she got closer and saw all these people and vehicles inching along. She slowed quick and pulled over to the shoulder, then sat in the car and looked at this caravan inching by. When she recognized Eli's pickup, she waved and got out of the car, crossed over, and asked Eli if he'd seen either me or Clem.

"I'm right here," I said, leaning forward a bit so she could see me.

"Well, where's Clem? And what's all this?"

I pointed with my chin. She either hadn't seen him or hadn't recognized him. Now she did.

"What's he doing? What's going on?"

"Clem seems set on walking home," said Isaac.

Linda pulled away from the window and ran up alongside Clem. His left hand was dangling at his side and slapping his leg every now and then. She grabbed it and held it in both of hers while taking little side-steps to keep up with him as she talked to him. She was asking him what was going on, what was it all about. It didn't seem like he was making any answer. I'm not sure he knew she was there. She clutched his hand to her breast and kept taking those shuffling sidesteps, then she started smiling and kissing his hand.

"Linda, let him be," called Isaac from my window.

She looked back at us, her face streaming. She nodded but didn't let go of his hand right away. I wondered if she was crying with relief, joy, or fear. Probably all of them. She lowered his hand very carefully, holding it in both of hers, then let it go. It started flopping around, slapping his leg again. She came back to the truck and sat on the hood.

About an hour later, Bear Dreamer Bordeaux pulled up alongside us in my Mustang. I got out of Eli's truck and got in the passenger door of my car. The old man was wearing jeans, moccasins, and a plaid shirt. "Gee, your brother," he said, shaking his old head with astonishment. "Some kind of tough skin." I wondered if he intended the double meaning. He continued, "I pierced him deep but this is *somethin'*. Must be a big vision."

"How was the library?"

"Libraries are a good thing," he said. "Wasitchu brought a lot of bad things, but not the library. I'll show you later what I found, but I can tell you now, something big's happening, and you boys are in the middle of it. Something wonderful, I think."

"Keep me posted, *kola*," I said, too tired for his stories. I got out and hopped on Eli's hood next to Linda, and I thought about how pathetic we must have seemed, how lucky it was that there were no anthropologists or journalists or photographers around to document it.

Many hours later, the sun moved behind us, westward as we headed east. It began its descent at the same time that the water tank of Wambli surfaced and slowly rose, glinting above the horizon of yellow plains.

Within a mile of Wambli, the skin ripped and the skewer fell. Clem toppled forward onto his hands and knees. I had to slap the hood to wake Elijah in time not to run over the skull. Then I ran with Linda to where Clem was down. When people realized what had happened, they ran up to help him and comfort him. They crowded around, many trying to hoist him on their shoulders, others just wanting to touch him, cop some wakan. Linda didn't know what to do. She was concerned about his getting enough air and not getting mauled.

Just then Clem started making a wild and tormented sound. I thought it was either his death rattle or maybe he was imitating an elk, because it sounded just like a buck elk I had shot up in Sweet Grass some years back: a whimper, a whine, and a fierce growl all in one. He started flailing with his arms to back people off, then he crawled around in circles, as if looking for something, or trying to pick up the scent of something. I wondered if he was doing some kind of hedgehog dance or something that he might have been given in his vision, some far-out dance to bring to the people, to mend the hoop, like Black Elk did.

Still on his knees, he reared up off his hands and started barking, "Thake! Thake!" Looking into people's eyes and howling, "Thake!" He looked into mine and barked, "Thake!" His eyes rolled a little bit, unable to focus on me. His tongue seemed too big for his mouth, and I realized then how swollen and spitless it was. "Kull, thkull," he barked.

Then, through a forest of shins and sneakers, his eyes spotted what he was looking for. As he scurried for it, the people retreated as if from a rabid dog. Now it was in plain view: the piercing stake, and behind it, ten or more feet, the skull. Clem grabbed the stake, removed the cord, lifted a fold of flesh away from his chest and forced the stake through. Then he hooked the cord up and stood.

He raised his hands up to the setting sun and began tugging the skull backwards into Wambli. As he got closer to town, he gained strength— a final surge of adrenaline, I suppose—and started high-stepping it, lifting his knees higher and higher, faster and faster, while never taking his eyes off the reddening sun, and never dropping his arms from its embrace. Then, beneath the water tank, he collapsed onto his back.

Linda began easing the stake out but I stopped her. I put my heel on Clem's chest, near the wound, and yanked the cord. His body jerked and the skewer flew over my shoulder. She looked up at me, first with anger, then with understanding.

We laid him on the hood of Elijah's pickup and drove him home. There we put him on the bed, his sage-crowned head sinking deep into the pillow. Linda began sponge-bathing him while Bear Dreamer mumbled stuff in old Lakota and purified the room with sage and sweetgrass. Linda cleaned his chest wound, checking every two or three seconds to make sure he was breathing. Next, we cleaned his back. Finally, we bandaged him up with gauze that a neighbor brought.

I moved over to the door where Elijah was peering in. "Gut's all gone," I said.

"What's that?" whispered Eli.

"Clem finally dropped his gut. Ain't so *cheppah* now," I said.

Eli just shook his head. "Who'd've guessed."

I started to say something, but my eyes kept falling shut. "I'm going home," I finally said.

I turned to wave to Linda, but she was seated at Clem's side, bending over him with her back to me.

Bear Dreamer Bordeaux was kneeling at the foot of the bed, a plastic basin by his knees. Clem's feet hung off the edge of the mattress and over the basin. The old man dipped a sponge in the warm water. Everything was silence except for the kissing sound of the sponge dabbing the cracked skin and busted blisters of my brother's feet. There was also the intermittent dripping sound of the pink trickle that fell from his heels back into the basin. Outside the window, a hundred people or more waited in dusk and silence.

Bear Dreamer Bordeaux started drying Clem's feet with bundles of sage. My brother was in sage from head to toe.

I woke to the creaking of the screen door. Then it slapped shut. "Who's that?" I called.

"*Kola*," came a voice. "Got something to show you." I sat up as Bear Dreamer padded into the room in his moccasins, his white hair flowing behind him. He gave me the cardboard on which Clem had drawn his dream mountain. "Yeah, I seen this already," I said.

"But you haven't seen this." He produced an old book from under his arm and opened to a page he had his finger in, then put it on my lap. On the right-hand page was a photo of a mountain that had the same shape and contours as Clem's sketch. There were even clumps of trees in the same places.

"Okay," I said. "So he sketched a real mountain."

"That's one of the *sacred* mountains."

"The Paha Sapa?" I said, which means "Black Hills."

He nodded. "He sketched one of our most sacred places. We called it the Six Grandfathers."

I shrugged. "Yeah, well, Clem's been to the Hills lots of times. Who hasn't?"

Bear Dreamer reached and turned the page for me. The same mountain appeared again, but the ridge seemed to have changed considerably, as if vast sections had been blown away. On the next page, areas below the ridge had also changed, displaying now bright sections where the outer, gray rock had been blasted off to expose a chalky inner whiteness. I turned the page again: Something like an eagle's beak grew out of the mountain. In the next photo, it looked more like a nose. And on the following page, a chin appeared, then eyes. I flipped a few pages ahead and looked upon the crudely carved and somewhat smug face of George Washington. Deeper into the book, the other three presidents appeared, first crude, then smooth. I looked again at Clem's drawing and scratched my neck, wondering if Clem could have been there as a kid before they started blasting and carving. The numbers didn't add up, though. Clem wasn't that old. I didn't know what to say, but there had to be an explanation.

"You must not be awake too good," said old Bear Dreamer.

PART II

THE RETURN OF THE BLACK HILLS

It was a cool night for July, but Shorty had brought some Wild Turkey, so we got a good burn going in the chest that soon spread warmly to the skin. It was just Eli, me, and Shorty in Eli's pickup. Shorty was at the wheel while Elijah loaded bullets into a clip. We were heading for Spirit Creek, in the Badlands. It was dark, no moon, which is what we wanted.

Up there on Buzzard Ridge, Shorty cut the engine and the lights. Eli and I got out and hopped into the flatbed. Shorty took his foot off the brake, so that we coasted silently in the darkness down to the creek. We stopped right near the water's edge.

Eli and I planted our elbows on the roof of the cabin and aimed our rifles into the darkness. "Now," whispered Eli. Shorty flicked on the headlights. Six deer appeared, wide-eyed and blinking, frozen in the high beams.

They come to Spirit Creek to drink at night because it's just about the only water in the Badlands. A beautiful buck with great antlers lifted his head from the water and looked directly into our high beams, but he didn't move a hoof. They never do.

It was like an invisible locomotive hurtled out of nowhere and clipped him. Part of the buck jerked violently and part of him disappeared. The echoes of Eli's rifle receded as I lined one up, also a male, and squeezed off a pop from my AR-15. This one stayed whole and just shivered for a moment. A front leg wobbled, then buckled. He flopped over and lay in the shallows.

The remaining four hadn't budged. "What is *wrong* with them?" I whispered.

Eli shrugged. "Hell, I ain't no deer psychologist. Guess it's instinct. Break their legs at night in gopher holes and such, so they freeze."

"Think by now they'd learn," I said.

"Guess they're traditionals. Like to do things the old way," he said. "Come on."

"Ask Shorty if he wants one," I whispered.

"That's too many. I'll give him half of mine."

We waded across the creek, making cowboy sounds to scatter the remaining four deer. I dragged mine out of the shallows by his antlers and laid him near the antlers of Eli's huge buck. Eli was looking for the other half of his buck with a flashlight. The carnage was unbelievable. It would take a couple hours just to collect all the strips and scraps of his animal. Clearly, he'd blown a gut, because the smell was strong and we hadn't even started cleaning them.

I picked up his rifle as he gathered his buck. I was thinking how crazy it is that every time someone pulls a McDonald's, there's all this hollering to ban assault rifles, when a deer rifle like Eli's is a hell of a lot more powerful than my AR-15. And since it takes clips, it's just as fast. One shot can stop a truck, while my AR just puts a few holes in the hood. I hunt with it because it leaves a nice hide for skinning, whereas Eli's loses you the hide and half the meat.

After we dropped Shorty off at his house, with a good chunk of my deer, I told Eli I wanted to borrow his rifle. He was silent for a while as we headed for my place. He knew right away, I guess, and was silent for the rest of the drive. After I pulled my deer out of the back, he said, "Come by in the morning."

He was up and dressed when I stopped in the next morning for it. "You sure you know what you're doing?"

I nodded.

I wanted to spend the day practicing and adjusting the scope, so I asked him for all his ammo. He gave me a number of clips and quite a few

boxes of bullets, then he looked at his rifle lovingly, like it was a son going off to war, like he knew the son wasn't coming home, not even his remains. Eli took such good care of his rifles, always oiling and cleaning
them. And this was his favorite. It was hard for him to picture it rusting
at the bottom of White River, or melting in a furnace somewhere.

I drove within two miles of McLaren's ranch, hopped the wire, and hiked in under the stars. It was a beautiful, warm night. I wore a dark T-shirt and Eli's rifle across my back. I had a pocketful of jerky and some candy bars. I headed to a knoll that was about a hundred yards south of the ranch house and overlooked it nicely.

As I cleared the crest of the knoll on my belly, lights from the house twinkled up at me through blades of buffalo grass. It was a pretty sight and I could faintly smell a fire going. I took the rifle off my shoulder and looked through the scope. It brought me right up to the windows so that I started imagining the voices inside.

Pogo would be stepping outside the kitchen for a smoke soon. He loved a cigar after dinner and one before bed, but Frannie didn't tolerate tobacco in the house. Neither had her mother before her. So Pogo had grown used to having his stogies under the night sky, even in winter blizzards.

I put some jerky in my mouth and waited. Now and then, a body would walk across a room, or from one room to another, a form crossing a window, and I would quickly train the scope on the kitchen door. After a few minutes of waiting for it to open, I took another piece of jerky.

I began to think I had missed the after-dinner smoke and would have to wait a few hours for the bedtime smoke, which would probably come after the eleven o'clock news.

To kill time, I started training the scope on each window for five seconds, counting slowly, then moving on to the next one, left to right, ending always with the kitchen door. At first, I just trained the scope on the lighted windows. Then, out of boredom, and to test my night vision, I included two windows that were unlighted. As I looked through the scope at a dark window on the second floor, I realized it was the guest room where I had discovered the spider magic. I started thinking about that night while I lay there waiting to shoot her brother.

The colonel and Pogo and most of the hands had gone to Wyoming for a cattle auction and a rodeo. Three hands remained on the ranch, but they were busy with the herd out on the rez—so Frannie and I got to enjoy the comforts of hearth and home.

Frannie's room didn't have a double bed, so we used the guest room upstairs. It had come to be more of a storage room, cluttered with junk that the family couldn't part with. To get to the bed, you had to make your way through an obstacle course of family heirlooms and keepsakes, ancient radios, TVs, dusty photos, and all kinds of junk.

Right near the bed, I stubbed my toe on this mother of a lamp. It should have been on a desk or a night table, but there was none. It was solid brass and it hurt like hell.

I helped her off with her T-shirt, then undressed myself and joined her on the bed.

We kissed for a while. When I entered her, I held still for as long as I could, savoring that first moment of absolute peace. I moved slowly for as long as I could, resisting the urge to go fast. Go circular, be gentle. Get her there and she's yours for life. My hands found their way down to her buttocks, which I held on to desperately. They were round and full. She was such a strong girl. I wanted to hold her breasts, too, but feared that if I let go of the buttocks for even a moment they might change shape or vanish into the night.

She murmured things that drove me to the brink. But I needed time to get her to the brink, so I stopped moving, hoping to lower my excitement and start again from zero. "Why'd you stop? It was nice," she said. I started moving again and realized immediately that I wouldn't last long. I found her mouth in the darkness and kissed it. I wanted it to be total and full-blown. I needed to look into her eyes, into her face. I needed to see her. I moved my hand down off the bed to find the lamp that I had stubbed my toe on. My fingers touched the base of it. She was starting to murmur things again that sounded beautiful. I wanted to see the look on her face more than anything in the world. I wanted to see those lips smiling or contorting or doing whatever they were doing. I groped for the switch, found it and turned it. Nothing. No light. Still rocking in her, I moved my hand up to tighten the bulb. My finger groped into an empty socket. An amazing jolt hit me in the darkness, bolted up my arm into my entire body, my brain, everything; she shuddered beneath me and screamed up into my face, dug her nails into my buttocks, and pulled me in harder. It was a scream of surprise that had flown from her lips, but also of joy. I buried my wounded hand back into her rump and speeded up.

"What'd you do?" she cried.

"What?"

"How did you do that? What did you do?" she gasped.

My arm vibrated from the shock. I knew I was in her house making love to her, but my body flashed on war. The body forgets nothing. Adrenaline coursed through my veins and jacked up my pulse. She dug her nails in my flank. "Oh my God. It's happening. I can't believe it," she murmured.

Then it started happening for me, too. Afterward, she wrapped her arms around me tight and said, "Don't leave. Don't ever leave."

It was too dark to read each other's eyes, but she cupped my face in her hands as if to lock my eyes into her gaze, as though that would force me to be solemn and truthful: "How did you do that?" she asked, "I felt a spark. It was like a spark that set everything else off. Then the fire just spread and spread."

"Old spider magic," I said. "Old as the stars. Iktomi asked the stars for help."

She laughed. I had already told her how I was nicknamed Iktomi as a kid because I was always pulling pranks on people. Iktomi is this mythological guy as old as the stars, as old as Time itself, but he's youthful in appearance and horny as an eighteen-year-old. He gets his magic from the spiders, they say, so he's also called the spiderman. He likes tricking virgins into sex. "No, really. How'd you do it?"

I shrugged. "It's chemistry, Frannie. You either got it or you don't. I guess we got it."

"I was beginning to wonder," she said.

"I know."

She put her face against the side of my neck and held me tight. I felt her body quiver, as if she were starting to cry. "What's wrong?" I said.

"Nothing. That's just it. For years I thought something was. Either in my head or with my body. It's never happened before."

"Not even . . ."

She shook her head. "And it makes ya feel so damn incomplete. I grew determined, you know. I mean, I was going about it with a vengeance. In Africa . . . Jeez, you wouldn't believe the things I did in Africa."

"Like what?" I asked, suddenly terrified.

"It's okay. I've been tested. But you're right, of course. It was stupid. Reckless as hell. That's how unhappy I was. Lost all judgment and control for a while."

I moved the scope off the dark window of the guest room and back down to the lighted ones of the first floor, counting off five seconds per window, then moving to the next, then finally to the kitchen door. After five Mississippis on the door, I started to swing left to the windows again, but a flicker of motion, a shift of light and shadow coming through the windowpanes of the door, made me stop. The door swung open and a figure stood in the jamb, backlighted by the lights in the kitchen. Like an idiot, I tried to read the face, which of course was in silhouette. Only then did I think to check for the peg leg, which would have been recognizable in or out of silhouette, but a fraction of a second before I moved the scope downward, the figure descended the two steps below the door and slipped into the darkness of the prairies.

Frannie didn't smoke and the colonel only chewed. I took the safety off, and waited for the light of a match, the glow of the stogie.

The problem was I didn't have him in my scope now and I didn't know how to get him back in. He could have gone anywhere within probably two hundred square feet of the house. The scope was too tight for a general search. And from that distance, my unaided eye would probably not pick up the tiny glow of a cigar, or even the flicker of a match, especially if the hands were cupped over it.

The only sure shot was to line up the kitchen door again and wait for his frame to fill it on the way in. That way, he could have his last smoke, and I could have a clear target. It would mean shooting him in the back, which is ugly, but then any sniper shot is a kind of back shot. And Pogo didn't deserve a lot of pomp and circumstance.

I kept trying to block two things from my mind. One was my mother.

She had always opposed vengeance and would clearly have been against this. The other was the fact that this body-burning son of a bitch was Frannie's brother. I had tried to separate the two in my mind, tried all sorts of things, but in the end, there was no getting around the fact that I was about to hurt Frannie terribly. I had figured that a guy like Pogo is going to get killed sooner or later, either riding bulls and broncos or in a bar fight. So I had convinced myself I wouldn't be causing her any more pain than what was already coming down the road. But as I lay on the knoll, aiming at the cozy light of the doorway, I sensed it would be Frannie who would first come running into the kitchen, slipping on the blood-slicked linoleum, to find him dead or gasping in his own puddles. And I wondered if it would do to her what similar sights had done to me. I told myself no. She's strong, stronger than me. I kept the scope on the door and waited for his body to eclipse the light.

What you doing in the grass? whispered a woman's voice. I didn't bother looking up or taking my eye off the scope, but I broke a second wave of sweat under my arms and felt a chill. It was the opera lady, the diva. *Are we hugging the planet again, or humping gopher holes? Don't hump Grandmother all by your lonesome. Come with me.* Yes, *precious, a mind* is *a terrible thing to waste."* She busted out laughing in her hideous way. It was so shrill and loud I thought it would split my head.

I wanted to cover my ears, but that would have meant letting go the rifle and the goal. And of course it would have made no difference. Focus on the door and stay calm, I told myself. Stay in control. Stay IN control. Check the safety, make sure it's off, OFF. Keep focused on the door. Forget her. Forget them both.

Sucky sucky, Joe? Fi' dolla, I suck you good, Joe. I clean. Clean as home fucky, Joe, she said, mimicking girls from long ago and far away.

Just keep your eye on the door. The door.

Right on witya right-ons, bro, she said, switching to mo-town. Then she sang, *Keep yo eyyyyyyyyyyyes on the priiiiiiize. Oh, Little Buffalo Chip, you as dumb as a nigguh but half as built.*

Then it happened. Pogo walked into the light that spilled through the panes of the upper door. He stepped up the two steps and filled the frame for a moment. I tilted down to see his legs, but light only came through the top half of the door, where there were glass panes. As he pushed the door open, though, his entire body appeared in bold silhouette. The slender shaft below the knee was finally out in the open. And the feeling was like when you turn over a big rock and find a snake glistening there. Instantly, I regained the center of his back and started to squeeze.

But I wanted him to see it coming. Lifting my head off the rifle and easing off on the trigger, I yelled his name. I hunkered back down and got him in the crosshairs by the time my voice reached him. He paused in the doorway, then turned slowly, unalarmed, as if wondering if he had heard something or if he was just imagining it. Deciding it was nothing, he began to turn into the kitchen again.

I got off my belly to get more wind in my lungs and yelled, "*Semper fi!*" He turned back around, still slow and unalarmed, as if he didn't have an enemy in the world or a thing on his conscience. He faced square into the scope, scratching his chin. It felt good to be the voice and not the one who's hearing it. "Good niiiiight, stoooooopid," I yelled in a high falsetto. I got back down on the scope and saw him cock his head slightly. "Yeah you, Noodle Boy," I yelled even louder. Noodle Boy had been his nickname in childhood, before Frannie was even born. She had mentioned once, many months before, how he had hated it and beat a kid up over it. Anyway, he probably couldn't make out any words from that distance, probably just caught a trace of the sound. Maybe he thought it was an owl or some other bird, or maybe a drunken hand running through the cow shit. I had the crosshairs right on his chest. My finger was sweaty, but I began to squeeze. I thought about the heart I was about to rip into, and the lungs and organs. The organs are what finally broke me. If I could have killed just his brain—that is, turned him into a vegetable without hurting the rest—I would have done it. He deserved slow torture for what he did, but a day might come when Frannie would need a kidney or liver, or some bone marrow or something only he could give her.

I swiveled to the left and started blowing away their vehicles, which were at the other end of the ranch house under a big floodlight. I used the scope to blow out at least one tire on each truck. I was careful not to hit Frannie's car, though, because I had a motel date with her the next night in Murdo and didn't want to get stood up. Then I put a few bullets through the engine blocks of the pickups, at least through the grids and hoods. And I took out a couple of windshields just for the tinkle of it. It took all of five or six seconds. I scanned the house. Pogo was crouched by the kitchen door, looking in different directions for Charlie in the night. Somebody was at an upstairs window and somebody at a downstairs window. A few hands ran out of the bunkhouse.

I picked up my cartridges and stuffed them in my pocket, then wriggled backwards down the knoll. I ran as I have only run a few times in

my life, feeling the full weight of the rifle in my arms, and the full weight
of what I had done—destroyed Property, white Property. This was
worse than burning down a House of God. I had defecated on the altar,
the very heart of the faith. Would they dare give chase in a night so dark?
I wondered. Would they dare give chase without their engines, lights,
and technology? I resolved to shoot the horses out from under them if
they pursued me. But in the end there was no need for such a slaughter.
The night indeed belonged to Charlie. I got in my car and drove back
to the rez.

She had just finished telling me how some bastard had shot up their trucks the night before and how her dad figured it was Indians but Pogo thought different. He thought it was somebody from Kadoka, from childhood, because he heard them calling out his childhood nickname. She'd either forgotten she'd told it to me so many months ago or else she just couldn't conceive of my doing something like that.

We were in a motel room in the town of Murdo, which is an hour east of Kadoka on the interstate. Murdo's not much more than a pit stop for the truckers going cross-country. It's got a couple diners in which they can eat steaks and pop pills, and there are some little motels for your tourist families who are too bushed to make Rapid or Sioux Falls.

We could hear the rush of trucks on the interstate as we kissed. "I'll be right back," she said, getting up and heading for the bathroom. She shut the door behind her.

I walked around to the far side of the bed and took the lamp off the night table. I removed the shade and shoved it under the bed, then I began unscrewing the bulb.

"How you makin' out in there?" I called, mostly so she wouldn't hear the bulb unscrewing.

"Okay," she said through the door.

I opened the drawer of the night table, put the bulb on top of the Gideon's Bible, and shut it. I placed the lamp on the floor between the bed and the night table, where it was in reach but out of sight.

Frannie came out of the bathroom and slipped under the sheet with me. Her mouth was exciting to kiss.

I hated putting my finger in the socket. Doing it accidentally is one thing, but deliberately is the worst. It's the anticipation that kills you. But I tried not to think about it. When I sensed she was getting near, I slipped an arm down over the side of the bed.

She screamed into my mouth and I groaned into hers. The shock to my arm was sharp and burning—a trauma—while what reached her center was much weaker, a flash of warmth, a spark and then tingling, a bit of static bliss, perhaps a gentle jolt to the G-spot. Not pain at all, but enough zap to break the cycle of self-consciousness and let slip the contractions that had eluded her for so long.

We lay about in bed for a while. Just when my arm stopped humming, Frannie wanted to have another go. I was surprised at how soon she was breathing hard. She was getting easier and easier to turn on. *You have such a good grounding in love,* whispered the diva. I wondered if I could bring it off now without the lamp. Maybe she was close enough that if I shuddered or did something spastic and sudden, it might feel the same to her.

The diva sang out in that taunting tune that kids use to hurt each other, *Iktomi's getting o-old. Couldn't kill the bro-ther. Can't please the sis-ter.* Then in a deep voice that sounded like a huge engine revving up, shaking everything, an engine that could split the earth: *So, pluck that chicken, stick that pig! Get your K-bar, skin her wig.*

Frannie was on the brink, right on the edge, and I hadn't used the lamp. I buried my face in her hair, kissing her ear, trying to block the diva out.

"*No* cojones!" the diva thundered accusingly, condemning me. *You're losing all your power. Barely killed the cow! Choked completely on the brother. And now you need GE . . .* She shifted way up into the high registers of the falsetto. *To bring good things to liiiiife.* Kettledrums thundered, cymbals crashed, then came an explosion so loud I thought a truck had jackknifed on the interstate and slammed into the motel.

Kill her. You need her power. Feed. Rip her throat out.

Suddenly, Frannie looked horrified and stopped moving. She just lay there, pale as the sheets.

I stopped. She didn't say a thing. Didn't move. "What's wrong, Frannie? Tell me what's wrong," I said, kissing her forehead. I could hear the diva laughing. Frannie was like stone, a statue.

Then, with great suddenness, she rolled over, turned her back to me. "What's wrong?" I asked again. After another thirty seconds of silence, she said, "What the hell do you *mean,* what's wrong? What's *wrong?* You tell *me* what's wrong. When the hell'd you turn so mean?"

"What do you mean?" I said.

"Mean and hurtful, you son of a bitch."

"How? What'd I do?"

"Oh, it ain't hurtful, I guess, if when I whisper loving things, you scream, 'Shut up, shut up, cunt. Shut up, fat lady.' No, that ain't hurtful *much.* I ain't fat, Joey Moves Camp. I've got big bones, is all." Her back was still to me. Her shoulders started to flutter and heave a bit, like she was quietly crying.

I was stunned and scared, my heart racing. I was now one of those who argue with the voices, fight out loud with invisible enemies. The diva had won. It's not over when the fat lady sings. It's over when you sing back. I recalled the promise I had once made to myself that I would end it all if I ever got to the stage where I could no longer hide it.

But what could I say to Frannie? Could I deny it completely, tell her that she was just imagining it all? Then she'd really think I was nuts. Could I tell her I was just joking around, that it was just a lapse in taste?

"Frannie," I stammered, my voice cracking, "I didn't mean a word of it, and I'm sorry. It was stupid. This guy Sylvester told me that his wife loves that kind of talk, says it helps her get there. It was an experiment." I was near tears right about there, but I pushed on. "It was stupid and I'm sorry. I should've known better."

Still with her back to me, she reached her hand around and held it open for mine. I put my hand in hers. "I don't need dirty talk, Joey. I'm not one of those. I never asked you to talk dirty."

"I know you didn't."

She turned to face me. "You're crying," she said, surprised. "Oh, baby, it's okay. It's not the end of the world," she said, squeezing my hand harder. She pulled me to her breast and we lay like that for a little while. Then she said, "Even so, Joey, just to think of those things means you think I'm fat."

"You're not even big-boned. I was just repeating everything this guy Sylvester said. Word for word."

And the fact is, I loved Frannie's body. She was strong and solid and very shapely. The diva, on the other hand, I had always imagined as a fat blonde with lots of jewels and gold around her wide neck.

Frannie drifted off to sleep. I went in the bathroom with the Gideon's Bible and prayed on my knees, committing my soul to Jesus, clutching the book to my breast and mumbling, " 'Though I walk through the valley of the shadow of Death, I fear no Evil, I *hear* no Evil, for thou art with me, O Lord . . .' " and on and on like that I mumbled. I said the prayer louder, faster. She broke into song, a lovely choir voice that I thought would lift the roof right off the motel and let the heavens in: *Jesus is my copilot, but Satan's in the tower. Sugar Daddies, Sugar Daddies, ooh-rah-raw.*

I dashed off a note and left it near Frannie on the bed. It said I had to go.

I took Eli's rifle into my room, lay on the bed, stuck the barrel in my mouth, and waited for her to sing. She didn't. My right arm, straining to reach the trigger, started to cramp. After a while, I kicked off my boots and put my toe against the trigger. I waited for her to say something snide, like *"Can't even die with your boots on,"* but she didn't.

I see now how pathetic I looked—sucking on a barrel and using my toe like a monkey—but I was too miserable to think about appearances or about what a mess would be left for someone to deal with. All I cared about was blowing the diva to kingdom come. I must have sat like that for hours, with my eyes closed, switching between my toe and my finger.

Then Buddy Levine's photographs popped into my mind, and I bolted up in bed. I hadn't looked at them in years, but they suddenly seemed like the most important thing in the world. I wasn't stalling or losing my resolve. Just the opposite. I felt I had to look at them again before checking out. I didn't know what was on the other side, and I thought maybe I could take some of those images with me. And if I couldn't, at least they would be the last thing I looked at.

I went to the closet, pulled a few boxes out, and there it was, a big album bound in red leather. He had given it to me the day I graduated from Crazy Horse High. I blew the dust off and took it back to the bed. Inside the front cover was a note:

6/10/71

For Joey Moves Camp, a tough runner, swift student, and good friend. Keep your head low. No more volunteering.

Buddy Levine

I opened the album and went through it slowly. There was a close-up of my mom, taken from a foot or two away. She was smiling softly, her lips parted just enough that you could see the one tooth overlapping the other. There was a mix of strength and tenderness in her face.

On the next page was a picture of me coming down the homestretch in the state cross-country championships, my hair long and flying back, my face drawn with exhaustion. I looked so earnest and innocent. I had never run or worked so hard in my life, and I did it for this guy Buddy Levine.

I met Buddy the day he showed up on the reservation. I knocked on the door of the little house they'd assigned him next door to the Crazy Horse School, one of the houses reserved for teachers. The door opened and this lean, wiry guy with dark hair and dark eyes leaned against the jamb, smiling. He had a cleft chin, a straight nose, and a broad smile. I handed him a loaf of bread that my mom had made for him and a bag of chokecherries, and I told him he was invited to dinner. He invited me in, and told me he would be teaching history. I watched him unpack as we talked. He had cameras and beautiful lenses, which he let me pick up. It was June and school didn't start till September. He said he had come early to build a cross-country team.

He and Clem were the same age and they became close. Clem took him hunting and took him into the Badlands. Buddy and my mother also became good friends. She liked the way he came to Pine Ridge with an open mind and with respect for the old ways. He really wanted to learn, and even paid her for Lakota lessons. During that year, he became like a family member. And he would always take pictures. The only times you would see him without his camera were in history class or during cross-country practice. He did every workout he assigned us, never asking us to do anything he didn't do himself. The guy had twelve years on us but could outrun every kid on the team.

The construction of Crazy Horse School had just been completed the

year before, so most of us had fled the Mission school with a sense of joy
and deliverance. Finally, we had a place where we could speak Lakota
without getting whipped, where we could learn math and English without it always being tied to heaven and hell. There was no more shame.

We had Indian teachers and white ones, but no more priests and no
more switches. Buddy was a history teacher, and he could really make it
come off the page. He could tell you about battles in such a way that if
you closed your eyes, you were there, you were in them. And he did im-
itations. He did Churchill, the speech about how We will fight them on
the beaches, in the skies, and in the fields. We will defend our island, we
will *never* surrender. It sent shivers down your spine to hear that stuff. I
even dreamt one night that I was one of those young pilots in the RAF
shooting down Nazi bombers over my home.

He told us about the gas crystals and how German companies competed for the contract to supply the poison. My uncle had been in Pat-
ton's army and helped liberate one of those camps and he said that what
Buddy had told us was true, and that it made you feel good about being
in the U.S. Army. The U.S. Army sometimes did very good things.

All facts and no spin was Buddy's approach. He didn't try to win you
over to any point of view, or to any set of beliefs. He didn't preach. History was a collection of facts that you needed to know to get on in the
world. But he didn't interpret them for us. He wanted us to reason things
out for ourselves, form our own opinions and outlooks. We didn't know
if he was a Democrat or a Republican or what. He never urged one position over another. And it was for this approach to history that we took
to him.

I wanted to please Buddy. And so I worked hard in history and ran
hard in practice, broke my hump for him in races. We all did.

Midway through senior year, it dawned on me that the whole point of
studying history was so you could get off the sidelines and into the game,
get involved. I wasn't going to piss away my life in tarpaper outhouses
with fall-down drunks while history was happening just over the horizon.
So, I hitched into Rapid and went to the Army Recruitment Office.

It was winter and Buddy and I were snowshoeing by Wolf Table when
I told him that I had signed up. He had sent away for snowshoes—several pairs, out of his own pocket—so that the team could stay in shape
over winter and be ready for track season. But that day it was just Buddy
and me, and we were out on this ridge and the wind was carrying us
along, whipping at our backs. You didn't want to stop for fear of freez-

ing. But Buddy stopped right in his tracks when I told him. "Are you sure you signed? It wasn't some preliminary form, or a statement of intent?" he asked.

I stopped and shoed back to where he was standing. His eyes were excited, waiting for my answer. And there was this *tell-me-it-ain't-so* look creeping into his face.

"No, I went whole hog," I said.

"Why didn't you come to me first?" He seemed angry.

I shrugged. "Wanted to surprise you."

He sat down in the snow, on his haunches, like I'd knocked him on his ass. "It's not World War II, Joey."

"I know. It's choppers and jungle," I said.

"I mean it's confusing over there. It's not black and white."

"You were *ov*er there?" I asked. He nodded. He had never spoken of it, probably—I realize now—because he knew how damn impressionable and hungry for role models we were.

"Marines?" I asked.

"I was in the Navy," he said.

"You a *pi*lot?"

He shook his head. "I rescued pilots."

I realized later when I was over in Vietnam that Buddy had been a SEAL. That meant more than rescuing pilots; it meant deep-penetration ambushes, snatches, assassinations. But back in high school, I'd never even heard of the SEALs.

He scooped some snow and scrubbed his face. Then he looked at me, his cheeks red from the scrubbing: "Which branch did you say again?" he asked.

"Army," I said.

"Maybe you'll just end up in Germany, chasing *Fräuleins*."

"You mean you wouldn't do it again?" I asked.

He shook his head.

"Not even if your country asked you?"

He sort of snapped at me then. "Your country didn't ask you. And it didn't draft you. God knows they've wasted enough Indians in foreign wars, but it doesn't have to happen to you."

"But *you* joined, right?"

"It's different. My family was getting raped and killed back in Russia. I mean that literally, Joey, raped and killed. There's a race of soldiers there called Cossacks and they had open season on us. They were our Seventh

Cavalry, only worse. For us, America was a haven. I owed. But you don't owe squat."

"So you can be the all-American but I can't?"

"That was part of why I went in. I admit it. But it doesn't work that way."

When I saw my recruiter again to find out when exactly I would be shipping out for boot camp, he told me that one of my teachers had been by several times, trying to convince him to rip up my enlistment forms. Even bribed him.

In the remaining months of school, something changed in Buddy's class. No matter what subject we discussed—whether it was Martin Luther King, or the Russian crackdown in Prague, or the future of space exploration—Buddy put a spin on it. He told us what was right and what was wrong. The Soviets were sons of bitches for doing what they did, Martin Luther King was a beautiful man, one of the best, Kennedy was wrong to try to kill Castro, and *man* did he screw up in the Bay of Pigs, and on and on like that. He steered the discussions, dominated them, injected them with his opinion all over the place, turned them into lectures about why we should believe this and not that. They were sermons, and you could tell he hated it.

On the next page of the album was a close-up of Wenonah, age eight. It felt like yesterday that she was here. It felt like yesterday that she gave me the medicine bundle. God, what a smile she had. Her eyes gleamed. She had dark brown eyes that always caught the light—whatever light there was, sunlight, lamplight, starlight—and sent it right back at you, gleaming. She had a wide smile and dimples. And you could see in this photo that her teeth were slightly overlapped like my mom's. Her hair was tucked back behind one ear and I could almost feel it pressed against my cheek, and her arms around my neck, and could almost hear her saying, like she did when I left for Vietnam, Be careful, Uncle Joey. I touched the barrel of the rifle.

On the next page was a wonderful shot of Clem and Linda at the table. He was in profile and seemed to be talking to someone who was not in the picture, and Linda was looking at him as he spoke, and there was such admiration in her gaze, and a hint of humor at the corners of her mouth and in her eyes, as if Clem was telling a funny story. But what struck me, too, was how incredibly young they both looked. Clem was lean and hard. You could see bands of muscle in his neck and shoulder.

And he was tight under the jaw. Linda was radiant. She had a kind of glow. I think she was all of sixteen when she had Wenonah, so she was only twenty-four or so in this shot.

There were shots of Mom, Linda, and Wenonah working on a star quilt together, and Mom teaching Wenonah how to sew on that same quilt. There was a close-up of Mom's hands, strong and creased with years of work, guiding Wenonah's little fingers, which were holding the needle.

A few pages further up, I found the photo I needed. I pulled the barrel up to my face. The picture was from a little outing we took in Wind Cave National Park in the Black Hills. It showed Mom, Clem, me, Linda, and Wenonah all in one shot. It was daytime, but we were roasting marshmallows around a fire and you could see woods in back of us and a ridgeline of the Paha Sapa. Everyone was happy and relaxed. It was like we were in heaven, and we were all together. I looked at each and every face in the photo, and tried to memorize it. And I tried to memorize the ridgeline and the smell of pine trees, and the smell of the fire, and all these things I love. I put the gun in my mouth, closed my eyes, and tried to see the faces in the darkness. Maybe if I saw the faces clearly in my mind's eye at the moment I hit the trigger, maybe I would take these images on through with me to the other side and they would be with me always. And if there was no other side, at least they would be the last thing I saw.

I waited for the diva to say something so that I could let her have it.

Mitakuye iyasin, I said over and over, though it was garbled because of the gun in my mouth. It means *all my relations.* It's like an embrace, but a huge embrace—of everything: brothers, sisters, wolves, birds, badgers, plains and mountains, little rocks, rivers, streams, everything, for everything has a spirit and is related. It's an embrace of our relatedness to everything, the whole balance.

C'mon, you little douche bag. Embrace this. I clamped my eyes shut, tried to see the faces of my family, and the ridgeline of the Paha Sapa behind them, and I groped with my toe for the trigger. But she said nothing more. I was too late, too slow.

I kept the barrel in my mouth and waited for her to chirp up again. My toe was now firmly on the trigger. I felt the weight of the photo album on my stomach. I saw Buddy's face in the darkness, that tell-me-it-ain't-so look in his eyes. "Why didn't you come to me first?" I could hear him say. "Are you sure you signed? It wasn't just a statement of intent?" I wondered if she was mimicking him, because it was like salt in the wound. I mean, things would have been different if I hadn't gone to Vietnam. The shrinks at the VA suspected schizophrenia, though they never said definitively. But what I did learn is that they believe there is a genetic "predisposition" for it, like you're wired for it but it doesn't have to happen. It has to be triggered by severe trauma: exposure to extreme or prolonged violence, loss of loved ones, that kind of thing—which is why there is so much higher a rate among combat vets than in the general population. If you have the wiring, the meat grinder of war will flip the switch. If I had gone to Buddy beforehand—or to Clem or to Mom—they would have talked me out of it, and then this bad wiring in my genes would never have been triggered, and I wouldn't have this goddamn bitch in my head, and wouldn't be sitting here with Elijah's best rifle. "Trigger this, you fucking bitch," I said, or thought, as I started to push with my toe.

"Joey! What are you doing?"

I opened my eyes. Clem. He stood in the doorway in a white undershirt and clean blue jeans. His hair was unbraided and freshly washed. Two bands of gauze around his rib cage showed through the T-shirt, a whiter white, and I saw dabs of pink where blood had mixed with ointment and seeped slightly through the gauze. He looked lean. He also looked stronger after his big sleep.

I shook my head at him, meaning Don't come in, leave me alone. The barrel rattled my teeth, the notch of the front sight scratching the roof of my mouth. My eyes burned and flooded. There were so many things I still loved in this world and he was one of them. He took a step forward but I shook my head again, more frantically. He stopped, then blurred into a column of black, white, and denim. I closed my eyes and got ready for the larger darkness.

He must've flown to my side because I felt his hand in my hair. He started combing my hair with his fingers. My mom used to do that to me when I was a kid, and I guess she must've done it to him, too. He didn't try to grab the gun or wrestle it out of my mouth. He just kept running his fingers through my hair, then stroking my brow a bit like she would have done.

"Nothing could be as bad as all this," he said.

I waited for the diva to mimic him or make fun of him, but she didn't. I kept my eyes closed. I couldn't face him. If I faced him, I wouldn't be able to hit the trigger. As long as I kept my eyes shut, I could sort of pretend I was alone. In solitude, we're capable of certain things. But who can blow his brains out in front of his brother? Who can be that fierce and hurtful? I hadn't asked him in. I couldn't help it that he came in. But with my eyes closed, I could still have the necessary privacy. And I knew he would one day understand all this.

A mix of steel, burnt powder, gun oil, and salt ran down my tongue into my throat. I think the front sight had cut the roof of my mouth and I was tasting blood. I felt like I was going to gag. If I gagged, the barrel would come out of my mouth. Maybe I should do it before gagging. One peep from her would have made it so much easier. Where the hell was she?

"Joey, is this because of what happened out at McLaren's?"

I opened my eyes. He put his hand on my right hand and gently pulled the barrel out. "The sheriffs and feds were out here rousting everybody again. Somebody shot up all McLaren's trucks a couple nights back. With a deer rifle." He paused a while, then said, "Was it you?"

I nodded.

"Where you been?"

"Murdo."

"What for?"

"Frannie McLaren and I go to a motel there."

He smiled and shook his head. "And you shot up all their trucks?"

"Her brother set the fire. Not the Mormon."

He looked terrified. "You didn't do nothing to *her*, did you?"

" 'Course not."

"Then what's all this?" he said, nodding at the rifle. "A few trucks ain't worth your life. Nobody'll catch you, anyway. Even if they could, a little jail time ain't the end of the world."

"I'm hearing these voices, Clem. Or one voice that likes to pretend to be different voices."

Clem perked up like I'd just given him great news. "It's the other side," he said. "It's spirits, something wonderful. They want to lead you somewhere, like I'm being led. It's like a vision, only it's with sound. Maybe you're going to become a holy man."

"They ain't talking Lakota, Clem."

"Still—"

"No!" I barked. He looked puzzled by my resistance to the beautiful. "There's nothing sacred in it," I said. I told him all about the sarcasm and mean-spiritedness of the voices, and I told him about the psych ward and the brain imaging and how you could actually see a difference, how this was real and not spiritual. And how there was no cure.

"But we got Yuwipis, Joey. I've heard of a girl who was haunted in this way and was cured by the Yuwipi. We'll get you to a good Yuwipi man. You'll be fine. You gotta be, 'cause you were in my vision, big part of it. I need you to make it happen. We're gonna take Mount Rushmore and get all our Black Hills back."

His face looked so bright and full of hope—as it hadn't looked in fifteen years. How could I tell him he was a dreamer? "I'm afraid I would be more of a risk than a help," I said.

"No, you wouldn't. Mom's looking out for us. She'll help you beat whatever this is."

"Clem . . ."

"I can prove it."

"Sure you can."

"I can. Look. Did you ever hear of anyone dragging skulls from one place to another before? I mean, no one was ever even asked to. At most, you just dragged them around the mystery circle, around the other dancers tied to the pole. But to go from one town to another, one side of the rez to another, that's *new*. I've never heard of that. Have you?"

I shook my head.

"That's right," he said. "So I asked Bear Dreamer how he came up with such an idea, and he said he didn't know. He said it just popped into his head. Well, Joey, it was Mom who put it in his head. When you were a kid, she walked fifty miles to get you underwear, remember?"

"Yeah."

"After her feet healed up, she told me she was glad we didn't have a car because she learned we have hidden pockets of strength. This is what she wanted me to learn, I think, so that I'd quit being so weak. So she gave Bear Dreamer this crazy idea of making me walk home to Wambli. And if she's looking out for me, well, you *know* she's looking out for you, too. Whatever this voice is, if it's bad, Mom will help you beat it. If she was here, she'd tell you to have a Yuwipi, Joey. She would."

Of course, nothing in what he said amounted to proof, but it felt good to have him at my side. He had a way of chasing off shadows and darkness.

He picked up the album and looked at the shot of us around the fire with our marshmallows. "Would you look at that smile?" he said.

Before I could give No Horse the tobacco offering and explain that I wanted him to do a Yuwipi for me, he called out through his screen door, "Hey, Joey Moves Camp, I was just on my way to fetch you. You and Elijah been chosen for the council." He stepped out into the weeds of his yard. The screen door slapped shut behind him.

"What council?"

"The strategy and tactics council," he said. I must've looked puzzled because he added, "Of the Tokalas."

"Who else is on this council?"

"Just a few of us. Fewer in the know the better. Ain't gonna be like AIM, all riddled with fed informers."

"Well, what the hell was that priest doin' there?"

"Oh, Waokiye? He's okay."

"What'd you call him?"

"Waokiye. One who helps."

"I know what it means. Why'd you give him *that* name?"

"You'll see."

"*He's* on your council?"

"Relax."

"Relax?"

"You'll like him."

"And you're making him *Tokala*?"

"Ain't makin' him nothin'. He *is* Tokala. And he's a council member."

Something that had been bothering me since the *Tokala* meeting, but only as a vague discomfort, now crystallized into words: "No disrespect, John, but where do you guys get off using the name *Tokala*? I mean what makes any of you Kit Foxes?"

"It's our heritage," he said.

"It's *all* of ours," I said. "But that don't mean we're Tokala. Did any of the old Tokalas pick you, find you worthy? You even know their songs or their dances? All you know is they were kick-ass warriors, so you took their name. What if you get your asses kicked? What if you run? Then what's the name *Tokala* worth? Where's our heritage then?"

No Horse folded his arms. I braced for something cutting. But his voice was soft. "Joey, you were named to the council because of your combat experience. I didn't think that was enough. It was Waokiye who pushed for you. I had doubts about you. The same doubts I'll bet you got about yourself, about your Indianness. But what you just said puts away my doubts, because you're right. We *do* risk destroying something of the past. I'm glad you see that. Most of us are not worthy of the name *Lakota,* much less *Tokala.* We're not the same people we once were. But what's the answer? To go to museums and look through glass cases at the war shirts of our ancestors—because we believe we're unworthy of wearing these shirts? Or should we *make* ourselves worthy? And if the clothes make the man, even a little bit—if putting on their war shirt helps give us the strength to become worthy—ain't that better than making no try at all?"

"You might stain the shirt."

"That's the risk. But what we stand to gain is land and dignity. If you treasure the past by locking it in a case, you end up being unfaithful to the very thing you treasure. It never gets dirty, but it never gets used. Don't you think the old Tokalas would like someone to at least *try?*"

I hadn't looked at it that way. He had a point.

He continued: "We see the spirits of the old Kit Foxes differently, you and I. Maybe you see them as proud warriors who would sneer at us for wearing their shirts. But I have met many Kit Foxes when I visited the other side. Before being warriors, they are fathers who love their children and would deny them nothing. Would a Sioux father deny his son a buffalo robe because that child is too frail to fill it out with the same majesty? Of course not. He gives it because it will strengthen the child, help him grow. And if the robe drags in the dust, what of it? You see what I'm saying?"

It might have been a load of bull, but I had to admit it made sense in a poetic way, which probably means it was just a higher-octane bull. I was too tired to argue analogies and poetry, so I cut back to the core issue: "But a *white* guy, John? You can't tell me the old Tokalas—"

"Spirits see spirit, Joey, not skin. Crazy Horse himself was wavy-haired and lighter-skinned. Some thought he had French trapper in him. Does that make him less Tokala?"

"That's bull."

"Well, are you saying you got less of a spirit than me 'cause you're part white? Or maybe you think you don't have white blood now? Back in school, I thought you was all white." He smiled slightly, then continued. "Look, I was skeptical about Quinn, too—and a lot more skeptical than you. But there's something different about Quinn, something special."

"Yeah, Special Agent Bacon."

"Why send a white dude when they could just buy an Indi'n?"

"Because they're counting on just that kind of simple logic," I said.

"He ain't no fed, Joey. He's a Jesuit."

"Oh, well, that's a lot different, isn't it? That changes everything."

"Been excommunicated."

"Having a beef with the Church don't mean we should take in crooked priests."

He laughed.

"I'm serious," I said. "The Church might've had good reason."

"So mighta he."

I wasn't gonna make a believer out of No Horse, so I let it drop. "Here," I said, pulling the tobacco twists from the pocket of my jean jacket. "I've got a sickness and need a Yuwipi. Will you help?"

He brought the tobacco to his nose for a whiff. "You got it," he said, not even looking at me or asking what's wrong. He opened the door to his car and got in. "But it's gotta wait till after we get things movin' with the Foxes. Anyway, you look fine to me," he said.

I remember thinking, *If this is Indian medicine, I ought to ask this Quinn Bacon for the name of a good exorcist.*

Eli and I slipped through the "hole in the wall," between the cliff and the big silt mound, then descended into the mini canyon of the Kit Foxes. No Horse was busy building a fire where the last one had been. Apart from his flashlight and Eli's, the canyon was dark. The night was starless.

Under a sloping wall toward the back were half a dozen crates that hadn't been there the last time. It seemed there were four or five people lounging on some of them. Here and there the orange glow of a cigarette would intensify, then grow dull, then arc through space to rest on a knee. I was curious who they were, but Eli was too polite to shine his light in their faces.

No Horse leaned forward on his hands, his braids hanging forward into the twigs as he blew softly from different angles. The little flames reared up after each jet, threatening to ignite his braids. But always he eased back just enough. Soon his skin glowed orange and there was no more need to blow. He sat back on his heels and said, "Let's get started," motioning for Eli and me to sit down by him and for the others to come over.

Pumpkinhead was the first I recognized, his shoulders giving him away before his face even entered the light. He squeezed in between No

Horse and Elijah, putting his hand on Eli's knee in silent greeting. Eli palmed it with his own, then let it go. The old Lerps were finally back together and waiting on a mission—maybe now one that would matter.

Speckled Hawk sat down on my right, and the fair-haired One Who Helps on his right. Speckled Hawk nodded to me, then stared into the flames. He had a nice ribbon shirt on and a bad-ass Uncle Joe hat, black, with a wide, flat brim—which was standard AIM attire and that cracked me up because he wasn't an AIMer and never had been. And he had short hair on top of it. His nose was sharp and hooked, giving him a beakish look to match his name. And he had liver spots on his hands and even some on his face, as if he was trying to become his name even more. It made me wonder about the notion of having spirit kin in other species, kin who guided us and spoke to us through visions and dreams. Maybe he *did* have hawk medicine, who was I to say no? Or at least maybe his granddad, the real Speckled Hawk, had received wakan from the hawks. Who knows? It surprised me to be taking all this old stuff seriously, to be making such irrational backward leaps. I chalked it up to the eeriness of the canyon, and the timelessness of the fire.

In broad daylight, I would probably be laughing at Speckled Hawk for his spiritual posturing, and at his toady priest for buying into it, trading one superstition for another. And I would laugh at No Horse for calling the group Tokala—as if we could slip back into the past just because the present sucked and the future looked worse. We were playing Indian and it was like guys in prison trying to remember what chicks are like, closing their eyes to re-create them, to feel ecstasy for a few seconds, to feel escape and beauty, to block out the surrounding reality of shanks and sharp spoons. That's all it was, a kind of circle jerk around a campfire. Once that image got in my mind, I couldn't get it out. I felt laughter rising, as unstoppable as vomit and just as bitter. I put my face in my hands and bit my lower lip until I could only feel pain. I realized that this might not be my own laughter at all but the opera lady's. Perhaps she was refining her own strategies and tactics, infiltrating deeper, attempting fusion—the parasite overtaking the host, the lodger now running the house.

I stared into the fire, hoping it would clean my mind. Chase the witch out with fire. "Your lip is bleeding," Elijah said. I licked it and tried to look surprised, puzzled.

Beyond Speckled Hawk's beak glimmered the blondish-white crown of Quinn Bacon, our excommunicated Jesuit, our blond lamb who helps.

His head was bowed, so I couldn't see much of his face. I wondered if he was acting humble or just avoiding eye contact.

To the right of him, old Isaac Sky Elk began lowering his huge frame. First he bent over forward, reaching both hands down to support his left knee, while lowering his right knee to the stone floor. Once he got his butt on the ground, he pulled his ankles in, one at a time, with both hands. I wondered if his old Korea wounds were stiffening up. He tilted back his hat, letting the firelight bathe his leathery face and forehead. He winked at me across the flames. So Isaac was on the council and had never even breathed a word of it, not even to me and Eli.

To his right was Abel Many Coups, a kid in his mid-twenties, just out of the Rangers. He had been decorated in Grenada and Panama, and I guess he figured that saving America's ass from foreign aggression twice was enough. His hair was getting long and he was obviously going for braid length. He was wearing an old football jersey from Crazy Horse.

With catlike ease and silence, Sharon Takes Gun entered the circle. I wondered if that meant there would be food. She sat by Abel. Sharon was twenty-six, about the best-looking Indian girl I knew. She smiled slightly and looked down at her sneakers. I didn't see any food, and couldn't smell any either. Maybe she was Abel's old lady, or one of No Horse's groupies. Hell, maybe the priest was doing her. Maybe that's the kind of stuff he got tossed out for. I looked back over at him but he was still looking down at his crossed ankles.

"Some warrior society. All we need now is blacks and *winktes,*" whispered Eli. "Have us a regular rainbow coalition."

"We'll get around to the introductions later," said No Horse. "First, let's lock the circle." We all swore on our ancestors and loved ones, and on sacred medicine bundles, that we would not divulge to anyone the identities of fellow council members, or any of the society's objectives until they were achieved. I wondered what the hell those objectives were, other than crawling around the Bad Lands and acting mystical. Each person framed his pledge with the things and people that he held sacred. To my surprise, Quinn pledged his oath in perfect Lakota. I wondered if Speckled Hawk had written it out phonetically for him to memorize. We sealed the oath with smoke from both No Horse's pipe and Speckled Hawk's pipe.

Speckled Hawk nodded to Abel Many Coups. Abel and Sharon left the circle and disappeared into the shadows.

It was funny to see old Speckled Hawk with his short white hair and

John No Horse with his dark braids presiding jointly over this meeting, because there had been bad blood between them over the years and they bad-mouthed the hell out of each other. *Ah, he's a charlatan, he's full of shit. He ain't nothing but a trickster. He's a sellout.* But now they were acting just hunky. I wondered how long they could keep it together. I also wondered how right it was to have medicine men in a war society.

Abel and Sharon returned carrying a wooden crate between them. They laid it down inside the circle but not too close to the fire. Old Speckled Hawk opened it and pulled out, to my amazement, a LAW. I looked over at Eli. His eyes were popping. Speckled Hawk handed it to Abel Many Coups. Abel popped it open, telescoped it out, and checked the sight. It was clear he had trained with this weapon in the Rangers. Speckled Hawk pulled out another and passed it to Pumpkinhead Pawnee-Killer.

"These are light armor-piercing weapons," Abel said. "They'll stop APCs and half-tracks and even some tanks."

"It is Waokiye we have to thank for these," said Speckled Hawk, extending his arm in Bacon's direction.

All eyes turned from the weapons to the provider. Bacon looked down quickly, too modest or humble to meet anyone's gaze. Then I realized he was trying to out-Lakota us Lakotas. In the old way, you showed your respect for someone by not daring to look them in the eye. You looked away, looked down. Kind of a pecking-order thing.

I wondered how he got his hands on armor-piercing weapons. He was probably a fed and we were in the middle of a trap. The weapons might be bait to draw out wanted AIMers like Pumpkinhead, lure them back from Canada and wherever else they were hiding. Bacon probably had a list of guys he had to round up before calling in the dragnet, so I guessed we were safe for the moment. Part of me, though, found it hard to believe that this odd bird with his split lip and sun-dance scars could be a fed.

But I couldn't believe the government would risk letting weapons like this fall into the wrong hands, unless, of course, they were dummies. "Has anybody tested these out?" I asked.

"Yeah," said Abel, returning his LAW to the crate.

So right there I started wondering if Abel had been recruited out of the Rangers and was part of the scam. They can brainwash you pretty easy in those crack units. They get you so gung-ho to fetch the carrot you don't care what the carrot is after a while, just so long as you get another letter for your sweater. "I think we should test another," I said.

No Horse looked at me like I was crazy. "They're one-shot deals. You fire 'em and throw 'em away. We already tested two. We're not wasting any more."

"Hey, you didn't test them on the road, did you, on 73, the night Clem tangled with McLaren's people? Anyone shoot a blank or something at McLaren's truck?"

"You think we'd risk all this on pranks?" said No Horse.

Speckled Hawk cleared his throat: "I don't know *what* that bullshit on the road was, but with enough booze people see what they want to see. Wasitchus see rockets. Broken Indians see the *other side*. Them spirit lights Clem says he saw was more likely another muscatel mirage."

"He doesn't drink anymore," someone said in a firm voice. To my astonishment, it was Quinn Bacon.

I leaned forward and peered around Speckled Hawk's beak. "Who doesn't?" I asked.

"Your brother," he said, looking me straight in the eye. He looked about forty-five to fifty, but tight as a drum. His face was lean, his cheeks sunken and cleanly shaved. The mouth had a lot of shape, like a woman's, but also bore the scar that crossed both lips. Most striking, though, was the fierceness of his unblinking gray eyes.

"You've met Clem?" I asked.

"No," he said in a tone of slight defeat. "Not yet." He looked back down at his ankles, perhaps to signify that our exchange was over, or perhaps attempting to regain his humility after speaking out of turn.

I was ready to make a snide comment about him being quite an expert on a man he never met. It would be fun to get Eli and Pumpkinhead chuckling at him, test his cool. It would also draw attention to the way he insinuated himself into our lives and pretended to knowledge of us. But I liked the way he had come to Clem's defense, so I held my tongue.

"Waokiye wanted very much for Clement to be Tokala," explained old Speckled Hawk to me. "Even wanted him on the council. But No Horse and I could not agree to this. Clement's drinking is too excessive, too great a risk."

"Yeah, I guess none of us here drinks," I said. "And I guess it was booze that fueled Clem for sixty miles of dragging buffalo skulls."

It was common knowledge that certain medicine men get hammered now and then. Only a few holy men, like Bear Dreamer Bordeaux, have never touched the stuff. So the real picture was beginning to dawn on me. Speckled Hawk and No Horse felt threatened by Clem's stunt. He had gone from being a pathetic drunk to being the talk of the rez, a larger-than-life figure who had received phenomenal wakan. Some were even saying that he was marked to be a holy man. Whatever deal No Horse and Speckled Hawk had worked out with each other concerning leadership of the Tokalas, they were not about to share that leadership with a third force.

"Let's discuss the objectives," said No Horse in a getting-down-to-business tone. He unsnapped one of his breast pockets and pulled out a map, which he unfolded and laid in the light of the fire. "What I want to learn from you military guys is how best we can use these weapons to take back the twenty thousand acres Wilson signed away in '76. And for that matter, we could also take back the Gunnery Range."

Gunnery Range comprised 382,000 acres of our reservation. It's a rectangle, forty-three miles by twelve. During World War II, the War Department "borrowed" it for bombing practice, and promised to give it back right after the war. In 1963 they finally returned a portion of it, less than a third of what they took. The other 250,000 acres remain in their hands. They won't give it back because infrared photos from NASA satellites revealed that the range, along with other sections of the rez, is all laced with uranium, which is also why they keep trying to force us to sell more land. That's what they were doing in the seventies through Dickie Wilson. It's what the GOON–AIM war was about. It's what the shooting of those two FBIs in '75 was about.

No Horse looked up at us and said, "Now I figure we can chase their miners and geologists out of there easy enough. But holding that turf once the government sends in the Army is another matter."

Pumpkinhead Pawnee-Killer nodded. "Don't get me wrong, this is an amazing gift," he said, sweeping his meaty hand out toward the crates and looking at Bacon. Then he turned his gaze to No Horse. "But even so, we haven't got enough men or weapons to hold down twenty thousand acres, much less the two hundred fifty thousand of Gunnery Range. I mean, hell, it's their bombing range. They're used to hitting it. Out on them plains we got no cover. It'd be over quick as a desert war."

"Quicker if they use Apaches," said Abel. "They wouldn't even need ground troops." He was referring to the Apache helicopter, a flying arsenal with every kind of ordnance and computer targeting you can imagine.

"Yeah, with or without Apaches they'll control the air," I said. "And that's the ball game."

"Didn't you control the air in Vietnam?" said No Horse. I couldn't tell if he was being snide.

"We're talking about prairie here, not jungle," I said.

Pumpkinhead cracked his knuckles, then spoke: "See, the real problem—with or without an air threat—is that to hold down twenty thousand acres, even with fifty times the men we got, we would be too spread out for the press to cover it all, which means the Army could hammer us with whatever weapons they liked and never have to worry about public opinion."

He reached over and pulled No Horse's map closer to him, chewing his lower lip with his jagged jack-o'-lantern teeth. After studying it for a minute, he shook his head slightly and said, "We got to take something we can hold, and something the press can cover. See, we're not gonna *beat* the U.S. Army. The best we can hope for is to create a stalemate situation. If we can do that, we get our story out there on the news for as long as the stalemate lasts. Once people learn the real history, they can write their congressmen, but that's our only hope. So we've got to take a small piece of terrain, dig in deep, and hold it for as long as possible. Hell, in '73 we held out for three months at the Knee. Personally, I think we should take it again. It's got mystique now. People's ears will prick up when they hear 'Wounded Knee.' They won't change the channel. It'll be Wounded Knee Three, which'll make 'em want to know about Wounded Knee Two, and some will want to know about the original Wounded Knee, the massacre and the whole shebang. And hell, it's the centennial of the massacre this year. Ah, man, this is fate. We'll make the cameras show the mass grave and copies of the Laramie Treaty and all the other broken treaties that have been denied the light of day. The longer we stalemate the government, the more we can show the people what was hidden from them in school. They'll call their congressmen and give us back at least some of what's ours. I mean, it'll be too embarrassing for them not to."

Quinn raised a hand slightly, like he was in school, then he looked across the fire at Pumpkinhead and spoke softly: "I agree the key is to take something we can hold. I wonder, though, if there isn't a better piece of real estate. Something more striking and dramatic. The Knee is a powerful symbol to the Sioux and to people who already know the history, but visually it's just a windswept hill with a shack, a store, and a church. Not even a one-horse town. A stalemate there would be like watching paint dry. There must be something more dramatic to take, something that will capture the country's attention more. And maybe something that's even more tenable."

"The Knee ain't much to look at, you're right, but then nothing on the reservation is," said Abel.

Pumpkinhead was probably nostalgic for '73 and wanted to relive his hour of glory. I mean, compared to ice fishing in the Arctic, holding the Knee had to be fun. But our Jesuit, too diplomatic to say so, was hinting at what we all knew; the country got bored in '73 and soon abandoned us for Watergate.

Bacon turned to me: "What about you, Joey Moves Camp? Can you think of something better than Wounded Knee?" It was spooky. All of a sudden I knew that somehow he knew about Clem's vision. I didn't know how he knew, but he knew. And it scared me, as if he was about to steal something precious from my brother.

Rushmore, of course, would be the perfect target. It was in the Black Hills and the Black Hills are ours, legally, morally, and by treaty—a treaty that was ratified by Congress, passed into solemn law. But of course they broke that law, or "abrogated" it, as soon as they found gold in them thar hills.

If we were to take Rushmore, our story would be front-page news the world over. That kind of world scrutiny might be enough to force the government to finally respect its own Constitution, its own laws, the treaty it had begged us for, and the "sacred honor" it had pledged toward upholding that treaty.

But I didn't know what Clem was going to do with his vision, or rather what his vision was directing him to do. I only knew Rushmore was his, and I wasn't about to let the likes of Speckled Hawk, No Horse, and a failed priest steal something so big from my brother.

Quinn Bacon was still looking at me, waiting for an answer.

"Well, yeah," I said. "Taking Wall Drug might ruffle their feathers."

He smiled and nodded very slightly, as if to say, *Fair enough. You check it out with your brother first.*

It was eerie.

◆

The next morning, I saw Sharon Takes Gun on the road between Kyle and Wambli. I saw her from afar, but there was no mistaking that slender build. Without turning around, she put her thumb out. I coasted, then stopped. She opened the door and got in. "How you doin'?" I asked. She nodded and said something under her breath, hey or hi. I pulled back onto the asphalt. After a minute or so, she finally asked how far I was going.

"Just home," I told her.

"How about a ride to Kadoka?" She flashed a half smile with a hint of cheek dimples, her lips parting just enough to expose bright teeth. She didn't smoke or drink coffee, that was clear. Her smile must have always got her what she wanted, and she seemed all too sure of its power. I wanted to take her down a notch: "I don't know," I said. "That's a lot of gas, a lot of time. Fifty miles."

"Yeah, might make you late for work, huh?"

"Well, don't you have a nice way of asking."

"I asked nice. You said no."

That may sound pushy, but she was right. Generosity had been a reflex once. If you didn't get lucky in the hunt, your family still ate. Others looked out for you. It was as natural as breathing. Without such reflexes, we would have perished long before the saviors arrived to teach us about property and charity.

"What is it you need in Kadoka so bad?" I asked, wondering if she had a white boy there, or a sugar daddy.

"My folks need groceries. And we're not exactly Latter-days."

The Takes Gun family had no car, no telephone, and no running water. A number of families are still without these things, especially traditionals who live way out. They have to trek many miles to fill up canisters and buy food. So the Mormon missionaries bought a fleet of vans to shuttle folks around in. It was a great idea that could have won them deep affection. But they made the same old missionary demand: *You've got to join the Church. If you don't join, you don't ride.* Keeping body and soul together is tricky on the rez. To maintain your body, you give away chunks of your soul. That's just the way of it. I figure that's why the sun dance is coming back so strong. It's the reverse. You offer your body to maintain your soul. Even spectators will give a little chunk from the back of their arms. Anyway, the point is that while some folks say, *Yay, brother,* and go along for the Mormons' ride, others just can't stomach it. They'd rather walk. And that was Sharon.

I passed the turnoff for my house and headed for 73. Sharon murmured, "Thanks," then turned on the radio, kicked off her sneakers, and settled in. Her cutoff jeans seemed to shrink slightly, or at least hike up, as she raised her knees and put her feet against the glove compartment.

She had perfect arches. And her thighs seemed to glow with health. Just the reddish-brown glow of life, of youth in summer.

"What cracks me up about Mormons," I said, "is they look so good on TV. They've got the best ads? I bet in five years the pope uses the same ad company."

"I wouldn't know," she said with a shrug, meaning they had no TV.

"Well, some of those ads just melt you, like the one of these little girls sharing a cupcake. You got to see it. I'd join that church in a second if—"

"Yeah, I bet they're great off rez," she said in a tired way. She rolled her window down and leaned a bit into the wind so it would blow her hair back. Then she said, "They just act the way they do with us because they think we're children. And they're right. We ought to grow up and sell Wakan Tanka on TV like so many cans of Pepsi."

"Coke," I corrected.

"Whatever."

"I mean they own Coke now."

"The Mormons?"

"Their church does, yeah."

"Can't keep a good faith down, I guess," she said, then turned to look out her window.

"What really cracks me up," I said, "is they always tell me I'm Jewish. They say we descended from some dark-skinned Jew, a bad seed named Manessah. Not just us, either. All the tribes in America. One day this anthro overheard them giving us that line and he laughed, said it was a load of horse dung, then started giving them all kinds of proof, like how there's no relationship between Hebrew and Lakota or any of the other four hundred–plus Indian tongues. And he started talking about DNA and stuff, degrees of relatedness, and that's when the Mormon kids started saying science is a trick of the Devil."

"Well, you can't say it's done the world any good," Sharon said.

"I guess I don't see it quite that black and white. Look at modern medicine."

She didn't respond, and I found the silence judgmental. *Enough of this small talk,* I thought, *let's get down to business.* "Hey, Sharon, I know why No Horse and Speckled Hawk asked me in. Why'd they ask you?"

"You mean the council?"

"Yeah."

"Bothers you, doesn't it, having a woman there?"

"Oh, I wouldn't say that. Everybody's got something to offer. I'm just asking what it is you're bringing—in the way of expertise, I mean."

"Beats me."

"Are you with that ex-priest?"

"Am I *with* him?"

"Yeah."

"I'm not against him."

"I mean, are you his?"

She looked at me sharply. "Only person I belong to is me."

"Well, what's your part in the show, then?"

She shrugged. "What's anybody's part? No Horse asked me in. I guess he had his reasons. What makes *you* so above it all?"

"My gut. Keeps telling me *Beware of geeks bearing gifts.*"

"You mean those weapons? The priest?"

"Yup."

She smiled and shook her head. "No, we're gonna get our land back. I can feel it. And I got a sense about people. He's okay."

"What's your sense about me?"

She turned to look at me straight on. "You're all screwed up," she said flatly. I took my eyes off the road again to look at her. Then she added with that half smile, "But not hopeless."

"I'm so glad I'm driving fifty miles out of my way for you."

"What exactly *is* your way?" she asked, meaning, I suppose, that it clearly wasn't the old way, that I wasn't a traditional. I let it drop.

"What's it like being *Iyeska?*" she asked. *Iyeska* means half-breed, mixed blood.

I looked at her like it was a stupid question.

"Well, what was it like having a white dad?"

"You got me."

"You must have *some* memories?"

"I never knew the man."

"Is that why you're Joey Moves Camp and not Joey whatever his name was?"

I shrugged. "My mom named me after her father." We were silent the rest of the way, and I thought about how no one ever talked of my dad. He must have been a piece of work.

In Harlow's, we went through the aisles together getting stuff that was on her list. When we were done, I loaded her bundles in the back. As I pulled onto 73 to head home, she dusted off a couple of peaches on her

T-shirt and offered me one. I could see a white bra through the white of her shirt. Her breasts were small and very pretty. No bigger than peaches themselves.

"Truth is," she said, "I was surprised to see *you* at the meeting, specially on the council. Word is, you're an apple."

"Is that the word?" I said, looking in the rearview and trying to sound amused, not hurt. Apple means white on the inside.

"They say you wanted the white world but couldn't hack it. Is that your dream, the picket fence, the blond wife, the golden retriever?"

"Black Lab, actually."

"But that's pretty much your dream, right?"

"I ain't a dreamer, Miss Takes Gun. I never have been."

"Sorry," she said. But I didn't know which way she meant it—you know, like *Sorry to have offended you,* or *Sorry to hear you got no dream, not even that one.* I felt like asking her what the hell her dream was, but I didn't. I kept it friendly. "Well, there was one thing that I wanted very much to do . . . to become."

She turned back and fixed her eyes on me. "What?"

I shook my head. "It's out of reach now, so there's no point in talking about it."

"So? You can still tell me. I'll tell you *my* dream."

"Go ahead."

"You first," she said.

"Well . . . I was studying astronomy. That's what I wanted to be more than anything. An astronomer."

"An astro*nom*er?" she exclaimed. "What for?"

"Because of that feeling you get when you look at the stars. Especially through a huge telescope, you know. You're *out* there. When I look at the stars, my mind just starts reeling. All those huge questions come at you. Thoughts about infinity, and other worlds that might exist, and how it all began. And did it begin because a previous one ended."

"A previous what?"

"Universe."

She looked at me with disbelief. For a split second, I thought she was impressed. "You don't think there are more pressing things to worry about?"

"Who said I'm worrying?"

"That's my point. Don't you think previous universes are kind of a wasitchu thing to worry about? You don't think we have more immediate problems?"

"Oh, like we're the only ones who can love the earth, and they're the only ones who can figure the stars, right?"

"Whatever," she said, turning to her window. After five seconds or so, she turned back. "So why didn't you stick with it?"

"I didn't have the math. It's mostly number crunching. And I was getting interested in psychology at the same time." There was another silence in which I felt I was being judged. "So what's your dream, Sharon?" I asked.

"The Paha Sapa."

"I mean, what do you want to become? What do you dream of being?"

"That's being enough for me. I dream about the Black Hills most every night. Every night I'm there."

"Wow, you must be tight with the spirits, huh? Bet the spirits voted you Miss Mystical Winchinchala 1990." I looked over, expecting her to be glaring at me, or flipping me the finger. She was smiling, though, all the way this time, dimples deep. And when our eyes met, she busted out laughing, not because I had said anything so funny, I think, but because she suddenly realized how she sounded—and she had a good enough heart to be able to laugh at herself.

"What makes you think I'm a *winchinchala?*" she asked, pulling a strand of hair off her face and tucking it behind her ear. *Winchinchala* means virgin.

I shrugged. "I was just being polite. You should try it sometime."

"Sometime I will. So, is it true all your girlfriends been white?"

"You think you got me figured, eh? Think you got my number." She shrugged.

"Well, you never see the whole picture. Just remember that."

"So?"

"So why judge? Sure, I like blondes. Some of them. But there's a reason for it, and it doesn't mean I want to be white. And it doesn't mean I don't like Indian girls."

"So what's the reason?"

"Something happened when I was a kid. It changed me."

"What?"

"I met a white girl. And I never felt anything so strong since."

"So you wander the earth, looking for her in other blondes."

"I thought you didn't have TV. You sound like the shrinks on *Oprah*."

She brought her ankles up on the seat, crossed them, then turned her whole body toward me so that she could study me straight on as I drove. "Tell me what happened with this girl," she said. Her smile was broad now, ear to ear. It was a smile of truce and seduction, a smile that said *I won't needle you anymore. You can trust me now, okay? I promise. Tell me what happened.* I thought of Charlie Brown running at the football.

"Well, I met her at this summer camp in Minnesota—"

"A *summer* camp?"

"Yeah, the priests at Mission school picked me to go to this camp. They picked a few of us from different reservations. The idea was that we would learn ambition from the white kids and bring it—"

"Learn *their* ambitions, you mean."

"Right. Do you want to hear the story or not?"

"How old were you?"

"Nine. So was Justine. She had such light hair it was almost white. It shone as she came out of the lake. So did her arms and legs. Everything shone about this girl. And her eyes were china blue, almost navy. I had never seen blue eyes, except for an old priest, but his were pale and washed-out. Eyes like hers never. I had never been off rez. She was so different from anything I'd seen, it was like falling in love with a Martian. When she looked at me, I froze. I near wet my pants. Twice that first day she wandered over in my direction like she wanted to say hi, but I feared I would start stuttering. I used to do that when I was nervous. I thought I spoke English pretty well, we all did, but those white kids were something else. They spoke like machine guns, and it broke my confidence. So whenever she got near, I would go play with the boys, wrestle, take dares, pretend I had nerve. Sometimes in crafts class she would look up from her macramé and catch me looking at her, and she would smile in a friendly way, but she had given up trying to speak to me.

"One day when the girls were eating over at our camp—their own camp was farther up the lake—she ended up in the food line next to me. She asked my name. My pulse was slamming in my temples, and I was sweating. We talked a bit about the counselors and activities we liked best. I never dreamt she would have more than a hello to say to me or that I could respond in full, unbroken sentences, but there we were, talking. When we got through the food line, she stood a moment, holding her tray at chest height. It didn't fully cross my mind that she was waiting for me to suggest a place to sit together. Actually, it did cross my mind, but I could feel everyone looking—or I imagined they were—and I had this feeling that Indian boys were supposed to watch their step.

" 'Well, see ya,' I said. Justine bit her lip and looked puzzled, then she flushed pink and walked away. I had no courage, see? And I hurt her with my lack of it. She thought I didn't want to sit with her. After that, I didn't dare look at her anymore in crafts class. I didn't deserve to."

I looked over at Sharon Takes Gun. She had her ankles crossed on the seat, her elbows on her knees, and her chin resting on her knuckles. Her face was expressionless. "Go on," she said.

"Well, the last week of camp I got whipped in a fight. I ran into the woods to be alone, deep in the woods because I knew I would cry. I stopped running when I was so far in the woods that I knew it was safe to cry. But out of nowhere a voice called my name. I looked around but couldn't see who. It was spooky. 'Up here,' the voice called. I looked into the treetops but just saw green everywhere. Then I saw a flash of white way up high, a white T-shirt and someone waving. It looked like Justine, but that didn't make sense. What would she be doing way out here, so far from the girls' camp? *I must be dreaming,* I thought. But it *was* Justine. She was sitting on a branch about thirty feet up, maybe forty, her back against the trunk. I raised my hand and waved, still wondering if it was a dream. You see, each night for weeks I had gone to sleep vowing that the next day I would talk to her, but in the morning it was always the coward who awoke. I had given up hoping for her, and suddenly there she is in a tree in the middle of the woods, her face and her hair as bright as ever, and all those leaves and bits of light around her.

" 'Joey, did the tree call you, too?' she asked, calling down to me. I didn't know what that meant, so I just said, 'What are you doing up there?'

" 'Sitting in the courage tree,' she said. 'Come up.' She pointed to various branches below her and explained the easiest way up—"

"This is a joke," Sharon said. "And I bet there's some dumb-ass punch line like *Joey and Justine sitting in a tree, k-i-s-s-i-n-g, first comes*—"

"Why don't you just listen? Okay?"

"*Okay.* Sorry."

"When I got within a few feet of her, she reached down to give me a hoist. We grabbed each other at the wrist and I can still feel the tight strength of her little hand, the flecks of bark pressing into my skin where she held me. I climbed onto a branch next to hers and looked at her. She wore blue shorts and the white T-shirt, but no shoes. 'Where are your sneakers?' I asked.

"She pointed down to where she had left them. It made me dizzy. When I looked back at her, she was staring at me. 'What happened to you? Your lip's all fat and your eyes are red.'

"I tried telling her I got hurt in Capture the Flag, but then she asked about my underwear, which were stretched and torn and hanging out over the waistband of my shorts. And that's when I lost it, just busted down crying. She put her hand on my shoulder. She rubbed my back gently, which calmed me, helped me recover my breathing. 'What happened?' she asked.

"I was too ashamed to tell her," I said, turning to Sharon. "But what happened is these three eleven-year-old boys wedgied me. It's this thing they do. You grab the back of someone's underwear and yank it real hard so the cotton wedges between the cheeks and digs into the tender skin there. It burns. Feels like all hell is in your ass. They lifted me clear off the ground by my briefs and hooked the waistband over a wooden peg in the wall, a coat hook. I was hanging on the wall like a goddamn painting. And the three of them are taking free shots at me. I didn't hit back, because I knew if anything got reported, it would be my fault. The people who ran the camp would say it had been a noble experiment that failed. No more slots for Indian kids. The priests at Mission would blame me. But the other reason I didn't hit back, the more important one, is that I was afraid if I made any sudden movements, the underwear would rip. They had stretched on the peg but not ripped yet. My mom had got me those underwear. She didn't want me to go to this camp in the first place, but the priests convinced her it would help me have a future. So finally she said okay. But she knew how cruel kids can be, especially to outsiders, and how viciously they tease. The only underwear I had were hand-me-downs from Clem, and they were too big and full of holes. *He* didn't even get them new. Mom feared those underwear would make me more of a target. So she took her coffee can full of coins and hiked twenty-five miles to Kadoka—same road we're driving right now—and she bought me Fruit of the Looms, a three-pack, still in the plastic. Her feet were still healing when I left for camp. And these bastards hang me on a peg? Anyway, I was keeping it together pretty good, but then the cotton started ripping—I could hear it—and I started slipping down the wall. My eyes burned and flooded and I thought I would lose it right in front of them, which would give them their victory. So when my toes finally touched the floor of the bunkhouse, I took off like a jackrabbit for the woods."

"And ended up by that tree?" Sharon asked.

"Yeah. And Justine calmed me down, just with the touch of her hand. Then she closed her eyes and leaned back against the trunk, her legs straddling the branch on which she sat. It was an amazing branch. It shot straight out like a line drive for a good twenty feet before it divided into smaller branches. Below it, a rocky slope fell away toward a stream. 'You should ask the tree for help,' she said.

" 'What do you mean?' I asked.

" 'Trees can talk.'

" 'You mean, to each other?'

" 'And to us,' she said. Her blue eyes were open again and she was looking at me. I wondered if she was making fun of Indians. This camp had been my first taste of ridicule. But she didn't seem like the type.

" 'Did the tree call to you, Joey?'

" 'I don't think so.'

" 'It called me,' she said. 'My bunk counselor took us through here on a nature walk, and I couldn't stop looking at this tree. I even had a dream about this branch. I had a feeling that if I could walk this branch, then I could do anything. Even choose which of my parents I'll live with. I have to choose before school starts. Last week, I snuck away and climbed up here, to try to walk the branch, but I started thinking about the rocks below and I got so scared I couldn't even climb down. But after an hour or so, Joey, something happened.'

" 'What?' I asked.

" 'The tree spoke.'

"I just looked at her. I was still wondering if she could be making fun of me.

" 'It did,' she said. 'It sent a feeling through the bark into my skin, my shoulder blades, all through me. It sort of gave me a nudge, like it was saying stand up, walk me, you can do it, I won't let you fall. You're safe in my arms. And suddenly I *was* safe, Joey, and I knew it. So I stood and walked all the way out to there,' she said, pointing to a far point on the branch. 'I've done it twice since then,' she said, 'but only when the tree says so. Close your eyes with me and rest your back against the trunk,' she said. 'Maybe the tree will tell you something, too.' "

Sharon snorted. "This is bullshit. You're making it up. Like you could really remember all her words, too, so many years after."

"Okay, then. I won't bore you with the rest."

"No, no. Finish it off. Please."

"Well, I tried to close my eyes and feel the tree. But my butt got sore, then numb. And I wanted to look at her, not close my eyes. After I don't know how long, she whispered, 'Do you feel it, Joey? It's happening. It's safe now.' She put a hand on my shoulder and got to her feet, then took a few steps out, not even putting her hands out for balance. I was so scared I stopped breathing. I wanted to tell her to get down and hug the branch, crawl back, but I was afraid my voice could break her concentration or whatever it was that kept her up there. It was like she was in a trance or in another world and my voice might yank her out of it, yank her back into this world of rocks, gravity, and hard things. She walked a good twenty feet out, maybe more, out to where the branch divided. It was no wider than her foot out there, and it was bending under her. Leaves and branches jiggled. She had gone too far. She couldn't possibly turn around and come back. And she was above the rocks. 'Use your hands!' I cried. And she did, but not the way I meant. Her hands came up and out to her sides, for balance. She took her lead foot off the branch, swung it slowly backwards through the air like a pendulum, and placed it half a stride behind the other foot. Then she flexed the branch a bit by bending her knees, and as it pushed back gently like a diving board, she spun on the balls of her feet like a gymnast girl on the beam, switching direction. Just like that. She looked at me and smiled for a sec, not with pride, just joy, then walked back easy as can be. I knew then she had a connection with *some*thing. She settled into the crook of the branch again, her legs dangling down either side of it, and she patted the branch like it was the neck of a horse. 'It's getting late,' she said. 'I better go. You want to meet here tomorrow, Joey? We'll try again.'

"We set a time. She touched my knee with her hand, then climbed down. She picked up her sneakers and disappeared into the woods.

"The next day was the second to last day of camp, so I spent it cleaning, sweeping, and scrubbing. After dinner, I snuck into the woods and waited up in the tree for her. I kept thinking about the boys who jumped me. I had all these revenge plans, and didn't know which one to use. As I got tired, I sat back against the trunk. Soon, I felt something like a current moving through my shoulder blades, like electricity, but pleasant."

"Don't tell me you walked that branch," Sharon said. "Because I don't even believe she walked it."

"I didn't walk it. But it dawned on me all of a sudden that those three boys had no idea what those underwear meant to me and to my mom.

Boys like that—I mean, coming from their world—they could never have imagined what my mom did to get me those briefs. See, they didn't know the larger picture," I said, looking over at Sharon. She rolled her eyes. I continued: "Which means they didn't fully know what they were doing. Sure, they were jerks for hitting me, but it was the underwear that really hurt. And I had this feeling that if they *had* known, they would never have done it. They would not have gone that far. So I let it go. I was beyond them."

"And you expect me to believe the tree told you all this?"

"I'm not saying it told me anything. All I know is I was up there when I had these thoughts."

"And what about Justine?" Sharon asked.

"I hung out two hours on that branch. She never showed. The next morning, the buses waited in a clearing between the two camps. One was bound for reservations in the Dakotas, and a dozen others for the Twin Cities and Chicago. I stashed my bag in the luggage hold, then got on and went to the very back seat. I lay low in the seat and closed my eyes on the summer. The sooner I got home and forgot her, the better. Now and then I opened my eyes and looked out the window at the hustle and bustle of kids and counselors saying goodbye, checking lists, and tossing bags into holds. There were shrill voices screaming, 'See ya next year, see ya, see ya.' A glint of blond hair caught my eye, but it wasn't Justine.

"Lakota kids started getting on my bus and settling in, trading candies and swapping stories of new friends and enemies. A counselor came on and started reading off names. Our driver started warming the engine. I felt sad when that engine turned over, felt completely whipped and empty.

"There was some kind of commotion by one of the buses. A ring of kids and counselors had formed around whatever this commotion was, so it was hard to see. It seemed like a fight, but I figured it must be two girls fighting because I heard a high-pitched shriek that any boy would be ashamed to make. Then some of the counselors started looking around and pointing at different buses. One of them pointed at ours. The ring opened up a bit and I could see Justine standing in the middle with her suitcase. I looked for the girl she was fighting, but there didn't seem to be one. A counselor at the edge of the circle was trying to talk to Justine, holding his hand out to her, reasoning with her, trying to convince her of something. She shook her head, stomped her foot in the dust, and shrieked, 'No. No. NO!' When he tried to come closer, she slapped his hand away and dragged her bag a few steps back from him. She was in a wild state. Something awful must have happened to her.

"The counselor threw his hands up. Another counselor whispered in his ear. They talked a couple seconds, then one of them came onto our bus and said, 'Is Joey Moves Camp here?'

"I panicked. What did she *tell* them? I mean, whatever it was that happened to her, how could she blame it on *me?* I raised my hand slowly 'cause my voice had gone south. The counselor walked down the aisle, slow and heavy, then squatted on his haunches so he could talk in my ear. In a quiet tone he said, 'Would you come with me, please?'

" 'What for?' I said, trying not to sound scared. Whenever something got stolen, they suspected us. He coughed into his fist, like to clear his throat. 'There's a girl who won't get on her bus till you come say goodbye. Kiss her goodbye, actually. She's holding everybody up,' he said. 'Seriously, she won't budge.'

"Some of the kids sitting near me overheard and started going Wooooh-wooo-woooooo, Jo-eeeeey. I walked down the aisle and out the door. When my feet hit the ground, our eyes connected, hers and mine, but as always I looked away. I looked at the crowd, the ground, then finally back at Justine. Her cheeks were stained with tears and dust.

"One of her hands went up to tuck a strand of hair behind her ear. Some of the kids and even counselors were smirking, but others weren't. Anyway, their faces soon blurred and I didn't care about them. Only her.

"I entered through the ring of people around her. She wiped her cheek with the back of her hand and smiled at me. Then she said, 'They caught me sneaking out last night. I'm sorry, Joey. Really, I'm sorry.' I didn't know what to say, so I just reached for her bag. 'Let's go behind that bus,' she said. As we walked, the others started to follow. I turned and said something to the counselor who had got me off my bus. He put some fingers in his mouth and made a high-pitched whistle, started ordering kids onto different buses. Justine slipped her hand into mine. I could hear kids on my bus going crazy at that, and I knew they would bust my chops the whole way back to South Dakota. But all I cared about now was this person who didn't care about making scenes, didn't care what people thought. Her hand was warm and it gave me strength. We got behind her bus, right by the taillights. Kids were crowding into the back window of that bus to watch us. 'Does your lip still hurt?' she asked. 'No,' I whispered. She put her lips to mine so lightly that I almost couldn't feel them at first. And she kept her eyes open. They had so much light and blueness in them, and happiness. That kiss was my first, and it was different from what I expected. It wasn't like red candy or smooth plastic, or any of the things I imagined. It was like finding an animal in the woods, or a bird, and touching it. I felt like I had entered another being and she had entered me. The back window of the bus thundered with little fists and a yell went up, but it had nothing to do with the excitement I felt. I couldn't have cared less about those kids whooping it up. Her lips were soft and I could feel the firmness of her teeth behind them, and behind the teeth the pressure of her soul. Then, she put her face against the side of my neck, her arms around my waist, tight. I can still feel her breath on my neck, her pulse and courage coming through the cotton of our T-shirts like a transfusion that I needed."

"Then what happened?" Sharon asked. She had a peculiar smile on her face as she studied me.

"The driver of the bus turned the engine over and started warming it, pouring diesel fumes into our little space. We were right by the tailpipe. The counselor leaned around the corner of the bus and knocked on the taillights like he was knocking on a door. 'Okay, sweetie?' he said. 'We've really got to go now.' Justine nodded without taking her face from my neck. He entered our little space behind the bus, took her bag, and disappeared. The diesel fumes grew thick, but I didn't want it to end. She looked up at me. She lifted my hand in hers and kissed it, smiling. Then, she turned and walked away."

"That's it?" Sharon asked after a long silence. She was staring at me. We were getting near her parents' house.

"Yeah, that's it. That's not enough?"

"You're saying that's why you like blondes so much?"

"Not all blondes."

"But that's why—"

"I'm saying you can't have someone like a Justine Moore happen to you—not at such a young age—and not be changed by it."

Sharon just gave me a blank look.

"Look," I said, getting frustrated. "Do you know what imprinting is?"

"No."

"Well, go back to college and read about it."

"Just tell me."

"It's hard to explain."

"Try, Mr. College Man."

"Okay, take ducklings. Did you know that when ducklings hatch, they follow the first moving object they see? They think it's their mother. If they see a fox or a man, that's it, that's what they follow. That's Mom. That's imprinting. It imprints on their brains."

Sharon started laughing uncontrollably.

"What?" I protested.

She calmed herself enough to ask in an even tone, "Are you a little duckling?" She immediately broke into a new fit.

"Sharon, I'm telling you, you can*not* have a Justine Moore happen to you at such a young age and not be changed forever. It marks you. Every time you see something in a person that reminds you of her, your body remembers and your mind relives it. Don't you see what I'm saying?"

Her eyes were red from laughing at me so hard. I pulled off the dirt road into the weeds and tall grass by her parents' house. I helped bring the packages to the front door. We were each holding a bundle by the door when she said, "Imprinting, huh? I think you're just a sucker for a good kiss on the hand." She took the bundle out of my arms and went inside, the screen door slapping shut behind her. "Thanks for the ride," she called over her shoulder.

The diva hadn't been bothering me since Clem suggested the Yuwipi. It was as though just the mention of that healing ceremony had already forced her to retreat for a bit. So I felt good. I phoned Frannie and asked if we could get together. She was glad I called, she said, had something important to tell me and could we meet at the Broken Spur?

Big Dori put a tall-necked Budweiser on the bar, then laid my change next to it. It was early afternoon and the place was quiet. There was a kid from the filling station shooting pool, and Squeak Hansen, who owned the filling station, was at the bar, slumped over a drink. He looked far gone already, just kept staring at the stuffed antelope heads on the wall behind the bottles, staring into their sad glass eyes. Farther down the bar was that cowboy Wade, nursing a drink and reading a Marvel comic.

Frannie came in the door and said hello to Dori and the other three, then slapped me on the back. "Heya, Moves Camp," she said, parking herself on the stool to my right. She ordered a Canada Dry. Dori put the soda on the bar. Frannie paid for her own and stood up. "What say we take a table?" I followed her to the back, to a corner booth with vinyl banquettes that came together at a right angle. She leaned her back against one wall and I leaned against the other, our knees touching for a

moment. Wade looked over his shoulder, nonchalant as hell, then returned to his superheroes. Frannie leaned close and spoke soft. "I'm late,
Joey. Actually, I'm way late. I didn't say anything at Murdo 'cause I was
hoping it would still come—been late before, you know, but . . ." She
shook her head. "I'm pregnant."

I was stunned. My next sensation was happiness. That there was a tiny
person coming together inside of Frannie's body—part me, part her, the
woman I loved—filled me with awe and joy. And it seemed everything
would come together now for us. "When?" I asked. "Which time d'ya
think?"

"Who knows?"

"And you're sure?"

"I bought a bunch of those home tests."

Scrounger, the gas station kid, had given up shooting pool and joined
his boss at the bar. The backs of all three men were to us. Dori was busy
loading beer into ice chests. I leaned closer and gave Frannie a real quick
kiss on the ear. Then we sat back apart, but I snuck my hand under the
corner of the table and put it on her belly. She smiled and shook her head:
"It's way too early to feel anything."

"It's never too early."

"Fine, but . . ."

"What?"

"The thing is, Joey, there's a big difference between being pregnant
and being a mother."

"I guess that's so," I said tentatively, not sure where she was going
with it.

"Well, think about it. It would be the end of my youth, my freedom.
No more travel. No returning to Africa, or ever seeing Europe. Joey, I'd
be anchored right here in Kadoka, the last place I want to be."

"We could move," I said lamely. "Anywhere you want."

"That's not what I'm talking about. I don't want to move to Califor-
nia or someplace and get anchored there, I want to roam the planet, keep
learning about other places and cultures. And life's short. In a way, it's a
good thing, this happening now. I might've dragged on another year or
two before getting off my butt. Dad has this way of sapping my will, making sure I don't jump the fence, you know? Every time I make noises
about leaving, I get a new pickup, or a prize mare. And he always tells me
how I remind him of Mom and how he misses her so. And God knows
you've made it hard to leave, too, Joey. I never could've lasted this long

without you here. But it's different now. Now I have to. I'm heading for Denver on Wednesday. Got a girlfriend there I can stay with till—"

"Okay," I said, raising my hands in surrender. "If you gotta go to Denver, you gotta go. But, Fran, instead of giving it to one of those agencies where it's all anonymous, let the tribe adopt it. Let my sister-in-law raise the child. She's great with kids. You'll love her. And this way you'd always know where your child is and you could visit whenever you wanted. You'll love Linda, she's—"

"Joey," she said, looking at me with a mix of pity and anger. "You know damn well if I have the baby I'll never give it up. Not to anyone. I'll be *trapped*."

"Then . . . ?"

"What else is there?"

"But . . ."

"Don't be so goddamn innocent, Joey. I didn't ask for this."

"You're only looking at the negative, the loss of freedom and stuff. Look at the positive—"

"It's not your lookout, Joey."

"You're saying I've got no say?"

"It's my body. My future."

"But *our* kid."

She shook her head. "Not yet. Right now it's just my body. And my mind's made up."

"Then why tell me? What did you have to tell me for?"

"I don't know . . . seemed you had a right to know, is all. Maybe I needed to talk out loud about it."

"Maybe you wanted to have your mind changed."

She shook her head.

Pogo walked in but didn't see us in the corner. He walked the length of the bar, his boot dragging on the wood floor, punctuated by the crisp percussion of the ivory peg. "Howdy, Scrounger."

"How're *you*, Mr. McLaren?" said the gas station kid.

"And how's old Squeak?" Pogo said, slapping Hansen on the back. Hansen slumped a little lower on his elbows. Pogo looked at his watch. "Guess I got time for one," he said to Dori, taking the stool next to Wade. Dori set him up with a beer and a shot. "Frannie been in?" he asked. Dori nodded in our direction. Pogo swiveled around on his stool and looked at us dead-on. Frannie gave him a wave. He had the powder-blue eyes of the father but lacked the McLaren chin. His face was weak and mean. He didn't return the wave, just shook his head and swiveled back around, said something under his breath to Wade, who nodded and turned the page of his comic book.

I looked at Frannie's strong features as she weighed her brother. I had daydreamed often of how our kids might look. A hint of reddish blond in their dark hair, and maybe light eyes against their bronze skin. They would have beautiful faces, Frannie's chin, my mother's cheekbones, my brow.

I looked down at her belly and wondered about the new life, and how large the embryo was. How many weeks? I tried to remember how long it is before an embryo becomes a fetus. It seemed arbitrary to call one human and the other prehuman. I had seen one in a jar at Berkeley once, pale and curled like a grub, but with the beginnings of eyes and little salamander hands. It looked so eager to grip the world. I imagined it pink and full of life, pulsating, then a tool hooking it, dragging it down from Frannie's warmth. I saw it shivering in a stainless-steel basin, torn and forever interrupted, the steam of life leaving it. Suddenly, I was vomiting on the table.

"Jesus, are you okay?" asked Frannie, putting a hand on my shoulder and getting up. She hurried to the bar to get paper towels. I got up, too, and followed her, to get the towels so she wouldn't have to deal with it.

"Ahh, for *Chrissake!*" Pogo cried. "The law's the law, Dori, but you could get around it with a good, stiff cover. Damn gut eaters can't hold their booze and never could." Gut eaters is a slight that goes back to buffalo days. We don't waste anything of an animal. Everything has a use or gets eaten. And it's still like that. Like that makes us dogs, you know? While Pogo's type used to shoot buffalo for the tongue and leave the rest to rot.

"Shut up, Pogo. He ain't drunk," said Frannie, heading back with some paper napkins.

Dori chimed in. "He ain't had but one beer, and not even that. Can't you see the man is sick? And how many times I gotta tell ya about usin' 'em racial epitaphs in my bar?" She came out from behind the bar with a steaming rag.

"Yeah, be nice to our feathered friends," scolded Scrounger.

"And that's enough out of *you,* Scrounger," snapped Dori. She laid the rag down on the table and started sopping up my mess. I tried to take it from her, but she brushed my hand off and said, "You just relax. This is part of the job."

"Yeah, kinda goes with the *territory*," said Pogo. Scrounger and Wade chuckled at that.

Dori paid no attention. "You need some Tums or something, Joey? Some solid food? What can I get ya?"

I shook my head.

"Some bad muscatel, was it?" said Pogo.

"I ain't drunk," I told him, wiping my mouth with a paper napkin.

"Dang," said Squeak Hansen, still locked into the glass gaze of an antelope behind the bar. "That poor darlin'. She musta been *flyin'* when she hit the wall. Look 'em all. Whole herd. What'd they go build a bar in middle of a antelope run for? I mean the hu*man*ity of it. The *humanity*." He put a boot down on the floor to get up and go, but he slumped forward and passed out, his head knocking over his glass. Scrounger ran over to help his boss.

"Another gut eater bites the dust," I said.

"Are you calling Mr. Hansen a drunk?" said Pogo. "Stand up and say it, you pukey maggot, 'stead of hiding behind my sister." Frannie, who was cleaning the table and had her back to her brother, spun around and shoved him hard. "Back off, Pogo. Just leave him alone."

She shoved him so hard he had to take four or five steps backwards to catch his balance. He forced a laugh. "Whadya do, get one of your witch doctors put a spell on her?"

"That's right," I said. " 'Course it helps if you like women."

"What the fuck is that supposed to mean?" he spat, peggin' his way back to us, fists clenched. Frannie shot me an exasperated look. "You calling me a faggot?" shouted Pogo. "Stand up and say it, you pukey maggot."

"Burned any women lately?" I said, getting to my feet. Wade's and Pogo's eyes met for a split second. Frannie looked completely puzzled by my comment and couldn't understand why I was egging him on.

"Are you calling me a fag?" he bellowed again.

"You know what I'm calling you." Adrenaline coursed in my veins and an overdue fury rose like foam in me. I wanted it out. "You're a woman burner, Pogo. I don't guess that makes you much of a—"

In one motion, he shoved his sister to the side and threw a punch over the table at me. It hardly connected, but it did overextend him across the table, making it easy for me to uppercut his chin. His teeth clapped together and he stumbled backwards. Wade caught him under the arms. Dori ran to the bar and hopped it to phone the sheriff. I'll bet even she was surprised she could hop it. I felt trapped by the table, so I shoved it aside. Frannie pleaded with me to just walk away with her. And I would have, but Pogo was staggering back and had a deer knife in his hand. Frannie saw it and shouted, "Are you crazy? Put that down. Put it *down!*" She jumped in front of me, facing him, and she put her arms straight back to prevent me from coming around in front of her. He held the knife close to his side, about rib high, and tried with his free hand to shove her out of the way. He was bleeding from the mouth and barking mad, cursing up a storm about gut eaters and telling her to "Just git the fuck outa the way." She was fast, though, countering his every move. "Get her outa the way!" he barked. I thought he was talking to me, telling me to have it out like a man, but Wade came from the side and grabbed Frannie's arm. She shook him off, but Pogo thrust from the other side, just missing me. Wade tried again and she kicked him in the knee, at which point Pogo tried to flank her on the other side. She countered him just in time, though. Then she folded her arms across her stomach and stood straight, speaking in an even voice: "Listen to me, Pogo. I'm pregnant and Joey's the father of my baby. And I love him. You touch a hair on his head and so help me I'll kill you. I'll see you get the chair. I mean it."

He looked at her for about five seconds, his eyes wide and disbelieving, then he blinked. "Tell me you're not that stupid, Francine," he said bitterly. He handed the knife to Wade and walked away, walked out the door.

By the time the sheriff showed up in his khaki uniform and dark aviator shades, we had righted the chairs and tables and were on our way out. Those Ray-Bans couldn't hide his disappointment when Dori told him I was just minding my own business and hadn't disturbed the peace.

I was very happy as I walked Frannie to her pickup. I almost felt thankful to Pogo for having brought about the crisis that led to this change in her. She opened the door and got in her truck. "So, Denver's off?" I asked.

She looked puzzled.

"Well, what you said in there."

"He had a *knife,* Joey."

"But you meant what you said, right?"

"Well, I do love you and I *am* pregnant, but I didn't say I'm going through with the pregnancy. Let him jump to his own conclusions."

"But you called it a baby. You admitted it's a baby already."

"It was a hairy moment, Joey."

"Frannie, don't go. We love each other."

She sighed. "Everything's a fence. I'm a slave to that goddamn herd and to my dad, and I've been trapped here too long. It's like we're slaves to our property. You Sioux used to float across the plains, do as you pleased. Now you're fenced on a rez. And me, I'm fenced on a ranch. I'm so sick of ridin' fences, Joey. I just wanna bust out of here. And I'm gonna." She leaned out the window and kissed me as she started the engine. "But that doesn't mean I don't love you." She put it in gear and drove off.

It felt strange crossing White River knowing I wouldn't camp on its banks with Frannie again. Other than that, the ride home was okay. I was numb.

I shot through Wambli, took the turnoff for Hisle, and barreled up the dirt road at about fifty or sixty. Locusts exploded on the windshield like greasy ack-ack fire. White, brown, and green splotches. From a quarter-mile off, I noticed someone waiting on my step. It was Bacon.

"How are you?" he asked as I got out of the car. He was standing now and was offering his hand.

I shook it, not to be rude. "All right," I said. I folded my arms and leaned back against the car.

"That's good," he said, making little rainbows in the dirt with the toe of his shoe. "That's good."

"What's on your mind, Father?"

"Please, call me Quinn. My name is Quinn Bacon." He took a deep breath. "I need an introduction to Clement. Will you give me one?"

"Knock on his door. Gotta trailer home off the main road leaving Wambli."

He nodded as if he already knew that. "It might go smoother if you introduced me. I want everything to go right."

I shrugged. "I don't really know who you are, or what you're really doing on Pine Ridge—"

"What do you need to know? Just ask."

It was too hot to stand around talking in the sun, and I wasn't about
to invite him in my house, so I suggested we take a ride.

I drove us to the foot of Eagle Nest Butte, a natural stronghold. It's the
only high ground around. Can't be snuck up on there. It's basically a flat-
topped mountain, an island rising steeply out of the prairie ocean. The
butte's not more than four hundred feet high, but even that, in such flat
country, gives the feeling of being up near heaven. You can see endless
prairie in all directions. To the south, we could see deep into Nebraska.

We reached the top and walked across the plateau, which is large
enough for a couple of football fields, and it's covered in tall grasses. On
the westward end, there's a little pine forest where it's shady and cool. We
entered the pine. Tobacco and flesh offerings were wrapped in colored
paper twists that were strung out across branches and boughs. They
quivered slightly in a faint breeze. No matter how still and blistering it is
below, there's always a breeze whispering through the pine on top of the
butte. That's probably why a lot of medicine men do vision quests up
here. After a four-day fast, your mind can do a lot with that whispering.

Above us, two eagles and two hawks circled on thermals, rising till
they vanished, then reappearing to check on their nests in the crags and
pines of the butte.

Two miles in the distance, the water tower of Wambli caught the sun.
The houses clustered beneath it seemed toylike and happy. And you
couldn't make out the herd of rusted heaps, stripped, sinking into the
prairies—serving as hiding places, homes.

A low-flying chopper thundered overhead, out of nowhere, bearing
west at a high speed. The trees shook and the strings of offerings jiggled.
The thunder scattered the birds, killed the spirit of the place, at least for
a while, and destroyed any sense I might have had that our land was secure. "They friends of yours, Waokiye?" I asked as the chopper dimin-
ished into the western horizon.

"What?"

"You got a homing device on you?"

He didn't act offended. He just took off his shirt, gave it to me, then
started to undo his pants. I guess the idea was for me to search the clothes
for a device, but I didn't bother; if he *was* a fed, they would not have
risked blowing his cover by coming so close. Also, the chopper shot by so

quick they probably didn't know we were below in the pines.

I tossed him his shirt. He buckled his belt. His dance wounds were closed but still pretty red-looking. That, also, made me think he wasn't a fed. I can't imagine a fed being that dedicated. He was covered with other scars of some kind. I was curious, but didn't want to be rude.

"How did you get your hands on those armor-piercing weapons?" I asked.

He seated himself on a ledge under the pines. I did, too. It wasn't pure cliff below us, but it was extremely steep. Black-and-white magpies flew out of crags below us, circled, then came back.

"Right about the time I got ordained, I received a call from one of my old college buddies. We had been in sort of a club or fraternity together as undergraduates—they called them secret societies, but it amounted to a club, a place to drink port and smoke cigars. Senior year, he and I were both approached by the Central Intelligence Agency—"

"So, we're talking about Yale," I said, interrupting him. I had read an article about Bush and other CIA guys who had gone to Yale and come up through that Skull and Bones thing.

Bacon looked surprised. "That's right. Anyway, I was drawn to the mystique of it. Very heady stuff, to be so young and have your government invite you into an elite wing. But I was also a religious kid aiming for the priesthood, and the mystique of the Jesuits was greater than anything the government would ever come up with. The only reason I attended Yale was that my parents insisted I try college before the seminary. They were hoping I would experience an enlightenment, discover something meaningful like stockbroking.

"Not long after I was ordained, I got a call from this buddy. Over martinis at the Yale Club, he told me about the Marxist threat in Guatemala, El Salvador, Nicaragua. The situation was made worse, he said, by a few priests who had gone native, turning a deaf ear to Rome and aiding the rebels.

"I was being asked to go down there and get close to an American Maryknoll priest. Nothing cloak-and-dagger, just get close to him and help keep tabs on him. He was constantly on the move, coordinating cells, putting university students—Marxists, of course—in touch with peasants, and peasants in touch with the guerrillas.

"I figured it could be the adventure of my life, that I could serve Church and country both. And I was excited by the chance of bringing back into the fold a brother priest who had lost his way.

"I told them I would have to check it out with my superior general. When I saw my SG, he said it had all been approved, both with our order and with Maryknoll and that I should pack my bags."

"You're saying the Church and CIA work together—"

"When their interests converge, absolutely. Iron fist in velvet glove. Look, you've got some priests and nuns down there who are all-out revolutionaries, and others who are on the Langley payroll. The only difference is that the second group is fine by Rome. The pope and Reagan were very tight, and not just on Poland." He paused, looking off into the distance while his fingers scraped moss from the ledge. He brought the moss to his lip, resting it there lightly against the scar. "This is a sacred place," he said as he gazed through the pine boughs at the prairies below. "I'm glad you brought me here." He put the moss in his breast pocket and continued with his story. "I received some instruction at Langley in different ways of passing information, meeting contacts, doing drops, all of that. And they brushed up my Spanish.

"This priest I had to get close to was named LaGuardia, and I admit I liked him right away even though he made a lot of claims that I thought were nonsense. He said that the Guatemalan government was killing off university students who had been trying to organize peasants. He said they were getting decapitated at night in a slaughterhouse and that mutilated bodies would be left here and there as examples. What's the point in turning the other cheek when they're lopping off heads, LaGuardia kept asking me. I didn't buy any of it, but of course I pretended to. When he told me the CIA trained the death squads, I almost laughed in his face. Anyway, after Guatemala, he had moved on to Nicaragua and then El Salvador, which is where I hooked up with him. Everywhere, he did the same thing, organized cells, coordinated students, peasants, Indians, and guerrillas.

"I pretended to be impressed with what I had read and heard about liberation theology. Over the months, we grew closer and he took me into the countryside. I met many guerrillas. And to my surprise, most were not out to get the Church. But they wanted a Church that would reform itself, would serve the poor. Not one that confers papal honors on landowners who pay their workers forty cents a day while making gifts of gold candlesticks and chalice cups to the bishops. They were seductive, these guerrillas, and they could be convincing. I had to keep reminding myself that they were funded by Moscow, trained by Cuba.

"One day, LaGuardia took me on a long trek into the mountains. He was bringing medical supplies to some guerrillas in the hills. We arrived at a village high up that wasn't much more than thirty or so thatched huts, a few acres of coffee beans and some goats and chickens. The villagers scratched the mountainside with hoes but mud slides usually washed away their efforts. I had rarely seen such poverty, but they were warm and welcoming, not only sharing the little food they had but insisting we accept most of it. And they were eager to receive the Eucharist and to have their confession heard. And above all they were proud to shelter and feed the four guerrillas who were among them.

"Two of the guerrillas were not even sixteen, but they had engaged the government troops many times already. There was no bravado, no machismo. They were quiet and modest and very tired. Don't be seduced, I told myself. They're killers, hit-and-run terrorists. Never forget that.

"We left the supplies with them and returned to the lowlands. A day later, I went into the city and met my contact. I was asked if I was sure about two of the names I provided. I told her I was.

"Later that week, LaGuardia and I made the long hike back up to the village, with more supplies on our backs. Before we saw what happened, we could smell it. Then we came over the ridge and saw. Everything was charred and burned. We couldn't understand it. No fire could spread so fast from shack to shack that no one would escape. And lots of the bodies weren't even near huts, and yet still charred. The earth itself was charred.

"It was the most deathly silence. Then, we heard faint weeping. LaGuardia disappeared behind the remains of a hut. After a minute I went back, too. He was on his knees and his back was to me, his arms were wrapped around someone. There was a little face, the chin resting on La-Guardia's shoulder. The eyes looked past me, oblivious to me, searching the sky. It was a little boy, maybe ten or eleven. LaGuardia was speaking softly in Spanish, in the boy's ear. Then, he loosened his embrace, put his hands lightly on the kid's shoulders, and asked him what happened. He asked again and again, but there was no response. The boy wouldn't even look at either of us. He didn't take his eyes off the sky behind me. I turned around to see what was there. Just some clouds over the next mountain range.

"LaGuardia asked him again what happened, shaking his shoulders very gently. The boy's lips moved but nothing came out. He pointed his finger at the cloud range and tried again. A raspy, broken sound—half cry, half whisper—rose out of his mouth, *'El fuego. El fue-go.'* It means 'the fire,'" Quinn explained, passing a hand through his short hair. He turned and looked directly at me. "They did an air strike."

"The Salvadorans?"

He shook his head. "A Navy A-6 from the *Independence.* They sent the Intruder, Joey, a goddamn attack bomber, fitted out with a two-ton payload of incendiaries. Napalm for good measure." He let out a bitter laugh. "Talk about your baptisms of fire."

"How do you mean?"

"Into liberation theology. Into the faith that justice must be had in *this* world, that two percent of the population should not own eighty percent of the land, the faith that it's better to vaccinate than to baptize, that cardinals and bishops should not wear gold while peasants starve, and that—"

"I get the picture," I said.

He blushed. "Of course, all that didn't hit me right away. First, I just wanted to die. While LaGuardia and I buried the bodies, I thought about suicide. But first, I would confess everything to LaGuardia, not as a Catholic to a priest, but as a soul to a soul.

"After smoothing the earth and planting crosses, I asked him to hear my confession. He said he had been laicized, stripped of those powers. I said it didn't matter. I knelt before him, head bowed, and told all. He had a charred shovel in his hand. Any other man would've used it. How badly he must've wanted to. I saw it lift off the ground and waited for the blow. Instead, I heard it land ten or fifteen feet away and the next thing I knew he had dropped to his knees, facing me. We looked into each other's faces. 'As a man, I forgive you,' he said. 'As a priest—if in the eyes of God I am still a priest—I absolve you.' I realized then, Joey, that this man who worked with guerrillas, and took part in their armed struggle, was perhaps the only really Christian priest I had ever met. In no one else had I ever encountered such strength. Over the next year, the death squads snatched many of our people, and finally LaGuardia. I went into the mountains and joined the guerrillas."

"As a priest?"

He shook his head. "All the way."

"That's some theology."

"I'm way past that. Theology of Liberation was a step in the right direction. But I kept going."

"So what are you doing here?" I asked.

"It's the same story. Land, minerals, and trying to keep a people down—dependent. And they go about it the same way. When tribes here stand solid, as you did with AIM, they discredit you as Communists. Then they organize death squads, Wilson's GOONs, equipped and supplied by the FBI. Hell, you know perfectly well what they did here, Joey, shooting people, blowing up their houses, abducting folks like Anna-Mae, killing them execution-style. There's no difference between the feds and the CIA. One's internal, the other travels."

"You still haven't told me how you got those weapons."

He shook his head. "Later . . . after we've gotten to know each other."

I shrugged. "I'm not gonna beat it out of you."

He laughed and said, "No kidding." We sat a few minutes, neither of us speaking. There was only the whisper and rustle of breezes weaving through the pines. I wondered about the strange scars on his body.

"How long you been back in the States?"

"Sneaked back three years ago, up through Mexico. Holed up on an Apache rez and been rez-hopping ever since."

"So, why is it you want to meet my brother so bad?"

"Joey, when I tell you what I'm about to tell you, I don't want you to laugh, okay? I don't want you to say anything. Just listen, think about it, let it sink in. Okay?"

I nodded, half-expecting to learn that Clem was his long-lost doubles partner from Yale.

He cleared his throat and turned to me, head-on: "Your brother, Clement, is the Messiah."

"What is that, code?"

"No. Listen to me carefully. Clement Blue Chest is the Messiah returned."

I didn't laugh. I didn't say anything. In fact, I was sad for him. Bacon was obviously a bright man, screwy as he was, and even if he'd done a fraction of the things he claimed—hell, even if it was *all* bull and he had never set foot in Central America—he at least seemed to care, which beats hell out of most. And I couldn't deny I had started liking him when he stuck up for Clem in the council meeting. He had won me over somehow, bit by bit, just as No Horse had predicted. And so it made me sad to see that he was deeply out of his skull.

"I thought Jesus was the Messiah," I said.

Bacon put up a finger. "He was *an incarnation* of the Messiah. But God sends the messianic spirit to us repeatedly. The Messiah keeps returning as a mortal man to lead the oppressed, against all odds, out of op-

pression. He repeats his suffering, just as the holy men of the Sioux perform the sun dance not once but *yearly*. It's an eternal recurrence."

I laughed.

"He keeps coming back, Joey. That's what makes him great. He hasn't
retired. He's not up there drinking piña coladas. He never gives up."

"So, you're saying Jesus reincarnated himself in *Clem?*" I kept a
straight face.

"No. The messianic spirit incarnated itself in *both* of them. Jesus isn't
the first or the last. Moses, David, Bar Kokhba, Spartacus, Che, probably
countless others around the globe. As long as men have been oppressed,
they've longed for messiahs to arise. But the deliverance is never total,
never global—it would put an end to history, it would be too easy—so
you have the eternal recurrence instead."

"Look, I've known Clem all my life and—"

"I'm not saying he was *born* the Messiah. The spirit can hit at any time.
Maybe a year ago Clem was the village idiot, but now—"

"You haven't even *met* him."

"I saw him dragging those skulls in a vision, weeks before he dragged
them. And they told me his name."

"Who did?"

"The Thunder Beings."

"Oh," I said, biting my lip. He wouldn't know a Thunder Being if it bit
him in the ass. Neither would I, come to think of it.

"They asked me if I would serve him and I promised, Yes, always."

"I suppose you saw all this when you danced?"

"Yes."

"We were there, you know, Clem, Eli, and me, watching you dance.
You probably saw Clem's face and worked it into your dream."

"It wasn't a dream."

"Fine, your vision. But don't you think that's a possibility?"

"They thundered his name. I saw him on Rushmore." The mention of
Rushmore startled me, then I realized Bear Dreamer might have shot his
mouth off, told someone about Clem's vision.

"Joey, I have to meet him."

"You're gonna get your bubble burst."

"Look, I'm not expecting him to speak Hebrew or Aramaic. I'm just
saying the Great Mystery placed some divinity in him, some wakan, just
as surely as He did in Jesus."

"I'm starting to see why they gave you the boot."

He laughed, shaking his head. "No. They did that long before I came to understand the Eternal Recurrence. They did that when I adopted a lifestyle of *works* rather than faith."

"You don't have faith?"

"Sure I do, but Christ challenged us to perform *works* for each other, not to swear up and down that he rose from the dead. What's the good of faith if it's not a predicate to action? Action toward justice, against oppression. As soon as I started trying to *really* live in the spirit of Jesus, they excommunicated me."

"So, if Jesus lived now, he'd be toting a Kalashnikov and ambushing government troops in El Salvador?"

Bacon didn't bat an eyelash. "There's no question he was a liberation fighter. But from Paul onward, the Church has tried to bury the fact that Christ preached resistance to Rome and that he worked toward expelling the invaders."

"Why would the Church do that?"

"To survive in the empire. Later, it would marry that empire, the very thing Christ struggled against."

"But his struggle wasn't violent."

"No? *I come not to send peace on earth but a sword.* And at the Last Supper he tells his disciples, *He that hath no sword, let him sell his garments and buy one.* Two of them immediately pull swords. A sword is a tool, Joey, neither inherently evil nor good. Its moral worth depends on how you use it. Do you think those LAWs I brought are evil?"

"How *did* you get those weapons, anyway?"

"When we know each other, okay? When you believe in what I'm doing."

"Fine. But about Clem, get one thing straight. He's just a guy with a family. He hasn't got a message. He doesn't even preach."

"What would you have him preach? It's all been said. You Indians, of all people, should know the Messiah would not come as a preacher. He would never come here and threaten you with hell or bribe you with heaven. His way is action. With action, he will inspire others to act, or inspire the oppressors to stop oppressing. It's always one of those two. He'll open their eyes somehow. Either way, he'll shock them so that they begin to see and to feel."

"Well, you're a funny kind of disciple, 'cause you sure can talk," I said.

His face went red, then he smiled. "I'm a windbag. Have been since I was a kid. But I'm serious."

That night, I woke up with the deer rifle against my mouth, the end of the barrel pressing against my upper lips and teeth. But this time I *knew* I didn't want to die. I did *not* want to kill myself, so how did it get there? I tried to pull the barrel off, but couldn't. It jerked in deep and broke off a tooth. I gagged so bad I thought all my organs would come up. The steel was cold and heavy, a lot of weight behind it. A flashlight flicked on, then tipped upward, revealing a sick grin under the brim of a Stetson. "Hey, lover, how's that feel?" It was Pogo.

I couldn't move my tongue. He settled into a tripod stance—his good leg on the floor, his rifle in my mouth, and his peg in my abdomen. The end was sharp and so was the spur.

"Whadja do, get one of your voodoo doctors put a spell on her?"

I tried to speak, but he just plunged the barrel deeper. "You lyin' gut eater. She told me everything. You were fuckin' her under our noses." I couldn't swallow and was choking on saliva and stuff from my stomach. Tears were blasting into my eyes. "Keep sucking, boy," he said. "Now, I want to hear you beg." He pulled the barrel out of my mouth and shoved it up against my nostrils.

I gasped, "You'll spend your life in jail. Ain't worth it."

He laughed. "Sioux season's twelve months a year in South Dakota. Anyway, I got buddies swear I'm drinking with 'em in Cheyenne."

"Don't even breathe," said another voice. The huge shoulders of Pumpkinhead Pawnee-Killer loomed in back of Pogo. Elijah had asked me to put Pumpkin up for a night or two, said we should move him around because of the feds. Probably, Eli's wife was just tired of their bullshitting all night long. Pumpkin had just wanted floor space for his air mattress and I was happy for the company. "Now. Pull that rifle up slow and aim it at the roof," said Pumpkin.

Pogo eased the barrel off my nose and tilted it upward. "We're just fooling around here," said Pogo, forcing a laugh. I saw the dark form of Pawnee-Killer's hand rising, and what looked like a .38 in it. The arm swept down like a hawk on a pigeon. Pogo's neck and head jerked back, then he crumpled down on me. He was heavier than his sister.

"Help me get him in the car," said Pumpkinhead.

The next afternoon, Eli and Pumpkin dropped by with a case of Buds. Old Isaac trailed in a minute later. Eli settled into the couch and tossed me a can. Everyone cracked a beer and slurped off the foam.

"Got a present for you," said Pumpkin from deep in my beanbag chair. He reached into his flak jacket and pulled out the ivory peg. He took the spur off, put it in his breast pocket, then tossed me the ivory. I rested it on my knee and studied the sweat-stained leather straps that Pogo had wedged his stump into every morning. I imagined the shrapnel ripping his leg, him looking up at the sky, disbelieving. Then the long road back, choppers, hospitals, the plane home, endless therapy, then walking, riding. The fucker had spirit, just too dumb to know what to do with it, and now it was gone.

"Batteries not included," said Pumpkin. He and Eli laughed.

"What'd you do with the body?" I asked.

"What do I look like, a killer? I just drove the fucker *deeeep* into the Badlands and stripped his ass. Then Eli and me drove east and dumped his truck in the Missouri."

"Dirty deeds," said Elijah. Then he and Pumpkinhead sang in unison, "Done dirt cheap."

"How deep?" I asked.

"It's way under."

"No, how deep in the Badlands you dump him?"

Pumpkinhead giggled. "Afraid he gonna hop to town and get a posse on you?"

"Only has to make it to a road," I said.

"I slit his Achilles'."

The screen door creaked and I jumped, half-expecting to see Pogo. Everyone laughed.

"Well, if it ain't the craziest fucking sun dancer who ever strode the earth," said Elijah.

"Hey ya, Eli," said Clem, walking in. He looked at Pumpkinhead quizzically. "Is that Harry Pawnee-Killer?"

Pumpkinhead grinned but didn't bother getting up out of the bean-bag. He just held up his hand and said, "Long time since the Knee, eh, buddy? How you been?" It was clear Pawnee-Killer didn't know Clem well, or even remember his name, but he obviously recognized the face from '73, and I'm sure that gave Clem a lot of satisfaction. Pumpkinhead had been a major player, right up there with Banks, Means, and Crow Dog. He was like a hero to Clem.

"Been all right," said Clem, smiling and embarrassed, like a kid meeting a professional athlete.

"Have a cold one," said Pumpkinhead, ripping a can free and tossing it up.

Clem caught it, then bent forward to place it gently on top of the others. "Thanks, but if I have one, well, you know . . ."

"Follow your heart," said Pumpkin with a smile.

"Never seen you say no to the Clydesdale wee-wee," said Elijah.

"Yeah, you have," said Isaac. "That morning he told us 'bout playing chicken with McLaren's truck. Drank the ice 'stead of the beer."

"Oh yeah," said Eli. "That truck musta scared the drunk gene right outa you, eh Clem?"

Clem smiled in that gentle, sheepish way he had, almost a blush, like he hated being the center of attention. He got up from the couch and went into the bathroom, shutting the door behind him. We heard the seat drop.

"What do you guys make of this white dude, Quinn?" I said in a low tone.

"Oh, I think he's on the level," said Isaac.

Pumpkin shook his head. "Not me. I'm the kind that don't trust nobody till I trust 'em."

Eli shrugged. "Well, he saved my boy's life."

"What better way to get him inside?" said Pumpkin.

"He was already inside," said Isaac. "Been tight with Speckled for a couple years now. And he brought us them weapons, don't forget."

"Maybe to lure guys like Pumpkin into the open," I said.

"He ain't no fed," said Isaac. "Too dang crazy."

"Or acting crazy so we don't think he's a fed. I mean, get a load of this," I said, lowering my voice so Clem wouldn't hear in the bathroom. "He says Clem's the Messiah."

"The what?"

"Thinks he's Christ or something."

"He *what*?"

"Seriously," I said, then explained as best I could. They laughed and came to a unanimous decision that I was full of shit.

There was a knock at the door. I jumped again, thinking it was Pogo with his rifle, or his dad. But it was Quinn Bacon that I saw through the screen door. "Well, speak of the devil," said Elijah as I opened it. Quinn was wearing a gray sweatshirt and jeans. I introduced him to the others as though they hadn't already met, because if Clem could hear through the door, it would hurt him needlessly to learn about the Kit Foxes, learn this white guy was in and he wasn't. Bacon said no thanks to a beer but accepted a chair that I brought from the table.

"What's new, Waokiye?" said Pumpkin, pronouncing the Sioux name with exaggerated care and a hint of mockery.

Quinn Bacon smiled and started to say something but stopped at the sound of the toilet flushing. Then came the trumpet sound of the faucet. The bathroom door opened and Clem stepped out, drying his hands on his shirt. "Ought to get a towel, you know, Joey?"

Quinn stood up. Their eyes met and Clem stopped drying his hands. He looked a bit surprised. Then he looked over at me for a clue, like what's *this* guy doin' here? Quinn took three steps forward and put out his hand. "You're Clement Blue Chest." There was a good four feet between them, and his hand waited in space there, in no-man's-land, trembling, waiting to be received and steadied by the mighty grip of the Messiah.

"Yeah, I am," said Clem, putting his hand out slowly. Quinn Bacon didn't so much shake it as grip it. He looked into Clem's eyes, as if expecting to see the eternal flicker of the burning bush in each pupil. Then he looked down at the floor, too humble to introduce himself, or maybe unable to look into the face of God.

"Clem, meet the Mighty Quinn. Quinn Bacon, my brother Clement," I said.

There was a silence. Clem was looking at Quinn and searching for something nice or at least neutral to say. "I saw you dance in June. It seemed to touch something in you," he said.

Quinn nodded slightly, still looking down. Then, lifting his eyes a bit, he said, "I've been trying to meet you. You're hard to find."

"Well, I've been off the rez for a few days," said Clem.

"Oh yeah?" I said. "I didn't know that. Where you been?"

"Oh, just working on the railroad," he said. I didn't know what that meant, but I figured he might have fallen off the wagon and didn't want to talk about it.

"So, what made you want to come out to Pine Ridge and dance the sun dance?" old Isaac asked Quinn.

"This was my third summer dancing. Two years ago, I had a vision in which wonderful things were revealed. The Thunder Beings showed me a leader who would arise and win back the sacred Black Hills for the Sioux and Cheyenne."

Elijah was biting his lip trying not to bust out laughing. He pulled his Stetson down low and held his can in front of his mouth to hide his face. Pumpkin was shaking silently.

Quinn turned to them, completely unfazed by their giggling, and said, "This year the Thunder Beings showed me the same man on top of a mountain in the Black Hills, and they told me his name, showed me his face. This is the man," he said, lifting his hand in Clem's direction.

Pumpkin and Eli lost it, crumpling into fits. Isaac was being more polite, and maybe wondering what this odd little guy's motives were.

"Have you been talkin' to Bear Dreamer Bordeaux?" Clem asked Bacon.

Bacon shook his head. "Never met him."

Clem sat down on the arm of the sofa, stumped.

Bacon spoke to the rest of us: "I swore in the canyon never to divulge information about the Tokalas to anyone *who might do harm to them.* That's how I worded my oath. Therefore, I can speak freely to Clement Blue Chest, for he's *in*capable of harming the Kit Foxes. He *is* the Kit Foxes. He's the very reason they exist again."

"The Tokalas were *your* idea?" I asked.

He shrugged. "Not altogether."

Pumpkinhead's face went from puzzlement to anger, the look of a man who has just learned all his diamonds are paste.

Quinn started telling Clem all about the reborn war society, explaining that he wanted Clem to join and to assume the leadership.

Clem shook his head. "Even if I was worthy, and if the old societies really existed still, I would not try for the Tokalas. I would try for one of the *Napesni,* the No Flight societies, the Badgers or the Sotka Yuhas," he said.

"Why?" asked Bacon.

"They wore long red sashes that they staked to the ground in battle, to make sure they stood their ground. Only a brother could unstake you."

"But the Kit Foxes were the best," said Elijah. "Crazy Horse was Tokala."

"Maybe so. But that night on the road, when McLaren's truck was coming at me. I couldn't understand why I didn't run—"

"Probably 'cause you crapped your pants," said Eli.

Clem smiled at that, then said, "I think it's because I staked my sash down. Or those spirit lights gave me a hand and staked it down for me. Anyway, that's the way I'm gonna make my stand. It's more defensive. I like that."

"Well, what's in it for you?" Eli asked Quinn Bacon.

Bacon paused, probably trying to decide how much to share with these two cynics who had already laughed at his vision. "Something wonderful," he said.

"You mean the chance to work with our Messiah of Muscatel?" asked Elijah, tipping his can in Clem's direction. He and Pumpkin broke into giggles. Clem looked a little hurt by the muscatel crack but clearly didn't understand the Messiah part.

A Bowie knife punched into the wall just above Eli's hat. Bacon swept down on Pumpkin, silent and swift as an owl. He had Pumpkin by a handful of hair, pulling it back hard so the chin tilted up. He had a second knife pressed into Pumpkin's neck, the edge pushing in just above the Adam's apple.

"You two Lerps have seen it all," he spat into Pumpkin's face. "You're so bad-ass you laugh at everything. Everything's a joke. You got so much swagger it makes me want to puke. As if in one war you grasped all the secrets of the universe, and because you couldn't really grasp shit, you decided there are no mysteries. Everything is meaningless. A little jungle training, a little snake meat and rat meat, a few claymores, and suddenly you're diamond-hard, and you're cynical about everything. You're so sure there's no Mystery that you dare laugh at believers. And all because of your precious Vietnam, because you've seen some killing and done some killing and you feel empty. Ah, poor baby. Let me show you the other war, *kola*. The one that's not empty."

He backed off of Pumpkin but commanded him not to move a muscle, and Pumpkin stayed still. Nobody moved. Bacon took off his sweatshirt and pointed to the different scars that I'd seen on the butte. "See that? Electric cattle prods. Those? Cigars, cigarettes. These three? Red-hot irons." He kicked off his sneakers. His toes were a mess. "Pliers. One at a time. Slowly." Then he unsnapped his jeans and ripped them down to his knees. He pulled down his boxers. I saw more scars on his ass, but I also saw the look on Pumpkin's face, and on Eli's and Isaac's, and on Clem's. It was a look of horror and sorrow. I saw tears welling in old Isaac's eyes. Bacon turned so I could see. His testicles were there, but that was all. There was a nub so short it didn't make it out past the hair. "Rose clippers," he said. "They did it slow, slow as they could, but they didn't get one word out of me." He turned to Pumpkin and Eli. "Because God is my strength."

"Who did that?" said Pumpkin.

Bacon pulled his pants up and did his belt.

"They didn't *kill* you?" I heard myself ask. I couldn't believe that the death squads or the police or whoever it was down there would do that, then let him live to bear witness.

"Of *course* they killed me. Shot me in the head and dumped me in a river." He parted his hair and bent forward. There was scar tissue stretched over a depression in the skull. It looked like a deep graze, but a graze. He looked at Eli and Pumpkin. "Everybody's got scars," he said, then turned and walked out.

We were silent for a long time. It was like a bomb had been dropped and no one knew what to say. General state of shock. Finally, old Isaac sighed. "That poor, busted-up son of—"

"You believe him, then?" I asked.

"Doubt he cut his own dick off."

Pumpkinhead took a deep drink from his Bud can. His hand was shaking from having that knife at his throat.

"I got a feeling he's on the level," said Clem.

"'*Course* you do," said Pumpkinhead, sputtering beer. "He says you're the fucking Savior."

We all laughed. Clem, too, but he looked puzzled. I don't think he even knew what the word meant. Probably he was just laughing at the way beer was coming out of Pumpkin's nose. "I just meant I doubt he's a fed," said Clem. "He pierced, went all the way."

Elijah gripped the knife above his head and pulled it from the wall. "Well, he comes on damn sincere, I'll give you that. But he coulda lost his tool a hundred different ways."

Pumpkin picked the ivory peg off the table. "Maybe we ought to fix new straps to this thing and give it to Waokiye." No one laughed, and Pumpkin was still sober enough that he flushed with embarrassment.

"Anyway, his sack's intact," said old Isaac. "And he got plenty of it."

They had a little fire going on top of Eagle Nest Butte, and all around the sky was full with bright stars. The night was cool, and the smoke from the fire smelled good. It was pine in the fire, cones and small branches. Every now and then came a sharp crackle and a swirl of sparks. Sharon and Abel were especially kind and respectful toward Clem, asking him to sit between them. No Horse and Speckled Hawk were cordial. Sharon said she had ridden in a car trailing Clem during the Porcupine-to-Kyle segment of his trek. She couldn't believe anyone could walk so long, much less pierced and dragging buffalo skulls.

Clem smiled and said he remembered almost nothing of it, just the visions.

"Can you tell us what was revealed to you?" asked Abel. "We want to make a stand and don't know where to make it."

"I can't talk too much about the visions," said Clem. "I'm not supposed to. But you talk about making a stand, well, I can tell you this much. In this one vision, me and my brothers and sisters, we make a stand in the Paha Sapa." Not knowing that Bacon spoke Lakota, Clem said to him, "That's the Black Hills. They're sacred to us."

Bacon nodded, then said, "Where in the Black Hills do you make this stand?"

"A place we used to know as the Six Grandfathers. It's very different now. It's been torn up. It's Rushmore now."

You should have seen the look on Speckled Hawk and No Horse's faces. They were stunned by the simplicity of the idea as much as by the boldness.

"That's it," cried Abel Many Coups. He was wearing jeans and a Ranger T-shirt. "It's totally defendable. Apaches and big guns would be out of the question, at least from any angle that could hurt the monument. They wouldn't dare. Plus, the press will be everywhere."

"And they can't do shit 'cause we got four hostages right in the rock," said Pumpkinhead.

"No," said Clem in a surprisingly stern voice. "We come from warriors, not lowlifes. Our fathers had a code and lived by it. You want to look like them PLOs and IRAs, taking hostages and blowing things up? You want to look like Custer when he took those Cheyenne chiefs hostage, then broke his word and murdered them? You want to look like him? End up like him?"

"Fine, but those faces shouldn't be there," Pumpkinhead said.

"We don't hurt one atom of the Black Hills. That mountain suffered enough," Clem said.

"Red paint, then," blurted Abel. "We dump red paint down the faces."

"Like drunken frat boys," Sharon said.

"Sharon's right," Clem offered. "We don't spit on what's sacred to them just because they do it to us. We show a little class. I mean, what are we trying to do? Are we trying to insult the American people or win them over?"

"We're trying to open their eyes," Abel said.

"Right. And you don't do that by making them see red."

"Okay, so if we take Rushmore," said Pumpkinhead, "then what? What are you going to do up there? You've got to have some kind of threat. I mean, what's your leverage?"

"We'll be an embarrassment to the government."

Pawnee-Killer shook his head impatiently. "Once they see you've got nothing rigged to hurt the monument, they'll just drag you down. Swoosh, bang, it's over."

"That's where the *Napesni* come in," Clem said.

"What are the *Napesni?*" asked Abel.

Clem smiled. "The No Flights." He turned to Speckled Hawk: "You remember about the No Flight societies? I will stake my sash down, just like a Sotka Yuha or a Badger."

"What *sash?*" said No Horse with a hint of derision.

"I will chain myself to that mountain, right on one of them heads, just like they staked their sashes down and held their ground. My sash will be a chain. We will hold our ground."

"So you stake yourself down, then what?" asked Pumpkin.

"Starve," said Clem.

Quinn Bacon sighed with disappointment. "You mean passive nonviolent resistance?"

"If you want to make a mouthful of it," said Clem. "I was thinking hunger strike."

Bacon leaned forward. "But look at the history, massacres, congressional cover-ups, sealed records. And all the disappearances in the seventies of folks who opposed more land transfers. Nonviolence can work against a decent opponent, like when Gandhi used it on the British, but we're talking about Congress, the guys who financed the death squads in El Salvador and Guatemala, and the GOON squads on Pine Ridge. There's uranium in those hills, and Congress plays hardball, Clem."

Abel nodded. "They'll cut your chain and drag you down before you miss a meal. Before the press arrives. You won't even make the six o'clock news."

Clem was silent. We all were. Pinecones popped in the fire, launching sparks against the starry night. Pumpkinhead cleared his throat. "We've got to be like the ants, the way they got their workers and their warriors. We should have Clem and the other hunger strikers chained down on top of the monument for the world to see, but we also must have warriors to protect their position, secure it, so that the feds can't storm in and drag 'em down. This way the hunger strike can last long enough for us to get the message out. We'll have a third group that deals with the press, tells about the treaties and how we just want what's ours by law. We can avoid violence, Clem, but only by bringing arms. A show of arms. They've got to know that if they act with force against our nonviolence, we can respond with force. Without that, they'll just kick our teeth in up there." He turned and looked Clem in the eye. "Bringing weapons is the only way you're going to lose weight on that rock, my friend. The only way."

"But I didn't see weapons in my vision," my brother said, puzzled.

"That's because we won't have to fire 'em," said Pumpkin. "It's a deterrence, is all."

Bacon and I drove to Rapid, then headed up 16 into the Black Hills. Keystone is the closest town to Rushmore. It's about a mile from the monument, more of a prop town than a real one. All the buildings are tourist shops, selling trinkets of Black Hills gold, and war bonnets and tomahawks made in Japan. And you've got "chuck wagons" left and right selling buffalo burgers, and prop shops where you can have your photo taken in a cavalry uniform or a Buffalo Bill or Calamity Jane getup. There are a couple of small motels, but no homes. The town is really nothing more than a hundred-yard strip of these joints and their flashing neon signs. Even in broad day, the signs are humming and glowing over the wooden boardwalk. This creation is nestled in a ravine of beautiful, dark pines. At the end of town is a small helicopter pad and a chopper that takes people up for a view of the monument and the surrounding hills.

We went into the office to inquire about a ride. A woman with huge mammaries and short blond hair snapped gum behind the counter. She looked blankly at Bacon as he explained that we were filming a documentary and wanted to take some aerial footage of the monument and the Hills. She shrugged. "Sure, I'll get the pilot." She disappeared into a back room.

A heavyset guy came out, wiping burger juice from his chin. He put out his hand across the counter and said, "Name's Larry. What can I do for you?" He had a large mouth and a gap between his teeth. He had a receding hairline and a shiny forehead.

Bacon explained the situation, that we were with the Smithsonian Institution in D.C. and making a documentary on the geological history of the Dakotas. He introduced me as his cameraman, José Martínez. Larry nodded and said, "Let me finish my burger and I'll take you up straightaway. By the way, what's it gonna be, the forty-dollar ride or the sixty?"

"What's the difference?" asked Bacon.

"Twenty bucks," said Larry, showing his gap and winking. Then he explained. "The sixty-buck ride actually circles the monument. That's a head, of course. Hundred and twenty total."

"That'll be fine," said Bacon. "Cash still okay in this part of the world?"

"Cash is great." Larry beamed.

"'Course, I'll need a receipt for the Smithsonian," said Quinn, handing him some bills.

"You betcha."

I hadn't been in a chopper since the war, and I've got to admit that even a little dragonfly like this one felt good. Within seconds of lifting off, Keystone looked like the toy village that it is. As we rose, the hills revealed their hidden valleys and ravines, their secret caches of cool beauty, deep pine and blue spruce, shimmering springs and flashing lakes. Seeing this lushness against the parched and yellow-gray backdrop of endless plains made it easy to understand why my forefathers believed these Hills to be the home of Wakan Tanka, and why they fought so much longer and more fiercely than other tribes. They were zealots, defending not just their home but the throne of God.

The heads of the four presidents appeared, glinting bright and chalky. The scale was shocking and the artistry stunning. They looked noble and majestic, yet so forced and unnatural—blasted into that tranquil and timeless garden of rock and spruce. Blasted. I felt a mix of awe, anger, and deep sadness at the irreversibility of it. Below me was the starkest definition of the differences between us and them. They were so ready to change the earth, to mine it, to make it serve them and glorify them, that they were willing to make mountains over in their own image. Mountains into mirrors. And if the earth offered resistance, they would blast it harder and explode it with more dynamite, just as they had blasted into

the bowels of the Hills for gold, coal, and now uranium, just as they had
blasted us with howitzers and exploding shells when we resisted. Perhaps
we Sioux would never have been capable of such monumental art, what
with our Stone Age tools and simple ways. But neither did we possess the
spiritual depravity to even dream of doing that to the earth.

"I take her up maybe ten times a day," said Larry. "And I still get a
lump in my throat every time I see those faces."

"You ought to get it looked at," said Bacon.

"Say again," said Larry.

Bacon shook his head.

I started filming as we circled, and I tried to spy fortifications or ob-
servation posts along the mountainside. There didn't seem to be anything
like that. Probably they sent park rangers up once or twice a day but that
was it. Maybe they had electric eyes and even hidden cameras in the
woods along the ascent, to alert some kind of a response team. But there
were no physical barriers to speak of, no guardhouses or anything like
that. On all sides but the southeast, it was cliffs. The gradient from the
southeast was easily hikable. The only deterrents to speak of were the
signs Bacon and I had seen nailed to trees at the foot of the slope when
we had visited the previous week. They promised six months in jail and
a $5,000 fine to anyone who ventured beyond.

Through the thunder of the blades, she crooned softly. *It was so much
like today, the day you had your empty vision, bright and full of chopper-
throbbing above the humming jungle heat. A sound within a sound, like
me in you. A kid from the Eighty-second flailed his arms up at you. Not at
God, but you, Joey. His squad was frozen. Mines, you thought. Poor grunts,
you thought. Chest-deep was he in peasant paddy. You helped Bill pull him
through the door, then saw he had no legs, and genitals no more, just shreds
in brilliant reds, a jagged, pearl-white pelvis, gleaming, splintered sharply.
Needles of bone and threads of gore, so at odds with his pasty face and owl
eyes. Halfway home, his intestines slithered across the floor—remember?
Slithered into the sunlit patch near your door, snakes quitting caves to
warm themselves in morning rays. By your boot. What a hoot when you
screamed and spat up faith.*

Back on the ground, stepping off the pad, Bacon explained to Larry
that we needed an aerial shot of sunrise on the faces. "How much extra
would it cost for you to take us up a bit before sunrise? Say in a week or
ten days?"

Larry stroked his chin. "That sure *would* be a beautiful shot. Tell you what. If you mention Keystone Air in the credits, you can have the next flight for free."

"You're a good man, Larry," said Bacon as they shook on it.

Larry handed him a card and said, "Just call me a couple days in advance."

"And we can really count on you to wake up that early?"

"Tell you what. That second one there is my home number. You can give me a wake-up call early as you want." They shook hands once more, and we left.

◆

Neither of us spoke for most of the drive back to Pine Ridge. I think we were both struck with awe at how takable Rushmore appeared. It was exhilarating but also scary, for I started believing that we would actually do it—and that's scary. But what terrified me was the thought that the diva would come along, just as she had come in the chopper. She might taunt me, warp my judgment, make me do something wrongheaded that could result in exchange of fire, in death, in many deaths. The only responsible thing to do, it seemed, was to exclude myself from the operation. I knew this would brand me a coward, and I wondered if I was.

"Do you believe in exorcisms?" I said, breaking the silence.

Bacon looked over at me, surprised by the question. "You mean, do I believe they can help people?"

I nodded.

"I believe the mind is deeply impressionable, open to the power of suggestion. Why do you ask?"

I told him about the diva. He listened quietly, respectfully. I told him what my concern was regarding Rushmore. I saw a muscle working in his jaw. When I finished, he said, "Joey, hearing a voice doesn't mean you're unsound. We've all heard voices at some point in our lives."

"But this one, it . . . it isn't good," I said.

"You think it's a demon?" he asked with a smile. "Remember what Nietzsche said, 'Think twice before casting out your demons, you may cast out the best part of you.' "

"I'm not saying it's a demon. I'm not saying it's not. Maybe it's a symptom."

"Of what?" he asked.

"I don't know. A schizophrenic brain about to melt down. I only know it's not the best part of me. I wouldn't mind at all casting it out."

"You don't seem schizophrenic to me. Has it made you do anything violent?"

"It tried."

"In other words, this voice or diva, or whatever it is, has never succeeded in making you lose control, right? It's never made you do anything irrational?"

"I'm still here."

"Okay, then."

"Okay what?"

"Ride it out. If you get weird, we'll get you off the mountain. But you've got to come. I mean, who knows what it could do to morale if Clem's own brother were to back out now? Everyone else might back out, too."

He was right. I hadn't thought of that. "Do you know what a Yuwipi is?" I asked.

"I sure do."

"No Horse is doing a Yuwipi for me tonight," I said.

"That's good. I've heard amazing things about the Yuwipi."

"Yeah, we all have, but it's always about a friend of a friend of a distant cousin."

"Isn't No Horse a good Yuwipi man?"

"I don't know. Look, if it doesn't work, can you do . . . like an exorcism?"

"The smart money's on your Yuwipi," he said.

First, we took the furniture out of No Horse's house and waited for the singers to show. "Singers are key," said No Horse. "Spirits won't come without 'em."

Pumpkinhead, Elijah, and Clem started nailing blankets over the windows, so that not even moonlight would come in. There was a guy who had come with Pumpkin named Ajax Whirlwind Horse. He was from Standing Rock. Pumpkin said they'd been buddies back in AIM and that Ajax was a good man. Dependable. "More dependable than his goddamn car. Piece of crap broke down near Kyle and we had to hitch. Got a ride from that old priest, O'Reilly. When the hell's he gonna croak, anyway?"

"Did he recognize you?" I asked. "He's the type that would turn you in without a second thought."

"He wouldn't know me from Adam. Hasn't seen me since fourth grade."

My stomach knotted up as Sharon Takes Gun entered the house. She was one of the last people I wanted to have learning about the diva. "Hey, Astro Man," she said, coming up to me and smiling brightly. "So there *is* more than science, eh?" She touched my arm reassuringly and said,

"No Horse is great. I had real bad spirits talking at me for two years until he did a Yuwipi for me. I come to all his Yuwipis now to help out, try to give something back." I wondered if she made that up about the voices to make me relax, or better still, to make me believe.

When the drummers and singers showed, No Horse lit a kerosene lantern, placed it on the floor, then shut the door and nailed a blanket over the cracks of the jamb. He lit a braid of sweetgrass and purified the room with it, wafting it over everybody. They drummed and sang for a while and prayed with the pipe, passing it around. The kinnikinnick was soothing and sweet.

Then we got down to business. Two assistants tied No Horse's hands behind his back with leather thongs, interlacing his fingers with rawhide bowstring, tying them tightly together. The wrists were also bound. They tied him at the ankles, knees, and thighs. They rolled him up in a quilted star blanket. It covered and overlapped his feet and head. This was bound around him, mummy fashion, with more rawhide thongs. In the old days, the Yuwipi man was wrapped in a huge buffalo hide and then tied up, just the way you prepare a corpse for the scaffold. The idea is that he's got to die to communicate with the other side. I was invited to tie some of those knots and I did. Tight.

Near the lantern was the altar with a buffalo skull and red, yellow, black, and white pennants symbolizing the four directions. A number of gourd rattles were also laid out. Everybody was seated in a circle around the altar and the horizontal mummy form of No Horse's body. The drummers and singers started up again, chanting some songs in old Lakota. One of the assistants, a kid with long hair and pimples, blew out the lamp. Everything went black. Just a black universe. No more pimples. No more altar. The chanting and the drum seemed to come now from inside me, and all the things of daily life that occupy our minds and distract us from the timelessness of the other side—all these material and trivial things vanished.

I had heard so many Yuwipi stories I didn't know what to expect. The Yuwipi is a crazy, crazy thing, but it gets results. It's a great healing agent, but that's not all. If you lose something, or someone steals your horse, you can go to a Yuwipi man and he'll get himself tied up in the blanket and thongs, and invite the spirits from the other side, enticing them with little flesh and tobacco offerings and of course with all these old songs. It's claimed that the spirits get right in the blanket with him. It is they who untie and free him. But first they tell him where your horse is, or your wallet, or whatever it is you lost. Even the anthropologists can't explain it. There were some anthros who put a wad of cash in a tin can and hid the can in a creek, then said to Frank Fools Crow that if he could find it, he could have it. The spirits didn't just tell him where it was, they brought it to him, can and all, same serial numbers on the bills. I've heard tell of stolen saddles and such materializing, too, but usually the whereabouts of the missing object is revealed to the Yuwipi man in a vision while he's in the blanket, and then, after the spirits untie him, he just tells you where to find your property.

The way it works for healing is similar. The spirits reveal a vision in the blanket, but this time it is a vision of medication. A root or a plant may be revealed, as well as its location and how to prepare it. Or the spirits might just heal you on the spot without prescriptions. I know a guy in Kyle who swears his tumor disappeared within three days after a Yuwipi, a tumor he'd had for years. And you hear all kinds of stories of full recoveries from all sorts of awful things. So even if it's just faith healing by creating a huge placebo effect with a lot of song and dance and mystical show, recovery is recovery, and I was in a hell of a foxhole.

I had heard stories about Yuwipi men sometimes flying through the room, lifted by the spirits and the Thunder Beings, the winged ones. I don't think that happened in my Yuwipi, but other things did. As the singing and drumming went on inside me, there was a heavy crashing on the floor, like someone lifting and dropping an anvil on the planks, and then there were many little blue sparks appearing all over the place. Probably, it *was* an anvil or a big rock that one of the assistants was banging for effect, as if the spirits were trying to break through from the *other side.* I wondered if the little blue sparks were just lighters without fluid. But they were more than sparks. They were something between a spark and the glow of a firefly. Then something struck me hard against the cheek, making a sharp rattling sound. It started orbiting my head. It sounded like one of the gourd rattles. Soon there were many of them around me. I reached out but felt no one standing there. I would say there were four or five of these gourds, and they started hitting my shins and then my shoulders and my head. From the other side of the room one of the drummers called out in a shrill voice, in Lakota, "You do *not* believe." I was more concerned with stopping these people from thrashing me with their rattles than I was with answering him right away, so I concentrated on one that was rattling near my left ear. Thrusting both hands in its direction, I grabbed it. I had the entire thing in my grip, in both my hands. There wasn't anybody else holding it. It vibrated harder and harder as if in a mounting rage. I got scared and let it go. Then, I swear to God, it flew from my hands and punched me on the nose. But I mean it bopped me *hard*. I had tears in my eyes. Then it flew away. They all flew away.

I don't care who you are, when something like that happens to you, you start believing. You may not believe it a week later, or even the next morning, but at that moment, you be*lieve*. And that's exactly what I cried out into the darkness. "I believe."

"Why are you having this Yuwipi?" came a voice that was not a voice. It asked neither in Lakota nor in English. I don't know how to describe it. I just know that that's what I was being asked.

I started to respond but then heard No Horse call out from within the blanket, "There is one among us who is haunted by voices, by spirits that are unknown to us."

An eagle cried out, very shrill, very loud, and I heard the beating of wings, even felt the powerful downdraft of those wings. I had goose pimples in the usual places plus inside my nose, my intestines, everywhere. I couldn't figure how such a massive bird could stay aloft in so small a space. The chanting and drumming stopped suddenly. That same moment, someone lit a match and put it to the kerosene lamp. It was No Horse holding the match. He turned up the flame and sat back on his heels. I searched the ceiling for the eagle. The blankets on the windows and door were still in place. Everyone was sitting just the way they had been and there was no bird anywhere. The star blanket was folded neatly a few feet from the altar, and the rawhide thongs were neatly coiled on top of it. The lights had only been out a minute or two, so I couldn't understand how anyone could untie him so fast. With the same match, No Horse lit his pipe. He got it going with four long drags, then passed it to the left. I couldn't believe the ceremony was already over. He got off his heels and sat cross-legged, his eyes on me. "It is done," he said in English. "That spirit will bother you no more forever, Joey." A rush of happiness and a sense of well-being flooded through me—through my toes and fingers, through the core of my body, my heart, my brain. I felt it everywhere, in every cell. I looked through the golden light cast by the kerosene lantern at this childhood rival, this classmate from the Mission school who had had the balls in seventh grade to rebel and travel his own path, and I silently thanked him for my life.

Then the front door blasted off its hinges and landed on the floor, skidding into the circle of seated people. A blinding light flooded through the doorway. I wondered about spirit lights and whether I was in the midst of something wonderful.

I heard the *pffhu, pffhu, pffhu* of mortar tubes or grenade launchers. Something whistled through the door, slammed into the back wall, and spun across the floor. Pumpkinhead jumped on it, covering it with his big chest. Next was the sound of glass breaking. A blanket hanging over a window billowed inward, as if punched by two fists from the other side. The fists tumbled down the blanket, hitting the floor with a clank and a clunk. Sharon lunged for one of them. I scrambled for the other. I could understand Pumpkinhead's automatic reflex. He had done a long stint in the Corps. But Sharon, man, that blew me away. If I hadn't seen her doing it, I would have chickened out. I know I would have because even as I lunged for it, I was thinking what a damn shame to kiss my life away fifteen seconds after being cured, fifteen seconds after being freed of the diva.

I heard hacking and coughing from people in Pumpkin's part of the room. Someone cried "Gas!" I unclenched my eyes. Pumpkin was up on his knees, backing away from a growing cloud, trying to wave it away from his face. Sharon and I got to our knees. I saw tears coming down her cheeks, which I guess were tears of joyful relief, because the cloud from Pumpkin's canister hadn't reached us yet. She smiled. Then my canister blew, then hers did.

My eyes and lungs burned—I mean *burned.* Everyone was hacking. Through it all, though, I felt tremendous relief. One more lease on life, I thought. One more shot at the mountain. And there flashed across my mind a realization that I loved Sharon, fell for her the moment I saw her lunging. And it was okay to love her, because I was healthy now.

A huge voice crackled, "The house is surrounded by federal agents. File out the door slowly, one at a time, hands on your heads. The windows and back are covered. Don't even think it."

People moved toward the door, squinting into the bright lights. Then came the thunder of a chopper overhead. It must have just arrived, must've been hovering a couple of miles away, waiting for the word to swoop in. No Horse's old plank house shivered under the thrashing rotors. You could feel it in your feet, feel it in the floor. I had my shirt pulled up to my mouth and nose, not that it did much.

From the doorway, I saw the high beams of twelve or more vehicles. Here and there, I saw the silhouette of a crouching fed. Then the chopper turned on its flood lamp, lighting everything like a small sun at high noon.

Three feds were on their bellies, just twenty feet in front of the door, M-16s pointed right up my nose. Others flanked them, standing and crouching, also with M-16s on me. There were two on each side of the doorway, one crouching, one standing, the crouchers with M-16s, the standing ones with pistols. They were decked out in camouflage and wore flak vests, combat boots, and SWAT hats. Others crouched behind their open car doors and aimed from behind their headlights. They were everywhere, some scurrying from car to car, some crawling on their elbows, others off in the brush. Two more choppers showed up, beaming more light in. Vultures and ants racing for the same piece of meat. A big feed they could smell.

I was probably the fourth one out the door. They had two of No Horse's singers and one of the drummers already lying on the ground, faces in the dirt, hands on their heads. A couple of feds covered them with M-16s while two others searched them, one doing the actual frisk, the other pressing the barrel of his rifle into the base of the skull. A fed from the corner of the house ran up to me, aiming his 16 at my temple and barking through a gas mask, "Hands on your head, motherfucker!" He looked like the Grim Reaper in that mask. I stopped pressing my shirt to my nose and did what he said. "Now, move it!" he barked, giving me a jab with the end of his rifle. I came down off the step, facing all their high beams. He was on my right shoulder, facing the house. As I walked forward, he walked backward, keeping an eye on the doorway. He walked me like that at rifle point to where the others were being searched. "All right, limp dick, lay down! Now!" So I lay down next to this drummer kid. He was really just a kid, maybe fifteen, sixteen tops, and there were tears running down his face. A fed pressed an M-16 to his head, really leaning on it, while another guy searched him. This kid didn't know *what* was happening, and the tears just kept coming.

"It's okay, little brother," I said.

"Shut your fucking hole," said one of the feds, kicking me in the ribs with his combat boot. That made it tough to keep my hands on my head. My body wanted to crumple into a ball, and I wanted to hold my belly. Then I felt the barrel of somebody's 16 pressing on my skull. The prick was really leaning on it, too. I thought my scalp was going to rip and that the bone might cave in. The other fucker started frisking me, started at my ankles and worked his way up.

"All right, hold those four over by the tree," one of them commanded. One of these Rambos led us to No Horse's cottonwood and sat us down there under it. Three others stood guard over us. The safeties on their rifles were off.

The next four to be laid out and frisked were No Horse, Sharon, Clem, and another of the drummers. Sharon got the same shakedown and barrel to the skull that we all did. No respect. These fuckers didn't respect anything. Then they were brought over to us. Clem was silent.

When Pumpkinhead was marched with some others to the frisking area, a voice crackled over a bullhorn from the direction of the cars, "That's him, third from left. The tall one. Harry Pawnee-Killer, this is *your* life." Three feds dropped to firing position, weapons trained on Pumpkin. His hands were already on his head, so all he could do further not to get shot was freeze. Two men ran over from the cars. It was those agents Maxwell and Dexter. Salt and pepper. They wore cammy jackets but had their fancy suits on underneath, trousers and silk ties flapping in the rotor wind.

They put Pumpkinhead on his belly and frisked him. Agent Dexter read him something off a card. I couldn't hear for sure what Dexter was saying because of the choppers, but he was reading off a card in the palm of his hand, so I guess it was his "rights." I wondered if they would violate your rights a little less if they bothered memorizing the fucking thing. Anyway, the only rights we ever had with these people were in the treaties, so how much could these ones on index cards be worth?

They cuffed him behind his back and brought him within a few yards of where we were sitting. The Rambos held him at gunpoint, jabbing him now and then for fun. Maxwell called for a car. A dark Ford Taurus sedan pulled up. They put him in the backseat, but before they could shut the door, Pumpkin blocked it with his boot, leaned his head out and shouted to us, "Hey, all my relatives. I will be like Waokiye. God is my strength." Which I took to mean, *They won't get a word out of me, so don't abort. Take Rushmore. Take it. Take it. Take it.*

The Taurus pulled out and so did one of the choppers. Maxwell slapped Dexter on the back as they passed us and said, "Fifteen years I've wanted that fucker." Then he turned to us and said, "Which one of you is No Horse?"

No Horse looked up and said he was.

"That your house?"

No Horse nodded.

Dexter started reading him his rights.

"What'd I do?" asked No Horse.

"Harbored a fugitive."

"He came to a healing ceremony."

Maxwell just smiled.

"I'm a spiritual leader," No Horse said. "You arrest priests for not phoning in fugitives?"

Maxwell smiled wider.

They brought another car around, stuck him in it and slammed the door.

Sharon was praying softly in Lakota, with a pipe.

"You gonna make-um big rain, little momma?" said one of the Rambos, squirting chew juice. "Heap-big rain wash away bad white man?"

His buddy laughed and bent down to examine Sharon's medicine pouch, which hung from her neck on a thong. "Hey, baby, what's this, Soap on a Rope?"

She dropped the pipe into her lap, punched his arm, and jerked the pouch out of his grip. He jumped back two steps, as if a snake had struck. Then he laughed, but it was a forced and nervous laugh. He was spooked by her strength. "Feisty, ain't she?" he said.

"You don't mess with their feed bags," said the first.

To regain his dignity, the other one stepped back toward her: "Come on, sweet pea, lemme see it. I know about them medicine bags. Bogeyman won't get you. I swear it. Be nice."

My head was spinning. I mean, a few minutes ago, I was undergoing this Yuwipi, most of which I had sat through wondering whether it was bull or whether there might actually be something to it. Then the gourd came along and beat down my skepticism, opened the door to belief. And now the tear gas, choppers, and Bureau pigs, who are *nothing* like on their TV show, start me doubting all over again, get me wondering why those rattles—if they really were animated by spirits—why they didn't warn us? If they can tell a Yuwipi man where a lost horse is, or where to find a healing herb, why couldn't they tell No Horse there was an army of feds approaching? Something didn't add up.

But Sharon kept praying with her pipe as if those pigs weren't even there. She was such a vision of faith that I started thinking about White Buffalo Calf Woman, who brought the pipe to the Sioux many hundreds of years ago and taught us how to pray. Suddenly, Bacon seemed less crazy to me for thinking my brother was the Messiah. Not that I agreed with him or even believed Sharon was White Buffalo Calf Woman, but it was as if *something* of her had entered Sharon. It's just a weird feeling that gets under your skin. And what's the harm in perceiving some holiness in your brothers and sisters? I mean, if it gives you strength. And if they seem to live up to it.

Two Rambos walked up with Ajax Whirlwind Horse on the end of their rifles. He was cuffed behind the back. These guys were gung-ho, even their faces were camouflaged with black greasepaint.

"Whadya got?" asked Dexter.

"Caught him darting out the back," said one of them. "Found this on him, too," he said, holding up a .38 snub-nose and handing it to Dexter. I got the feeling these Rambos weren't crazy about having to report to a black superior. They looked like spooky Al Jolsons in their blackface.

"What's your name?" asked Dexter.

Ajax kept his mouth shut. One of the Rambos handed Ajax's wallet to Dexter and said, "Minnesota license. Says his name is John Lame."

Dexter examined the gun with his long black fingers. "Well, Mr. Lame, it appears your weapon has lost its serial number."

Ajax said nothing. Dexter told the Rambos to read him his rights and put him in the back with No Horse. When Ajax bent forward to get in, I could see his hands were bluish-black. That's how tight the cuffs were fastened. They were those plastic cuffs that you can make tight as a noose. Ajax settled onto the seat but quickly stuck his leg in the door before they could close it. "Hey, Shaft," he said. Dexter turned and looked at him.

"That's right, baby. I'm talking to you. Just a buffalo soldier. Man says, *Sic 'em, boy.* You say, *How high?* and you sic away on us, like them buffalo soldiers did. Man tosses you a bone. *Atta boy.* Bone for ob*eee*dience. Lapdog happy now, sits, begs, rolls over for the man, gets another bone tossed his way. Nice suit, fancy badge. But the man ain't never gonna let his dog sit at the table. Is he, Rufus?"

I saw Dexter's big Adam's apple move up his throat, quiver slightly, then slide back down to where it hovered above the starched collar and the silk tie knot. "Get your leg in the car," he said, barely controlling his voice. He slammed the door and walked off. For a split second, I felt sorry for Agent Dexter. But Ajax was right, those buffalo soldiers were just attack dogs. They had no quarrel with us. But what's also true—and it breaks my heart—is that even Crazy Horse, once penned up on the rez, finally chose to scout for the Army against the Crow. Just like the Pawnee scouted against us.

Maxwell and some agents came out of the house, still in masks. They were carrying the rattles, sacred eagle feathers, and the buffalo skull.

They dumped it all in the dirt near the car, just dropped it like it was junk. Maxwell took off his gas mask and noticed a second prisoner in the back of the car. "Who've you got?"

"John Lame," said Dexter.

Maxwell opened up the door and bent forward to take a better look. He turned back real slow and looked up at Dexter. "John Lame, my ass. That's that fucking Ajax Whirlwind Horse." He stuck his head back in the window. "Where the *hell* you been hiding all these years?"

Ajax said nothing.

"Where'd you nab him?" Maxwell asked.

"Round back," said a greased-face Rambo.

"Was he packing?"

"A thirty-eight, loaded," he said.

Maxwell shook his head. "Should've shot the cocksucker right there. Wouldn't even have to flake him." They took their prisoners and cleared out as quick as they must have come.

◆

I helped clean up No Horse's place, then gave Sharon a lift home. We'd been through quite a bit together that night, but when she got in my car, I was nervous like on a date. After some silent miles, I managed to say, "I can't believe how quickly you jumped on that grenade—that canister, I mean. Did you know it was tear gas?"

She shook her head and whispered no. The light of the dashboard glowed lightly on her skin. "I was at my uncle's in '75 when the GOONs drove by, lobbed a grenade in. I lost two cousins."

"I'm sorry," I said.

"It was a long time ago."

"I don't think I could have done it if I hadn't seen you diving first," I said.

She studied me, a slight smile on her face, her even teeth picking up the glow of the dash. "That's silly."

"Why?"

"We did it for the same reason."

"And what's that?"

"Your brother," she said.

I didn't know what to say to that, so I just murmured, "Yeah."

We drove for quite a while on a gravel road, then I turned onto a dirt one that leads through a prairie to her place. "Pull over here, okay?" she said when we were still a hundred yards or more from her house. "I don't want to wake my folks."

I turned off the road and into a field. Tall grass and weeds rushed into the beams of the headlights, slapping the grille, caressing the rusty underbelly of the car with long, rasping strokes. I stopped, cut the lights, the engine. Absolute silence, then crickets.

We got out and closed the doors real slow, leaning into them to click them quietly shut. I walked around to her side. "Wow, there's a lot of stars tonight," she exclaimed, her head tilted back. I felt like kissing her, but it didn't seem right given all we'd been through in the last few hours. "Seems the longer you look, the more of them appear," she said, still looking up.

"That's your eyes adjusting."

"How many are there?"

"Hard to say. Always some dying and others getting born."

"Hasn't anyone ever counted them?"

"You can't. I mean, some of them look like lone stars but they're actually clusters. Hell, some are entire galaxies, but they're so far away they look like one point of light. You'd be off by billions. Take that fuzzy one there," I said, pointing and leaning over her shoulder to line it up. "That's Andromeda. It's a galaxy, billions of solar systems in it. About two billion suns in that one galaxy. But it's so far away it seems to us like a single star. It's much bigger than our own galaxy."

"How far *is* it?"

I explained to her what light-years are, then told her Andromeda was more than two million light-years away.

"No way!" she said, taking her eyes off the sky and looking at me.

"And that's the closest galaxy. There are billions of them farther out. But even stars in our own galaxy are hard to count. Know why?"

She shook her head.

"Some of them don't even exist. You *think* you see them, but you don't. They're not really there."

"I don't get it."

"They burned out long ago. They're gone forever, *mashke*. But they were so distant that their light is still traveling to us, still crossing the universe to make that all-important rendezvous with Miss Mystical Winchinchala 1990."

She laughed for a moment at the crack, then looked some more at the stars in silence. "So, it's like ghost light," she said in a sober tone. "Like spirit lights."

"If you like." I touched her shoulder with my hand. We started walking toward her house.

"How do you know which are which?"

"What?"

"The ghost stars from the still-burning?"

"There's a way, but I forgot. Or never got that far. It's very mathematical." We crunched through the dry grass for a while in silence.

As we approached her folks' house, she slipped her hand in mine and said, "Good night, Joe Moves Camp." Then she kissed me on the cheek. The kiss was quick but left a lingering warmth on my skin. For a split second, I imagined how a real kiss with her would feel: the firmness of that broad arc of teeth from behind those soft lips, the warmth and gentleness of her tongue. But I was too slow. Her slender silhouette was already floating through the weeds toward the little shack she grew up in. But then she turned around, and in five steps was back in front of me. She held her hand out between us, and gazed into my eyes. I didn't know if I was supposed to shake her hand or what. And she didn't explain. Her eyes gave no hint. They just kept looking into mine. I figured it was a handshake she wanted, and that it was her way of saying we were friends now—that she wouldn't needle me anymore, that I had won her respect, or at least her understanding—but that we were to be friends and not more than friends. Deflated, I placed my hand in hers, her smooth fingers closing lightly on it. She held it out there in the space between us for a while, as if weighing it, weighing me, my worth. Then she raised it slowly toward her face, and tilted her head down to meet it. Her thick hair fell forward on either side of my wrist. I felt her lips touch my skin. She must have held her lips to the back of my hand for three seconds, maybe more. The moist warmth went straight through me to the center of my brain, then down my spine. There was heat in my chest and I thought my knees would give out. Her head tilted up off my hand and her eyes took me in again, large and wide like the eyes of a deer. "Night, Joey," she said, then slipped away into the house.

Bacon was waiting at my shack. "I heard about the raid."

"I'll *bet* you did."

"What, I'm the enemy again?"

"Funny how these old AIMers turn up on account of your weapons, then *swoosh,* the dragnet comes down."

"Don't you think they would have extracted me at this point?"

That made sense. I shrugged.

"Look, I heard they busted No Horse and Pawnee-Killer."

"Yeah."

"We've got to move the schedule up," he said.

"Why?"

"They could crack."

"Maybe they're stronger than you think, Quinn. Maybe you're not the only pair of brass balls on the planet." It angered me that he had so little esteem for men who had virtually invoked his name while being led off.

"They may hold out awhile," he said. "They may not even get beaten in a way that leaves marks. But every other trick will be used, including booze, and threats of hanging them in their cells like it's suicide, threats to their families, threats of shooting them while they're trying to *escape,*

you name it. Meanwhile, the nice fed will pop in every now and then offering promises of relocation, new identities, steady incomes, if they just
play ball. Sure, maybe they won't talk, but I figure we've got two, possibly three days."

"We need a day to get the rest of the food together."

He nodded. "I'll call the chopper guy, tell him we want to move the
flight up."

"What if he can't?"

Bacon shrugged. "We don't need it. It was just for style," he said, flashing a grin. Then he paused and his expression changed.

"What is it?" I asked.

"It's possible the feds have figured out who I am, so—"

"You're not a priest?"

"Oh, I am, very much so, but listen, I've got to lay low. Go to my tent,
okay? It's out in back of Speckled Hawk's place. In a thicket. Speckled,
Isaac, No Horse, Sharon, and I have been working on a letter to the press.
It's taped to the bottom of my typewriter. Photocopy it at Crazy Horse,
but don't let the secretaries or anybody see what it is. Make around forty
copies. We'll mail them the night before we move on Rushmore."

Bacon's tent was large, the kind you can stand up in. The canvas was a
sun-bleached yellow, so everything was bright and cheerful inside. It felt
airy, and yet it was cramped because of all these piles of books all over the
place. On the desk, which was a door laid over two wooden horses, there
sat an ancient black typewriter. I turned it on its side and found the press
release.

I poked around a bit before I left. The stacks of books on the tent floor
were arranged by subject. There was philosophy, theology, American and
European history, history of the Church, of the Reformation, and there
was another stack of books in Spanish. There were books on the Dead
Sea Scrolls and histories of the Jewish Wars by Josephus and Pliny. And
there were books about the Sioux, and a Lakota-English dictionary.

He had an upside-down vegetable crate for a night table. On it were
a kerosene lamp, a Bible, and about six Nietzsche books. There was a
funny-looking crucifix hanging over the bed. It was two wooden sticks
lashed together with a rawhide string. Each stick had a sharpened point
and was darkly stained along the shaft. Clearly, he had made it out of his
piercing skewers. I put the press release inside my shirt, made sure my
tails were tucked in, then I left.

LETTER TO THE PRESS

The Lakota (Sioux) Nation greets you from the heart of our sacred Black Hills. We are camped on one of our most sacred sites, a granite ridge known to us for generations as the Six Grandfathers. This same ridgeline has become known to the rest of the world as Mount Rushmore, into which the government carved the heads of four Presidents.

WHY ARE WE HERE?

The history of this territory has been deliberately concealed; it is our aim to lay it bare for you.

Subjugation has rendered us a voiceless people. But now we have a podium from which to speak. The podium, of course, is the message. We never sold nor ceded these Hills. They were stolen by force in flagrant violation of U.S. law and of the Treaty of 1868.

WHAT YOU NEVER GOT IN SCHOOL

In the eighteen-sixties we were powerful, thus the U.S. government recognized us as a sovereign nation.

We repelled incursions into our land with such force
that the U.S. finally came to us, hat in hand, asking
us to sign a peace Treaty at Fort Laramie in 1868.
The Treaty stipulated that if we would permit the
U.S. to build a railroad across our territory, as
well as grant safe passage to pioneers on a desig-
nated trail West, the U.S. government would guaran-
tee the inviolacy of our lands in perpetuity. It even
went so far as to commit the U.S. Army to keeping
whites from penetrating the boundaries of our lands.

Out of the Laramie Treaty came the Great Sioux
Reservation, which comprised the western half of the
Dakota territory (what is now North Dakota and South
Dakota), plus about a fifth of what is now Nebraska,
a quarter of what is now Wyoming and a good section
of Montana, even a piece of Colorado.

The vastness of our land would allow us to continue
our life of following the herds. Of even more importance, it provided a huge buffer zone between whites
and our sacred Black Hills, which lay in the heart of
the reservation. The Hills are an oasis of green in
the middle of what the whites used to call the Great
American Desert. For us, Sioux, these Hills have always been the center of the world and the Heart of
Everything That Is. They are the home of God. They
contain our most sacred places of worship. It is for
this reason that our fathers fought longer and more
fiercely than any other tribe. And it is to this zeal
that the government finally bowed, putting forth the
1868 Treaty with its guarantees of the inviolacy of
the Black Hills in perpetuity.

ARTICLE 12

There was one more condition that our fathers insisted on before signing, and they made sure that it
was explicitly written into the Treaty. It is Article
12, stipulating that no portion of our reserved lands
can pass out of our hands without the signed consent
of three-fourths of all living Sioux males. We knew
about the practice of abducting individual "chiefs,"
boozing them up, or just beating them physically until they touched the pen to the paper, thereby relin-

quishing reserved lands. We had seen it happen to our
Dakota Sioux cousins in Minnesota. With Article 12,
our lands would be safe, for we numbered in the tens
of thousands and were spread far and wide; even the
task of finding and consulting three-fourths of us,
much less getting our signed approval, would be impossible. So we signed the Treaty, as did the representatives from Washington. Congress then ratified
it, passing it into solemn law.

The railroad men worked unmolested. The completion
of the Union Pacific Railroad in 1871 hastened the
government's hidden policy of wiping out the buffalo.
The goal of that policy was to reduce the Sioux and
other tribes of the plains to starvation and depen-
dency. Congress quickly decreed that "no Indian nation or tribe shall be acknowledged or recognized as
an independent nation . . . with whom the United States
must contract by Treaty." So, through the "peace,"
they had continued the war, wiped out our food supply. Having crippled us, they now felt free to dic-
tate to a subjugated people. No more sovereign nation
status. Congress would simply legislate down to the
tribes whatever new policies or land transfers it desired.

CUSTER'S MISCHIEF
In 1874, George Armstrong Custer, in criminal violation of the Laramie Treaty, sneaked into the Black
Hills with a company of soldiers and geologists. He
quickly sent word back East that there was "gold in
them hills," prompting, as he knew it would, an invasion of armed prospectors and a return of violence.
Custer was hankering for a new Indian war by which to
regain the glamour and lofty rank he had once enjoyed. He wrote his wife that such a war would be his
path to the Presidency.

GRANT'S PERFIDY
The law still prohibited non-Indians from entering
the Great Sioux Reservation, and it still committed

the Army to preventing such incursions. Nevertheless, in 1874, President Grant secretly issued orders to Generals Crook and Sheridan that "no further resistance shall be made to miners going into the Black Hills." The military should look the other way and offer no resistance to the miners, Sheridan reported in a letter to General Terry. He also reported that the President wanted this decision to be enforced "quietly," and to remain "confidential." Grant's faithlessness achieved its desired end: invasion of the Hills by armed miners and the escalation of violence.

In his State of the Union address, President Grant claimed to be unable to staunch the flood of miners into the Black Hills, and pleaded, therefore, that his next moral duty was to protect the lives of U.S. citizens, namely the trespassing miners. At long last Custer would have his Indian war. He and his Seventh Cavalry were dispatched to hunt down the truculent Sioux. After exterminating a number of camps (of mostly women and children), he attacked another encampment near the Little Big Horn on June 25, 1876. It was larger than expected, and this time the men were home.

The annihilation of the Seventh Cavalry, and the reporting of it back East as if it were an ambush or a dirty trick, a trap, enraged the American people. After all, how else could a band of savages liquidate the entire command of a gifted Anglo-Saxon officer? Throughout the States, men signed up for the Army. The shift in mood enabled Grant to open full-throttle the engines of war. And it enabled Congress to enact, with head held high, its most cynical legislation: The Black Hills Act of 1877, transferring ownership of the eight hundred square miles of Black Hills from the Sioux to the federal government. This, of course, was a unilateral and shameless breaking of the 1868 Laramie Treaty, and of a government's oath. They called it an "abrogation."

Aware of how shabby a naked landgrab would look, the government sent the Manypenny Commission out to Sioux country to negotiate a post-factum "purchase" of the Hills and thereby make the theft legal. "Sell or starve" was the ultimatum of the commission. Deprived not only of buffalo but now of arms with which to hunt the vanishing small game, our fathers survived on government rations—barely. The rations, of course, were cut off and withheld for months until the deal went through. And yet, in fact, it never really did go through:

Only 10% of Sioux males voted—a far cry from the 75% required by Article 12. So, quite apart from the coercion used, the purchase was legally unsound. As to its moral soundness, Bishop Whipple, one of the men on the Manypenny Commission, remarked to the *New York Times*, "I know of no instance in history where a great nation has so shamefully violated its oath." He and most of the other men on the commission were clerics and were morally opposed to the sale. They negotiated it on behalf of the government because they believed that if the Hills were not sold, the tribe would be exterminated.

Clearly, these Black Hills are still ours.

But even the Hills, with all their gold and lumber, did not satisfy the government's appetite. In 1889, Congress split the reservation into six small and scattered reservations, and appropriated eleven million acres in the process. What land was arable was taken. That which was deemed worthless was left to us.

The following year, 1890, winter came early. Our Sioux cousins on the reservation called Cheyenne River began dying off as the promised annuities of food and clothing failed month after month to arrive. Measles, whooping cough, and influenza made easy work of the malnourished people. In desperation, Chief Big Foot and a few hundred followers left Cheyenne River to trek one hundred fifty miles east to the Pine Ridge Reservation, in hope that we their cousins would have food.

Eating the horses as they fell, the dwindling band pushed on through the frozen Badlands and deep snow, losing members to exposure and exhaustion. Three hun-

dred forty reached Pine Ridge at a place called Wounded
Knee. It was there that the rebuilt Seventh Cavalry,
almost five hundred strong, encircled and disarmed the
340 wraiths. They were made to camp the night in a deep
ravine. The next morning, having surrounded the ravine
with a steel band of Hotchkiss guns and repeating rifles, the Seventh Cavalry restored its regimental honor
and settled a twenty-four-year-old grudge. Of the 340
who had survived the trek, only forty survived the
Hotchkiss guns. As ever, two-thirds of the body count
were fleeing women and children. That marked the end of
the Sioux Wars.

SO, WHAT EXACTLY ARE WE DOING ON RUSHMORE, AND DO WE MEAN TO HARM THE MONUMENT?

Our aim is to have a dialogue with Congress, for
only Congress can undo what it did. We would like
this dialogue on TV, for the country and the world to
see, and we will speak from right here on the mountain by way of satellite hookup, ideally on Koppel's
Nightline. It is our hope that Mr. Koppel will also
bring into the dialogue bona fide historians and university professors whom he deems to be impartial.
They will shed more light and go into further detail
concerning Congress's "acquisition" of the Hills. We
are convinced that once the American people see what
has been kept from their high school textbooks, they
will make their feelings known to Congress.

THE MONUMENT

Though the sculpture of the four Presidents is an
abomination of nature, we have absolutely no desire
and no intention of harming or defacing it. This mountain has suffered more than enough blasting and
drilling (as have all the Black Hills) and our goal is
not to make enemies or to insult what is sacred to
others, but to regain what is ours and sacred to us.

The FBI will try to discredit us. They will say
that we are militant, armed, crazy, and Communist.
Unless they have recently become more sophisticated,
they will try to tell you that Castro trained and
supplied us.

Yes, we do have arms. The rest is nonsense. We are armed purely for defensive purposes and will not fire unless attacked. We want only to hold our position, and to voice it. In 1971, our brother, Russell Means, and a handful of others took this same mountain and tried to be heard. Being unarmed, though, they were swiftly dragged down by federal forces and never got to say their piece. We are armed to make sure that we will not be dragged down. We will be heard.

It is sad that we had to bring arms, because they detract from the real action up here, which is a hunger strike. We hope it will create a time frame and lend a sense of urgency to the dialogue. It should make it difficult for Congress to stall and give us the runaround.

Understand that in light of what happened to Russell Means, we had to fortify our position. Ironically, it is the guns that enable us to make a nonviolent protest through hunger. Having sworn not to harm the monument, we see the hunger strike as our only leverage on the government.

At least one of the hunger strikers will make his stand on top of Abraham Lincoln. This is to remind people that at the same time that blacks were emancipated and enfranchised with full rights of citizenship (13th and 14th Amendments), Native American tribes were stripped of their sovereign-nation status and made wards, not citizens, of the U.S. Obviously, the same stroke of the pen that enfranchised the blacks could easily have bestowed citizenship on Native Americans. But that would have recognized our inalienable right to own property and to defend it in court, and thus would have brought to a grinding halt the westward expansion.

Not until 1946 would we be permitted by Congress to pursue our grievances in court, and even then we would have to apply to Congress for permission to bring suit against it. Permission depended on how much a tribe was daring to ask for.

And always the verdict was along the lines of, Yeah, you got screwed. It was unfair and ugly, a shameful chapter in our history, but we can't turn back the clock. Can't just displace those white settlers. They've been there too long now, put down roots (as if we Lakota were negligent in not having brought suit before '46), so here's some cash. Be happy.

Well, we don't want cash; we want our land. And furthermore, the government *does* displace whites whenever it pleases. When building highways, dams, railroads, or anything else of "national importance," the government displaces and compensates the people who are in the way, regardless of how long they've been there. We think the American people will feel, as we do, that honoring one's solemn oath, one's own laws and Constitution, should also be a matter of national importance.

1980 SUPREME COURT DECISION

In 1980, our Black Hills claim went before the Supreme Court. The Court said we were right, but that it did not have the power to return the land. Only Congress could undo what Congress had done. The best the Court could do, it said, was to uphold the decision of a lower court to compensate us with money. We were awarded $106 million, not one penny of which have we accepted.

Despite the fact that our present reservations comprise the poorest counties in the United States, and despite the fact that we could do much with that money toward health care, nutrition, and education, we refused it. True, this was far and away the largest judgment ever made in the history of Indian land claims, but the award is worth a tiny fraction of the mineral and lumber wealth extracted each year from our Hills, to say nothing of the worth of the Hills themselves (both in the monetary sense of the white world and the spiritual sense of our world). Distributed on a per capita basis, the award breaks down to roughly $1,000 a head. No matter what the sum might be, we would never take it, for that could constitute a sale retroactively.

So, what do you do when the highest court in the land says, *You're right, but there's nothing we can do about it. Only Congress can give you back your land.* What do you do? You try to speak to Congress, but Congress won't listen. Some people would then hijack airplanes and school buses and blow things up. That is not our way.

On the hundredth anniversary of Wounded Knee and the tenth anniversary of the Supreme Court decision, we have come to Rushmore to take our case to the American people and to the citizens of the world.

The Supreme Court told us that an Act of Congress may supersede a prior treaty, be it with a foreign nation or with a Native tribe. In simple English, Congress reserves the right to break treaties. Naturally, this was never mentioned in 1868, nor was there a clause to such effect in our Treaty. We remind the Congress that *unilateral abrogation of Treaty obligations by legislative order is illegal under international law.* We will go to the World Court if we have to.

THE SPIRIT

It seems America has more religion than any other country. Airwaves are saturated with preachers, and yet we all know in our hearts that with each disappearing species, each poisoned lake, we become more estranged from our Creator. It is no secret that this nation has lost its way. Americans know how they acquired this land, and they know what they're doing to it. But they avoid learning the details. For only by knowing the details (the facts, the treaties) can one begin to redress the wrongs. This willful ignorance separates them further from the *path back,* the force that we all long to be with. The preachers talk a lot of redemption. Is there such a thing, or is it poetic nonsense? Would not a return of land, at least *some* land, be a redemptive measure? Might it not be the beginning of a return to the high path? Why should God redeem a nation that makes no effort to redress its wrongs, even labors to conceal them? At the very least, such a return would restore much national honor and good will.

This epistle is sent to you from the Council of the
Kit Fox Society:

Peter Speckled Hawk, John No Horse, Sharon Takes Gun,
Isaac Sky Elk, Elijah Hunts Alone, Harry Pawnee-Killer,
Abel Many Coups, Q. Waokiye, and Joseph Moves Camp;

And from the Lakota holy men, Bear Dreamer Bordeaux
and Clement Blue Chest.

The word had been passed to meet on top of Eagle Nest Butte at midnight. I sat up there under a pine and watched for the others. They drove the rutted dirt road without their headlights. When the breeze was right, I could just make out the sound of car doors being closed down below. Then, ten or fifteen minutes later, a group would arrive at the top, silent and winded. It's a steep climb, on which you often have to use your hands.

Speckled Hawk came over to me by the lip of the butte. "Joey, listen," he said in a quiet voice. "Much of what I'm going to tell these guys tonight will surprise you. No matter how much you want to pipe up, don't. I'll explain later. I don't have time now."

By 12:40 or so, all thirty-six Tokalas had shown up and were huddled in different groups, some pulling on cigarettes and talking in low voices. Someone wanted to build a fire but Speckled Hawk said no. "All right, gather in tight," he said. "Got a lot to go over. Tonight we're going to tell you what the target is. Day after tomorrow we take it. How many of you know about Gunnery Range?"

Only seven or eight men raised their hands, the old guys. Speckled

Hawk nodded. "Well, it's a big chunk of our land. During the big war against the Nazis, the Pentagon asked to borrow land for bombing practice. We didn't want the land getting beat up that way, but they said it would help beat Hitler, and that it was our patriotic duty. Most important, they promised to return it right after the war ended. So we loaned it out, a strip forty-three miles by twelve. A lot of families had to move off that land, and they've never been able to move back, because the government refuses to give it back. It's Air Force property, they say, and off-limits. What they're doing there now is digging up uranium, robbing the earth after beating it. We're going to get back this Gunnery Range once and for good."

"How can thirty-plus men take something that size?" asked one of the younger guys, a kid with long braids.

"By taking Ellsworth Air Force Base," Speckled Hawk said.

"You're crazy! We can't take no Air Force base," the kid said. And he was right. I'm glad he said it, so I didn't have to.

"No, we can't take it exactly, but we can lock ourselves to it, to the front gate, with chains. And we'll have the press there. And if they try to blowtorch us off, we'll have other men with rifles to hold them at bay. It'll be a standoff and the press will get it all. We'll have information pamphlets like this to give out to them." He held up a piece of paper, a single sheet folded in three, and passed a few copies of it out. "In forty-eight hours, the whole world will know about Gunnery Range and how the U.S government keeps its promises."

"I don't know," said a young guy in the front row. "I was in the Air Force and those security guys are crazy."

"Are they going to boil us in oil?" Speckled asked. This was met with muted laughter. "Look, with the press there, they can't do shit to us. And we'll have our own riflemen backing us up. We're going to tie up their base, at least for twenty-four hours, and that will be enough to get the press interested in Gunnery Range. All right, then, all those who are game, go stand by Isaac Sky Elk there."

Only about half the guys went over to Isaac.

"Hang on," someone said. It was an older guy from Kyle. He had gray braids coming out from under a broken Stetson, and he had a handsome face with a big scar down one side. "Gunnery is a big chunk, but it's nothing compared to the Black Hills. We should try to get back the Paha Sapa."

Speckled nodded. "Once we have the TV on us, we'll talk about the Hills. Before we win the war, though, we've got to win some battles. Right? This is just round one. Okay, then, who else is in?"

The kid who had been in the Air Force walked over and joined those who were already standing with Isaac. This prompted most of the remaining guys to join, too.

Speckled turned to two guys who were opting out. They were looking sheepish. "That's okay," Speckled said. "Sometimes your wakan is off, and it's your right to stand down. Just like the old days. You're still Tokala. But remember this, your brothers here are depending on you to keep your mouths shut. Do we have your word on that?" They each nodded and swore silence. "Shut means shut," Speckled said. He paused to let it sink in, then said, "All right. Why don't you fellas go home, then." They turned in silence and walked off toward the lip of the butte to find the path.

Speckled turned back to us. "The rest of you guys, you show up here tomorrow night at ten. And I don't mean Indian time this time. Ten means ten. We'll go over what you need to know before we head out. Don't worry about chains and locks. We've already got them. Since we haven't worked out yet who'll be hunger-striking and who'll be protecting them, I want each of you to bring his rifle. Don't worry about your vehicles. You'll leave them here at the butte, and leave the driving to us. Okay, that's about it," he said. The meeting broke up.

At the foot of the butte, I stood by my Mustang and waited for Speckled Hawk. After the last of the Tokalas drove off, he walked over. "What about Clem's vision?" I said. I was hardly able to hide my rage.

"What about it?"

"RUSH-MORE," I said.

He smiled. "What if one of those guys is an informant? You ever think about that? Or if someone gets drunk in a bar tonight and shoots his mouth off? You want the feds waiting on top of the presidents with a big butterfly net? It's better this way."

"They have a right to know what they're getting into. How do you know they'll even want to *do* Rushmore?"

"Because park rangers don't carry M-16s. Air Force Security does. All I did is find out who's committed and who's not. They'll be overjoyed when they learn it's Rushmore. They'll be relieved. Smaller risk. Bigger payoff."

It made sense, but I didn't like it. Clem would never have done it that way. He would have had faith in each and every man to keep his mouth shut. And the feds would have busted us at the foot of the mountain.

❖

"You're going *hunt*ing?" Linda said. She clearly didn't buy it.

She was standing in her kitchen, leaning against the fridge with Jenny at her breast. Clem was in the bedroom loading T-shirts and blankets into his old Scout pack—which I had returned to him after fishing it out of White River.

Jeb, their five-year-old, was playing on the floor of the main room with an old cement mixer, a Tonka truck that a priest gave me when I was about the same age. I think he gave it to me because I had no dad and he wanted me to have a good role model. Go pave the world.

"Clem, did you hear me?" called Linda. Still no response came from the bedroom. She rolled her eyes slightly, then looked at me: "You're not really going hunting."

I nodded earnestly that we were, then looked over at my other nephew, Rafer, the eight-year-old.

Rafer was sitting at the table drawing pictures with a crayon and scrap paper that he got from school. He drew surprisingly well, much better than Clem or I could at that age. The table jiggled under his crayon. It was an old card table with collapsible legs, quite wobbly, but it had held up many years.

When I was a kid, we used to eat dinner off that card table. It was the only table in the house, and we had it set up in the kitchen. Clem always sat across from me, facing the door. When I was a little kid and he was a teenager, he would do this trick that fooled me every time. We would be eating and he would say something like, *Wow, what's that eagle doing sitting on our doorstep?* Or, *My God, what a huge grizzly bear that is at our door.* Once he said, *Gee, there's that girl Missy that you like.* And I would always turn around, but there would never be anybody at the door. Not a soul. When I turned back, though—sometimes because I felt the table quiver—there would be more meat on my plate than I remembered. It took me a while to catch on. He did it especially on nights when we were eating some little animal he had shot or trapped. He wanted to make sure we little ones—my sister and me—had full bellies. But also, I think he believed that if our bellies were fuller, the animals he had bagged would seem bigger, the hunter better, and the old way still within reach.

Clem came out of the bedroom, stepped carefully over Jeb and the cement mixer. As he passed in back of Rafer, he touched the nape of the boy's neck and said, "Looks good, Rafe." He entered the kitchen area and stood in front of Linda. He looked at his daughter in Linda's arms and touched the fuzzy head lightly with his thumb. The Scout pack was slung over his shoulder.

"So, you're going hunting?" she said again.

"Yeah, hopefully deer, maybe even antelope," he said.

She shook her head. "Right."

"What?" he protested.

"You haven't gone hunting in fifteen years."

"And I miss it."

"So why now all of a sudden?"

"I *miss* it."

"Oh, I bet you do."

There was silence, just the sound of Jenny suckling. "A bunch of us are going to drive up to Standing Rock, maybe even up into Canada. More game up there. Make it worthwhile. So it might be a while," he said.

"Don't give me this bull," she said. "You're going to tangle with the authorities. I can tell."

"You can, huh?" he said, trying to act amused, as if she couldn't be more wrong.

"You're going to do some dumb-ass thing like try to break No Horse out of prison. Right? You're a dreamer, Clem. You're going to land your own ass in prison, or get it shot off."

The word was that they had No Horse in a small jail in Custer. And it's true that some fools had talked loudly and brashly in a bar about busting him out, but it had nothing to do with us.

He laughed. "We're just going hunting, is all. Hell, we're doing it to *avoid* the feds."

"Look, I'm proud you beat the booze, Clem, and proud you danced— like no one ever danced before. I'm proud to be Clem Blue Chest's wife. But don't start thinking now about becoming a warrior, like that's going to make me prouder. Don't even think about warrior societies. I hear talk, you know, whispers about the Tokalas coming back. Don't think for a minute that would make me proud. That's for fools, Clem. Those days can never be had again. They won and we lost. Not fair and square, but it's over. Over. The only victory now is survival."

"I'm not Tokala," he said, which was true.

"You're lying to me!" she said, almost shouting. "I'll leave the kids with my sister and follow you. I will. I know you're lying."

Her following us was the last thing we needed, and she would have done it, too. "Look, Linda," I said, stepping between them. I spoke in a hushed voice so that the boys wouldn't hear. "We're going to Ellsworth, okay? We're going to chain ourselves to the gate and get us back Gunnery Range. It's completely nonviolent, nobody's going to shoot anybody. Here, you see?" I gave her one of Speckled Hawk's flyers about Gunnery Range.

"Are there women and kids going along?" she asked, scanning the flyer.

"No," I said firmly.

"It'd be safer if there were. The press will be there, right?"

"They'll be notified at the right moment. We can't have them showing up before we do."

"Having women and kids along would be stronger, make a deeper impression. And it would be harder for the feds to paint you out as criminals, or radicals or terrorists or whatever it'll be this time. Plus, they'd keep their safeties on."

"It's just a hunger strike," I said. "Nobody's going to take his safety off."

Clem bent forward and kissed Jenny's fuzzy crown. "See you later, Jenny," he said. The boys were still playing and drawing. Clem walked over and kneeled by his eight-year-old at the card table. "How's my man?" Rafer looked up and smiled, then looked back down at his drawing. "I'm going off with my friends for a while. Can I count on you?" Clem asked.

The boy nodded. "Are you going to bring home a deer?" Rafer asked.

"Better than that. You ever tasted buffalo?"

Rafer shook his head.

"There'll be buffalo. But I need you to take care of Mom and the little ones. Will you do that for me? Will you do what Mom asks? I'm counting on you to be the man while I'm gone."

Rafer nodded again and said okay.

"Put her there, buddy," Clem said. Rafer put his crayon down and placed his hand in Clem's big palm. Clem pulled him right out of the chair into a tight hug and kissed him on the side of the neck, just below the ear, where it tickles. "You're so serious, Rafe," Clem said, as he planted more kisses. Rafer started giggling and couldn't stop till his dad set him free with a slap on the bottom.

"And how's my bucky one?" Clem asked, pivoting on his knee so that he faced his five-year-old. Jeb got to his feet, raised his hand, and blurted, "High five!" in an excited voice. Clem raised his palm, and little Jeb high-fived it with surprising force. He smiled triumphantly, looked at his mom, then me, then back at his dad.

"Is that all I get, a high five?" Clem asked.

Jeb shook his head, his cheeks dimpling into a wide smile. He took a step back, then launched himself into his father's chest. Clem kissed the top of his head. "You know what?" said Jeb.

"What?"

"It's a secret," Jeb said, gesturing with his index finger for Clem to bring his ear close. Clem lowered his head and tucked his hair behind his ear so that the boy could whisper in it. Jeb reached up and slipped the top of Clem's ear into his mouth, biting down hard and holding it.

"Ow!" cried Clem. "What's this?"

The boy laughed through clenched teeth but wouldn't let go. Rafer laughed, too, and so did Linda and I. "I've got to go," Clem said.

Jeb shook his head without relaxing his jaw.

"You're hurting me," Clem said.

Jeb laughed through his teeth at that.

"You're going to make me late for my friends," Clem said.

"Good!" blurted Jeb through his teeth.

Clem stood up, and Jeb hung on with his arms around his dad's neck and his teeth on the ear. "Okay, that's enough now. Let go, Jeb." Clem tried to sound angry, but still the boy wouldn't let go. "Uhn-uhhhn," he said in a mischievous voice. I looked at Linda. She had an odd expression on her face, as if she were charmed and at the same time puzzled, even scared.

"Maybe the tickle monster will help set me free," Clem said. He got down on his knees again, so that Rafer could help him tickle Jeb. Overcome by laughter, Jeb finally had to gasp for air and let go the ear.

"What does he do, sharpen those with a file?" Clem asked as he got to his feet and looked at Linda. She smiled but seemed preoccupied. Clem looked down at his younger son. "You help your mom out, too. Right? You do what she says."

Jeb nodded.

We walked out the kitchen door to the car. "You swear you're not try-ing to bust No Horse out?" asked Linda.

"I swear it."

"Okay, then, just don't do anything stupid."

"I love you, too, Linda," he said with a smile. He kissed her cheek, then touched the baby's head once more, this time with the back of his hand. He looked into Linda's eyes. "See you soon."

"You better," she said.

◆

Bacon and I walked up to the chopper in the dark. The dew on the grass soaked through my sneakers. There was no sign of the pilot yet.

I sat on one of the skids, leaning my back against the bird, and stuffed some jerky in my mouth. The little town of Keystone was dead. The shop-keepers and merchants were probably still asleep twenty miles west in Rapid. It would be a good three or four hours before they would drive out here in their Broncos and Chief Cherokees and turn on the player pianos and go through the motions of living like miners, panhandlers, bad-ass frontiersmen, Calamity Janes, and saloon whores. It was a sham town, to make money off the old myths, and to continue clouding the truth.

I checked my watch. "Quinn, we don't need the chopper," I said. "We could still join the U-Hauls."

"Twenty years they've been dropping in on you with gunships. This time *we'll* come from above. Can you imagine how pumped it'll get the dog soldiers?"

We had three plans by which to get Larry to put the chopper down on Rushmore. Plan A was the Smithsonian bullshit. Plan B was a water pistol at the base of the neck. Plan C was a loaded Colt.

Headlights appeared at the far end of town and moved up the drag, re-vealing cartoonlike chuck wagons, wooden boardwalks, hitching posts, and swinging saloon doors. The vehicle passed the little Gutzon Borglum museum, then pulled into the driveway of the Air Tours office, the high beams lighting up the chopper and the two of us. They blinked off and the engine stopped. The door opened and a voice called out, "Morning, boys." Larry came up through the grass and shook hands with us, then shook his head and said, "Ain't been up this early in a while. The wife brewed me a thermos. You want some? I'll go in and get some cups." He came back out with two foam cups. "Too bad you've got to hurry back to D.C. I hope everything's okay."

"Yeah, just administrative headaches," groaned Bacon. "I'm gonna have to quit one of these days and just make films full-time. Be my own boss, like you."

"Yeah, I got it purty good," said Larry. "Aren't too many folks love their work the way I do. Don't need no hobbies for this boy. Got her right here. Just my bird, the sky, and my Black Hills."

We all sipped to that, Larry from his red plastic thermos cup. Then he went to pour a couple canisters of fuel into the chopper. I wasn't quite done with my coffee when the rotor started turning, building up speed, blew the cup from my hand into the tall grass. He let the engine warm a bit, then motioned us in. Bacon scrunched himself into the little seat behind the pilot. I got in the front seat. As cameraman, I needed the view.

We climbed fast through twilight. The stars were fading but the sun was still below the horizon. I saw the morning star and pretended to film it. Then a single ray broke over the eastern horizon, beaming upward at us over the endless sea of prairie. I wondered if that tiny section of the sun was visible from ground level, or even from the level of the presidents, or were we, from our altitude, looking over the natural horizon. I looked down but didn't see the monument. The hills were still dark and at rest. I looked through the camera at the first ray and watched it grow.

"I'm getting that lump in my throat again," said Larry.

"What's that?" said Bacon.

"Ain't it *some*thing," said Larry, pointing. Washington's forehead caught the first ray squarely. The neighboring foreheads also gleamed. The light expanded downward onto the brows, then slipped into the depths and recesses of the farseeing eyes.

Bacon leaned forward and shouted in Larry's ear, "Why don't you circle it for a bit so that José can film from all angles?" Larry nodded.

Behind the ridge in which the heads are carved runs a parallel and higher ridge. It rises straight up like a wall. You don't often see it in postcards because they're usually taken from the ground at such a steep upward angle that the heads block it. But that second ridge probably runs 100 to 150 feet higher than the presidential ridge.

Hidden Canyon is what they call the dip between the two ridges. It's like a long alley or corridor that has the backs of the heads, so to speak, on one side and the steep wall of the second ridge on the other. The tops of the heads are maybe twenty feet higher than the floor of Hidden Canyon, and they slope down into it. You could hide up there and never be seen from the ground. It's a natural fortress.

I could also see the gaping portal of the Hall of Records, another creation of dynamite, another insult to the mountain. The sculptor, Gutzon Borglum, had dreamt of a huge chamber inside the mountain in which would be displayed all the wonderful documents of the Republic, the Declaration of Independence, the Constitution, and of course the deed to the Louisiana Purchase, the proof that all these tribal lands of the West rightfully belonged to the U.S. because Jefferson had paid cash to the French. It was the coup of the Purchase, they say, that won Jefferson a spot on the mountain. Anyway, the sculpting crew had blasted out this giant hall in the second ridge, right behind Lincoln's head. There's a huge doorway, thirty feet high by twelve feet wide, that leads into a large rectangular cave about seventy feet deep. It was supposed to be a lot deeper, but they ran out of money and abandoned the project. So no doors were ever mounted on the entrance and no archives were put in the Hall. It was just a big, gaping wound. We had our own archives we would fill it with, copies of the 371 treaties that Congress had ratified and then broken. Most prominently displayed, of course, would be the 1868 Laramie Treaty. When *Nightline* and the others arrived, we would take them on a tour of the Hall of Records.

We would also use the Hall as a shelter for our supplies. It looks out on the back of the emancipator's crown, like you're sitting behind him at the theater.

As Larry swung the chopper around the southeast side of Lincoln's head, I could see the convoy of three U-Haul trucks and Elijah's pickup turning off 244 and taking the service road. The service road was just for the use of park rangers, and was clearly marked as such. But Bacon and I had reconnoitered the woods down that way and knew that the service road led to the sculptor's studio, which was at the southeast foot of the mountain. The mountain—really a very high ridge—is sheer cliff on every side but the southeast, where it's a long, gradual rise through a pine forest. An eight-year-old could hike it. Of course, when we reconnoitered the base of the southeast hill, we found on every tree down there a bright orange sign promising six months in prison for anyone who traveled beyond that point. It was clearly an easy ascent. What was less clear was whether there would be ranger posts in the woods along the way. Now we could see there were no bunkers, no defenses. Even if there were hidden ones, how could a few park rangers stop thirty armed Tokalas racing up the hill?

"Must be some kind of work crew," said Larry, pointing at our trucks on the service road. The Kit Foxes were on time. I hoped Clem and old Bear Dreamer had not had any problems. They were to be the first ones on the mountain and should've climbed it already. When we circled around in front of the heads for the second time, I could see two tiny figures on top of Lincoln. They were just specks, but I knew it was them, and, man, that was a feeling.

"The rangers are up early. Wonder what they're doing?" said Larry, pointing at the specks. I zoomed in as much as I could with the camera. It looked like they might already be staking themselves down, hammering wedges into fissures in the granite and chaining themselves to the rock, but I couldn't tell for sure. "Can't see," I said. "Why don't you take her in closer?"

"A bit, but we've got to stay at least two thousand feet out and two thousand higher than the rock. That's the law." He moved us in a hundred yards or so.

"You can do better than that," said Bacon.

"Nah, my ass 'ould be grass," said Larry, shaking his head.

"Who's gonna know?"

He looked at me like I was stupid. "The rangers."

"They don't look like rangers to me," I said, looking through the camera. "They look like kids or something pulling a prank. Seriously, it looks like they've got buckets of paint or something. Let's buzz 'em, scare 'em off."

"No way. If they ain't rangers, the best thing is to just call it in."

"It'll be too late then," snapped Bacon. "Could take months to clean off paint. And what if it's not paint? They could be Shi'ites or Iraqis. They could have explosives."

We went in another thousand feet. It became clear to the naked eye that these were not park rangers. Clem was hammering a metal wedge into a crack in the rock, to anchor his chain. You could see his arm going up and down. "They're driving dynamite into the crevices!" shouted Bacon. "Put her down on that back ridge."

"Are you *nuts?*" said Larry.

"I'll take full responsibility. I'm a curator of the Smithsonian and the

National Archive. You're off the hook. Trust me. It'll be a lot worse if we *don't* act."

Larry was sweating above his upper lip and the vein near his temple was bouncing. "I don't know," he said.

"Set us down on that back ridge, over the Hall of Records. They'll probably take off like rabbits."

Larry hesitated.

"Take her down!" thundered Bacon in a tone I didn't know he had. Larry looked over at me. I just put the camera on him. He tried not to look scared.

"I'll approach from the back. That way, if anything happens to the chopper, it'll at least pose no threat to the monument," he said. I guess he was imagining an FAA review board watching the film. We swung around behind the monument, then hovered lower and lower till the skids were brushing the granite of the back ridge.

"Did they take off?" asked Bacon. He couldn't see down that far from his backseat.

"Not yet," I said.

"Then we gotta get out and chase 'em off."

"No way," shrieked Larry. He started cursing when I opened the door.

"Relax. You'll stay with the bird," yelled Bacon in his ear.

I put one foot on the skid and the other to the granite. "*One small step for wasitchus,*" sang a voice through the rotor thunder. "*One huge leap for lesser primates,*" then the shrill laugh. A wash of anger flooded through me and I hated myself for having placed hope in the Yuwipi, for having been so naïve. I should've known it was bullshit. But just as quickly as the anger came, so did it pass, and I slipped into a state of detachment. If I was fucked, then I was also free to do brave things.

I turned around and watched Bacon maneuver out from the backseat. "Thanks for the ride," he shouted. Larry was totally perplexed, his mouth hanging open. I felt sorry for him. Bacon shut the door and grinned. Larry pulled off the ridge and hovered, puzzled, scared, and still without a clue, I think.

We were right above the Hall of Records, and about eighty feet above the presidents' heads. Clem waved and cried out a greeting, which was mostly drowned by the rotor thunder. He was sitting on the rock, ankles crossed, and I could see a glint of chain around his waist. He was already staked down. Just then, the first wave of dog soldiers exploded out of the pines on the southeast hill and sprinted up the mouth of Hidden Canyon, and some of them onto Lincoln's head. Hearing the chopper, they looked up, saw us on the ridge and the chopper behind us. One of them lifted his rifle and fired, thinking, no doubt, that our position was already being attacked by feds. I started to yell for him to hold his fire, and at the same moment Elijah came up behind the guy and ripped the rifle away. Meanwhile, Larry and the chopper had peeled out of there at a sharp angle.

Some of the Tokalas ran out onto the heads and greeted Clem and Bear Dreamer. They were pumped, out of their skulls with excitement. Some had their faces painted red and their hair roached in the old Tokala way. Most wore jeans and T-shirts, some flak jackets, Uncle Joe hats, the black, flat-brimmed hats that the AIMers used to wear. And they lugged packs, each humping enough food for two weeks if rationed carefully. Some would run up and touch Clem's shoulder or his hair. Some howled with joy and adrenaline, joy to be here, to be alive and part of this homecoming, greeting this bright and fantastic day. One guy kept shouting, "Paha Sapa, Paha Sapa," again and again. "The heart of everything that is," he shouted. Speckled Hawk had been right. They did not mind in the least having the target switched.

Bacon and I shinnied down a cleft in the high ridge behind the presidents. By the time we made the tricky descent into Hidden Canyon, 'most everyone had arrived. Elijah and Eli Jr. were passing out little trench shovels and burlap bags. We were greeted by old Isaac, Abel Many Coups, and Sharon. Her eyes were bright with excitement. "Joey, I can't believe it. We're really up here. We're gonna get our Hills back."

I nodded. There were a couple of park rangers with them, wearing these beautiful Smokey the Bear hats. "We made some friends on the way up," said Isaac. "Thought we ought to hang on to them till we're all dug in."

"Did they have time to radio?" asked Bacon. Isaac shrugged and the two rangers wouldn't say. They were trying to act like big P.O.W.s, divulging nothing. "Well, give 'em some grub and send 'em down in about an hour."

"We should send them down right away," Elijah said. "So it can't be said we're taking hostages."

"Can we dig in on time?" asked Bacon.

"They're already digging in the pines," Abel said, meaning the southeast hill.

"Well, it was nice meeting you gents," said Elijah with a big grin. "We'll get you an escort, see you safe down the mountain."

"We *know* how to get down!" snapped one of them. "We know this mountain like the back of our hands."

"Whoo, look out. They know how to get *down*," Abel said.

I relieved them of their hats. It would be hot on the presidents, and the hunger strikers would need protection.

Eli, Isaac, and Abel started deploying men and weapons at strategic points along the mountain, especially in the woods of the southeast hill, as this was the only real avenue of approach. Kit Foxes were digging bunkers and trenches and filling sandbags with dirt. Everybody worked quickly. I was supposed to keep a general lookout.

I walked out onto Jefferson's head and stared out at our Paha Sapa, green and sawtoothed, carved with roads here and there, but still beautiful. I looked left, over at Lincoln. Clem was sitting peacefully with his legs crossed, his elbows on his knees. I waved at him with one of the ranger hats, but I guess he had his eyes closed. Praying, maybe. Far down below me, the two rangers bolted out of the woods and ran to the Tourist Center. I sat down on the cool granite. I heard hawks calling out to one another. Everything was peaceful. Everything was ours. The sun was full above the horizon, and the granite slightly warmer when I saw two squad cars of the South Dakota State Police speeding up 244. They pulled into the huge, fan-shaped parking lot on the other side of the tourist canteen, less than half a mile away from where I sat. I reported this back to Speckled Hawk, who nodded. Twenty minutes later, three unmarked Fords appeared, no doubt from the FBI office in Rapid City.

Then, an olive-drab Huey without markings buzzed by at three thousand feet. It circled once at a safe distance, then began its descent into the parking area where all the Fords were gathering.

Isaac had joined me out on Jefferson's head. He tipped back his old black cowboy hat and folded his huge arms across his chest. We watched the Huey gentle herself down near the Fords. The engine was cut and the rotors slowed. "Well, it's done," he said, letting some chaw juice fall onto Jefferson's white wig. "We got ourselves a sit-chew-A-shun." He looked at me and smiled, with all his deep lines.

We secured a perimeter just above the base of the southeast hill. Old Isaac and I trekked down through the pines. Abel Many Coups and Elijah were running from bunker point to bunker point, checking on the construction, telling the guys how to do it. Some worked with picks, some with shovels, others stood guard, aiming ancient Winchesters into the pines below.

Burlap bags, flour bags, even grain sacks from the Rapid Feed and Seed were quickly filled with the excavated earth and built up into sandbag walls along the trenches.

We had these shallow bunkers all over that slope, three tiers of them fanned out as you descended the hill. On the lowest tier, there were four bunker stations, about fifteen yards apart. The most southerly of these bunkers was within sixty yards of the service road. The guys who volunteered to man that bunker were all combat vets. Nam, Korea, and even a couple from World War II.

Thirty to forty yards uphill was the second tier, comprising three bunkers about fifteen yards apart.

At the top of the hill, where the pine forest ends and a cluster of soaring granite formations begins, we dug our final fortification, a long trench that arced around and blocked off the two routes to the presidents. One route was a path that veered to the left, southward, dipping down the south side of the slope a bit, in view of the Tourist Center, before feeding up into the flight of stone stairs that are hidden behind a tower of granite to the right of Lincoln's head. The stairs, which had been blasted and chiseled into the rock, reached all the way up to the mouth of Hidden Canyon, feeding into it just behind Abe's crown. I think they were made with the idea that tourists would be visiting the Hall of Records, and that some kind of chairlift or gondola system would carry folks up to the foot of the stairs.

The second path led over jagged ridges and between soaring rock formations to the high ridge that Bacon and I had landed on. From there, you would have to shinny down a cleft into Hidden Canyon. In all other directions it was cliff.

The bottom level of the three-tier system would repel any attack that might be launched. The second tier would not enter the fray unless the first were overrun. This way we avoided the risk of casualties by crossfire—that is, having the second tier accidentally hit men in the first tier. Likewise, the third and top level would not fight unless the second level were overrun. The men in each tier had staked themselves down, *Napesni*-style. Of course, no one thought it would come to that.

Isaac and I walked back up the hill, then up the granite stairs into Hidden Canyon. Sharon and Bacon were storing provisions in the Hall of Records. LAWs had already been deployed to the three bunkers. We used the empty weapons crates to store food, mostly canned goods. We also had fresh fruit and huge blocks of cheese that had to be eaten within the first few days. The cheese was unsliced American, each block about a yard long. It was government surplus that we had bought in Pine Ridge village. It was just like the blocks that the government used to include in the food allotments to our fathers, the allotments that the missionaries would intercept and withhold.

While Sharon prepared burlap bags full of food for the bunker teams, I went outside onto Abe Lincoln's head to check things out. Another unmarked Huey was putting down in the distant parking lot, then a double-rotor Chinook troop transport arrived and landed farther back. A column of four Army trucks came up 244. Bringing up the rear were three armored personnel carriers. I kneeled by my brother. "How do you feel?" I asked.

"I feel good," he said, smiling. "My chain's a bit tight, but it oughta fit fine in a day or two."

"Why don't I loosen it a link or two?" I offered. He had the chain locked around his waist with a padlock, but there were yards and yards of extra chain. I didn't know why he made it so tight. He shook his head. "It's fine."

"Can I get you some water?" I asked.

"I'm okay just now. Thanks. Did you know, Joey, that the old *Napesni* way, when a No Flight staked his sash down in battle, he could not unstake it himself? Not even to advance. Only a brother could unstake him."

"Yeah, I think you mentioned that before."

"Well, this is the key to my lock and chain," he said, taking a leather thong off his neck and passing it over his head. A shiny, pale key dangled from it. He put it over my head and I tucked it in my shirt.

I was impressed with the way his body had changed over the last month. His gut had disappeared, while his chest muscles had become hard from all the push-ups he'd been doing. The push-ups puzzled me. It seemed vain, like body-building, and yet I knew he didn't have a drop of vanity in him.

"All right," I said, touching his shoulder with my hand. He put his hand over mine and kept it there for a moment. Then I stood and walked off Lincoln, down the sloping backside of the head into Hidden Canyon. Elijah was sitting by the portal to the Hall of Records, working his rifle with a rag. "Fine time to oil your gun," I said.

"Oh, she's oiled. I'm just getting the road dust off her before I give her to Junior," he said, nodding his chin out toward Roosevelt. I turned and saw Junior standing on the old Rough Rider, looking out at the Hills, his back to us. "That boy's the best. He deserves the best," Eli said. "I can't wait to see his eyes pop when I give it to him. Come on," he said, getting to his feet.

"Son, I got something for you," Eli said, holding out the rifle. Junior turned, looked at us, then smiled faintly. "Well, take it," Eli said. The boy looked at his dad. He took the rifle in his hands, seeming to enjoy the weight of it, the solidity. He caressed the polished stock, then brought it to his shoulder and looked down the sight, squinting one eye. "It's beautiful," he said. "But I can't." He held it out for his dad to take back.

"Why?"

"It's your best one. I know what it means to you."

"It don't mean nothing to me next to you, Junior. I want you to have it."

"It'd be wasted on me."

Elijah looked perplexed.

"Remember when I had that Winchester in the federal man's back," Junior said. "Well, I just did it to make them leave Clem and Joey's mother alone. But the whole time my gun was there, all I could see was this guy's back. And I don't mean the jacket and big FBI letters. I mean his back, Dad, like he was naked, and had no skin suddenly. I could see muscles and tendons, veins throbbing, ligaments, bones, nerves, so many nerves, all the things the bullet would rip into, and I could see it would never heal up right. Something was telling me it would never heal up right. And I started thinking about how he was a kid once, this fed, and how he must be somebody's son, and maybe somebody's father now, too, and I knew that if it came to it, I wouldn't shoot. What I'm saying is, I want to try it Clem's way. I want you to stake me down, Dad."

Eli was speechless. Junior kneeled and took off his pack. I thought it was loaded with food, but when he opened the flap, I saw chain, a hammer, and something like a huge piton wedge. He stood up and held the end of the chain out to his father. "Will you?"

Eli blinked a few times. When finally he spoke, it was with a mixture of anger and admiration. "No," he said, shaking his head. "And you will not hunger-strike. If you don't want to carry a rifle, you can help out in other ways. But you will not starve. Not even a day. Our family has done enough of that in the last hundred years. You lost more relatives than you know to hunger. It makes me sick. Why don't *they* starve?" he said, pointing down to the federal forces. "My own grandparents starved to death and so did two aunts. You're not even full-grown, son. It can stunt your growth. And then there's dehydration. You can hurt your kidneys and liver. My God, Junior, don't you realize that if you keep growing and stay healthy, I mean, with an arm like yours, you could go all the way, college ball, maybe even—"

"Dad . . ."

"No!" Eli said, shaking his head. "I'm not going to have my son sitting out here like a target."

"With the press coming, I don't figure it's too dangerous. And neither do you or you wouldn't've brought me. I'll drink plenty of water. I promise."

"I'm not going to help you do this," Eli said. He turned on his heel and walked off of Roosevelt. Junior started the work of staking himself down. He took the piton wedge and started driving it into one of the fissures with the hammer. At the sound of the hammer, Clem looked over from Lincoln. Junior waved across the abyss at my brother, then smiled. It was just the two of them. He fastened the chain to the piton, then sank the piton all the way in. All that remained was to lock the chain around his waist.

"I can put it on here with Clem's key," I said, showing him the thong around my neck.

"Let's give my dad a few minutes."

Sure enough, Elijah came back onto Roosevelt. "You're as stubborn as your mother," he said, getting down on one knee. "But you've always made me proud." He locked the chain around his son's slender waist, then put the key on his old Marine Corps dog-tag chain. "At the first sign of trouble, I'm unstaking you. Is that understood?"

The boy nodded.

I brought Clem a bowl of water. We looked over at Junior. He looked so young against the backdrop of ancient hills and ridges. I hated the idea of his starving and maybe hurting his growth. "He's got strong wakan," Clem said, as if he had read my thoughts. "He'll be okay."

Just then, an APC rolled down from the Tourist Center and crashed its way along the footpaths, then up through the ponderosa pines approaching the foot of the monument. It stopped at the foot, way down below Lincoln. I crawled to the edge to get a better look. The hatch on top of the vehicle opened slowly, a head emerged, then a megaphone. The names of the council members crackled through the bullhorn. They wanted us to meet with them. Speckled Hawk came out to the edge, too. We were on the crest of Lincoln's thick wave of hair, a good twelve feet above his forehead. Speckled turned to Clem: "What should I say?"

"Tell 'em we spoke our piece in the letter to the press," said Clem. Speckled Hawk turned and yelled that down. He had to yell it three or four times before they stopped saying, "Say again."

"Meet us so we can give you a radio," said the megaphone.

"We got a radio," yelled Speckled Hawk, but actually we didn't. We'd forgotten it in the rush.

"A two-way radio," said the APC.

"Tell them to bring it up to the stone staircase," I said.

The staircase winds its way up between two towers of granite to the side of Lincoln's head. Like Hidden Canyon, the staircase was out of view from the woods and therefore protected from FBI snipers who might be out there. We, on the other hand, would have men all over the granite towers and ridges with their weapons trained down on the stairs.

Speckled Hawk, old Isaac, Elijah, and I waited about halfway down the staircase. It would probably be a good ten minutes before the feds could hike up that steep slope to the right of Lincoln and make their way behind the granite tower to where the stairs begin.

Speckled Hawk pulled one of these yard-long blocks of cheese from a burlap bag that he was going to deliver to one of the bunkers. It was about 11:30 now and none of us had eaten since well before dawn. "Who's for some belly timber?" he asked. Old Isaac handed him his big hunting knife. Speckled Hawk cut the plastic and then a slice for each of us. There was a second yard of cheese still in the burlap, so we knew the guys in the bunker wouldn't mind. If we had too much of anything, it was cheese.

We chewed and talked and decided not to say shit to these feds, not to give 'em one inch. Just accept the radio. If they started breaking us down with the radio, we could always toss it off the cliff.

I was just finishing my slab when we heard their voices. I stood and looked up to make sure that the Foxes on the granite above were awake and ready.

Special Agents Maxwell and Dexter came around the bend in the staircase, and with them were Colonel Hank McLaren of the National Guard, in full battle dress, and an Air Force major in a black beret. They stopped within five steps of us. The Air Force guy was no doubt from Ellsworth, the big bomber base near Rapid. Those black beret guys are the security corps of the Air Force. They're good. What with all the nuclear weapons stockpiled on bases, they've got to be good, but guarding a base and attacking a mountain are two different things. I figured he and his men were just here until the heavies arrived from Fort Bragg or Coronado.

"Mr. Moves Camp," said Agent Maxwell. "You *do* get around." He was wearing a tie and a starched white shirt, but he must've left his jacket in the APC or down at the tourist canteen. He had to look up at me from a few stairs down, which I didn't mind. They were all having to look up at us. "You do know, of course, this is an exercise in futility," he said. "You'll never get back the Black Hills. I think you understand that. Now, I've been authorized by the president to promise that if you come down peacefully and immediately, we'll set up negotiations between representatives of your group and a presidentially appointed negotiating team toward the end of apportioning to the Sioux some *limited* piece of Black Hills territory, perhaps a section of Wind Cave National Park or Custer State Park. I'm also authorized to promise you amnesty regarding your seizure of the monument, provided you lay down your arms immediately. This offer expires in half an hour."

"Presidentially appointed negotiating team, eh?" said Elijah. "We're still waiting for Nixon's team." He was talking about how at Wounded Knee, AIM had been suckered into laying down their weapons with the promise that there would then be negotiations with a team of Nixon's people. The weapons were laid down, everyone got busted, and there were never any talks. Elijah let some Skoal juice fall from his lips onto the white steps between us and them.

Dexter, the black agent, held up his long, two-toned index finger: "You people are either stupid," he said, "or suffering from a collective death wish. Do you have *any* idea what kind of force we can bring to bear against you, what kind of force is being assembled as we speak?"

Well, isn't he the fancy house nigger. Do re me fa-so-la-ti . . . She was starting her warm-ups. She didn't sound too close, but I broke a sweat under my arms and down my spine. She cleared her throat and moved closer in the darkness. *Do re me fa so la ti do.*

"We don't have to settle this with force," I said. *We don't want a hand job, just a hand.* She giggled. Then, in a commanding tone, no longer melodic, *Knife him. He's such a stringy bull. Take his sack.* I tried to block her out. I cleared my throat in my fist, trying to make noise in my head, to jam the frequency.

"If you want this monument," I said. "All you gotta do is ask. Nicely." Maxwell looked puzzled.

Oh what a friend, she began to sing.

"Because, I mean, you're right. The whole thing *is* futile. And we know it. We knew it from the start. You'll never give us back these Hills. First there was too much gold, then too much coal, now too much uranium, so we know you'll never give us back what you stole. We ain't dreamers. But you feds have been shitting on us and humiliating us for so long that we want you on your knees this once. Just once. Okay? And one of the guys up there will snap a photo. That's all we want."

Oh what a friend we have, she sang again.

"Sir, we don't have time for this crap," said Dexter, touching Maxwell's elbow with his long, skinny hand. "Let's go."

But Maxwell wouldn't take his eyes off me. "Give 'em the radio," he said. Dexter took the radio pack off his back and held it out at arm's length. Old Isaac took a couple steps down and grabbed it. As he slung it over his shoulder, turning his back to them, he shot me a look like what the hell're you doin'? I looked back at Maxwell, who hadn't taken his eyes off of me.

Oh what a friend we have in him, she sang at a higher pitch.

"Look," I said, trying hard to focus on my words. "Your mission is to get us off this rock." I stuck a finger out as Dexter had: "Now, you can wait us out and starve us off, but that takes time, and the longer we're up here the more press we get." I held up a second finger: "You can pull a Hamburger Hill, very messy because we're dug in deep, and if you use big weapons, you'll get even worse press." I held up a third finger: "Or, you can kneel right now and just ask nicely."

He kept looking at me and I could see the little wheels turning in his head. He was working out equations and probabilities, weighing the risks versus the payoffs. If he recovered the monument by simply kneeling, he would be hailed as a master psychologist, a genius in reading the criminal/aboriginal mind, which is what his job is all about. But if he kneeled submissively only to be hoodwinked, he would disgrace himself and the Bureau. He would blow his career. I knew he would never kneel. I was just fucking around and didn't know why.

He moved his eyes off me and searched Isaac and Speckled Hawk to fathom if I was on the level. I guess they must've given him stone faces, because, to my astonishment, he lowered himself to one knee. "Will you please remove your people from this national monument and surrender your arms?" I guess he figured that if a photo ever turned up in the papers, he could just say that there were all kinds of rifles trained on him from above. Or they could say the photo was doctored.

"You've only got one knee down," I said. "I want all four of you guys on your knees. Eight knees, and put your hands together and pray. Especially you, Air Force. You never returned Gunnery Range."

Oh what a friend. She laughed. *Do it!*

The Air Force major looked at Maxwell, got the nod, and started to put a knee down. But McLaren spat on the stone stairs and said, "Get serious."

Oh what a friend we have. She giggled. *Do it.*

"Come on, Colonel," I said in an even tone. "Get with the program. On your knees and kiss the cheese." They suddenly looked scared. I think it crossed their minds that they were being set up to be offed execution-style. I grabbed the two bars of surplus from the burlap. I held up the unopened one, vertically, then raised the one we'd eaten from and placed it horizontally against the other. I took two steps down to McLaren. "Get on your knees and kiss it, Hank," I commanded. I quickly sidestepped over to Maxwell, before he could get to his feet, and I thrust the cheese in front of him and shouted, "Kiss it, Special Agent Man. Forsake your brutal ways. Oh, my simple red children, such a friend we have in Cheeses! Swallow it. Swallow. Don't fight the spirit." I started shaking with something like laughter, but it wasn't laughter. I don't know what it was, fear, maybe, for having given in to the bitch. I had not repelled her. Her sickness was mine. I dropped the cheeses and walked up the stairs.

"Gonna sit tough, eh, Joey?" called McLaren, getting to his feet. "We'll see how tough when the buckin' starts."

"Yeah, fuck you, Hank," I said, not bothering to turn around. I heard them start down the stairs.

I went out and sat on Lincoln for a while, watched them get in their APC. Clem asked me how it went. I just told him they gave us a radio. We sat there, silent together. Clem had a wonderful quality of knowing when a person didn't want to talk. After a while, Bear Dreamer and Speckled Hawk joined us.

"What you looking so down in the jaw 'bout?" Speckled Hawk asked me.

"Had a Yuwipi and it didn't work."

"Give it time," said Bear Dreamer Bordeaux.

I laughed.

"Why you laugh?" he said.

"*Ta-chesli,*" I said, which means "bull, it's a load of bull." "It's no realer than a Christian faith healing. Just a motherload of placebo."

Bear Dreamer cocked his head. "What's that?"

I explained how we used to give fake injections onboard the chopper when we were out of morphine. It quieted the wounded. No matter how bad they were shot up, they quieted right down.

Bear Dreamer scratched his scalp, his white braids clean and shining in the sun. He was gentle. A lot of people would have gotten defensive, but he just said, "Hmmn."

"See, you make them believe there's strong stuff in that syringe, just like you Yuwipi guys make us believe there are spirits coming to help. Your little lights and rattle tricks. The mind has to buy into it. Deep down, the mind wants to be tricked. Tricked *all* the way, or it's no go." I thought of my old nickname, Iktomi, and wondered if the problem was that you can't trick a trickster. Can't bullshit a bullshitter.

"Who did the Yuwipi?" asked Speckled Hawk.

"John No Horse."

Under his beak, Speckled Hawk's thin lips broke into a sly smile. "Well, there you go," he said.

"There I go, what?"

"John lost the power 'bout a year back. Carved a guy with a buzz saw," Speckled said.

"Bullshit," I blurted. He was always slamming No Horse behind his back.

He shook his head slightly. "Up around White Clay, it was. Over a chick and a six-pack. Cut this Rosebudder bad. Can't carve folks up and keep the power."

"I don't know about that story," Bear Dreamer said, "but joining a warrior society was not the Yuwipi-man thing to do. Don't get me wrong. It's great you brought the Tokala back," he said, looking at Speckled Hawk. "You should bring all the *akicitas* back, the Badgers, the Plain Lance Owners, all of 'em. But if you're a Yuwipi man, you're a healer, not a warrior. Try bein' both, you lose the power."

"I never claimed to be Yuwipi," said Speckled Hawk defensively.

Bear Dreamer nodded.

"But if he lost the power," I said. "How come he was untied?"

"Spirits got a sense of humor, like to tease. But they never heal nobody for him. Not since the buzz saw," said Speckled Hawk.

"What was ailing you, anyway?" asked Bear Dreamer.

"A voice. Won't leave me alone. Taking me over."

Speckled shook his head and shrugged. "No Horse couldn't have helped you there, nohow. Only medicine works on that is bear medicine." He slapped old Bear Dreamer on the shoulder. "Ain't it so?"

"I ain't saying it's the *only,* but I never heard of no other medicine doing it. I cured a girl of voices maybe fifteen years back. And a young man at Standing Rock about three years back."

"You're a lucky boy, Joey," said Speckled Hawk. "Bear Dreamer here is the last bear-medicine man alive."

Bear Dreamer nodded wistfully and turned to Clem. "When this mountain stuff is settled, I'd like to teach you what I know."

Clem beamed back at Bear Dreamer. "Thank you." Then he said, "Junior would be better, though. He's young and got so much wakan a'ready." We all looked over at Roosevelt, at the slender kid chained to the rock.

"I'll teach you both. First we're going to fix up old Joey here. Tell you what, Joe. Bring me a twist of kinnikinnick and a pipe. We'll do it right

in the Hall of Records on a dark night. Don't even need no puppy soup.
I know what you got."

A great weight lifted off my shoulders at the thought of being cured.
Then I reproached myself for buying into the same scam again. How
many times would I let them jack my hopes up? But I couldn't control
these sudden flashes of warmth for the old guy. And even if it was bullshit, it seemed better to live in groundless hope than in resolute despair.

We heard some tinny pops, like the sound of M-16s on semi, then the
heavy crackle of rapid fire. The sound was coming from the pine hill,
from down near the bottom, it seemed.

I took the ridge path back to the Level Three fortification. From there,
we could see that Level One was repelling the attack of an unseen force.
We wanted to pour some extra fire into those woods but refrained. So did
the guys in Level Two.

The first tier seemed to be fighting well, keeping low, using the sandbags, firing at where they heard fire. A sharp cry shivered through the
pines. A guy in cammies darted from one tree to another. Through binoculars, I could see he was working his way toward a fallen man. He
reached a tree that was maybe a yard away from the fallen guy. He wanted
to drag his buddy behind the cover of the tree but didn't want to get his
ass shot off—so he peered around the trunk, looking uphill to our guys
and making the T sign with his arms, like Time-out, please, like it was just
a shirts-and-skins pickup game. "Take him and get," shouted Sparky
White Thunder, the captain of Bunker Two, Level One. The Time-out
guy dragged the wounded man behind the cover of the tree. Another soldier materialized, also making the sign of the T, then ran up to help carry
the wounded one. They took his arms over the backs of their necks and
shuffled down the hill, his feet dragging through the pine needles. He was
the tail between their legs. I scanned back and forth with the binoculars
and spied here and there a figure quitting a tree and heading downhill
toward the service road.

There was a lot of yelling and celebrating in Level One, and somebody
let off his weapon a few times to hurry up the retreat. "Well, that's fine,"
said Eli. "But you can bet it was just the Guard. The feds are using them
to feel us out before the pros get here."

"Yeah. They'll probably bring the Deltas," said Abel.

Sparky White Thunder was so pumped he got out of the bunker and
ran a ways down after them, firing shots over their heads. We had to yell
at him to bring him to his senses. On his way back up, he stopped by the

tree where the fallen man had lain and he picked something up. "Yeah!" he shouted triumphantly, then ran back the rest of the way. We went down to Level One. They had dropped a walkie-talkie. Isaac took it up to Hidden Canyon.

We made a small fire in Hidden Canyon, set a tripod over it, and cooked our first dinner on Rushmore, beans and dogs. It was warm in the belly. Clem and Junior must have smelled it. I brought them water, then climbed to the high ridge, where I did a three-hour watch. After Isaac relieved me, I laid out my bedroll in Hidden Canyon. It was foam rubber and a cotton quilt. Too excited to sleep yet, I turned on the walkie-talkie and listened for transmissions as I lay on my back and looked at the stars. They were out in force, brightly, as if they had learned what we had done and wanted to witness the outcome. I lay on my back and took it all in. And I wondered if there would be more bloodshed. The mountain felt solid and good beneath me. Everything felt right. It felt right to be up there. Opera lady or not, I was overcome with a sense of well-being. Every now and then, the walkie-talkie crackled. "Post One?" "Check." "Post Two?" "Check." And on like that for six posts. I looked at the Big Dipper for a while and wondered if all the stars in it were in our galaxy, or were some of them not stars but galaxies themselves, just way, way out there. I wondered about other worlds, and if the universe really goes on forever. I had all those thoughts you have when you look at so many stars. There was so much I didn't know. "Smiddie, this is a job for the ATF," crackled a voice from one of the posts out there, below us.

"Why's that?" crackled Smiddie.

"They're drunks, got firearms, and they pray with tobacco."

Day Two

The next morning, huge NBC and ABC trucks rolled up 244 and pulled in to the parking lot of the Tourist Center. So did an assortment of vans with little satellite dishes on the roofs. Through the binoculars, I could make out different markings of TV and radio stations.

In the next couple hours, we saw camera crews filming reporters on the patio of the Tourist Center, always setting up the shot so that the monument would be in the backdrop. I wished we had a big banner to unfurl across the presidents' foreheads.

Bacon came out onto Lincoln with me. He had been taking supplies to the bunkers all morning. "That ABC one is probably *Nightline*," he said,

resting his hand on my shoulder. "Pretty soon everyone in America is going to know about Article Twelve." He laughed. "I can just see it now.
They'll have a stable of slick government lawyers talking *res judicata*, but
Ted will just keep sticking it to them in that way he has, you know, like, Yes,
that's fine, but please, sir, answer the question, what about Article Twelve?"

That afternoon, Eli and I received the first group of reporters on the staircase and led them up into Hidden Canyon. There were twelve of them,
including the cameramen, and they represented a range of stations and
papers. Maxwell wouldn't let more than twelve up at a time. Most of
them were decked out in action vests with zipper pouch pockets. One
lady even had a full safari outfit. It was like they had looted Banana Republic. Bunch of greenhorns trying to look like war correspondents.

"Before we take your questions, we'd like to show you one thing,"
Isaac said. He turned and entered the Hall of Records. Everyone followed. We had on display photocopies of the 371 treaties that the U.S.
Congress signed with native tribes. They were pasted to the stone walls
inside the Hall. Three hundred seventy-one is a large number. They hung
side by side and ran all the way to the back of the cave, where it was dark.
Luckily, the camera guys had battery packs and lights, so that they could
film them all. As they did, Isaac explained that each of the treaties had
been broken by Congress the moment a tribe was rendered weak. Not
one of the 371 treaties had been respected. "Not one. Ask any historian,"
he said, then walked back outside.

We stood in Hidden Canyon. The reporters held copies of our Letter
to the Press in their hands and would often refer to it before putting
questions to us. Speckled Hawk, Sharon, and Isaac fielded them. I was
supposed to field questions, too, but I was afraid the opera lady would
mess me up again, so I hung back. Bacon had made himself scarce.

"Do you really think you can get back the Black Hills?" asked the
woman in the safari suit. She had straight brown hair with blond streaks.
She smiled pleasantly, showing her even teeth as she held the mike out
to Sharon.

"Of course we do," Sharon said.

"How long are you prepared to stay on the monument?"

"Long as it takes," Speckled Hawk said.

"Meaning you have an endless supply of food and water?" asked a guy
with slicked-back hair.

"Plenty of both," Speckled lied. Water was my main concern.

"Can you be more specific?"

"I don't imagine I could. Don't you think your viewers want to know what it's about?"

"Will you be able to hold out as long as you did at Wounded Knee in 1973?" asked a balding man in his forties. He wore a blue shirt and chinos and had a *Chicago Tribune* tag on his breast pocket.

"This is completely different," Isaac said. "We held out three months there, but had no leverage. This time, the government has to do the right thing, or else the world will see two good men die of hunger on a national monument. And one of them's not even sixteen."

"You think they're just going to hand you the Black Hills? What about all the people who settled here?"

"When the American people learn how the Hills were acquired, they'll talk to their representatives. It won't be Indians versus whites. It'll be about what's right."

"How many other women are along? Are there children, too?" asked the safari lady.

"No comment," Speckled said.

"Why doesn't your tribe accept the one hundred six million dollars that the Supreme Court awarded you in 1980?" asked the bald guy from the *Tribune*.

"It's an insult," Isaac said.

"Aren't you just holding out for more cash? Isn't that what this stunt is about?"

"Look at all this! Look around you," Isaac said, sweeping his great arm across the seemingly endless shoulders of mountains and pine forests. "Would you sell this for *any* amount?"

"So you do want more cash?"

Isaac shook his head. "Our wealth is this, these mountains, these trees and lakes. Money is *your* invention."

"But you sold it," the *Tribune* guy said with a smile, then added, "Technically."

Isaac kept his cool. "If you have a horse that you love, don't you have the right *not* to have to sell it? Do you think I should be able to wave a rifle in your face and say that horse is worth five bucks, so here's five bucks, now take it and shut up. Do you think that's a sale? Even the Supreme Court said that ain't a sale."

"Tell us about the Kit Foxes. Isn't that an old warrior society?" asked a plump little guy from an NBC affiliate in Detroit.

"No comment," Speckled said.

"How do you reconcile a warrior society and a hunger strike?"

"No comment."

"So who's doing the hunger strike?"

"That would be Clement Blue Chest and Elijah Hunts Alone, Jr.," Isaac said. He pronounced their names like they were royal titles.

"Blue Chest is the holy man, right?" asked the safari woman, consulting her copy of the letter to the press.

"That's right," said Isaac. "He is at that."

"And who's this Eli Hunts Alone, Jr.?"

"Just the best fucking quarterback in South Dakota," I blurted, almost shouting. They all looked at me, surprised. The various cameramen pointed their lenses at me, and even the lenses looked surprised. "Well, he is," I said with a shrug.

"And who are you, sir?" asked the safari lady.

I didn't want to say any more, but then I realized it would be on national TV and that there was a fair chance Justine Moore—wherever she was—would hear my name and look up. I pictured her preparing dinner for her children, in a bright kitchen, a small TV on top of the Formica counter. She hears my name and looks over, sees my face and wonders *Could it be?*

"Joey Moves Camp," I said, then stepped back to end further conversation between us.

The woman turned back to Speckled Hawk. "If this is such a peaceful operation, why are only two men fasting and all the others armed to the teeth?"

"Because we know what we're up against," said Speckled.

"Look at Tibet," Sharon said. "Tibetans tried nonviolence without rifle backup and look where they are. Refugees in India."

"How many of you are AIM?"

"I'll say it again," said Speckled. "We brought weapons simply to protect the hunger strikers. So that nobody takes them down."

"So, can we speak to your hunger strikers?"

"No," said Speckled Hawk flatly. I looked at Isaac, like to say, Who the hell made him captain? Isaac cleared his throat and said, "Yeah, right this way. I don't see any harm in it."

Speckled looked pissed as hell to be undercut like that, but Isaac wasn't the kind you could argue with.

First we took them onto Roosevelt to meet Junior. He seemed embarrassed by the attention and didn't answer any of their questions. He only said that he had read the Letter to the Press and that it was all in there.

On Lincoln, Clem wore a towel over his head to protect his shoulders from the sun. He was facing out toward the Tourist Center. "Clem, you got company," I said. He turned around slowly. He was already getting sores on his butt.

The reporters generally introduced themselves before asking a question. They asked many of the same things that Sharon, Speckled, and Isaac had already answered. Then the guy with the slicked hair said, "Mr. Blue Chest, we learned on your reservation of some of your amazing feats. Some say you're a deliverer, a messiah. Are they correct?" He stuck a microphone down in Clem's face.

Clem looked perplexed. I don't think he knew what those words really meant.

The babe in the safari jacket said, "Are you concerned about repeating history? Aren't you setting up another powder keg like the 1890 Wounded Knee massacre?"

"We're not repeating history," Clem said. "We're here to lay it bare for you. It's been hid too long."

"But surely you remember the massacre at Wounded Knee in which three hundred of your people were needlessly gunned down—surely you know that that tragedy resulted from *Wovoka*'s claim to be the Messiah."

He shook his head. "It was the Seventh Cavalry getting even."

"Are you the Son of God, Mr. Blue Chest?" She said it with a straight face, holding the mike to his mouth with one hand and tucking her brown-and-blond hair behind her ear with the other. The cameraman kneeled to get in tighter on Clem's face.

Clem smiled. "What kind of question is that?"

"Are you, or aren't you . . . the Son of God?"

"You mean of the Creator? Sure, we all are. Gotta start treating each other that way."

"Are you telling the people of Pine Ridge that you're not the Redeemer sent down to expel the whites from your land?"

"Lady, I'm a drunk on the mend. But we do aim to get our land back."

After the press went back down, the feds radioed up that they wanted another parley. "What for?" said Isaac into the radio. He pushed back his black hat with his thumb. He looked tired.

"Can't make headway unless we communicate," Maxwell crackled.

"When Koppel arrives, there'll be plenty of communication."

"That's one of the things we have to talk about, the logistics of the *Nightline* thing."

"You can come up to the staircase. No more than three of you."

To my surprise, it wasn't Maxwell and Dexter who came up, only Colonel McLaren. He was flanked by two soldiers. He said he needed to talk privately with me. Speckled Hawk and Isaac withdrew and joined the others up on the ridge. "Give us some room, boys," said the Colonel. His flunkies withdrew a respectful distance down the staircase, but with rifles at the ready.

The Colonel pulled a pack of Camels from his pocket, then lit us both up with a Zippo. He exhaled twin jets from his nostrils, rubbed his big chin with the back of his hand, then held the hand out and studied the back of it. He took another drag, then said, "Ever since you fixed my truck on the highway, I've liked you, Joey. I really have. I know you're sore on account of my letting you go, but it wasn't personal. I'll give it to you straight. I let you go because I didn't want half-breeds for grandkids. Sounds harsh, but I know you understand. I know lots of Indians feel the same way." He coughed a bit and spat something up. "You and Frannie thought you were pretty clever sneaking around, but I knew what was up. And to be honest, I admired the hell out of her for picking the one hand on the ranch with some real character. I never had a hand who put so much pride into no matter what job he was asked to do. Never had to ask you nothing twice. But I've got a standing in the community, Joey."

He looked at me like I should respond somehow.

"What I'm trying to say ain't easy," he said, taking off his helmet and scratching his scalp through his short-cropped hair. "It's a bit like what happened with my wife. This'll sound like a hell of a leap. But bear with me. Eleanor, God rest her soul, was never what you'd call beautiful in the skin-deep way. And I didn't want to get tangled up with no plain Jane. I wanted beauty. My plan was to marry a glamour girl, a Marilyn Monroe. The dang thing is, I so enjoyed Eleanor's company that we started spending time together, as friends, you know. Then I started to have feelings for her, and that scared the bejesus out of me. I panicked. It was like she was threatening my plan of having a flashy wife. And what would my buddies say? So I stopped calling her, stopped seeing her. Just froze her out of my life. Then one day it hit me like a diamond bullet."

"What hit you?"

"That the whole point of beauty—the whole point of being beautiful—is that it helps folks get together, helps love along. Well, I already loved her, see? . . . So the hell with beauty, and the hell with what my friends would say. I went to her home and asked her to marry me." He flicked some ash and squinted at the orange tip of the cigarette and then at me. "See, Joey, life is always throwing us curves, and sometimes that's good. I mean, a good curve can make life so much richer than what we had planned for ourselves. I don't know if it's Fate, Destiny, or God, but whatever it is, it's got loads more imagination than we got."

He stopped and looked at me with those powder-blue eyes, waiting for me to make some kind of connection, or waiting for some meaning to knock me over. Waiting for me to be touched, I suppose. Clearly, I had to say something, but I didn't want to get sucked into whatever his game was.

He smiled. "But you see what I'm driving at?"

I shook my head.

"Well, I wanted half-breeds 'bout as much as I'd wanted a homely wife. Neither was part of the plan. But our plans are never too imaginative."

I looked blankly at him.

He put his hand in the pocket of his field jacket and pulled out an M-16 banana clip. He started turning it over slowly in his hand as though it would start spinning out words for him. "When Frannie told me she was pregnant and that it was yours, I immediately thought of abortion, just like I had first tried to cut Eleanor out of my life. But then the diamond bullet hit me again. I already love that grandkid, and to hell with what people think. I want my grandkid, Joey, and I don't give a good goddamn what people say. I love him already—or her—and that kid deserves to have its own daddy. You and Frannie can marry or not marry. Do as you please, but I want that kid to have his own dad, his real dad, nearby and accessible. Because I know that man and he's a man of character. I mean that. But how can you be his dad with this kind of crap?" he said, tipping his chin up the staircase. "You won't be *no*body's dad rotting in prison or six feet under." He paused for a while to let that sink in. Then he leaned closer and said in a lower tone, "Now, I've got a Jeep down there and an extra uniform in it. Your hair's short, that's good. We'll get you off this rock before it starts raining death. And it will, Joey. SEALs, Deltas, the Bureau's tactical team, SWAT teams from Denver and Minneapolis, they all want a piece of the action. The ATF is clamoring to try out its new dynamic entry party. Everyone wants a piece of you guys."

I knew most of this was bluff and scare tactics. Even if they tried something, they wouldn't use that kind of overkill in front of the world press.

"But it doesn't have to end in tragedy," he continued. "I know you could never sneak off if you thought your friends were going to get wiped out. You got too much honor in you. But the beauty is that if you *do* leave the scene, this thing will defuse itself. See, your friends don't realize what they're up against. They're too pumped up 'cause you took this mountain. They feel like they can do anything now, like they're unkillable, wearing those ghost dance shirts that your granddads thought were bulletproof and wore at Wounded Knee. You're setting yourselves up for another tragedy, my friend. But if a key player like yourself was to disappear from the scene, it would take the others down a notch, you know, deflate 'em enough to see reality again. At which point they'll want to leave the mountain, too. Some'll sneak off, others'll trade surrender for amnesty, and bit by bit we'll defuse this keg before it blows. You've got to give up this obsession with the past and start thinking of life, Joey. The future. Your kid."

"Are you saying she hasn't left for Denver?"

"*Den*ver? No. No, she's at home," he said. But he had perked up a bit too much at the mention of Denver.

"And what kind of a future would I have when everyone would know I was the first to quit the mountain?"

"We'll tell them the SEALs snatched you in the middle of the night." He paused, looked at his wedding band, then continued. "Now, it would be best if you snuck down tonight. I'll have the Jeep and a driver waiting for you on the far side of the sculptor's studio."

"So, she's not going to have an abortion?" I asked.

"God no, son. She *wants* your child now. And she wants you." He rubbed the stubble on his chin with the edge of the ammo clip and looked quite philosophical for a moment, probably contemplating how tough it is to get a good shave in the field. Another one of life's curves, I guess.

"Why isn't she here?"

"It's a war zone. I wouldn't let her."

No doubt it was Pogo that told the Colonel about the pregnancy, probably when he got home from the Broken Spur that day. Frannie had probably left for Denver and had the deed done. By now she could be anywhere, chasing whatever she was chasing. "I'm not leaving this rock," I said.

"Why?" he asked, genuinely puzzled.

"I got a standing in the community."

"Come on, son," he said, smiling with a flush, as if to say, Don't tease an old man with his own words.

"Plus, I shot your cow," I added.

"Hell, that's nothin' now. We'll have a steak in Kadoka."

"And I shot up all your vehicles."

The smile disappeared and the watery blue eyes turned to ice. But he remembered his mission and regained his goodwill. "The insurance covered it, every last cent," he said. "Hell, I would've been resentful, too, if I'd been laid off like that."

"And I burned your son's body for burning my mother. Did him up on a scaffold with gasoline."

He looked puzzled, then the blood drained from his face as his mind crashed into two conclusions: that Clem's mother was my mother, and that Pogo was not just off on another drunk in Rapid or Cheyenne.

"It sounds harsh," I said. "But I know you can understand." I turned and walked up the stairs. I heard a strange sound come out of him, like a puppy being strangled, and I heard him start to rush me, but the sound of Eli clearing his rifle from up above on the granite tower froze him. I heard the two M-16s of the Guardsmen snapped up to eye level, no doubt aimed at Eli. I looked up. Eli was staring down his barrel from under his black ten-gallon, his shiny rodeo buckle glinting in the sun. Some Kit Foxes were on either side of him, staring down their barrels at the two Guardsmen on the staircase. "Turn around and walk away," Eli commanded in an even voice. There was a long silence. I heard the Colonel breathing hard and fast. Then I heard his boot swivel on the granite step. "That's right," said Elijah, talking down the barrel. "Now, the same for your men."

I didn't even know if Pogo was dead or alive. I said what I said to hurt the Colonel. But I guess the main reason I said it was to make sure that I could never change my mind about that goddamn Jeep. Because a big part of me wanted to believe she was on the ranch, and that there could be a new life.

Day Three

The sun was just rising and I was still half-asleep. Clem pointed a finger out at Route 244 as I handed him a bowl of water. A transport trailer was unloading three tanks onto the road, old World War II vintage. They hit the asphalt, lumbered fifty yards or so in reverse, then took the turnoff onto the service road. I lost them in the trees for a while, but it seemed they had stopped on the far side of the sculptor's studio.

The pines on the southeast hill were scrubby. Tanks would be able to move right through them, then sit on our bunkers. I guessed they didn't want to risk their infantry on anything but mop-up. The tanks could do it all, pouring machine-gun fire at close range into our bunkers.

"We gotta take those out," said Abel Many Coups from behind my shoulder. I got on the radio and told Maxwell he'd better withdraw the tanks.

"Or what?" he said.

"Or we'll take them out."

He laughed.

"We've got the armor piercers you were looking for."

He laughed again. "You're quick on your feet, Joey, I'll give you that. But it appears those weapons are in Central America, or headed that way. You've got one hour to surrender." He clicked off.

I called back. "I want to speak to the Army commander of those tanks."

"I'm in command of the whole turkey shoot," said Maxwell.

"Tell your tankers that they're up against armor-piercing weapons."

"Give it up, Moves Camp."

"It's on *your* head if you don't."

"One hour," he said, and he clicked off.

I turned to Abel. "Get down to Level One. Make sure they're ready."

"That ain't enough," he said. "We gotta hit that armor before it gets anywhere *near* Level One."

I shook my head. "We can't look like the aggressors."

"Fuck the PR war," snapped Abel. "It's real war now, and we go the way that risks the least men. I could sneak out solo and whack all three before they even get near our people."

Isaac agreed with him. "The bunkers aren't deep and the ammo's limited. If we don't whack 'em first, it could be over in an hour."

"All right, but we just cripple the treads."

"That's about all a LAW *can* do on a tank," said Abel. "It'll pierce an APC's armor, but not a tank's."

Frankly, I was glad to hear it. At Level Three, Abel, Elijah, Isaac, and I each took a LAW. We took a fifth one just in case, then ran down through the forest, past Levels Two and One, and then beyond into no-man's-land. We each had a rifle as well. We got to a knoll from where we could see the end of the service road. We hid behind a big log and could hear the tanks revving. Thirty seconds later, we saw them, rolling out, coming our way. Eli and Abel advanced another thirty yards or so, out on the left flank, crouched, darting from tree to tree. Eli had a LAW slung over his shoulder, Abel had two. They disappeared into some bushes. The lead tank was now sixty yards from old Isaac and me. We kept low behind our log, but we could feel the rumble in the ground, slow and steady, like nothing in the world could stop them. I tightened my ass, terrified of crapping my pants in front of a sixty-year-old Medal of Honor winner.

Right before the tanks reached the end of the service road and started into the brush, Abel and Elijah let them have it. Three explosions ripped the morning, two in rapid succession, then a third. It looked as if the tread on the right-hand side of the lead tank had been blown off. We couldn't see the other two, as they were in single file, but we figured they were also crippled. The turret of the lead tank started to swivel to the right. Elijah and Abel streaked out of those bushes. The tank opened its machine guns on them. Old Isaac put his big hand on my shoulder to push himself up, then he ran twenty feet into the open, fell to one knee and fired his LAW, like it was a bazooka in Korea. It took off from his shoulder and covered the forty yards at a speed that was both fast and slow. You could see the streak of it, the way you see the streak of an arrow or a rocket. It slammed into the turret, leaving a fire shroud all over the thing. Inside, they were probably fine. He just did it to draw them off of Eli and Abel.

He turned around and shrugged. "Indi'n-owned and Indi'n-operated," he murmured. I motioned him back. He was a sitting duck out there, though no one was firing on him yet. I guess all the infantry still had their faces in the dirt, or maybe they hadn't made it down from the parking lot yet and were still somewhere in the woods near the Tourist Center.

Isaac scrambled back and hunkered behind the log. "Beats hell outa bingo," he said, grinning. Every cell in his old body was made to count coups and do pony raids. He hadn't tasted anything like it since Korea, but Korea had been joyless. And this was not.

Elijah and Abel were running back our way. A Huey swooped in low out of nowhere, buzzing the trees, shooting up the bunkers of Level One, strafing everything. It broke away from the bunkers and swooped on down the hill right over Elijah and Abel. The door gunner opened up with the 60. They dove behind a boulder that wasn't big enough for both of them. The Huey circled and kept firing, so that they had to scramble around the rock. Then only Eli was scrambling. The Huey hovered lower. The door gunner was lining Eli up. It was low, and coming lower. I could see the bastard clearly. His shaded helmet lens was down, so I couldn't see his eyes, but his mouth was all bad-ass, like he was shooting rats. I unsnapped the last LAW and telescoped it out. The sight popped up. I put it to my shoulder and lined the bird up, but hesitated: I was thinking that there was a good chance the tank crews were fine—just treads and scorched paint—so blowing up a chopper crew would ruin everything. The door gunner started firing again. Elijah did his best to scrunch up behind the rock. Isaac grabbed the LAW off my shoulder and brought it to his. Quick as I could, I shouldered my AR-15 and lined the door gunner up. *You'll never squeeze off.* She giggled. The fucker was hammering the rock. My fingers were so sweaty I thought I'd slip off the trigger. I kept thinking that I hadn't shot a living thing since I shot McLaren's cow and hadn't shot a human since I was up there in the door gunner's seat. I was scared that she was right, but then I felt the kick against my shoulder and saw his body snap back off the gun. His helmet rolled right out the starboard door and hit a pine tree on its way down. The pilot swerved out of there like a bat out of hell, and not a moment too soon, as the smoky tail of Isaac's LAW moved right through the space where the cockpit had been a split second before.

Elijah hoisted Abel across his shoulders in the fireman's carry and we ran as best we could up to Level One. Everyone there was okay, except for one kid who caught a bullet in the thigh, but it went in and out. I took a turn with Abel on my shoulders, up to Level Two, and she was singing in my ear, *I am the very model of the modern major succubus. I'm very fond of algebra and very hip to calculus.* Then old Isaac insisted on carrying Abel the rest of the way. He made it look easy.

He laid Abel down in the mouth of the Hall of Records. There were two holes in his back that came out his chest, so we didn't know which way to lay him down. Elijah had taken his shirt off and was pressing it against the chest wounds. I took mine off and wedged it into the back wounds. He had already lost a lot of blood. "I'll get some sage and sweet-grass," said Speckled Hawk. Sage and sweetgrass, I whispered. Sage and sweetgrass. Sage and fucking sweetgrass. It's their cure for everything. "He needs a goddamn doctor!" I shouted. "Get me the radio!"

Down at the Tourist Center they wouldn't pick up.

Elijah and Isaac were fixing a blanket around Abel when he came to and whispered something. We all moved in closer. He had blood on his lips. "Don't let them take me."

"No one's gonna take you nowhere," said Eli. "You're with us."

"Don't let them take me down."

"You're staying right here. You're staying with us. You're on the Six Grandfathers. No one's taking you down."

"I don't want to go down. Get me a priest." His voice was just a hoarse, terrified whisper, inflating a pink bubble at the corner of his mouth.

"Where's Bacon?" I shouted.

"Right here," said Quinn, from over my shoulder.

"*Real* priest," whispered Abel. "No hell. No hell." His eyes rolled back into his head so that just the whites showed. Bacon kneeled down, taking Abel's hand in his, trying to comfort him.

"Nobody's going to hell, Abel. There's no such place."

"Real priest," he pleaded.

Sharon gave me the radio pack again. Maxwell took his sweet time before picking up. "We need a doctor and a priest," I said.

"You cocksucker."

"I told you we had the LAWs. I told you not to move those tanks up."

"I'll see you fry in hell," he crackled. "I will personally blow your head off."

"We need a doctor and a priest."

"Fuck you."

"You're refusing us that?"

"Our medics have their hands full, you fucking—"

"When can you send them up?"

"You get nothing!" he screamed, then clicked off. I called back.

"Agent Dexter," said a voice.

"Put him on," I said. There was a long silence, then Maxwell came on.

"Send us a medevac chopper," I said.

He laughed. "That's all you people can do, make demands, give us this, give us that. Always want something for nothing. Surrender the mountain and we'll fly out your wounded."

"You shot a decorated Airborne Ranger. Doesn't that mean squat?"

"You got that right."

"He's a kid. He's dying."

"There's a priest here from your reservation. That's all you get."

"What about the doctor?"

"Use your medicine man."

"You're going to let him die, an Airborne Ranger? Give us a goddamn doctor."

"How about some more ammo and food, too?" The bastard was enjoying himself.

"He's bleeding to death, Maxwell. He's a kid."

"How many LAWs do you have left?"

I hesitated.

"How many?!" he snapped.

"One," I lied.

"Give it up and I'll send a medical team when they're done with our tank crew. But you surrender the weapon *now!*"

"Send the team up now."

"The weapon now, the medics when they're done with our wounded. It's a one-time offer, Moves Camp."

I clicked off. "Run and get a LAW," I said to Sharon and she was off. She sprinted back a few minutes later from Level Three with one in her hand. I got back on the radio. "I'm on Jefferson. I'm throwing it over." I tossed the weapon as far out as I could and watched it sail down, wondering if there would be an explosion on impact. There was none.

"I'll send a man to check it out," he said.

"It's *real.* Now just send the medics."

"They're still tied up. You can have your priest in the meantime. Meet him on the stairs."

"Fly him up or it will be too late."

"So you can try for that chopper again?" He clicked off.

The priest turned out to be Father O'Reilly. "What are *you* doing here?" I said.

He looked up as he climbed the stairs. "I go where my flock goes."

"More like where the feds go," I said. "And they go where you tell them."

"Just what's that supposed to mean?" he asked, straightening his back and trying to sound indignant.

"How'd they know Pawnee-Killer was at No Horse's? You gave him a ride that night."

"Pawnee-Killer was a *wanted* criminal," he said.

"Anyone who resists more land transfers is a wanted criminal."

"Not like Pawnee-Killer," he said defiantly.

"He was your student for three years at Mission."

"He was a boy then. He went bad."

As we stepped up into Hidden Canyon, we could see the others gathered around Abel, near the mouth of the Hall of Records. O'Reilly pulled his scapular out of a pocket, kissed it, mumbled Latin, then kneeled. Sharon touched Abel's forehead, to open his eyes. She told him the priest was here. The lids fluttered, then lifted, revealing glazed, already dead-

looking eyes. He said in a choked whisper, "Bless me, Father, for I have
sinned . . ." I walked away, feeling kind of sick and kind of terrified, because Abel had been one of the stronger voices calling for the running off
of priests.

Bacon was watching from about fifteen feet off, and trying not to look
hurt. "Don't take it personal, Quinn," I said, touching him on the shoulder. But he wouldn't turn away.

We sat on the back of Lincoln's head, where it slopes into Hidden
Canyon. I opened up a can of peaches, plunked a fork in, and offered
some to Bacon. He waved it off, probably wondering how I could think
of food while a brother dies. I learned long ago, though, that in combat
you eat when you can, and frankly I felt betrayed by Abel's big surrender.
I scrunched down a few feet lower into the canyon so that the smell of the
syrup wouldn't reach Clem. I imagined the odor snaking through the air
and tickling his nose, like the smell of picnic baskets in Yogi Bear car-
toons. Bacon kept his eyes on O'Reilly, on the performance of the last
rites.

"You miss all that?"

"Not all of it. But I liked giving absolution."

"Yeah?"

He nodded. "Some people come in desperate, I mean so completely
without hope, because they've done something they think is monstrous,
and they hate themselves for it. *Hate* themselves. Well, I could hear them
out, say a few words, tell them it was okay, they were forgiven and had a
clean slate." He smiled. "You should see the way their faces would *light*
up, Joey. Like a, a poison suddenly drains from their body. They can start
to forgive them*selves,* and start liking themselves again." He nodded.
"Absolution was nice."

"Nice enough that you'd join up again, if you could?"

He laughed. "You make it sound like the Army. *Join up.*"

"Sorry . . ."

"Nah, join up's right. I mean, uniforms, chain of command, absolute
obedience, worldwide deployments, opportunity to wipe out exotic cultures." He smiled weakly but kept watching O'Reilly doing the rites over
Abel. Then he said, "But, Joey, you don't have to be ordained, you know,
to do absolutions. Everyone can do them. It's our human duty."

"So, you wouldn't become a priest again, would you?"

"Oh, yes, I would. Absolutely, I would. And I'd get tossed out again.
I'd do it all over again the exact same way. I don't regret a thing."

I laughed. He had a weird sense of humor.

He shook his head. "I don't. Not a thing."

I thought about his butchered penis, all his burns and electric-shock scars. How could he not regret that? Or the mountain village?

"Everything you live through," he said, "can be turned to your advantage, turned into a strength. But only if you refuse to regret." He finally took his eyes off of O'Reilly and looked at me. "A soul that has overcome itself would choose the same life, the same circumstances, again, wanting nothing to be different, no matter how tough that life had been."

"Quinn, you've said a lot of crazy stuff that I thought was kind of beautiful in a screwball way, but that's just stupid. Take Clem. You say he's the Messiah, so you must think he's one of these great souls that regret nothing, right?"

He nodded.

So I told him all about Wenonah and how she got killed on the road, and how it tore Clem up and set him on the bottle. "Now, are you telling me that Clem has *overcome* himself to the point where he would say to his maker, *'I want to repeat my life exactly, so please make sure my daughter gets killed again, just the same way'*? And are you saying that if on the other hand he *does* regret her death, then he isn't the great soul you thought he was?"

I liked Bacon, but it felt good to shut him up.

He wasn't silent too long, though. "Everything's connected," he said. "For all we know, it was Wenonah's death that shifted Clem's life toward this mountain. Without it, he might never have sunk to the point where he became receptive to his destiny, to his vision. Pain opens the eyes. Men who have never known pain are blind. I mean, that's why one pierces, right? For vision. Your niece's death might have been the thing that opened the door in him, set him on the path. See, Joey, the Black Hills *will* be returned, and it'll be the result of Clem's pursuing his vision. Which means that his other kids, Rafer, Jeb, Jenny—and all Sioux kids from here on in—will finally have their land back. And I'll bet my right arm that neither Clem nor Wenonah would regret that, or any of the steps they had to take to make it happen."

I resented how smoothly he fitted her death into his scheme of mystical cause-and-effect. It was all so pat, so like a Jesuit. Listening to him, you would almost think Wenonah had been given the choice—the *opportunity*—to sacrifice herself for a *cause,* you would almost think her death was meaningful and not senseless. I also wanted to tell him not to preach the sun dance to me, that I had danced it long before he or Clem had. But I didn't, because there was also something comforting in what he said, perhaps the optimism of it. And I had come to like the guy.

"Look, Quinn, if you really have no regrets, how come you can't come clean about how you got those LAWs?"

He shrugged. "There's a black market right out of Fort Benning. Abel told me about it." He reached for the peach can and took a sip of syrup. "I knew it would come to tanks. I've seen U.S.-built tanks used on Indians in Salvador and Guatemala. They used APCs at Wounded Knee on you guys. Now they're using tanks on Mohawks in Canada."

We watched O'Reilly wrap it up, putting on the final touches and flourishes, so that Abel could die in the comforts of the Church. Quinn got to his feet, crossed the canyon, and disappeared into the Hall of Records. A minute later, he emerged with a plastic bowl filled with water. He walked out onto Lincoln, knelt beside my brother, and helped him drink.

◆

We cut saplings from the southeast hill and built a scaffold on Roosevelt, just behind Junior. When we picked up Abel's body, O'Reilly commanded us in the name of the Lord not to touch it, as if he had some claim on it now. I shoved him back with my rifle. "You got his spirit. Don't get greedy," I said. A scaffold on top of Roosevelt would make every front page in the land. It would be worth the flies and the odor, and I wasn't about to let an old buzzard like O'Reilly get in the way.

We took O'Reilly to the bottom of the staircase and showed him how to get down the mountain on foot. But he wouldn't go, he said, until he conducted mass on the mountain for all who wished to attend. He said it was our moral duty to inform our men of this. "More than half of your boys are Catholic, and you know it," he said.

I shook my head. "Ration days are gone, old man."

"Was Abel Many Coups just looking for grub?" he asked, his voice rich with sarcasm. He figured he still had a grip on us, at least on the so-called Catholics among us, and that he could reactivate all the old programming by pushing the right buttons in his sermon. He would hellfire-and-brimstone us off the mountain, create doubt as to our goals and leadership, break our momentum, get us to fight among ourselves. Doubtless he would seek to create factions that would give in to the feds, give up the Black Hills for the boundless expanse of Paradise. I could just see him and Agent Maxwell working out the homily together, smiling slyly over coffee in the Tourist Center.

"What are you afraid of?" he said, like it was a dare.

"Ain't a question of afraid," said old Isaac. "We got a limited number of men deployed at strategic points. We ain't moving 'em for no hocus-pocus."

"Then, let me take it to *them.* I'll administer the Eucharist in the bunkers."

"The hell you will," I said. "So you can tell Maxwell about our positions and numbers."

"They already know where your men are. You've got three levels of bunkers on the southeast hill in the forest. That's where eighty percent of your force is. I'm not here to gather intelligence. I want to talk as many of your boys off the mountain as possible, because you're going to get hit hard, Joseph. There's going to be a heavy, heavy attack, maybe even an air strike—"

I laughed.

"I overheard them," he pleaded. "A low-level, precision strike. They've talked about it. Listen, I know most of your boys will tell me to bugger off. I doubt any will follow me down the mountain. But it's my human duty to try. And failing that, it's my priestly duty to administer last rites before such probable death. That's the least I can do for them, Joseph, so that they won't be denied heaven. Please. Their souls are in your hands."

He spoke all this with such earnestness that I believed he actually believed it himself. And it crossed my mind that he might not be intentionally sinister, just simple—and that he was being used expertly by the feds to unnerve us.

Thoughts of hell are infectious in a sneaky way. I caught myself wondering if there might be some special circle in hell reserved for those who obstruct priests from administering the Seventh Sacrament. I wondered how the tortures might be different there from the other circles that we had studied as kids.

"What about it then, Joseph?" he asked, as if I were suddenly the man in charge.

Old Isaac took a step forward, tipping back his dusty hat, crinkling his face into a broad smile. "Come now, Father," he said. "No one's goin' to hell or limbo. Them places can't exist, because how could heaven be heaven without the whole family there? The Great Spirit would never split a family up for eternity. That would be *small*-spirited and vengeful. It would cause sadness in heaven. How can you have sadness in heaven?" He paused, and then, just before O'Reilly could bounce back with some fancy Church bull, Isaac said, "We're having beans for supper. Naturally, you're welcome, but after that, you best hump it down the mountain."

The last two nights, Clem and Junior fell asleep at sundown, so we waited till then before cooking dinner. On a stretch of granite between Roosevelt and Jefferson, Sharon kindled a fire while Isaac emptied five or six cans of baked beans into a pot. He hung it from a tripod that he had placed over the fire. It started smelling good real quick and I was glad Clem and Junior were asleep. We sat around the fire in a semicircle, facing out toward the Tourist Center and the federal forces. We could see the flicker of campfires and occasionally Jeep lights.

Bacon was delivering food to the bunkers. He went every night to check if they needed provisions. He looked tired and sweaty from all the climbing up and down, but he smiled as he joined us, armed with an aluminum spoon and a plastic bowl.

We were an odd little tea party. You had old Isaac, Congressional Medal of Honor and baked-bean chef, stirring the pot, humming "Waltzing Matilda" in his deep voice, as relaxed as if he was doing a cookout in his yard. And I guess he was. I mean, that was the whole point. Next to him was Speckled Hawk, the least impressive of medicine men, but he had a knack for landing on his feet, probably had a book deal in New York and a film deal in L.A. Next to him sat Sharon, silent and mysterious, but looking at me from time to time. She had more wakan in one glance than Speckled Hawk had in his entire being. There was Elijah on my left, ex-Lerp, great shot, decked out like a rancher, checking Jefferson's head every two seconds to make sure Junior was okay. Next to Eli was Father O'Reilly, Defender of the Faith, deigning to eat with his simple red children. And now, joining the circle, slipping in between O'Reilly and me, was the Mighty Quinn, bizarre preacher-creature and all-around bad-ass.

Father O'Reilly squinted at Quinn. Old Isaac said in a cheerful voice, "Father, I guess you don't know our friend Quinn Bacon. Quinn, this is Father O'Reilly of the Holy Rosary Mission, largest landowner on the rez."

"I've already met the good sun dancer," said O'Reilly to Isaac, "but I didn't know back then that he was a son of the Church, much less a member of my own order." He turned his gaze back to Quinn, who was waiting for Isaac to hand him back his bowl of beans. Squinting once more, O'Reilly said, "Yes, Father *Gallagher,* once the tanks were hit, they realized you must be a part of all this. And here you are. In the flesh."

As he accepted his bowl of beans from Isaac, Quinn smiled and said, "*Ecce homo.*" Then he kneeled and sat cross-legged. O'Reilly put his hands on the granite and shifted himself away from Bacon, as if Quinn had something he could catch. When everybody's bowl got filled, the old priest took it upon himself to say grace. It was a good grace. He thanked God for the food and asked Him to bless it and to bless the hands that prepared it. I liked that bit about the hands. I looked at old Isaac's huge mitts, still powerful and well shaped, free of arthritis and other ravages, and I thought of countless hands of migrant workers, picking beans and putting them in baskets, sorting good ones from bad ones, and I thought, *Yeah, O'Reilly knows a trick or two. Good thing we're not letting him near the bunkers.* But then he started beseeching the Lord "to guide His wayward sheep back to the manger, lest they . . ." He paused, searching for a new image of hell, no doubt. I felt the beans losing heat through the plastic bowl.

"Lest we perish of hunger *again,*" said old Isaac, shooting the priest a look that said we may forgive but sure don't forget. A chorus of *amen*s went up, along with some muted laughter. We dug in. After a couple of spoonfuls, I glanced at O'Reilly. He hadn't lifted his spoon. He looked at us with disgust, as if his words had indeed been pearls before swine.

We ate in silence, except for the sound of spoons scraping the plastic bowls. O'Reilly picked at his beans, then put the bowl down with disgust. "How could a man of your training abandon the Church and sink so low?"

We were all silent.

"I was never too serious about the Church in the first place," said Isaac. We laughed, but not O'Reilly. He looked at Quinn real hard. "Well, Mr. Gallagher? No answer for us? Or is it shame holds your tongue?"

"I never discuss religion, politics, or women at the table."

O'Reilly let out a bitter laugh. "Never discuss women, poli— Oh, you're a clever one. But I think we're all done eating, and I'm sure your Sioux brethren are quite as curious as I to know how a man of your training comes to abandon the Holy Roman Church?"

Quinn closed his eyes and rubbed his temples with a slow, circular motion. I wondered if he was trying to massage away the pesky presence of Father O'Reilly. Then he opened his eyes: "Your Church is *exactly* what Jesus preached against—"

O'Reilly laughed. "And what have we here, a new Luther, is it?"

"The Church insists people conform to it in matters of faith, and to the state in matters of action. That's precisely what Jesus preached against— the Temple answering to King Herod and Herod to Rome."

O'Reilly snorted.

"Jesus espoused theology of liberation. You practice theology of empire."

"You're so lost I don't know where to begin with you. Your whole world is one great distortion."

Quinn smiled. "Rome claims credit for the drops of progress in Central America, as if it had a hand in liberation theology. But in truth we had to fight the Church every step of the way, getting silenced, estranged, excommunicated. Ratzinger and the pope hated us, wanted to crush us— even Romero was against us. And when he finally joined us, the Vatican turned against *him.* But when he became a martyr and started a groundswell, *then* the Church scrambled to embrace him. The glorious underground Church that Jesus founded on liberation became venal the moment it merged with Rome. It became obsessed with power and gold, brutally siphoning wealth from the corners of the world to the throne. It became the very thing Jesus had struggled against."

"You're out of your bleedin' gourd, man." O'Reilly laughed, but it was forced. We ate in silence. Then O'Reilly started up again with his right to do a mass and administer precautionary last rites.

Sharon put her bowl down. "You're saying without baptism and last rites you would be refused heaven?"

The old man nodded. "The best you can hope for is purgatory."

She laughed. "Kind of skin-deep, your God."

O'Reilly bristled and straightened his back. " 'There is only one path to the Father and that is through me,' said Jesus. Only Jesus can forgive your sins. And I, young lady, as a performer of the Holy Sacraments, make that path accessible to you and your brothers. But make no mistake. It is the only path."

Bacon laughed. "The real Jesus would never have—" But Sharon had spoken at the same moment and he gave way to her.

"Why would the Creator of the universe," she asked, "the Creator of so many peoples, religions, cultures, languages, the Creator of countless *galaxies,* for crying out loud, offer all that diversity just one path home?"

"That's just the way of it, young lady. One path to heaven."

"Well, these Black Hills are our church, our heaven," she said. "Grandfather says there are many paths through the mountaintops but the view is all the same. We come here to be with the Creator, and so do our spirits after us. But there are countless paths into the Black Hills. You can enter from any direction, come by foot, horse, car, come alone or with friends, you can even come with Jesus, or you can come through dreams. Doesn't matter what path you take, long as you walk softly and respect the place. If you don't, you don't love the Creator. Not really. Not in the right way."

"Very poetic," said the old man. "But it has nothing to do with—"

"We're talking about the same Creator, aren't we?" she said.

"But you're talking about *this* world."

"You say *this* world like it's something dirty, Father. To us, it's not, which is why we don't consume it like a runaway fire."

After dinner, I radioed Maxwell and told him we were sending the priest down. O'Reilly protested some more, but finally walked down the granite stairs and into the woods.

Day Four

"Surrender by five o'clock or we slam your bunkers," said Maxwell. He and Dexter were squinting in the bright morning light that ricocheted off the granite steps. They were in shirtsleeves, which were pitted out from the hike up the mountain. Maxwell's nose and cheeks were red from all these days in the sun.

"Do what you gotta do," I said.

"Thanks for the green light. We're bringing in a SEAL team."

"They gonna swim up and speargun us?" asked Elijah. Isaac and I laughed, but it was a nervous laugh. Things were getting out of hand.

"Of course, there are folks in D.C. who feel no serviceman's blood should be risked on a bunch of rebel Indians."

"What are you driving at?" asked Isaac, staring Maxwell in the eye.

"Your bunkers are comfortably far from the presidents," said Maxwell.

Isaac turned to me: *So they* are *thinking air strike,* his eyes said.

"It's a bluff. They can't take the mountain without losing men, so they figure we're stupid enough to be bluffed off it," I said. "What are they gonna do, air-strike thirty Indians while the world press looks on?"

"We're not concerned with the press," said Maxwell.

"Yeah, or with gold, coal, and uranium," I said.

"What's that old line, 'If a tree falls in the forest' . . . how's the rest go again?" Maxwell asked, turning to Dexter.

" 'And there's no one there to hear it, does it really make a sound?' " said Dexter.

"Yeah, that's it," said Maxwell.

"What are you driving at?"

He smiled. "You really are one dumb fucking Indian after all, Joey."

"You saying those press people are bogus?"

The smile widened.

"That's a crock. Why would you've gone to the trouble?"

"As long as you believed you were in the public eye, we knew you wouldn't harm the monument."

"And now?"

"We know all about your plan now. You're just going for the sympathy vote. You would never hurt one atom of your sacred Hills."

"Maybe so, maybe not," I said. "Either way, your choppers won't fly over us again. We still have LAWs."

He thought a few seconds. "Maybe they won't, but your story won't ever see the light of day. So the question is, Joey, are you gonna let your brother and that teenage kid starve for nothing? Because we've sealed everything off in a ten-mile radius. No reporters. No link to the outside world. So, no bleeding hearts are going to see the hunger strike. No one will be moved by what you're doing. Let's wrap this up without more death. I'll get you guys light sentences. I swear it." He pulled a folded newspaper from his pocket and handed it to me. It was the *New York Times.* "Check it out, my friend. Not a word about Rushmore." He also handed me the *Rapid City Journal.* Both papers ran photos of troops landing in Saudi Arabia, tanks unloading out of Hercules planes onto airstrips in the desert. Nothing but Desert Shield. The only mention of the Black Hills was a headline in the *Rapid City Journal* about a train wreck a few days earlier.

"Maybe these are genuine and maybe not," I said, handing him back his papers. "But what you're overlooking is, I'm not my brother. I don't believe in hunger strikes or in appealing to the conscience of Congress, so I don't need the media. I'm like you, Maxwell, I believe in force. It's the only mover. I knew one way or the other Clem's plan wouldn't work, so guess what we did? We wedged charges into fissures in the monument. Did you know there's cracks and fissures all over this rock? Now, I'm no demolitions expert, so it might only blow a small chunk away, but then again it might cause you a huge loss of face."

"Harm one inch of that monument and your people will never stop paying."

"Here's the deal," I said. "There's a guy at Time-Life named—"

"Did you hear me? Harm one inch and your people will never stop paying. Acknowledge."

"That's the first straight thing you've said all week, Maxwell, because we've never stopped paying for defending ourselves against Custer. Only problem is, we've got precious little left to pay you with. Now here it is and get it right. Buddy Levine, he's a photojournalist. You can reach him through Time-Life. Have him here by noon tomorrow. Write it down and don't bungle it."

He looked at Dexter, who dutifully pulled out a small pad and a golden pen.

◆

"I didn't know you knew," said Isaac with a relieved smile. We had just reached the top of the staircase and were stepping into Hidden Canyon. "I been tearing my hair out over whether to tell you, but I was sworn."

"What are you talking about?"

"The charges."

"I was bluffin' them, Isaac, to get leverage." We walked a little farther, then it hit me. "What are you saying?"

"Speckled Hawk," he said. "Back on the rez, Speckled was holding charges for Pumpkinhead, ten pounds of plastique. He brought it along. Wedged it in a crack in Washington's forehead."

"I been out on Washington. I didn't see any fuses."

"It's a radio signal fuse."

"Is he crazy? You know how many frequencies they're using out there?"

He shook his head. "It's gotta be armed. I seen the control. Two switches. One arms it and the other sends the frequency. You can send the frequency all you want—if it ain't armed, it won't blow."

"Show me." We walked the canyon behind Lincoln, Roosevelt, and Jefferson, then climbed up the back of Washington's head. Elijah came with us. Isaac took small steps out toward the top of the forehead. He kneeled and pointed. I kneeled and saw something white down there, but I couldn't reach it with my arm. It was too far down and the crevice got too narrow.

"Your word's worth a lot, Mr. Medal of Honor," someone said. I turned around. It was Speckled Hawk.

"*His* word?" I said. "What about yours? We swore to Clem, swore in the letter to the press, that we weren't going to hurt the monument, not one atom."

"Yeah? Well, I just heard there ain't no press release, and that all the reporters are feds. We're sealed up. Which is why you've always got to have a Plan B with these snakes. They want to take us down and never let the world know why we're up here. Never let our claims see the light of day. I don't want to blow the monument, Joe, but it gives us a handle on them. Now they've got to bring the press in. It's our ace in the hole."

Of course, his logic was the same that I had used in my bluff. But there's a world of difference between a bluff and a bomb. It changes the nature of everything. "Who else knows about it?" I asked.

"Just us and two guys in the bunkers, but I'm not saying who. And maybe the feds if they've beat it out of Pumpkin."

"They ain't beat shit outa Pumpkin. And I'll take that detonator," Elijah said, putting out his hand. "The nerve of you, Speckled. My boy is chained to this rock and you rig it with explosives. Give it over. Now!"

Speckled shook his head. I grabbed him and Eli frisked him. He just laughed. "I got it hid, Elijah, and it'll stay hid, so don't worry about Junior. We won't actually have to use it. Anyway, the charges are way the hell over here on Washington and Junior's way the hell over there on Roosevelt. At best, all it could do is blow a chunk of forehead out. It won't touch the others."

"If we even scratch the monument, it's open season on the Sioux," I said. "Rednecks will come in caravans from all over and swarm the rez and shoot everyone up. Vigilantes armed to the teeth. And the feds and State Troopers won't do shit. The government will take the rest of the land. You ain't got kids, Speckled Hawk. You got no right."

"Relax, Joey. Nothin's gonna get blowed up. Elijah, I won't even go near the detonator without telling you first. Okay?"

◆

I tried with pine branches to get the plastique up out of the crack, but it was useless. Clem asked me a little bit later what I had been doing on Washington. I told him about the explosives. A look of sadness came over him. "I think I understand now," he said.

"What?"

"My vision. There were things that confused me in it, things that did not fit together. But now I believe I had two visions on the road. Not one. And I think they were battling each other."

"How? Why?"

"I would see one thing, then another would replace it for a while. Then the first would push its way back into my mind. I thought it was all one vision, like in two parts. And I hoped that if I did the first part right, the other part wouldn't be necessary. But I see now they're very separate visions, and I'm guessing only one of them comes from Wakan Tanka."

"You mean the second one came from somewhere evil?"

"Oh, no. Not at all. The one about a hunger strike—I see now—it came from Mom. It had to come from Mom."

"And the one from Wakan Tanka? What happens?"

He shook his head, meaning he couldn't talk about it.

"Well, are you saying Mom and Wakan Tanka want different things?"

"They both want us to have our Paha Sapa back."

"So it's about how. This other vision has you take up the gun?"

He shook his head again.

"Did you see explosions? C'mon, Clem, you've got to tell me."

"Don't you worry about Speckled Hawk," he said. "I'll reel him in."

Day Five

From twenty feet down the staircase, Buddy Levine smiled up at me, taking big strides, two or three stairs at a time, his feet making no noise on the steps. He was wearing gum-soled shoes just like the ones he had when he taught at Crazy Horse. No cowboy boots or hard heels for Buddy Levine. Buddy had always walked softly through the halls of our new school. My guess is that he walked softly wherever he went.

The leather tops of his shoes shone in the sun, which did not surprise me. It had been Buddy who got me in the habit of caring for my boots. I used to stop by his house on Saturday mornings with a couple of friends. Buddy would always offer us fruit or coffee or whatever he had, then he would get back to saddle-soaping his shoes and a leather Navy jacket. Same routine every Saturday. We would bust his chops for it, like *Don't you have nothing better to do, old man?* And he would laugh with us, but then say something corny like "Take care of your gear and it'll take care of you." Then, when my mom gave me a pair of boots for my eighteenth birthday—which she bought by selling a buffalo robe that had been her granddad's—Buddy said, "Bring them by and I'll show you how to make them last forever." So it wasn't the Army that got me polishing my boots. It was Buddy Levine.

As he floated up the granite steps, I could see that the lines in his face had deepened, but he was still fit and had all his hair. He wore khaki chinos and a white cotton shirt. No tie. His jaw and neck were still lean, and his chin strong. At the waist, too, he was as slim as any high school runner. His white shirt, billowy and extremely bright in the sun, added to the illusion that he was floating upward like something lighter than air. Clearly, he was still a runner, probably doing marathons.

His smile widened as he came within a couple stairs of the one I was on. I held out my hand and could feel myself grinning. It was good to see him. So many memories came rushing in on me. He gripped my hand, but didn't so much shake it as yank it, pulling me down a step into his hug. I could smell soap and shampoo, and it made me wonder how I must've smelled after all those days on the rock. He asked how my mother was, then seemed genuinely saddened to hear of her death. He said nice things about her, remembering good times and funny moments at our house, some of which had slipped my mind. He asked about some of my old classmates and guys on the cross-country team, then asked about Clem.

"Well, he's okay," I said. "He's up here, too."

"I know. I meant how's he holding up? They say he's fasting."

"Yep. Ain't so *cheppah* now," I said, smiling.

He shifted out of the reunion tone. "These guys are serious, Joey."

"So are we," I said.

He nodded. "But they're bringing in SEAL Team Six."

"I've been hearing nothing but SEAL talk for quite some days now. Maybe the SEAL teams got more pressing business in the Gulf."

He shook his head. "SEAL Team Two is on its way out to Saudi so that Six can come home and take care of this. Joey, Six specializes in take-downs. All they do all year long is practice antiterrorist ops."

"We're not terrorists. Didn't you get the press release, the letter to the press?" I couldn't believe how goddamn slow the mail moves. Probably it was sitting on his desk in New York, unopened. "This ain't terrorism, Buddy. We're not pulling any terrorist shit here."

"Joey, you're splitting hairs. Who are you going to split hairs with? The SEALs? This is no different to them than rag-heads taking embassies. They *live* for this. They want to take you out, put your feathers in their caps, and get back to the Gulf before the fun starts. They'll be landing at Ellsworth soon."

"Good for them. What are they gonna do? It's cliffs all around but the southeast hill," I said. "They'll die coming up that hill. We're armed to the teeth and dug in deep. We got the high ground. And I mean the *high* ground."

"Come on, Joey, you really think SEALs are going to hump it up the mountain like a bunch of jarheads? You think they're going to do a *frontal?*" He shook his head. "They'll HALO in. Man, they can land on dimes now. They'll come in with night goggles, and silenced Heckler-and-Kochs, Swedish grease guns. You'll never see them. Never hear them. It'll be over before their boots touch the mountain."

"We've got a Stinger."

"No, you don't. Even if you did, their plane'll be too high. They'll jump with oxygen and zero in on you with cues from the ground forces. When they're in range, they'll see you with their night goggles. They'll see you clear as day and you won't see them. They'll land *in* your bunkers, right on your shoulders."

"Can't you get us night goggles?" I knew he still had connections in the SEALs. Over the years, we had exchanged letters, and he had mentioned in one of them that he attended the reunions every summer in Little Creek.

"I'm a journalist now."

"Then why don't you *tell* our story? How come it isn't out there in the papers or on the air, or in your goddamn magazine?"

He pulled a rolled-up *Newsweek* from the pocket of his chinos, opened it to one of the back pages, and showed me an article about a collision of cargo trains in the Black Hills of South Dakota, involving chemical tanker cars. It said that civil defense authorities had evacuated everyone within a twenty-five-mile radius of the spill, because of a poisonous cloud that had formed in the area. Special cleanup crews were going into the area before the chemicals could leach down into the water tables. That was pretty much the gist of it. There was also a photo of a couple of guys in chemical suits and gas masks working with pumps and hoses near a smashed-up tanker car. I handed him back the paper and started shaking with a sort of silent laughter. The water tables of western South Dakota were already fucked up from the coal and uranium mining. I mean, these feds were just so snaky. Not only were they trying to cover up Rushmore, but they were creating an excuse for the next dismal set of water purity tests, which, obviously, they were expecting to be worse than the last set. Now it would all be the fault of a drunken railroad switchman or some bullshit like that.

"Well, that's clever, but we sent out fifty press packets all over the country. Reporters'll be snooping round soon enough."

"Did you put postage on them?"

"Pretty funny."

"Seriously, did you put the right amount of postage?"

"Of *course* I put the right postage," I snapped, but immediately wondered if I had botched it somehow.

"Well, where'd you mail them from?"

"Stuffed them in a box in Kadoka the night we drove out."

"*All* of them?" That tell-me-it-ain't-so look was back in his face. "You mailed them all from the *same* town? The first town off the rez?"

My stomach knotted up. "Hey, we had to move fast. We got raided. Everything got rushed. What was I supposed to do, drive cross-country and mail each one from a different zip code?"

"Might have been quicker to stop in Rapid and leave them at the FBI office."

"Jeesus! Is the idea of returning a chunk of land that fucking terrifying? Or are they afraid that if they honor our treaty they'll have to go back and honor the other three hundred and seventy?"

"That's part of it. But it's mostly about uranium, Joey. Anything for energy. Hell, that's what this thing in the Gulf is about, energy. Oil. Bush and Baker been knocking themselves out drumming up support for a war. And it worked, the country's behind it. All systems go. We've got Saddam in the black hat—and he *is* a prick—and us in the white. No shades of gray. But if your story gets out, then everything gets murky, everyone gets reminded that we're a land-grabbing bully just like Saddam. And the high note in Bush's bugle call is to save the Kurds from Saddam. How will that wash when they've got you on Rushmore trying to get back land that Congress stole? You are the fucking Kurds, only more so. Your story would ruin the black-and-white effect. And the last thing this administration wants is people thinking about murky situations like Vietnam. They're scared out of their shorts that the country will lose its nerve again."

"Buddy, write it for us. Write everything, the Gulf, the train spill—"

"I'm a photographer, Joey."

"So take pictures *and* write it."

"I can't."

"What do you mean you can't? You mean there's some union law?"

He shook his head. "What would it accomplish?"

"Everything. *Everything.*"

"Disaster is what it would accomplish. A personal one for you and a general one for the Sioux."

"That's bullshit."

"No it's not."

"What is wrong with you? Who the hell am I talking to here?"

He didn't say anything.

"I remember when you had balls. What the fuck have they got on you?"

He paused a long time, then said, "The point is, if you ever make the news, it'll be as terrorists attempting to destroy Rushmore. Do you know what kind of reprisals would happen to Sioux all over the Dakotas and Montana, and to Indians everywhere? I mean, with all the fucking militias and rednecks. It would be open season. They showed me the stuff they prepared on you in case the story breaks. You're a pack of terrorists armed to the teeth, led by a schizophrenic Vietnam vet named Joey Moves Camp, who acts under the orders of a voice he hears, a voice that commanded him to blow up Mount Rushmore. They yanked your VA records, man, and twisted them all out of shape. You're the Son of Sam. I don't know if you guys sabotaged that train or not, but they've got some convincing evidence that says you did, that you did it as a diversion."

"So you're telling me the train wreck is real—"

"They have photos of Clem messing with train tracks—"

"Bullshit!"

"I've seen them. Pictures of him pulling up railroad spikes. And I'm a photographer, Joey. Those photos were not doctored."

"That's bull. You know we're not terrorists and they know we're not."

"What *they* know or think is not the point. What they can make the country think *is* the point."

"Buddy, if a train *did* get derailed, it's either unrelated or they did it themselves. I only made that threat about the monument to get some leverage, to get you out here to bear witness. We are not terrorists."

"The bottom line is, they're going to take you off this mountain even if they have to body-bag every one of you, in which case you were definitely about to blow the monument. It's that simple. You were supplied by Hezbollah or Saddam, or whoever the flavor of the month is—just like they did to the AIMers, linking them to Castro. A lightning strike was the only way. Had to be done."

"And the press will fall for that?"

"See, you want me to bring the press in, but here's the snafu: as it stands now, the derailment is just a derailment, and all you've done is trespass on Rushmore. If I bring the press in while you're up here, those agents are not going to sit back and let you win hearts and minds over the TV. They'll produce evidence that the train was sabotaged, and evidence that you aim to blow the monument. And that unfolding will lead to rampant reprisals. Once you're down and waiting for trial, you can tell the press all the stories you want—"

"Because they don't figure anybody will believe us?"

"Because they don't figure anybody will care. The drama would be over. Nobody wants to hear a lot of old history about treaties."

"Don't you think some journalist will ask why they covered up Rushmore?"

He shrugged. "To avoid reprisals, save Indian lives. They're tired of seeing so many good folks suffer for the stupid actions of a few hot-heads."

"Buddy, did you come here to help me get through to them, or to help them get through to me?"

"I came because they said you asked for me. And because they said you would blow the monument if I didn't."

"But they sure did a lot of brainwashing on you during the trip."

He shook his head. "They're just holding all the cards, is all." They had obviously convinced him that our goose was cooked. I guess he just wanted to save our butts from getting greased. "Joey, you're out of your league. We're both out of our league."

There was silence for a few seconds, then I said, "You've come this far, might as well come up and see Clem," I said. I don't know why I said it, because suddenly he was the last person I wanted talking to my brother.

"I'd like that."

"Only don't tell him about how they put the lid on us. It could break him. He's weak now and he thinks he can set everything right just by reaching the American people."

We sat down next to Clem. His chain was now loose around his waist. When he opened his eyes and took in Buddy's face, he smiled weakly. "How about some water?" I asked. He nodded. I got up to get some. When I came back, Clem was explaining how the chain in the rock was like the red sashes that the *Napesni* warrior societies used to wear, how you would hold your ground by staking your sash. "The sash meant no retreat. No Flight. This is my ground."

Buddy nodded. "Yes, I think I remember hearing of them, the Bad-gers, right? And the Plain Lance Owners?"

"That's right," Clem said. We were all silent for a bit. Clem drank water from the margarine bowl, then said, "If people write their representatives, we'll win. They'll put pressure on their congressmen. And if they don't, well, at least we'll have our, our— Hey, Quinn, what's the name of that butte again, where they never surrendered?"

"Masada," said Quinn as he walked up the back of Lincoln's crown. He sat next to Clem, nodded hello to Buddy. I introduced them. They shook hands.

Clem continued, "Yeah, at least we'll have our Masada for the world to see. Then maybe in two thousand years we'll get our Black Hills back."

Levine looked out at the Tourist Center, at the forces gathered below, the choppers, half-tracks, APCs. I wondered if he saw them, even for a moment, as the Roman camp, the invaders. Did he understand what was really going on the way he used to? I stood up and waited for him to say goodbye to Clem. We walked through Hidden Canyon in silence, Quinn trailing behind us. At the bottom of the staircase, we shook hands. A few hundred feet below, an APC waited for Levine. *There's your limo,* I thought.

When Buddy Levine had taught at Crazy Horse, he was really one of us. He used to seek out the old folks to learn all he could of the Lakota way. He loved everything Lakota and tried to get us kids to see the beauty in it. But maybe that was only because he was disillusioned with America after his tour in Vietnam. Maybe by now he had bought back into the system. If it came down to us versus the SEALs, who the hell would he be pulling for? I wondered.

"Can I call you Buddy?" asked Quinn.

"Of course," said Buddy.

"Well, Buddy, this really *is* Masada. It is. They're not coming down, these guys. The government can shoot us up, napalm us—hell, they can neutron-*bomb* us so long as it leaves the monument unscratched—but none of these threats will scare these guys down from this mountain. These guys in the bunkers, man, they're staked down. They've sung their death songs, they're ready to go if it comes to that. They'll make the same choice the Jews made on Masada. These people want their land, just like those zealots did. And if they can't, well . . ."

"Is that the message for Maxwell? Some stuff about Masada?"

"Are you saying you're nothing but a messenger boy? Because if you're something without a shred of free will left, I won't even waste my breath."

Buddy flushed. For a moment, I thought he was going to swing on Bacon, but he swallowed the insult and listened.

Bacon switched out of the hostile tone. "Did you know the Romans had a historian at Masada to record the fall? That's how proud they were. The horror of it would keep the other colonies in line. But the days of might makes right are long over. We've got higher principles now, especially in the Constitution. So the government has to hide this Masada, not record it. The Shrine of Democracy, they call this monument. It's the Arch of Titus, my friend." He paused, looked Buddy up and down, then said, "Joey tells me you're some kind of photojournalist now."

Buddy nodded.

"They must really have a handle on you to let you into this area and count on your silence."

Buddy made no answer.

"Josephus was the historian they brought to Masada to record the fall. You know about him?"

"I've heard the name."

"He was a Jew who became a Roman citizen. I wonder how he felt when he got to the top of Masada with the legionnaires and found those nine hundred and sixty men, women, and children with their throats slit and their message scrawled in the dirt that they would remain free men. I wonder if it stirred his Hebrew blood, or if he looked on the scene with Roman scorn? I wonder a lot about him. But it doesn't matter which way he felt, because either way, he still recorded the basic facts. The world *did* get to see that some people just won't be dogs for others. Do you know what I'm saying? Whether you think we're criminals, hoodlums, or heroes doesn't matter. But the basic facts *must* see the light of day."

"They'll discredit me, and you'll come off as terrorists, but the worst kind. And all the Sioux will pay."

"Contact other journalists. How many people can they discredit?"

Buddy let out a long sigh. He put a hand to his head, grabbing a fistful of dark hair. The muscles in his forearm were tight. Without looking up, he said, "I have a friend at the *Toronto Globe and Mail* and one at *The Times* of London. It's best to go with the foreign press. Realistically, we're talking forty-eight hours. And it can't be linked to me."

"You said the SEALs are arriving today," I said.

"Yeah, but they'll need at least a day to reconnoiter and set a plan," he said. "They never trust any intell but their own. Don't be spooked if you see a few skulking in the woods this afternoon. They might feel you out with a little fire, see what you've got, and where you've got it, but that won't be the attack." He shook my hand again, and then Bacon's.

He started down the steep hill and veered to the right, toward the APC that waited way down there below Lincoln. I watched him stepping lightly, placing his soft-soled shoes on sharp granite chunks that had been blasted off Abraham's face forty-nine years ago and never hauled away. I wondered what the hell they had on Buddy Levine. Maybe nothing. Maybe he just knew there was no chance of anything positive coming out of all this, and he was trying to do damage control.

◆

I sat with Clem, and watched Buddy's APC crash through the woods back up to the Tourist Center. "Have you been messing with the railroad?" I asked, turning to look at him.

"What do you mean?"

"You didn't try to derail a train or anything, did you?"

"Of course not. Why would you ask me that?"

"Buddy says they have photos of you messing with some tracks."

He smiled. "Really?" He seemed both surprised and flattered that they would pay him that kind of attention.

"Yeah, really."

"I just took a couple of spikes."

"What the hell for?"

"Had this hankering."

"Clem, seriously."

"Seemed like the thing to do."

"C'mon, Clem, why would you do that?"

"Just in case these piton wedges wouldn't fit the cracks here," he said, nodding with his chin toward the wedge anchoring his chain in the rock.

I wondered if the removal of two spikes could cause a derailment. It didn't seem likely. "Was it here in the Black Hills that you took these spikes?"

"Oh, no. I took one from an old track north of the rez and one from a track south of it. Nowhere near here. Why. What's going on?"

"Nothing." I knew then that if there actually was a derailment, it had nothing to do with him and the spikes he took. And that was a good feeling. I undid the plastic wrapper of some jerky, then realized what I was doing. "Go ahead," he said, smiling gently. I lodged the meat in the right side of my mouth, between the teeth and the cheek, like it was tobacco. That's the way I like eating jerky, letting it dissolve slowly, first the salt, then the meat, trying not to chew it as long as possible, just letting the saliva soften it up, letting it bleed. When the salt's all leached out and the meat's easy, then I break down and chew. It's just something I do to make it last longer and kill time.

Through the binoculars, I could see Buddy get out of the APC and follow someone into the Tourist Center. "I suppose they've got to debrief him," I said. It cracked me up to imagine Buddy in there with all those FBI hard-asses, amid their maps and telephones and field radios, telling them it was Masada all over again. Of course, he was probably just feeding them some worthless intell, or telling them we were solid and sitting tough. Whatever it was, it didn't take too long. I was just starting to chew the jerky when I saw four men walking away from the Tourist Center across the asphalt in the direction of the choppers. Their backs were to the mountain, but one appeared to be Buddy—white shirt, khaki pants—and two of them were probably Maxwell and Dexter. The fourth wore an olive-drab flight suit. He and Buddy got into a chopper that was already spinning its screw. It rose quickly and headed in the direction of Rapid.

◆

That night, we ate Hormel chili on Lincoln, and it was good. We were about thirty feet from Clem's bedroll. He had conked out about an hour earlier. "I guess by now you all know we've got charges in Washington," Speckled said, looking up from his bowl.

This was met with nods and silence. *What's this "we," white man?* I wanted to say.

"Which means we've got a realistic chance of getting the press in on this. To make it happen, though, we need a deadline, like forty-eight hours. What do you say?"

"Or what?" said Elijah.

"Or we flip the switch," said Speckled.

Isaac shook his head. "Some warrior society."

"But it won't come to that," said Speckled. "They'll bring the press and the rest is like we planned, talk and dialogue."

"We'll still look like Arabs," said old Isaac.

"At least we'll get the story out."

Bear Dreamer shook his head slowly, pensively, his long, silver hair jiggling around his collarbone. "For so many years I have seen and heard stories of PLOs and IRAs doing these ugly things. They blow up passenger planes and school buses full of kids, shoot machine guns into crowds. And always they say it's because they lost their land, or somebody is oppressing them. Well, we lost more than those people will ever lose, and we live in worse conditions, far as I can tell. But do you see us blowing up airplanes or carrying on like that? Do we go killing people in department stores at Christmastime like them IRAs? Have we *ever* done this?" he asked, looking across the fire at Speckled. "Of course not. And this is because we have always had a backbone that is not capable of stooping so low. And you know what that backbone is?" he asked, again looking at Speckled Hawk. "It is that we have always had the sun dance, always had men among us who *know* what suffering is and so would never inflict it on innocents."

"I'm not talking about hurting people. I'm talking about rock," protested Speckled Hawk.

"It's still ugly, and where does it end? What has come over you, Speckled Hawk?" .

"You lecture *me* about the sun dance? I was piercing at fourteen," Speckled said.

"Yeah, but when'd you dance last?" I asked.

"When'd *you,* college boy?"

"I don't pretend to be in touch with it. You're the one holding sun dances every summer. You're the big intercessor."

"Look," said Bacon. "I don't like the idea of threatening with a bomb, but how else do we force them to bring in the press? And without the press, they can do anything they want to us. There's nothing holding them accountable."

"Levine will get the press."

"You're gonna bet the farm on him?" said Speckled. "On Mr. Photo-journalist? He didn't even have a camera on him. What does that tell you?"

"Look," I said. "You've got a bomb and now they know it. Fine. That alone will keep them from attacking. But if you create a deadline, you *force* them to attack. They'll go for broke," I said. "They'll blitz us."

We voted him down, and that was that. I did a three-hour watch on the high ridge that night, then came down and laid out my bedroll in Hidden Canyon. As I looked at the stars and played the day over in my head, I realized Speckled was right about one thing: Buddy Levine didn't even have a camera on him.

Day Six

The first rays of dawn woke me from an uneasy sleep. Clem was still lying back on his bedroll. I pulled my boots on, folded my blanket, then shouldered the Armalite by the strap. I turned to head for the Hall of Records. It was in the Hall that we kept the water in jerry cans. My first move each morning was to get Clem a bowl of water. As I walked across Hidden Canyon toward the Hall, I saw Speckled Hawk by the big portal, crouched over the radio. I dropped the blankets and ran at him. "What are you doing? What'd you do?" I shouted.

He looked up and smiled. "I just gave them twenty-four hours to bring in *Nightline* and CNN. Told 'em it's got to be Koppel or at least people we'll recognize," he said, getting to his feet.

I reached down for the radio. He laughed. "Tell them whatever you want, boy. They know who's calling the shots now."

"You fucking hijacker. You're stealing everything from everyone."

"You won't call me a hijacker when I deliver the Hills."

I stuck the barrel of my Armalite into the base of his neck, just under the Adam's apple. I saw the vein pulsing. *Do it,* she said, calmly. *He's not good, like Clem is.* "Give me the detonator," I said.

"Whoa, what's going on? Easy, Joey, easy," Elijah said, as he and Bear Dreamer came up beside me. I told them what Speckled had done.

"I ain't actin' alone," Speckled said. "So, shooting me won't get you the detonator."

"Yeah? Well, can you use it with me sitting out on Washington? Keep your gun on him," Elijah said. Then he squatted down by the radio and asked to speak with Maxwell. Maxwell came on. "This is Elijah Hunts Alone. I'm calling to let you know that there won't be anybody blowing anything up. Is that clear?"

"Why should we believe you?" said Maxwell.

"We had a little fringe movement, a very small one, but we got it under control."

"You mean Moves Camp and the medicine man?"

"Moves Camp wasn't the problem, but we got the problem under control. Nothing's going to explode. Okay? No deadline. No pressure. Let's everybody relax."

"Why should I believe that? You guys have about fifteen different leaders."

"The charges are in Washington's head, okay? And I will personally go out and sit on them like a hen."

"Unacceptable. Remove the charge and throw it down."

"We tried. It's too deep. It's out of reach. But I'll sit right on top of it." Bear Dreamer was gesturing that he would, too. "So will another man, Bear Dreamer Bordeaux. We'll sit right up front where you can see us."

"Unacceptable. How do I know the other presidents aren't rigged?"

"Because we've got one man chained down on Lincoln, right? My own son is chained down on Roosevelt. And I'll sit on Washington. I'll chain myself, if you want."

"What about Jefferson?"

"Okay, Bordeaux will be on Jefferson. And we'll both be right up front where you can see us."

"What you're telling me is that there's no fuse, no wires, it's a radio detonator, and the naughty boys have it. Right?"

"They'll never use it with us sitting out there. Never."

There was a crackly silence, then Maxwell said, "Right," and clicked off.

Eli put down the hand mike. "You're a real team player," he said to Speckled.

"And you're a red-white-and-blue hero. The good Indian. Gonna die to save Mount Rushmore. *Semper fi.*"

"Fuck you," Elijah said, and he cuffed Speckled across the face with his open hand.

Speckled staggered back a step and looked shocked. His hand rose to his face, his fingers touching the corner of his mouth, of his thin lips. Then he looked at his fingertips to see if there was blood. "You slap a *medicine* man?" he said.

"You ain't no medicine man," Elijah said over his shoulder, heading off for Washington.

"Some Kit Fox," Speckled said, wiping his nose and looking for blood.

"He's *Napesni* now," said Bear Dreamer. "And I'll tell you something, Peter Speckled Hawk, you don't know the first thing about the real Tokalas. Not even the first thing."

"We'll see who gets us back the Hills," said Speckled.

Bear Dreamer shook his head, then walked out onto Jefferson, out beyond Abel's scaffold. He stood a few moments, just looking at the world, then he slowly sat down.

I walked onto Lincoln and sort of snapped at Clem. "I thought you were going to talk to Speckled. You said you'd reel him in." My tone was pretty unpleasant. He looked at me but didn't say anything. He looked weak. I explained to him what was going on with Eli and Bear Dreamer being on Washington and Jefferson. We sat for a few minutes in silence. Then he got to his knees, and slowly to his feet. I held on to his elbow because he looked dizzy. "Please unlock the chain," he said.

"You want me to go get Speckled?" I asked.

He shook his head. "I need to talk to Sharon."

"Sharon? It's Speckled who needs talking to."

"I'll get through to him. And to the feds. First, I need Sharon."

"What the hell for?"

"That's between her and me."

"Fine," I said. I was fed up with his mysterious airs. I helped him down the back of Lincoln's head, and held his arm as we crossed Hidden Canyon. Happily, Speckled Hawk wasn't around. He had probably gone off to the bunkers. Clem steered us toward the Hall of Records. We entered the shadows of that rectangular cave. It was an unnatural place, but the cool darkness felt good.

"I'll be fine now," he said. My eyes were beginning to adjust and, to my surprise, I could see Sharon's slender figure way at the back of the Hall, where it was darkest. She was sitting on one of the weapons crates near some bedrolls and air mattresses. She wasn't packing food or cleaning weapons. She was just waiting by the bedrolls. And it seemed like Clem knew she would be there. "See you back on Abe," he said. Then, as an afterthought, he added, "If the others come around, whistle 'em off, will ya? Don't let anyone come strolling in."

My cheeks burned when I heard that. I turned and walked out into the sunlight, which glinted everywhere off the granite, dazzling, dizzying. Clem obviously had something going with her, and I never saw it. I was angry and felt like a fool.

I walked onto Lincoln and sat down by the chain that should have held him. How many times had they already met like this? I wondered. Did she sneak out onto Lincoln in the small hours of the night and caress him? Had she loved him since first seeing him drag those skulls?

Bacon emerged into the canyon from the staircase. I motioned him over. "What's up? Where's Clem?" he asked.

"Sharon's washing and dressing his sores," I said, which was believable because he had plenty from sitting on the rock so long.

Bacon sat down next to me. "They're getting stir-crazy down in the bunkers, starting to bitch at each other."

"They may have their action soon enough," I said. Then I told him what Speckled had done. He shook his head. "Who knows, though, maybe it will get us *Nightline.*"

"It'll get us all killed, more likely. Where's he now?"

"He's talking to the guys in Level Two. Getting everyone all pumped up. Hey, how come Elijah's not guarding the ridge?" he asked, looking at the high ridge we had landed on. As Eli was the best shot, it had become his lookout.

I pointed to Washington and Jefferson and explained why they were out there.

Speckled and old Isaac emerged from the stairs into the canyon. I waved them over so that they wouldn't wander into the Hall. Isaac looked tired as he sat down. "Where's Clem?" he asked. I gave the same answer about a sponge bath.

I was telling Isaac how Speckled had called in a deadline, and how Bear Dreamer and Eli had staked themselves down, at least figuratively, to cool out the feds, and I was in midsentence when Clem stepped out of the Hall of Records. He was wrapped in a blue-and-white star quilt that Mom had sewn for him years back. I was surprised to see it, but I must say it looked good on him, hanging all the way down to his ankles like he was an old-time blanket Indian. He must have kept it locked away all these years, because it was in perfect condition. It was crisply white with triangular patches of rich, unfaded blue in a kaleidoscopic star formation. But it was an odd choice of clothing on a scorching day. Probably it was to protect his burnt shoulders while Sharon washed out his T-shirt, which had many days of sweat in it. How lovingly she would scrub the threads of her guru, I thought.

As he approached, I noticed that his braids were combed out and that his hair was wet and clean.

Bacon rose immediately and went over to help Clem get up the back of Abe's head, putting out an arm for my brother to grab hold of. But Clem didn't notice and kept his own arms inside the quilt, taking small, careful steps up the sloping rock. He seemed weak, as if each step required great effort and concentration of balance. I noticed that the quilt was fastened shut around his neck with a big safety pin on the right shoulder, which looked stupid and ruined the beauty and power of the blanket. But I kept my mouth shut.

Bacon sat again, but Clem stayed on his feet. He was standing to my left and I had to crane my neck around to look up at him. His face was just running with sweat. He looked awful. He gazed at the federal forces, and bit his lip, then spoke. "Starving is not the way to get through to these people . . . they never knowed hunger. Not even a day."

I figured he was looking for an honorable way to start eating again. And who could blame him? I couldn't have gone half as long as he went.

But with Junior over there on the next rock, Clem was looking a bit shown up. I felt like pulling out a piece of jerky and giving it to him before he fell on me.

"So much for the *Napesni*," said Speckled, unable to hide his smirk.

"I'm not giving up on No Flight. I ain't quit this rock," Clem said. "I just see now that hunger won't work on these people. It is time to dance—"

"To *what?*" I said.

"To sun-dance," he said.

Speckled Hawk laughed out loud.

"Get some food in your belly, Clem, 'cause you're talking crazy," I said.

"Ain't crazy," he said.

"Haven't you had enough fucking visions for one summer? Aren't we far enough up the creek with your visions?" I said.

"This ain't *for* a vision, Joey. It *is* the vision. The other vision. The hunger thing, that was from Mom. I understand it now. Gonna dance to make those people *see*. Not just the feds. All of them. And I'll dance for healing, to get the wakan to heal folks, heal the Hills, the land. Gonna dance for the health of the people, for yours, Joey, for the *world*. And it's gonna work."

"You're putting my bullshit meter on overload here. The dance ain't about healing and redemption. It's about saving your hide in battle. Period. And ours is about to be greased."

He shook his head. "You take the pain so others won't have to. You don't dance for yourself, but for the people."

"That's bullshit. It was a warrior's dance, pure and simple, Clem. It was a rabbit's foot and a bribe rolled into one. If you had a close shave in battle, you offered up *some* of your flesh to thank the Great Mysterious for not taking *all* of it. And you did it to flatter Him into saving your ass the next time. All this talk about dancing to heal folks and redeem folks is just a lot of crap to please the missionaries," I said. "We had to twist it into Christian terms so that those fuckers would stop trying to stomp it out. 'Course they just stomped harder."

"No," he said. "Missionaries wanted to snuff it out because it proved we already had what they claimed only they could bring. But we really *had* it. Wasn't just talk with us. We had our own traditions of sharing and sacrifice and selfless love—and *healing*—and they were ancient, Joey, much older than the wasitchu been here. Old as time. And the sun dance is at the heart of them traditions. But you know what? Let's just say for the hell of it you're right. You're not. But let's say the reason we dance the way we do—that is, to help others, instead of just each man to save his own hide—let's pretend it's because of the missionaries. Well, what I'm saying is, hey, if that's the case, then at least one good thing came out of it all. I'm not saying it equals all the ugly things, the beatings and shame and withholding of food till you kiss the cross. I'm just saying that what's good is *good* and you can't throw it out with the bathwater just 'cause you think it's a mixed blood, a child of rape." His eyes softened when he said that, and I suddenly knew what I had long suspected. My stomach knotted. He continued, "You can't dwell only on the sorry things, Joey. I mean, don't you see we've already won? What you've done here—whether we live or die—what you and all of us have done is bring the sacred Black Hills back to our people, at least to our kids and their kids. It may take time, but it's gonna happen. These Hills *will* be returned. People out there just don't know the history. They don't know about Laramie, or any of it. Now they will. And they'll talk to their people in Washington. You'll see. There's a change happening."

"The reporters were feds!" I blurted. "They're fakes, Clem. Everything's sealed off. Nobody's gonna see your little sun dance and—"

" 'Course they're fakes," he said, smiling gently. "This is Mount *Rushmore*, Joey. Rushmore would get the big guys, Jennings, Brokaw, Maury Povich's wife. Not these faces we never seen before."

I stared at him for what must've been ten seconds. I was surprised he had figured it out, and puzzled he didn't seem to care. I looked around at the others, then back at Clem. "So, you know that nobody would see it, but you'd still—"

"*They'll* see it," he said, turning slightly toward the forces below. "We'll do it for them. Them feds and SEALs. At least one of them will understand, or feel *some*thing. Maybe not right away, but as the years go by and it plays in his head, and in his dreams, he'll come to understand, and he'll see it's more important than any oath of silence. They'll start coming forward. It'll all come out, and we'll get our Hills. But everything takes time."

"You're dreaming, Clemmy. To them, it's backward. They'll never understand the sun dance."

"Then I'll give 'em one they *can* understand."

"Clem, our only hope is Levine getting through to the foreign press."

Clem shook his head. "It won't happen. They own him. I heard him talking to the agents in the Tourist Center."

"Listen to yourself. Would you *listen* to yourself? You might as well be on drugs, you're so hungry. How could you hear him talking to agents in the Tourist Center?"

"I saw it in the Hall of Records. The Six Grandfathers musta showed it to me. It was toward the back. Like I was watching big-screen TV, only brighter. The mountain just opened up and showed it to me. There were shadows on Buddy. They got him on a string."

Gee, another vision, I almost said out loud.

Bacon raised his hand slightly. "All this sitting and waiting is killing the guys in the bunkers," he said. "A quick dance could boost morale. We could rotate them out of the bunkers and spell them. Some of them are getting spooked by the talk of SEALs. A dance would jack up their confidence, restore their wakan."

"No such thing as a quick dance," Speckled said with great authority. "It takes four days."

"Where is it written we cannot do a quick one?" Clem said. I was glad he countered Speckled and finally stood up to him a little bit. But I still thought a dance was crazy.

"Go ahead and do one," said Speckled. "But it won't have power."

"Where would you set it up? What would you use for a pole?" I asked, meaning there were no cottonwoods around, and no space for a Mystery Circle.

Speckled Hawk laughed. "There's a time and place for sun dancing, and this ain't it. You dragged those skulls a long way, Blue Chest, but that don't make you a medicine man or an intercessor. And it sure don't make you a strategist. The best thing to do now is hunker to the bunkers and show these feds we'll tough it out."

"You mean blow their monument," Clem said.

"It won't come to that. Anyway, those honky faces shouldn't be on the Six Grandfathers."

"Wind and rain will rub them out in time," Clem said.

"Yeah, in five thousand years."

"That's nothing to a mountain."

"It's a lot to a tribe."

"You want the whole country to hate the Sioux even though we're in the right?" Clem asked.

"They already hate us," Speckled said.

"No, they don't. The government is just blind with greed. We'll open their eyes."

"With what?" I asked.

"The vision."

"The vision, the vision. *What* vision? I thought the vision was to hunger-strike. Lot of good that did," I said. I hated arguing with him, especially as it put me on the same side with Speckled.

Clem looked at me, his face still running with sweat. "Could you undo this pin, Joey, and take Mom's blanket?"

I looked at him, puzzled, and I was sort of thinking, *What are you, the king of Siam? Take it off yourself.*

"I'm very stiff," he added.

Bacon started to get up but I motioned him to stay put. I stood and came around behind Clem to undo the safety pin at his shoulder. I lifted the blanket off and started folding it. "This vision," I heard him say softly, as I placed the blanket on the granite. That's when I noticed the look on Bacon's face, and on Isaac's and even Speckled Hawk's. They were gawking at Clem, their eyes wide and astonished. Speckled's mouth was open. I stepped around to see what all the fuss was about.

Bursts of silver, yellow, and red glinted brightly in the sun, shocking the eyes. My mind would only accept the colors at first. The rest I could not take in. His chest was like a final explosion of energy from a star going out. More shocking than the brilliance of color was the reality of what these colors were. Not war paint made of old-time pigments, nor fluorescent spray paint from a can. They were not colors for their own sake, or for ornamentation. But still my mind rejected the meaning.

Speckled was the first to find words. "Metal? You can't pierce with . . ." But his voice trailed off into disbelief.

"You can do whatever a vision tells you," Clem said. "Are you going to tell me metal does not come from the earth?"

Speckled was finally silent.

Just above Clem's pectoral muscles, the sharp ends of metal spikes emerged from his flesh, pointing skyward, glinting. Beneath the pectorals, near the armpits, the blunt heads of the spikes protruded. Each head flared out an inch or so wider than the shaft, like the heads of giant nails or railroad spikes. But these shafts were longer than railroad spikes, and the points were needle-sharp. It was as if they had been heated up and hammered out.

Blood from the insert wounds trickled down his flanks, and some slid down the blunt metal heads, slow as honey, then dripped off to the granite, speckling it. From the exit wounds above his pectorals, two rivulets worked their way down either side of his sternum, and then down his abdomen, seeping red into his lucky pants.

Most shocking was the depth. My Uncle Jesse had told me stories about how in the old hunting times, you had guys actually pierce the muscle—not just the skin. A ripped muscle, though, could take months to heal. Those old-timers could afford to do it because they could count on friends to supply food and to protect them and their families while they healed up. That communal spirit was the first thing the agencies tried to break in us when they set out to make us over into white farmers. They wanted each man out for himself. So maybe Clem was right that the dance was about more than just saving your own hide in battle. Maybe it *was* danced for others. But these spikes in Clem were not just piercing the muscle. They were *deep,* maybe even under the pectorals, skimming the ribs. I thought I was dreaming, but part of me knew I would not awaken from this.

Yellow nylon cord ran up the centerline of his abdomen, then branched in two, like a *Y.* Each branch blossomed into a yellow noose that hung from a shiny spike. The loop of each noose had been placed over the sharp point and behind the blunt head, then made so tight that the flesh encompassed by the loop went white. It was upsetting to look at.

The yellow cord that hung from the spikes appeared very long. It was coiled into a thick bundle that was stuffed between his belt and his lucky pants.

Sharon came over from the direction of the Hall of Records. She had blood on her hands and looked very scared.

Clem looked at me, then tilted his chin downward at the spike in his left breast. "Pulled this up from the Union Pacific," he said. Then he tilted his chin to the right. "And this one from the Northern Pacific."

I began to see the logic in the madness. Those two railways, built by grace of the peace treaties, had been the weapons that finally destroyed us. First, they were used to wipe out the buffalo, millions being killed from open windows of sports-hunting cars, then they were used to speed the troops around us, to box us up. The Union Pacific ran below us, and the Northern Pacific above us, belting us in. Cavalry columns were whisked east and west on the rails, and would descend from the Northern and rise from the Union to strangle us. We never should have let them finish those rails. The spikes in his chest were the nails in our coffin.

But even as I thought these thoughts, I could hear my voice saying, "Why so deep?" I heard myself ask over and over, my throat tightening, my eyes burning. The sight of what he had done to himself, to his poor body, was starting to wear through the initial shock and numbness that had first shielded me. "Why'd you go so deep? You'll never pull free," I said. "He'll never pull free!" I shouted at Sharon. "What's wrong with you?"

"I did it the way he told me," she said, then quickly looked away from me, looked down.

Then I had a thought that was even scarier than the image of him trying to pull free from skewers so deep: it was the thought of infection so close to the heart. My beautiful, simple brother had probably killed himself with dirty spikes—and for what? For some hokey symbolism, because nothing else could get through to those bastards in D.C. As if that would.

"There are no cottonwoods up here," said Sharon, meaning what should we do for a sun-dance pole.

"Are you crazy!? You want to kill him?" I was ready to rip her in two.

"Me and Bear Dreamer spotted a cottonwood when we arrived," said Clem. "Would you all go look for it? Sharon is a maiden. She can harvest it. I would like to talk to Joey for a spell. Oh, Peter," he said, addressing Speckled Hawk. "Could I ask you something private?" After a few seconds, everyone but Speckled Hawk and me had got off Lincoln and headed for Level Three.

"I would like that detonator, please."

Speckled Hawk stared a long time at my brother's chest. He couldn't take his eyes off it. Finally, he bent over and pulled the cuff of his pants up. He reached into his boot and pulled out a small aluminum box. Clem nodded at me. I put out my hand and Speckled Hawk placed the detonator in it. I opened the cover and found two switches, just like Isaac described. There was also a red light that was not on. Speckled Hawk explained that when you arm it, the red light goes on. I closed the cover and considered throwing the box off the cliff, but feared the impact might trigger it. So I pulled up the cuff of my pants and stuck it in my boot the same way he had.

"How about helping them cut that cottonwood?" said Clem. "I'd like some time with Joey."

Speckled Hawk nodded, then walked away off Lincoln. He kept looking back in disbelief. Clem was shaking and sweaty, but he looked me in the eye and said, "Don't be sore I asked Sharon 'stead of you. I knew you wouldn't do it, Joey."

"How could you do this to yourself?"

"For the Hills," he said.

"Fuck the Hills! I'm unstaking you. We're going down and getting your chest cleaned out. It's over, Clem."

He stared at me with big, soft eyes, the same look that McLaren's cow had used on him, so that he couldn't bring the hammer down. *Give it up, Clem,* I was thinking. *I'm the one that shot her, remember?*

"I'm taking you down," I said. How could he want to dance again? How could he possibly want to dance again? I had promised myself I would never do it a second time. He shivered and started pouring out more sweat. "Are you okay, Clem? Maybe you should sit," I said.

He shook his head. "Been sittin' too long. Just put the quilt back on me." I picked it up and draped it over his shoulders. "Would you pull this coil out? It's diggin' in." I eased the coil of nylon cord out from between the belt and the pants. I undid a few coils to create slack, so there wouldn't be any pull on the spikes, then I laid the coil gently on the granite.

"Jesus, Clem. I thought you were—I don't know what I thought—that you were *poking* her in there, then you come out like this."

"Only one Linda," he whispered hoarsely.

"Right," I said absently. I was looking for the field radio. I wanted to call Maxwell and tell him Clem and I were coming down on the condition that they send up a medevac chopper. But all there was on the rock was Bacon's police scanner, which only received. The field radio was back near the Hall of Records. As I turned in that direction, I heard him say in an almost panicked tone, "Joey, you gotta stake me down. Stake me down till the others come back."

I turned. "Clem . . ."

"I'm a No Flight," he said.

"And I unstaked you," I said. But I suddenly realized that staking him down again would make it hard for him to scurry away from the medevac guys. I picked up his chain and passed it around his waist. "Where's the lock?" I asked.

"I left it in the Hall, I think."

"I'll get it," I said in a reassuring tone. I would grab his lock and quietly radio Maxwell for the medevac.

"Wait!" he whispered. "They could swoop in and snatch me while you're gone. Tie my sun-dance cord to my No Flight chain."

"A nylon cord won't stop them. They'll just cut it."

"Still. I'll be staked down. *Napesni.*"

I kneeled and threaded the yellow cord through a link in the chain, then tied a slipknot. "One more," he said. I tied a square knot to make him happy, then left for the Hall. I was just starting down the slope of Lincoln's head when I heard him cry, "Oh, wow!"

"What?" I said, spinning around to make sure he was okay.

"Look!" he cried, pointing his chin into the western sky behind me. "An eagle."

I turned west again to look, but all I saw above the back ridge was blue sky. The sun was past its peak but still very bright in our eyes. "I don't see any eagles, Clem," I said and kept walking.

"High, little brother," came his voice over my shoulder, like a greeting. "Look higher."

Without breaking stride, I looked up again but still saw nothing. "You're seeing things, Clem. You're tired."

"Higher," he pleaded.

I made a visor with my hand, trying hard to see whatever he saw. "Okay, you're not seeing things," I said. "You're just full of—" But as the words came out of my mouth, I shuddered and felt a tremor underfoot, my body remembering the quivering card table and the way he used to sneak meat onto my plate: *Look at that big old bear at the door,* he would say, or *What's that eagle doing on our front step?* The table would quiver and there would be more meat. Something definitely shuddered under me, and through me, a tremor in the mountain. Something.

I spun around, and in the split second that it takes to turn, I already knew I wouldn't see him. There was just the white granite of Lincoln's tufty hair, and on it I saw the yellow cord wriggling furiously like a snake, uncoiling, then the chain following it over the edge, wriggling the same way, fast and frantic. The chain snapped taut and his scream blasted up, ripping the blueness of the sky, cracking the mountain. I thought the universe was ripping. Every leaf and pine needle in the Black Hills must have shivered at that sound.

The radio scanner went crazy. "They're on Lincoln! Man on Lincoln!"

"We know, Miller."

"I mean *on* him, in his face! Rappelling, sir."

"Train a marksman! Bandit on Lincoln. Could have charges. Bandit on Lincoln. Get a team on him. Double. Double!"

I ripped off my T-shirt, which was white, and started waving it frantically at the Tourist Center. I was screaming that he had no explosives, no
charges, nothing—as if they could hear me. Bacon and Sharon came running onto the head, shouting at me, "What's going on?" "He fell," I
shrieked. I stuck the shirt in Sharon's hand and told her to wave it. Then
I turned my back to the Tourist Center and grabbed the chain. His
weight pulled it flush against the rock, but I managed to wedge my fingers under. Holding on like that, with a foot on either side of the chain,
I started taking little backward steps down Lincoln's wave of hair, which
was about fifteen feet above the forehead. I could grip the chain well
enough, but what about when the chain would end and the nylon would
begin? Even if I could hang on long enough to reach him, how would I
get him back up? My arms would give out on so skinny a cord. I would
have to either hang on to him, which would kill him, or jump to my own
death. I started scrambling back up the chain and trying to figure out another way. But I couldn't think because all I could hear was his screaming. I couldn't for the the life of me figure how to get to him. Then I
realized I had it backwards; I had to get him up to us. I scrambled back
up the chain, cursing the slowness of my mind. "Help me pull him up,"
I screamed. By this time, Isaac and Speckled Hawk had shown up.

We were able to pull up about eight feet of chain, but that was it.
When we tried getting him higher than that, the screaming got worse. It
felt like there was another rope tied to his ankles and anchored to the bottom of the mountain, a rope that had eight feet of play in it but no more.
Some mysterious force was holding him down there.

I started walking backwards down the chain again, to go over the wave
of hair, at least far enough out there to look down and see what was holding him. I leaned back away from the rock as far as I could and twisted
my head around to grab a look. He was down there, all right—to the
right of the gigantic nose, twirling slowly, looking tiny.

I didn't have a full view of him, because Lincoln's brow was in the way.
Clem's bloody shoulder and part of his head would twirl into view, then
disappear under the stone brow as the other shoulder appeared, traveling the same orbit. So it was the brow that was jamming us up. He was
eight feet below Lincoln's noble brow.

◆

"There's more rope!" said Sharon, turning on her heel and sprinting off
Lincoln. She darted across Hidden Canyon and into the Hall of Records.

Bacon had had the presence of mind to get the field radio while I was out on the edge. He was on one knee and shouting into the receiver. "Don't shoot the man on the rope. Repeat, do not shoot the man on the rope. He's unarmed and wounded. . . . What does it matter *who* I am? Just put Maxwell on . . . put him on. . . . Fine, then tell him it's the Seventh Priest. . . ." He looked up at me as if to say, Now he's coming to the fucking phone. "Maxwell, don't shoot the— Yes, this is Gallagher. . . .Okay, you'll see me fry, don't shoot the man on the rope. He's unarmed and badly wounded. Did you hear me? Maxwell, *did* you hear me? Acknowledge. Agent Maxwell, we are broadcasting this conversation on ham radio, and we've got friends taping it. The record will show you know he's unarm— Maxwell!" Bacon slammed the receiver down into its compartment, looked up at me and said, "The bastard laughed and hung up."

I didn't know what was keeping her. I started to run for the Hall, but just then she came flying out, carrying a huge spool of red nylon rope. I had been worried there wouldn't be enough to get me down, pulley fashion, to the brow, but this was plenty. My only worry now was whether the piton in the rock would hold our combined weight. I threaded the cord through the ring in the pin and hoped everything would hold. I tied a big loop around my waist, fastening it with square knots and other nonslip knots. I pushed it down under my butt, so that I could sit in it like a harness swing. I picked up the spool, let some slack out, then heaved it over the edge—to the left side of Lincoln's face, so that the heavy spool would not fall on Clem but go down the other side of the nose. Then I flipped the line over the nose onto Clem's side by whipping my arm around and sending waves down the cord.

I took small steps backwards, feeding out the rope slowly as I went. Right after the ridge of Lincoln's hair, where the rock starts to turn vertical, I leaned back away from the monument and did a feeble kind of rappelling. It was tricky getting below the thick wave of hair, because it protruded so far beyond the upper forehead that I had no place to put my feet for a while and had to lower myself in a dead hang until I regained the rock at midforehead. Down at the brow, I took the feed line and tied it to the loop of my harness.

With my hands now free, I eased myself around so that my back rested against the rock and my knees pointed out toward the federal forces, which I tried not to look at. I yelled up, "Start pulling. Go slow."

They must have had Sharon lying close to the edge to listen for my voice and relay the commands, because I could faintly hear her echoing my words. Clem's yellow cord, which was just a foot to my left, began inching upward.

From my awkward perch, it was difficult to lean far enough out to see below the brow, so I watched the cord and estimated how many feet Clem had risen. When it seemed to have advanced five or six feet, I told them to hold up. Planting my heels wide apart against the brow, I slipped my left hand under the yellow cord and pushed it out away from the rock, then brought it directly in front of me, where my right arm joined in the effort. With both arms locked straight out, I yelled for them to start hoisting again, slowly.

As the cord crept up, I slipped my right hand, the upper one, below my left, then in a few seconds slipped the left below the right, and continued like that, "walking" my hands down as the cord inched up. He was rising slow and steady.

First I saw his chin and neck. His head was tilted completely back, so that the Adam's apple and chin were the highest points on his body—except, of course, for the twin peaks of his pectoral muscles, which were grotesquely stretched. The yellow nooses clenched the flesh around the spikes. The flesh there was white and bloodless. I concentrated on keeping my elbows locked, on walking my hands down smoothly. His body twirled a bit on the line and his inside shoulder brushed the granite brow. I leaned forward more against my line and strained to push my arms out still farther, until my left shoulder began to dislocate.

He slipped above the brow and then up to my level. I could see two triangles of blue sky through his chest muscles. And I glimpsed little sections of rib peeking through the gore, like pearls. Then I saw a throbbing stretch of artery that had been laid bare and I knew there was still a chance. "We're gonna get you out of here, Clemmy," I said. "We're gonna get you out of here." I think I was saying it over and over.

His eyes were open but rolled back—white. His lips mouthed the words *Mitakuye iyasin* over and over, mindlessly and without sound. He didn't even have the breath to whisper. I couldn't tell if he was conscious. I yelled his name, but his lips just kept mouthing *Mitakuye iyasin*. All my relations. All my relations. The embrace of everything, his relatedness to everything, the whole balance. All I could do was keep telling him we would get him out of there.

I heard the drone of a plane and saw it shoot past on the other side of the great nose, maybe a hundred yards off. It was a small bastard and unmarked. There was also the sound of something hitting the mountain, a series of popping sounds. I couldn't see the southeast hill, but the trajectory of the jet made it clear that it had just passed low over the hill, and the sound suggested that something had been laid down on the bunkers.

There was a bit of shooting, but it didn't last long. I wondered if Bunker One had checked an advance. Then there were choppers all over, not giving a damn that we might have serious weapons. Some went around the corner out of my view to shoot up the southeast hill. Another circled the mountain slowly, door gunner squeezing off a round here and there at the high ridge. The gunners, it seemed, at least for the moment, had been ordered not to shoot at anyone right on the presidents, for fear of chipping them, I guess. So, Isaac, Sharon, Speckled, and Bacon were able to hold on to Clem's chain and keep pulling.

A black-and-silver Huey came out of nowhere from behind Washington and swung in low to the base of the monument, hovered there a second or two, then rose straight up like an elevator in front of Lincoln. The sliding door was all the way back and there was a guy in a seersucker suit who was strapped in at the waist to a cushioned seat. He had a polished black shoe out on the skid, shining in the sun, and he was leaning his torso out the door and looking through a scope on a rifle. Real clean Ivy Leaguer. His short brown hair fluttered above his dark Ray-Bans. He let off three rounds and Clem began to slip down past me and below the brow.

I didn't know whether most of them had been hit or had fled, but at least one or maybe two of them up there managed to hang on and let Clem down as easy as possible. I undid the knot of my feed to my harness and went down after him. Below the brow there was nothing for me to anchor my feet against. It was just a dead hang. That's how serious a brow it was. The rock went straight back at practically a right angle, straight back like a ceiling until it reached the deep-set eye. The upper eyelid came far forward of both the pupil and of the lower lid, but even that was far out of reach.

I kept looking across at Lincoln's giant eye. If I could get Clem over to it, he might have a chance. They had achieved the illusion of a pupil by drilling out a huge, deep circle from the eye. The pupil was big enough for a couple of men to sit in and deep enough to lie back in. If I could just get us over to it, I could prevent his muscles from ripping further. My other fear was that he was slowly suffocating. His breaths were very shallow and faint. If I could lay him in the eyeball, I could pull his stakes out. But we were suspended so far forward by that goddamn brow that I couldn't get near the eye or any part of the face. It was all out of reach. Everything was out of reach. I was just dangling in space. The haven of Lincoln's pupil was out of reach and always would be. Think of something else. God, help me think of something else.

The best I could do would be to get him on my lap, so that the tension would leave his line. I secured my position a couple feet above him by knotting my feed line into my harness loop again. Holding both lines in one hand, I leaned back and reached down to his waist. I slipped my fingers under the blood-soaked corduroy, grabbing as much material as I could, and I pulled him up. After a long struggle, I managed to maneuver him across my lap. I wanted to pull his spikes out right there, but he was so slick with blood and sweat that I feared I would drop him. And I was losing strength all over the place, couldn't even feel my legs.

The black-and-silver chopper reappeared, doing the exact same maneuver as before, coming in around Washington from around back of the mountain, dipping low near the base of the monument, forty or fifty yards out, hovering a moment before making its elevator ascent. The light-blue seersucker suit flashed below me in the open door, the black shoe out on the skid again. As the chopper shot up, I saw he was still wearing his Ray-Bans. By the time the bird was eye level with the presidents, he had his rifle readied and was leaning out the door. I thought for a moment he had come for me, but they kept rising till they were level with the top of Roosevelt's head. I screamed Junior's name to try to warn him. The suit let off two shots, then pulled his rifle in and turned to say something either to the pilot or to someone else.

There was the sound of a third shot, and the guy in the seersucker suit jerked around as his lower leg dropped out from under his knee. He looked down in disbelief. No black shoe. Nothing. And it was a beautiful sight. He started screaming and dropped his rifle out the door, as if to destroy the evidence of what he'd done, as if to distance himself from the sin, so that the gods might reverse their judgment and give him back his leg. I could see his mouth open in horror, and I wished he didn't have the shades on. I wanted to see the eyes of a man who had just found God. I thought about getting the detonator out of my boot, but was afraid of dropping Clem. It was awful to feel unarmed with these bastards all about.

I guess I sat on that rope harness with Clem on my lap for a half hour or more while they rounded up—or maybe hunted down—the last of us. I kept trying to shift around a bit on the rope to get some blood into my legs, but it didn't really work. I also kept calling to them to pull us up, yelling that my brother was bleeding to death. But no response. I think they were probably taking an inventory of the weapons, making sure all the missing ones were present and accounted for, and that there was no more danger to their hardware.

Every now and then, Clem's lips would move. Once there was a faint cry, not even as loud as a whisper, yet there was voice in it. Joey, I think he said. I know he said my name.

I had him well enough in my lap now that I could hold him with one arm. I had my elbow cradled under his neck, and the forearm and hand of that same arm were wrapped around his outside shoulder, pulling him in tight. With my other hand, I ran my fingers through his hair, combing the strands back, caressing his scalp. I stroked his brow. I pulled him in more and kissed his forehead, and I was speaking in Lakota. He smiled faintly, or I think he did. The words came more easily and fluently than Lakota ever had to me. Then gradually I realized I was watching myself and him from a few feet above. It was like I'd left my skin and was just looking at my body clutching his body. I watched my lips talking in his ear. Was I dead? Did they shoot me? How could I be seeing this? Was my spirit leaving? How could my spirit be leaving and my voice stay in my body? I listened and watched my lips. I was telling him how I loved him, and telling him about the day he was born—my firstborn—and how happy I was. How proud he always made me and his father, how things would get better now. Then I floated away from us, floated up the monument, passed the brow and forehead, passed the wave of hair, and I saw blood and I saw clouds of gas up there, and Sharon vomiting. I saw men in masks and black outfits all over the rock, and choppers above the high ridge. I saw blue skies and sun. I saw men kneeling and crouching around the crack that Clem's piton wedge was anchored in. They crouched in a circle like wolves feeding.

Next thing I knew, I was back down by Lincoln's eye with Clem in my lap. His cord snapped taut and I felt a shudder through his body. His torso started to rise. I waited for my own cord to jerk and rise, for we were hooked into the same ring up top. In a split second I realized that they had cut his chain from the ring in the piton and were trying to take him separately. I didn't trust them with him. I scrambled to get his stakes out, but the nooses were too tight and slicked with blood, and he rose too quickly out of my arms. I grabbed his hips for a moment, but realized this would only rip him. So I let him go. I had to. He rose at an incredible speed, bumped into the brow and flopped up over it, then disappeared.

After a couple of minutes, I felt a jerk in my own line. Then I thought the line broke or was cut, because I fell. I must have fallen six or eight feet before the line went taut again. Just as quickly as I had fallen, I started to rise. I smacked into the brow, bounced up over it, then shot up the forehead so quickly that there was no time to brace or prepare for the overhanging wave of hair. It hit me like a shithouse. Broke my left arm. A moment later, I saw what was pulling me. Over the back ridge, above the Hall of Records, a chopper was reeling me in and rising at the same time. They had attached my line to a chopper rescue cable, and had probably done the same with Clem's chain. I wondered if he could possibly be alive after a rise like that? They could have hovered directly over us and spared us the wear and tear, but that would have put the choppers over the presidents' faces. A risk they wouldn't take.

As I rose, I saw a lake of blood on Lincoln where Isaac, Sharon, Bacon, and Speckled had been hauling Clem's line. Over on Roosevelt was another pool of blood and an empty chain. There were men in gas masks coming out of the Hall of Records carrying our provisions and dumping them into a huge tarp at the mouth of the doorway. Another guy came out carrying an armload of papers, the 371 treaties. He tossed them on the tarp.

As I rose, I swung toward the back ridge. Two guys in gas masks with Heckler & Kochs reached out and grabbed my line. There were about eight others all along the ridge. My feet touched the rock and I collapsed. I tried to get up but my legs were dead. I couldn't feel them. I tried again but these fuckers started kicking me.

"Where's my brother?" I shouted. The fucker was busy pulling the harness down my legs and off my ankles. "Where is he?" I shouted louder.

He grabbed my hair, brought my face close to his Grim Reaper mask, and barked through the rubber, "Shut your fucking hole." Then he threw me down and someone started to cuff me from behind, which is when I knew for sure my arm was busted. It hurt like hell and I screamed and tried to turn and plead with them, and that's when I saw a dagger of bone sticking out through my triceps muscle. It was as white and jagged as the pelvis of the kid I pulled from the rice paddy.

"Just cuff his ankles," said one of them. The other started fumbling with my boots. "With your MP5," said the first. There was a pause, then a burst from the H&K, then a second burst. I felt the impact above my ankles, like two blows of a bat, but no pain right away. My legs were still dead.

"Where is he?" I shouted.

"I said stow it!" barked one of the rubber masks. They walked thirty feet or so along the ridge to where Maxwell had set up his command post.

I recognized Maxwell by his big shoulders. He was in a flak jacket and gas mask, speaking into a walkie-talkie, maybe ten feet from me. Guys were coming up to him and making quick reports. He would nod or shake his head, then say something, sometimes point down the mountain. I guess this was the mop-up. He started barking into the radio, and looking west. I managed to get to my knees and looked where he was looking. Hovering on the other side of the ridge was another Huey, and my brother below it on his yellow line, twirling. "Clem!" I cried. He looked like a helpless fish, dangling above his element.

"Which LZ?" crackled a voice from the walkie-talkie.

"Alpha," barked Maxwell. The metallic voice crackled back, "Roger," then the chopper slowly turned its nose west. Clem looked dead.

I felt deserted. He had had his vision, danced his bogus dance, then checked out, leaving the rest of us to pick up the pieces. Part of me hated him at that moment. And I realized Speckled Hawk had been right all along. I pulled up the cuff of my jeans and took the detonator out of my boot. My ankles were hurting now like a bastard. I opened the case and armed it. The red light came on like a warm ruby. Maxwell was still giving orders, but more calmly now, already anticipating the secret commendations that would fill his dossier, the pats on the back, the atta-boys. I looked down at Washington's crown—I knew right where it would blow—then back at Maxwell and his bastards, then at my brother twirling beneath his Huey. I had the power now. I had it in my hand. Till the day he died, Maxwell would be the man who botched Rushmore. I moved my thumb to the second switch. I shut my eyes to block out Clem. But I saw him clearer, his cow eyes, round and wet, and Linda and the kids, and Bob Walking Eagle's teenagers, and Joe Conquering Bear's little whelps, and all the old folks who would be defenseless and would never stop paying. *Fuck 'em, just do it,* I thought. But I snapped the cover shut and whipped the box hard as I could at Clem's body. The box cut through the air between us. I wanted it to hit him, strike him in the face, yank him back long enough to see just what he'd done—all the death and disarray—but the box died in the downdraft of the rotors and didn't come close. I watched it fall, half of me praying the impact would trip the switch, half of me praying it wouldn't.

I thought I saw Clem's leg twitch. I wondered if he could possibly be alive still? Could he see the chopper above him, feel its thunder around him? Was it terrifying, or was it distant and faint, even lulling?

It must have been reflexes. He must be deep in the darkness and silence of nonexistence, I told myself, or in a brighter world somewhere. His body sped away over the gutted Black Hills, over mines, power plants, and poisoned rivers, hurtling low above the spruce and firs, into a swollen, fading sun.

1996

It was January and beginning to snow. The trucker I'd been riding with for two days pulled off the interstate at Kadoka. I wanted to ask if he would take me to Wambli, but it would have been twenty-five miles out of his way, fifty really, and I knew he had a schedule. I thanked him. "Take her easy, Joe," he said, flashing his gold tooth in a broad smile. I got out, put my collar up, and watched him roll back down onto the interstate, heading west toward the Black Hills on the horizon. I thought of calling Shorty Shangreaux for a ride, could phone him from the Broken Spur and warm up over a coffee. But I feared someone in there would remember me and make trouble, so I just started walking home down 73. If my mom could do it back to back, I figured I could swing it one way.

It felt wonderful walking those open spaces after six years in a cell. The prairie ocean rolled in from the east, seeping into the crags of the outer Badlands, forming a patchwork of dry-grass plateaus between red rises and fall-away canyons. It was pretty, and the falling snow came gentle like gauze. I tried to prepare for the different things Linda might say, and for the possibility of her continuing the silence. I had some visitors over the years, but never her or her kids.

Eventually, I came to a pothole by the yellow divider line. The snow was sticking on the prairie and starting to stick on the asphalt. I wondered if this was the same pothole Clem had sipped water from instead of cracking a beer open. I pictured his yellow corduroy knee at the edge of it. I pictured a puddle in the hole, summer rain tinged with motor oil. I kneeled, cupped my hands, and brought them to my lips, pretending I was him. It seemed strange that the pothole still existed while he did not. The pothole had been the first witness to his comeback. It was more than a witness and more than a rupture in asphalt. It was the earth coming up again from below the wasitchu road, coming up to renew itself by renewing him, setting him on a different path. At least that's what I told myself late at night sometimes in my cell. And other nights I had lain awake, imagining the road unblemished, the pothole never existing, Clem at home, maybe drunk, but at home with Linda and the kids. Some nights I even dreamt it, and it was convincing and wonderful, but I always awoke to the same reality.

I spent most mornings trying to convince myself that Clem had gotten dizzy and lost his balance, that it was *not* intentional. He was weak, dehydrated, in pain; *of course* he'd gotten dizzy. How could he *not* have lost his balance? I would repeat five hundred times a morning that his intention was to dance from a cottonwood pole, not go over the edge. He sent them off to get the cottonwood. The problem, though, was that I could not forget the feeling of him sneaking meat onto my plate while my back was turned. I can live with a senseless accident. I can accept the meaninglessness of accident—barely. But a deliberate act of that size and kind is too horrible, too huge.

Pushing on down the road, I thought about Wolf's Pass, where we received due process. It's a remote cow town up north near the border. Two stop signs and a courthouse. The explosives sealed our fate, of course, while our letter to the press was nowhere to be found, and any attempt on our part to make reference to it, or to treaties, or to why we were up there in the first place was ruled immaterial and deemed to have no pertinence to the charges. It was all about explosives, and the sad truth is they didn't even have to frame us on that. We were quickly dispatched to federal prisons across the land. I read the papers in the prison library every day. Finally, an AP blurb of a few lines appeared in the back pages of various papers, never better than page 12, though, filler really. We couldn't compete with the daily barrage of stories about war preparation,

scuds, and possible gas attacks in the Gulf. Those stories had been going on since summer. I read that blurb a few hundred times.

A.P.—wᴏʟꜰ's ᴘᴀss, s.ᴅ. Twenty Sioux Indians
were convicted of trespassing on federal property, seizing and threatening to deface a national monument, and attempting to extort the
release of a federal prisoner.

I guess somebody started digging, though, because the story grew a bit
before it died. Two weeks after the first blurb, a second one appeared,
also in the back pages.

A.P.—wᴏʟꜰ's ᴘᴀss, s.ᴅ. Twenty Sioux Indians
were convicted of placing explosives on Mt.
Rushmore and threatening to detonate them unless the government released from prison Mr.
Leonard Peltier, the celebrated AIM leader
convicted in 1973 of shooting two FBI agents
on Pine Ridge Reservation, S.D.
A statement, issued this summer by the militants to the Park Service, claimed that the
FBI framed Peltier in '73 as part of a larger
effort to destroy AIM, and further claimed
that the FBI suppressed evidence (its own bal-
listics tests findings) which strongly indi-
cated Peltier's innocence. The militants claim
to have gotten this information through the
Freedom of Information Act. "Leonard is a po-
litical prisoner of a government that glibly
champions human rights around the world while
abusing those of original Americans," con-
cluded the Indian statement to the Park Service.
Commenting on the nine-hour standoff at
Rushmore, an FBI spokesman said in a phone in-
terview, "The threat to the monument left our
tactical team little choice but to move
swiftly and decisively. The team accomplished
the removal of the militants without sustain-
ing losses. The Bureau regrets the unavoidable

```
deaths of Abel Many Coups, of Kyle, South
Dakota, fatally wounded in an exchange of
fire, and of another man, probably Clement
Blue Chest, of Wanblee, S.D., killed when an
explosive device detonated prematurely in his
hands."
```

The next day, the deadline in the Gulf ticked out and the bombing of Baghdad started. Bush and Baker were home free.

I learned from Shorty Shangreaux and others who came to visit that folks were trying to tell the real story to the press, trying to explain the true objectives. A couple of pieces appeared in alternative magazines and in Indian papers like *Akwasasne News,* but that was it. While these pieces contradicted the government story, they couldn't disprove it, and worse, they often contradicted each other, which just made us look like liars.

By the time the Gulf War ended, people who had read anything about Rushmore only remembered the explosives. *What about the explosives?* was always the retort to any claims against the fed story.

Soon, there were bigger stories, of greater historical injustice, like Tailhook. That was everywhere for a good six months. Can't beat sex and women's rights and officers who aren't gentlemen. Waco stole the spotlight, too, but at least Americans got used to seeing feds with M-16s and tanks. And there was that shit up at Ruby Ridge, where FBI snipers shot and killed a guy's wife and child. He got a Senate hearing and three million bucks. Then came O.J., cameras in the courtroom, lawyers attacking police methods and appealing to the court of public opinion. I think about Wolf's Pass and what we got, how speedy and efficient it was. No cameras, no nothing. But those other cases were not about land.

My ankles started hurting, but it felt good to be out in the open spaces again, so good that every now and then I sprinted for twenty strides or so, shuffling as fast as I could. The light was dimming when I came to the little bridge over White River. I went down to the bank, right by where I had pulled up Clem's Scout bag full of beers. I drank a few handfuls of icy water, sat a bit, then shoved on.

It was getting dark. The thought that McLaren might barrel down the road any moment made me nervous. I wanted those spirit lights to appear, the ones that had protected Clem that night. Then the part of me that doesn't believe in that kind of stuff tried to laugh at the part that does. But I'm less skeptical now, because I've gone six years without hearing the diva, not a peep since my brother began mending the hoop for us.

Finally at the crossroads, I turned west on 44, a narrow ribbon of asphalt that rises and dips with the gentle hills. The snow was still coming, tender like a bandage. The road, which had been growing pale in the off-and-on flurries, soon vanished, making the land whole again, undivided. It was on this road that a car had shot over a hill and clipped my niece Wenonah and her friend. So much would have been different had the road never been paved. It felt good to watch it vanish. As I crested that same hill, Wambli came into view. The lights of the homes twinkled under the huge gray sky. I heard a coyote cry and the yip of a dog, then silence. The air was clean and sharp. Against the backdrop of whitened plains, the houses looked tightly clustered, as if they had drawn closer to share warmth. Overhead, the cloud front broke apart, letting in stars and a shaft of moon. I shuffled on.

Near Bob Walking Eagle's house, a yellow shadow slipped over the snow, low to the ground, circling me, moving closer. There was the sound of a sneeze, then a friendly whimper. Her head held down submissively, her tail wagging low, Ooly crept up and touched my feet with her snout. When I said her name, her tail went faster and she reared up, putting her paws on my waist. I held her head and kissed her. Her dark eyes stood out against her pale coat. I let her down and she stood patiently while I tried to decide whether to surprise Bob and get something warm to eat, or push on for Linda's. I pushed on and Ooly followed, running off here and there to sniff things out in the snow, but always circling back to let me know she was with me.

Clem and Linda's trailer home is about a half mile out of Wambli. As I got closer, I got scared. But at five feet from the door, I heard a deep and lulling voice singing, *"I'll go a-waltzing Matilda with you."* I only knew one person who sang that song, old Isaac. He learned it in Korea from an Australian soldier he was tight with, who got killed. You never heard anything so moving as Isaac singing that jingle-ass kangaroo song. And I think it's because the tune reaches so high and low while the words make no sense, which was Korea for him.

I went up the two front steps soft as I could. I peered through the windowpane of the door. Isaac's huge frame was sitting on the old couch, and a little girl of six or seven slept against his chest. The last time I saw Jenny she was feeding at Linda's breast. I backed down the stairs and walked around the corner of the house. I looked up through the kitchen window.

Linda was doing dishes at the sink, looking older but just as strong, just as beautiful. She scrubbed something, a pot or a pan, with great concentration and purpose.

"What are you doin'?" challenged a voice hoarsely. The tone was firm but not rude. I put my hands out to my sides in plain view, then turned slowly. A boy of twelve or so was looking at me from fifteen feet back. No weapon. He wore a zip-up corduroy coat that was too short in the sleeves. He had Clem's brow. I wondered if he was Rafer or the younger one, Jeb. "You hungry, mister?" he asked. There was something about the word, or the question, that confused me. For six years, I hungered for a moment like this, a moment of return, of homecoming. And I was starved for moments and people that I knew could never return. My lips and tongue were dry and spitless in the cold air. I felt them move, but nothing really came out. "We got food," he said. "We got stew."

"Jeb," I whispered.

He paused, his breath appearing twice in the cold air before he spoke again. "How you know my name?"

There was a long silence. I was scared to tell him who I was, because I felt Linda had bad-mouthed me to the boys. It was clear she blamed me. Jeb walked closer, his eyes never leaving my face. I got down on a knee so we could see each other better. Jeb took another step. He was looking right in my eyes, his face blank. "I know you," he whispered. Then he put his arms around my neck. "I remember you," he said, his cheek now against my cheek. "Do you remember me?" he said. His arms pulled me in tighter and it was like the day Wenonah gave me the medicine bundle for Vietnam and hugged me so tight around the neck. It was like the welcome-back she never got to give me. "Of course, I remember you, Jeb. Of course I do."

He took my hand and tugged me in the direction of the door.

As I got up off my knees, I turned and checked the window. Linda was still scrubbing away, eyes in the sink. Jeb led me around the corner of the house and to the steps at the front door. I think he knew what was up, because he looked back at me and squeezed my hand before pushing the door open, like to say *It'll be okay, really.*

"Uncle Joey's home," he chirped as I followed him in. Isaac struggled up out of the sofa, Jenny still sleeping against his chest. Isaac's leathery face creased up as he smiled. "Well, I'll be hanged," he murmured in his deep voice. He supported Jenny with his left arm. The right arm dangled limp at his side. At the trial, Isaac and I each had an arm in a sling. His had been a bullet wound, and I gathered now it must have severed the nerve. I had learned from Bacon that a chopper marksman fired at them—Bacon, Isaac, Speckled Hawk, and Sharon—when they were trying to haul Clem's cord. That's when Clem slipped below the brow. He said Speckled took off, but that Isaac held the cord with one arm till it was over.

Jeb skipped past Isaac to the kitchen. "Uncle Joey's here." There was silence, then the sound of a drawer being shut with some excess force. She whispered something sternly that we couldn't make out. The boy answered in a plaintive whisper. Old Isaac looked at me reassuringly. "It'll be fine," he said.

"No, I wrote her and wrote her. She never wrote back."

"Same here," he said. "Give her time."

The whispers in the kitchen area continued. "It never came back?" I asked, nodding at Isaac's right arm.

He shook his head. "I get by, though." Then there were the sounds of the fridge opening, a pot put on the stove, a match struck. Isaac smiled. "You're in for a treat."

I was dying to ask Isaac if he had seen a cottonwood out by Level Three, dying to hear him say, *Yep, we sure did.* It would strengthen my theory that Clem went over by accident, that fatigue and dehydration got the better of him. But I knew that if they had not seen a cottonwood, it would shatter my mind. So, I swallowed and said nothing.

Linda walked in, drying her hands on a dishrag. "Hi," I said. She put the rag on the back of a chair. "Go wash up for bed, Jeb," she ordered. Jeb came and said goodnight, shaking my hand. Isaac bent down for a kiss. Linda retreated into her kitchen, coming out minutes later with a bowl of stew and four slices of white bread. She set these things on the table. It was the old card table. "C'mon," she said, in a flat tone.

I sat, picked up the spoon, and looked up at the two of them. Sensing my discomfort, Isaac joined me at the table, Jenny still in his arm. I took a spoonful in my mouth. It was hot and tasted good. Linda walked away, then returned with three cups and a pot of coffee, which she placed on the table. I looked up at her but she wasn't looking back. She sat and reached over for Jenny, taking her onto her lap. Isaac poured the coffee.

"Stew's delicious," I said. She rubbed Jenny's back and ignored me. "How's Bear Dreamer makin' out?" I asked Isaac.

He blew on his coffee. "They released him 'bout a year back. Same as me. 'Fraid he passed on last month, though."

"He was a good old spirit," I said.

Isaac nodded thoughtfully. "The good news is he taught his medicine to Eli Jr. Junior's quite a healer now."

"How about Elijah?" I asked.

"Not so good."

Elijah had been shot bad. Bacon and I were in neighboring cells and he told me that Elijah had scrambled off Washington to unlock Junior and get him out of there, and that a chopper marksman shot him while he was unlocking his boy. He said Junior didn't miss a beat, though, just picked up his dad's rifle and shot the bastard's leg off, clean off, then carried his dad into the Hall of Records.

They never prosecuted Junior for taking that shot, because it would have exposed the fact that he was chained to the rock, which would have exposed the hunger strike—which they went to great lengths to bury. They buried it with our letter to the press, and with Clem's fast. They buried everything but Speckled Hawk's explosives.

Linda got up to put Jenny to bed. "Where's Rafer?" I asked.

"Out with the wrong crowd. Raisin' hell," she said over her shoulder. She stopped and turned. "I can't control him. Just hops out the window." She disappeared into the bedroom with her little girl.

Isaac scratched his scalp through his short hair, which was finally going gray. "One thing I never did get," he said, picking up his limp arm with the other and placing it in his lap, "is why Bacon didn't stand trial with us? They cut him a deal?"

"Quinn tried to kill himself," I said. "They were holding us that night in Rapid. Where were they holding you?"

"Fargo, I think."

"Well, we were in Rapid. Quinn was convinced he wouldn't get a trial, felt sure they would 'extradite' him down to Guatemala or Salvador, where the puppets could put screws to him for names of old contacts down there. He didn't think he could take it a second time. And he didn't want to finger anyone. So he opened his wrists with a paper clip."

"And died?"

"I don't know. He either made it, or they sewed him up and sent him south."

Isaac shook his head.

"What I never did get," I said, "is how they took us down so quick."

Isaac shrugged. "A plane blanketed the southeast hill with stun grenades, or some stun device. The mighty SEALs only had to cuff and carry. And there was gas on the monument. Half a whiff and you were blind and puking."

"Is Sharon okay? She back?"

"Been back awhile." He smiled.

Linda emerged from the bedroom. "Joey and I have to talk," she said.

"I'll take a walk," offered Isaac.

She shook her head. "Jeb's wide awake, he'll try to listen. We'll walk. You mind the kids, okay?"

He nodded and reached for the coffeepot. She went to the closet, put on a coat, then pulled two Army blankets down from a shelf. She handed me one and threw open the other, wrapping it around her shoulders. We walked up the hill behind the house. I got cold and wrapped myself in the other blanket.

Just beyond the crest of the hill was Wenonah's headboard and my mother's, and there was a third. All three were roped off inside a huge rectangle made by four posts and some twine. The twine was heavily loaded with colorful paper twists of tobacco offerings, red, yellow, green, and white, all of them now capped with snow. I ducked under the string. The headboard was made out of hard cherry, and the word "Clem" was handsomely carved in it. "Is he really down there?" I asked.

She shrugged. "I suppose. Parts. His lower half."

"Did you build a scaffold?"

"What do you think?"

I ducked under the twine again, and we walked over the spot where my mother's scaffold had been. I remembered it blowing around under the FBI chopper and how Linda held it steady so it wouldn't collapse.

She walked back to the top of the hill, then sat down in the snow. I followed, lowering myself slowly to my knees and sitting a couple of feet away. Down one side of the hill were the dead, my mother, brother, and niece; down the other was the trailer home with Isaac and Jeb and Jenny safe and warm. Between Linda and me lay an icy silence that I found unbearable. Ooly came up the hill, circled us twice, then trotted up to Linda and nuzzled her ear. Linda broke into a smile, wide and unchecked in the moonlight. "Hey, girl," she whispered, then quickly put the smile away. But I had seen it. The dog lay down between us and curled up, tucking her snout inside one of her hind legs. She had left a perfect circle of paw prints around us, which made me feel warm and protected. I wondered if Linda felt it, too, the power of the circle, the sacred hoop of the people mending. Or was I kidding myself again?

"How come you never wrote me back?" I asked.

"You know why," she said without looking at me.

"Not for sure, I don't."

"You introduced him to that Bacon," she said, her voice cracking with rage. "It was Bacon put that Savior stuff in his head. That's right, Joey, I've heard all about it. Half of 'em make Clem out to be some kind of god, and that freak Bacon his prophet. Others prefer the fed story, say Clem was a kick-ass warrior, another Crazy Horse, went down fighting. Well, which was it?"

"You should give him credit for having his own mind. His own plan."

"Oh, really?"

"He never bought a word of that Messiah stuff. If anything, it just made him feel sorry for Bacon. But I'll tell you this, you got Bacon all wrong."

"Fuck Bacon. This is about you, Joey Moves Camp. *You* were his brother. You and nobody else. You were his lookout and he was yours. You were supposed to—"

"What? What could I have done? He acted out a vision. He never told us what it was, so how could I see it coming?"

"You hooked him up with Bacon," she shrieked.

"He had his vision while dragging those skulls, Linda. That was before he even *met* Bacon."

"Look me in the eye and tell me he wasn't under that bastard's influence. Tell me *Messiah* is a Lakota word."

I looked her in the eye, but she looked away. "It was Sioux to the bone, what he did. It had nothing to do with Christianity, Linda, other than maybe to say, Cut the bull and *live* it, quit beating on your neighbor."

She laughed bitterly. "So he was a reformer, Martin Luther Blue Chest."

"Don't twist."

"Then tell me what he was, Joey. I want to hear you say it. Goddamn it, *say* it!"

"What?"

"That he was a fool. That he was always a fool. And that he died Bacon's fool."

I looked at my breath in the cold night and wondered what to say to her. "Linda, in prison I used to think a lot about something that I hadn't thought of since Vietnam. There was this Buddhist monk who wanted us out of there. So he sat down in the street, lotus position, and emptied a jerry can of gasoline on himself, soaking his robes, his skin, his scalp, everything, then he torched himself up—to get through to us, you know, to Washington. Christians didn't invent that stuff. It's always been around."

"How much you want to bet Buddhist monks don't get married and have kids?"

A horn blared just then and headlights flew up the dirt road past her house. There was the sound of skidding on snowy gravel till the car stopped, then cursing and laughter coming out the open windows. A bottle hit the road, bouncing end over end, another one breaking crisply. The car shot backwards and stopped by the trailer home. The passenger-side door opened and someone struggled out of the backseat. More cursing back and forth, then the door slammed and the car speeded off in reverse.

A slender shadow walked unsteadily toward the front door of Linda's house, tripped, got up, then leaned against the house for many seconds before shouldering the door and slipping through. Linda bit her lip, pained, but also relieved that her fourteen-year-old had survived the roads another night. She turned back to me and repeated her question with some hostility: "So what *was* he?"

I looked at Wambli twinkling in the distance. For six years, I had tried to understand what my brother was, and how he died. It seems that everyone—that is, every people—has a glory age, a time of freedom and greatness, and when it ends, especially if smashed by invaders, then the longing for a Tecumseh begins, a Crazy Horse, a Moses, a Joan, a messiah, one who can push back the invader and regain what was lost. Redeem it, get it back. It's so basic a hope, so universal a reflex that I figure it must be wired into every human brain. The whites didn't invent it. The Christians don't own it. A messiah is just one who rises to the needs of his people in desperate times. He's not picked or preordained, he's not tapped by some larger Messianic Spirit, like Bacon believed. He or she just feels the desperation and tries to respond, tries harder than most. I wanted to say to her *You're damn right he was a messiah,* but there was too much baggage attached to that word—and to redeemer, deliverer, savior. They were all inflated beyond usefulness by centuries of exaggeration and mythmaking. "He was a father to his people," I said flatly.

"And how about to his kids?"

"He gave them more than you know, Linda."

"Like what?"

"The Black Hills."

A sharp laugh escaped her lips. She shook her head. "You, too, eh?"

"You'll see," I said.

"And how're we gonna get the Hills back?"

"Those feds will talk. At least one of them will. As it plays over in his head, year after year, haunts his dreams at night, he'll come to understand what he saw, and he'll realize it's more important than any secrecy papers they had him sign."

"So you're counting on some fed to wake up, is that it? That's crazy, Joey. You've got to write it. Spell it out. Every detail."

"They'll just say we're dreaming, that we've got no proof. It's got to come from *them,* Linda."

"It's already been six years and no fed spoke up. You *are* dreaming."

"It'll happen. Might be a deathbed confession—I don't know—but it *will* happen."

"And just what are we supposed to do in the meantime, nothing?"

"Raise the kids, I guess. No one raises kids like you, Linda. I mean that. That Jeb is really somethin', got all the old ways. Like Wenonah."

In the moonlight, I could see the corners of her mouth turn slightly upward, then she put away memory and satisfaction and returned to business: "Well, his older brother's all screwed up. And who can blame him? The kid hears nothing but tales of his legendary father, the mighty Blue Chest. They crack him up to be God Almighty, ten feet tall and purer than snow. Holier than holy. How's a fourteen-year-old supposed to deal with that? Or live up to it? They come from all around to pay their respects, leave offerings. And they jabber on like you, *a father to his people,* they say." She shook her head. "But he took the high road on his kids. That's the bottom line, Joey. He took the high road on his kids."

I wanted to tell her that Clem lost his balance. I wanted to tell her that his intention was only to dance from a pole, not die. But I feared that the meaninglessness of an accident—another accident—could break her, make her go crazy. She was the kind who needed meaning, even if she was lashing out at it. "C'mon," I said lamely. "That's not fair."

"Nothing is," she snapped. Then she hung her head forward, her hair curtaining off her face from my gaze, her shoulders beginning to shake. A hand came out of the blanket and settled on Ooly's shoulder. "He was such a good man, a . . . lovely man," she said, stroking the dog's coat. "Even when he was a drunken mess he was never ugly, never mean."

"Let me help you with Rafer," I said, placing my hand on Ooly's shoulder but not daring to touch Linda's hand. "I'll take him out to Junior's. We'll do sweats. If he wants to pierce come summer, I'll pierce with him. I will. And every summer. And if he doesn't, that's fine, too. But I'll tell him who his father was, who Clem *really* was, how none of it came easy, I mean the struggle of it, beating the booze, all his struggles, the choices, the constant choosing, the overcoming, the—"

"Yes!" she blurted, grabbing my hand, squeezing it hard, and now looking me in the eye. "All of it, Joey. Weaknesses, too. There's so much more helpfulness in Clem, in who he *really* was, than in these damn myths, you know, these perfected myths that come after."

We sat awhile without speaking, then Linda stood. My ankles had stiffened in the cold, so I moved quite slowly off my haunches and onto my knees. She offered a hand from out of her blanket and helped me up. Ooly untucked her snout from the warm pocket of her hind leg and looked up at us, blinking. She rose and stretched her legs, one at a time, luxuriously, then shook her coat to wake up more. Her coat was full now, free of mange, even lustrous in the moonlight. She trotted downhill, padding through the powder without a sound, as sleek as her wolf cousins, long gone from these plains.

We followed her slowly. I could feel buffalo grass under the snow and it got me thinking about the gritty soil underneath, about the countless bones and untold stories in the dirt, the splinters of horn and antler, chips of beak, tooth, and claw, flecks of gold, shards of glass, the stories of animals and of men, *all* our relations, the vanished and the still-hungry, all sinking into the layered record of struggle and sleep, sinking but burning to live.

I saw embers under the snow, all across the plains, smoldering. A great heat rose in my legs and something real hit me across the thighs, and again across the calves, like an iron bar, breaking my muscles, cramping them, forcing me down. I fought to stay up, staggered, then fell to my hands.

"Hey, are you okay?" Linda cried from behind me. Then she was at my side, kneeling, speaking softly. "What happened? God, I thought you were having a— Hey, it's okay. It's okay," she said even softer. "Hey, c'mon. It'll be okay."

"So much is *gone*," I said.

"I know. And never coming back. None of them. But nothing's over, Joey Moves Camp."

I was staring at my handprints in the snow when I realized it doesn't have to be just one or the other, doesn't have to be purely deliberate on one hand versus pure accident on the other. I mean, what drives a person to the edge, anyway? Why do we lose our balance? Why did *I* just fall? We never just lose it. Something has to knock us off center—a shove, a gust, fatigue, a tremor—*some*thing has to whack us, stagger us, wrestle us down. And even then there's a whiff of choice, I think, a split-second acceptance, a letting go, a stepping off.

A heaviness slipped from my shoulders as I thought about this middle version. An odd happiness crept into me. The mountain shuddered. *Some*thing staggered him. He staggered and said yes.

I sat back on my heels and watched the front moving out, countless stars angling in. I wondered which of those distant suns were still burning, and which had burned out long ago, their light still traveling to us. I couldn't tell the lights from the ghost lights, and that was fine with me. "No, nothing's over," I murmured. For a moment, I thought about other worlds that must be out there, circling their suns. I wondered if any of them—or any piece of ground anywhere—had ever been held as high and as fiercely as my brother held ours. "He was a No Flight, Linda. A sun dancer, and a No Flight."

She trailed her fingers through the snowy buffalo grass, caressing it. She did this quite some time before she nodded.

Historical Note

On July 6, 1971, twenty members of AIM scaled Mount Rushmore, set up a camp above the immense heads of the presidents, and demanded that the government honor the 1868 Laramie Treaty. Honoring the treaty would mean returning the Black Hills and all of South Dakota west of the Missouri River. Within twelve hours, Rangers dragged the group off the monument. The members were arrested and charged with trespassing.

◆

While setting up sports clinics for children on Pine Ridge, Bill Bradley of the New York Knicks learned how the government acquired the Black Hills.

In 1985, Senator Bill Bradley remembered Pine Ridge and put forth the Sioux Nation Black Hills Act on the floor of the U.S. Senate. The bill called for the return of federally held lands in the Black Hills to the Sioux. It posed no threat to privately held properties in the Black Hills, nor to sections owned by the state of South Dakota. After recounting to his colleagues the history of government deceit in dealing with the Sioux, Senator Bradley pleaded that "history and other nations judge us by our deeds. . . . We now have the opportunity to write a new chapter in the history of the deeds dealing with the Sioux people. This chapter could describe a nation of honor, a nation of understanding, and a nation that affirms its great principles with great deeds. Let us write that chapter."

South Dakota senators and congressmen killed the Bradley Bill with ease. It was reworked and reintroduced in 1987. Again, it perished.